Courting Sarah

Deborah Lawrence

JOVE BOOKS, NEW YORK

FRIENDS is a trademark of Penguin Putnam Inc.

COURTING SARAH

A Jove Book / published by arrangement with
the author

PRINTING HISTORY
Jove edition / October 1999

The Penguin Putnam Inc. World Wide Web site address is
http://www.penguinputnam.com

ISBN: 0-515-12480-X

A JOVE BOOK®
Jove Books are published by The Berkley Publishing Group,
a division of Penguin Putnam Inc.,
375 Hudson Street, New York, New York 10014.
JOVE and the "J" design
are trademarks belonging to Penguin Putnam Inc.

PRINTED IN THE UNITED STATES OF AMERICA

10 9 8 7 6 5 4 3 2 1

For
my granddaughter, Taylor Rylie.
Happy birthday, sweetheart,
with love and joy
and for
E. C. Thompson, M.D., a real hero

Acknowledgments

The research for each book is different. With this story I needed to consult with a physician who could understand my sometimes strange curiosity. Fortunately, I discovered just the man.

My heartfelt thanks to Errington C. Thompson, M.D., former Asisstant Professor of Surgery and Director of Trauma/ Surgical Critical Care at Louisiana State University Medical Center, Shreveport. Errington, you helped make my vision possible, generously sharing your experience, knowledge, and time with me. You answered my numerous questions and cared about Gil as if he were your own patient. You have ''our'' gratitude.

A special note of gratitude to Laura Taylor for being my sounding board. If the best mirror is a good friend, then I must be drop-dead gorgeous and multitalented.

Courting Sarah

Prologue

*H*olding Esmee, her favorite doll, in the crook of her arm, ten-year-old Sarah Simmons darted through the tall grass. Her bonnet slipped off and hung down her back by the ties. "Phoebe, hurry up—we're almost there." Phoebe Nelson was her dearest friend in the whole world.

The old elm tree, their secret place, was just ahead. It was late afternoon and if Phoebe was too late getting back home, her mama'd tan her hide good. Sarah reached the tree first and looked to see if the dried black-eyed Susan was still under the rock where they had hidden it.

Phoebe ran up to her. "Is it there?"

"Mm-hm." Sarah held up the flat blossom. "See? I knew no one would come out here. It'll always be our place."

Phoebe sat down and rested her doll, Linnet, on her lap. "I don't see why we had to come all the way out here. We could have done it at the house or behind the barn."

Sarah wrinkled her nose and grinned. "I don't want to seal our friendship forever-and-ever near the barn or the Joe."

Phoebe straightened Linnet's mobcap and kissed the doll's cheek before she looked at Sarah. "Are you ready?"

Sarah made sure the bow on Esmee's pinafore was tied, kissed her, and nodded. Holding Esmee out to Phoebe, Sarah said, "We will always be best friends, and I promise to keep Linnet safe with me always."

"And I vow to care for Esmee, and be your beloved friend till I die," Phoebe affirmed. They exchanged the dolls that each of their mothers had made for them, and then they hugged each other.

Sarah sat back, her gaze locked with Phoebe's. "I'll *never* move away from you. Not ever."

"No, never, even when we get married." Phoebe cradled Esmee in her arms. "And our little girls will grow up and be best friends, too!"

"Phoebe!"

"That's Mama," Phoebe said, scrambling to her feet. "We better go."

Sarah sprang to her feet also, grabbed Phoebe's hand, and, with their dolls, they ran until they reached Mrs. Nelson at the edge of the field. "Hello, Mrs. Nelson. We took Esmee and Linnet for a walk with us."

Mrs. Nelson shook her head. "It's suppertime. I'm sure your mama's looking for you, too, Sarah."

"You're not going to whoop Phoebe, are you?"

Mrs. Nelson fixed Sarah with a fierce glare before she turned to Phoebe. "If I have to chase after you again, I certainly will." She grabbed her daughter's hand from Sarah and started walking.

Sarah winked at Phoebe and ran along with them. She was never sure if Mrs. Nelson would follow through with one of her threats, but Sarah didn't think so today. When they reached the fork in the path that led to Sarah's house, she grinned at Phoebe, hugged Linnet, and skipped along the dirt track leading to her farmhouse.

1

Gridley, Oregon, 1873

The Wedge Saloon was deserted. Gil Perry stepped from behind the bar, got the broom from the back room, and swept the grimy sawdust toward the doorway. He hadn't seen anyone walk by since before he sat down for dinner. If he didn't know better, it would be easy to believe he was the only person in town.

He shoved the broom and sent the pile of dirt and sawdust flying out onto the boardwalk. A shrill "Agh!" broke the silence before he had lowered the broom.

Sarah Hampton shook her skirt with a viciousness she should have reserved for the lummox who had just hurled the sweepings at her. She had ironed the tartan plaid dress just that morning and now it was covered with dirt, wood shavings, and only the Lord knew what else.

She sure was a sight, flailing her skirts around as if a pack of rats had attacked her. "Mrs. Hampton. I didn't see you."

"Of course not," she said, glaring at the man. It was the beer jerker, Mr. Perry. "You didn't even *look!*" He was grinning at her, the dolt. She supposed that some innocent women might be easily enticed by the resonance of his voice, the long dark lashes that hooded those brown eyes, but she was not.

The scent of lilacs floated around her. He inhaled the delicate fragrance and smiled to himself. For all her high-falutin ideas, she was in the habit of wearing her hair unbound. He knew he wasn't the only man ever to think about running his hands through her dark brown, wavy hair, but those blue eyes of hers could unman a fellow as easily as entice him. A lock of her long hair now rested over her shoulder. She moved her hand and the sunlight caught on her gold wedding band. Gil had heard that her late husband had been gone for over a year; he wondered what it would take for her to remove that ring.

In the last three months he had watched her sashay down the street, overheard her rich laughter, and read her spirited articles in the *Gridley Gazette*, but he hadn't approached her.

He hadn't planned this meeting, either, but he had definitely gotten her attention.

"I'll brush off the rest." He dropped the broom and advanced a step toward her.

She jumped back and whipped her skirt aside. "Keep your hands to yourself." She turned on her heel and proceeded down the street.

After Sarah's husband died, Phoebe had written to her about life in Oregon, the beauty of the land, the new-found freedom women enjoyed—but she had failed to mention the men. Thankfully not all men were like Mr. Perry and, to be honest, Sarah had not been at all interested in men.

Not then.

That was why the suffrage movement appealed to her. When women became independent, men wouldn't have the right to control women's finances, or their lives, or their property. Sarah did not dislike men. However, she had learned that she did not *need* a man in order to have a fulfilling life. Meeting Mr. Perry did nothing to change her mind.

She stepped down from the end of the boardwalk and

paused in the sunlight. As she brushed at her skirt again, she glanced back at the saloon. He had the temerity to grin at her a moment before he went back inside—just where he belonged.

"Phoebe, you must do something about Sarah—"

Phoebe Abbott looked up from the mail she was sorting to glance at her husband, Charles. "You're her employer. I'm her friend. I'd say that is something you should do."

He paced across the newspaper office. "Her column for the ladies was good. I'd sure like to see another one right now." He held up three sheets of paper and shook them. "Did you see what she wrote this week?"

Accustomed to his outbursts—age hadn't dampened his temper—Phoebe knew this one would not last long. "Not yet. She finished writing it late last night." Sarah hadn't confided in her, and Phoebe didn't think Sarah would be surprised by Charles's reaction. Her last two articles had received a similar response from him. "Is the editor of the *Gridley Gazette* asking? Or my husband?" His light brown hair now had a dusting of gray, and he had gained a few pounds, but his warm brown eyes still sparkled and had the power to make her feel like a girl again.

"The editor."

Phoebe smiled. "Is it so terrible?"

"I can't print this in the *Gazette*! Half the men in town want to lynch her, and the rest double up laughing when they see her walk down the street. She has to stop this female suffragist foolishness."

She stared at him in disbelief. "Surely you don't mean that." After fourteen years of marriage, she knew he didn't really feel that way. "You've encouraged her to write for the women in town and that is what she's doing."

"This time she has gone too far." He tossed the papers onto his office desk and ran his hand through his hair. "Talk to her. I don't want all the husbands in town marching on this office."

"Charles . . ." Phoebe stood, stepped over to his side, and linked arms with him. "Sarah just wants women to think for themselves." She pressed her cheek to his shoulder. "Why don't you ask her to write a different kind of article?"

"What would you suggest? She said she can't do one more column on receipts, stitchery, or house cleaning."

"I don't blame her. She was never interested in the running of a house." Phoebe gazed up at her husband and grinned. "How about a column on etiquette?"

He burst out laughing. "That's perfect, my dear. It is. I hope she will be as enthusiastic about this as she's been about the suffragists."

"I believe she's been feeling a little restless. This might be just the thing for her. She hasn't been here very long, and I'm sure the change hasn't been easy for her." Phoebe glanced out through the front window and saw Sarah crossing the street. She was an attractive woman, though Phoebe knew Sarah gave little thought to her appearance.

"She's coming. You can talk to her now. Maybe she'll have time to write a few paragraphs for tomorrow's newspaper." Phoebe leaned up, kissed his stubbled cheek, and returned to the desk.

Sarah marched across the road to the *Gazette* office. The sign hanging overhead squeaked on its hinges. She charged into the office and, as she pushed the door closed, she caught a glimpse of the saloon. "Someone should teach that beer jerker some manners," she declared. "The man's a menace."

"Mr. Perry?" Phoebe eyed her. "What happened?"

"Look at my skirt!" Sarah grabbed a handful of cloth with each hand and shook it. "I ironed this just this morning and now it's a mess."

"I know how much you dislike ironing," Phoebe said, smiling, "but I don't see anything wrong with it now."

"The fool brushed the saloon sweepings all over my skirt." Sarah frowned and released her hold on the fabric with a flick of the wrist. "I suppose I should be grateful he wasn't emptying chamber pots."

"I'm sure it was an accident. Mr. Perry seems like a nice

man." Phoebe grinned at her. "He's rather attractive, don't you think?"

Sarah rolled her eyes. "A pleasant face is certainly *no* indication of a person's disposition. I learned that lesson well enough, and I'm not about to repeat the experience."

"John wasn't the same after the war. It affected some men like that."

"No. He was worse," Sarah intoned. "He had been attentive, charming, and oh, so very handsome. I believed each and every sugarcoated promise . . . until I could no longer avoid the truth. He was *primed* the better part of every day."

"I didn't know—" Phoebe gave Charles a bewildered look. "You never told me."

"I didn't notice how much he imbibed until he returned after the war; then we moved to New Jersey and I hoped he would change." Sarah glanced at Charles. "Enough. I left all that back in Camden County."

Not really, Phoebe thought.

Sarah glanced at Charles, who appeared decidedly uncomfortable. Men, she had concluded, rarely liked hearing women discuss men with such honesty. "Charles, you look as if you've read my article and don't like it." He was as close to a big brother as she could hope to have and, like siblings, they were not always in agreement.

He shook his head in his weary fashion.

Here it comes, she thought, the same old objections. "It might be an unusual experience for a few of our readers, but what is wrong with giving people something to think about?"

"No. You're not talking me into it this time, Sarah. But I do have an idea. . . ." He glanced at his wife before he faced Sarah. "You could write about etiquette—forgotten manners."

Sarah stared at him. "Manners? Yes sir, no ma'am, please, and thank you?" She hadn't thought he was *that* angry.

"Well . . ." He rubbed his hand over the back of his neck. "Phoebe, help me out."

Phoebe smiled. "I believe what he had in mind was a column that would help people know how to behave in social situations. Each week you could write about a different problem."

Sarah gaped at each of them. "You're serious?"

Phoebe nodded.

Sarah rolled her eyes. "That sounds about as interesting as how to launder soiled bed sheets." She paced over to the front window and back to the desk she shared with Phoebe. "You teach your children how to behave. Every mother does. What could I possibly add?"

Phoebe tried again to pique Sarah's interest. "You were just complaining about Mr. Perry, and the loggers could use a few reminders on how to approach a woman, speak to her, or, for that matter, how to tell the difference between a lady and a soiled dove. You have said a woman isn't safe on the streets from Saturday afternoon to Monday morning while the loggers are in town." When Sarah stared at the far wall with that gleam in her eyes, Phoebe knew she had captured her interest.

" 'How a man should greet a lady' may be a good subject to start with," Charles said with a nod, as if to himself. "Then you could give advice on different ways a lady may respond to a gentleman to show her interest, or lack of interest, appropriately. You have complained often enough about what rude louts the drifters and loggers are. Here's an opportunity to—"

Phoebe noticed the look of horror on her husband's face as he cut himself off. She realized that he understood he had come close to putting his foot in his mouth by giving Sarah an excuse to isolate the men even further than she had already. "Sarah, it doesn't have to be more than a page or two. Will you do it?"

"Mm-hm. . . ."

Sarah pulled the shawl from around her shoulders and hung it on a peg. Manners. Raucous, ill-behaved men. Mr. Perry. His name topped that list in her mind. "It might be fun." She absently smirked, her mind warming to the subject.

Charles sighed. "Good."

"I'll start on the article now—while it's fresh in my mind." She went over to the window and cast a speculative grin in the direction of the Wedge. Maybe she could repay Mr. Perry.

Phoebe set the mail for her husband on his desk, went over to him, and kissed his cheek. "I'll keep your supper warm if you're late." She put on her bonnet and took her cloak off of the peg. "I'll see you at the house, Sarah."

"Yes—this shouldn't take very long."

Sarah settled at the desk. She had considered finding other employment, but she truly enjoyed writing articles for the newspaper. She didn't set out to write pieces that would irritate Charles, but the result was almost the same as if she had. A couple of her columns had almost doubled their sales, though. Maybe her etiquette articles would do so as well.

She made a list of topics to use in the following weeks, but her opening column would be on how men should and should not approach women in public. She quickly filled three pages, then went back over each line, revised, and rewrote it on fresh paper. She refrained from naming Mr. Perry, although she hoped that when he heard about the article he would know who she had had in mind.

She handed the pages to Charles. "This should give the men the guidance they need."

He quickly read the first paragraph and nodded.

She considered that a welcome sign.

"Hmm." He scanned the second page and eyed her. "You have to rewrite a couple of lines." He marked the place with a pencil and handed the papers back to her.

She read aloud the lines he had indicated. " 'Too many men feel it is their right to accost women on the street and in the stores, forcing their unwanted attention on the ladies. It is time these men realize that women are not unclaimed baggage waiting for the nearest male, who usually reeks of cheap whiskey and stale tobacco, to rescue them.' "

She looked up. "I don't see anything wrong with that."

"You are insulting nearly every man in town."

"Only the rude, offensive ones, the ones who won't take

no for an answer." She handed the pages back to him. "Why not let the readers judge it for themselves?"

"You're responsible for my gray hair," he said, shaking his head. "You'll never find a man to marry in this town."

She arched one brow at him. "What makes you think I'd want to marry any man in this town? Or in any other town, for that matter?"

"Most women don't choose to be alone."

"That may be true for some, not for others. Most women are very capable of managing their own affairs, although few realize it."

"You're a fine-looking woman, Sarah. I hope you won't turn against men. We're not all like John."

"I know." She gave him a fun-loving grin and whispered, "I'm holding out for a man like you."

He chuckled. "I hope I'm around when you meet your match. Should be most interesting."

"Phoebe needs to give up matchmaking and find a new pastime."

"She just wants you to be happy." He sighed and walked over to the printing press. "Oh, all right. I'll run this. Who knows, I may learn something from these columns, too."

"I'm sure Phoebe will tell you whatever you want to know."

"And more." He looked at Sarah. "I think you should use a pen name. Your last articles caused quite a stir."

"This should give the men something else to think about, other than whiskey and brawling." She mulled it over for a moment and decided that writing under another name appealed to her. Besides, she had given him enough trouble for one day. She had a favorite aunt, and she didn't think Aunt Lucy would mind. "Lucy."

"Lucy what?"

"Just Lucy."

"Miss Lucy?"

She nodded. "I believe she would approve." She would have to send a copy of the newspaper to her aunt, one to her mother, too, with an explanation why she was using her aunt's name. She felt sure they would get a chuckle from that. "Would you like help setting the type?"

"Thanks, but I've got my routine."

She understood, but occasionally she asked in case he changed his mind. She put on her shawl and left him to his work.

She walked down River Road. It was a lovely September day. The red maple leaves were turning gold and the cottonwoods near the Mill River were the color of butter. Two boys ran out from between the buildings and darted straight at her. She jumped aside, just managing to save her toes from being trampled.

Laughter drifted from the saloon across the road, and she glanced in that direction. Mr. Perry was standing in the doorway chuckling. At her? The deep rumbling sound had the strangest effect on her. It was a pleasant effect, or would have been had if it had not been directed *at* her.

"This seems to be your day for mishaps, Mrs. Hampton."

She gritted her teeth, tempted to return to the newspaper office to add another line to the article. Instead she glared at him, squared her shoulders and continued down the street, determined not to allow him the satisfaction of ruffling her yet again.

With his broad shoulders, muscular arms, and rough bearing, he kept the peace in the saloon, or so she had heard. It was time he learned that the ladies in town were not the inebriates he kept company with, nor were they easy women.

Gil watched the Hampton woman stroll down the street. It was plain as the tracks in the road she wouldn't spare the time of day for him. If he hadn't accidentally swept dirt on her earlier, she wouldn't have spoken to him then either. For a woman who wrote articles about free love and said it was every woman's right, she wasn't too friendly.

She continued walking, but she couldn't help wondering if he would read her new column. All of the businesses in town subscribed to the *Gridley Gazette*. From what she had observed about him, though, he was as rough as the men he served, and he probably didn't even look at the news-paper.

Maybe he didn't know how to read.

From the way he had smiled at her it seemed obvious that he was accustomed to using that smile to gain what he wanted. Well, it wouldn't work on her. She had been mar-ried to a man who depended on his persuasive countenance in every situation, and she had learned it was best to ignore that type of man.

Relegating Mr. Perry's image to the far recess of her mind, she turned down the side street to the Abbotts' house. Charles and Phoebe had insisted Sarah stay with them. As much as she felt a part of their family, she wasn't. She worked for Charles in exchange for room and board, but she couldn't live with them forever. However, whenever she mentioned having her own small house, Phoebe pes-tered her until she agreed to stay a while longer.

Phoebe enjoyed the early mornings. The air was crisp, the house quiet, and the aroma of fresh coffee for Charles and Sarah filled the kitchen. Soon the children would wake up. Clay was thirteen, and Cora was nine. Sarah had helped raise them, until she moved east and they moved west. Phoebe finished her tea and smiled. She hoped Cora would someday have a friend as dear as Sarah.

Sarah entered the kitchen, bringing her pitcher to fill it with warm water for her morning ablutions. As usual, Phoebe was seated at the table. "What are you grinning about?"

"Memories." Phoebe refilled her cup with tea and poured coffee for Sarah. "Do you miss New Jersey?"

"When John and I moved to Camden the city seemed so noisy compared to Jackson County." Sarah turned the plain gold wedding band around on her finger. "I've almost stopped listening for boat and train whistles, but I'm not yet used to the delay in getting news from the East."

Phoebe watched the way Sarah twisted her wedding ring. "I wish I'd been able to go back and help you after John's death. We couldn't manage it but you were always in my thoughts and prayers.''

Sarah lowered her left hand. ''You were in mine, too, and settling John's affairs kept me busy for the first weeks. Then I attended a symposium on the suffrage movement. That's when I started writing letters to the editor of the *West Jersey Press*.'' She chuckled. ''I bet he doesn't miss me.''

''You probably brightened his days.'' Phoebe sipped her coffee. ''Last night Charles brought this week's paper home. I read your column. It's good. The women should like Miss Lucy.''

''I hope so, but I want the men to read it, too.'' Sarah sipped her coffee. ''Do you know how many loggers actually *read* the *Gazette*?''

''Not really.''

''I suspect most of them are told about what's in the newspaper rather than read it themselves.''

Phoebe couldn't disagree with her. ''I'm sure they will hear about the new column. Since it's written by ''Miss Lucy,'' you will be able to hear firsthand what people think. You could even take issue with some of the points in the article, just to keep your distance. It might be fun.''

Sarah beamed. ''Yes. Indeed.'' She sipped her coffee. ''We should agree on what to say when people ask about Miss Lucy.''

Phoebe nodded. ''We can't say she sends her column to us. Mr. Seaton sorts the mail. He would be the first to figure out we haven't received any mail from a Miss Lucy.''

Sarah flashed a conspiratorial grin. ''But we do receive newspapers.''

''And they quote from other newspapers—''

''Charles can credit her column to another paper. . . . The *Danbury News*. The *New Northwest* always reprints items from that paper.''

''Or simply say, Danbury, Connecticut.'' Phoebe laughed. ''No one will know the difference.''

''I wish we'd thought of this yesterday, but it's not too late. We'll just have to make sure the Miss Lucy column isn't run if the *New Northwest* doesn't arrive that week."

"I'll tell Charles."

"Okay." Sarah glanced at the pitcher. She was anxious to wander around town and see what people thought of the new column, but the paper wouldn't even be delivered until later that morning. "Do you realize we probably won't hear any comments before Monday?"

"Don't be so impatient." Phoebe grinned, took another sip of her tea, and watched Sarah. "You haven't changed. Once you make up your mind about something, you want to make it happen right then."

"No one lives forever," Sarah said with a shrug.

"That's a cheerful thought. I'd better introduce you to some of our eligible bachelors. Maybe one of them will tame your impulsive spirit."

Sarah, in the process of swallowing when Phoebe spoke, choked on her coffee. Once Sarah stopped coughing, she stared at Phoebe. "That's a fine thing to say about a friend."

"I want to see you happily settled so you'll stay here."

"If that's all, I will see about purchasing a piece of land. It shouldn't take long to have a small house built."

"Oh, Sarah, that's not what I meant." Phoebe reached across the table and held Sarah's hand. "You were happy with John, at one time, and I—"

Sarah sprang to her feet. "I am quite content with my life. Marriage does not guarantee contentment or security. Would you rather have me miserable and desperate?"

"Of course not—"

"Then please leave me to my own devices." She set the pitcher by the stove and ladled warm water into it. On the way out of the kitchen, she paused and looked at Phoebe. "Not everyone is suited to marriage, but if the right man comes along, I won't bite his head off."

"Let's hope he has the stamina to survive the courtship," Phoebe said, grinning at her.

2

$\mathcal{G}$il finished wiping spilled beer from the table. The loggers would soon fill the place. They wouldn't notice if the tables were clean or the sawdust on the floor was fresh. If they paid attention to anything besides their drinks, it would be the large painting of the lovely Lorinda baring her charms for all to appreciate. It was the only touch he had added when Jack Young, Gil's friend and the owner of the Wedge, built the place.

Jack was seated at the back of the room at the table nearest his office door. Gil finished cleaning off the table, drew two beers, and joined him.

He slid one glass across the table to Jack. "What's the tally?"

Jack tapped the pencil on the ledger. "I knew this place would make money. But who the hell woulda thought I'd have an account at the bank?" He took a long swig of beer.

"Who would've believed a town would spring up around a logging camp's weekend sport? When I set Vonney up in business, I figured we'd be here a couple of seasons."

"I kinda like stayin' in one place."

Gil chuckled. "Especially since Ben Layton moved to town last spring with his pretty, blonde daughter."

"Miss Tess's nice. And she don't mind my ownin' the

saloon. What about you? None of the women in town seem to interest ya.''

Gil took a swig of beer and was struck by the jolting memory of Sarah Hampton's image and the scent of lilacs. He felt a strange restless sensation, and downed another gulp of beer. If it had been any other woman, he might have been interested in pursuing her. But not Sarah Hampton. Riding a key log out of a jam on the river would be safer than chasing after that woman.

''I'm sure Vonney ain't complainin'.''

Yanked out of his reverie, Gil frowned at Jack. "She has a good heart.''

''When the mill opens up again next month we'll see more newcomers settlin' here, and she won't have much time for ya.'' Jack raised his glass to Gil. "Thanks for talkin' me into buyin' land.'' He finished the beer and set the glass on the table.

''Vonney and I are just friends now. Have been for some time.'' Gil smirked at him. "You're one of the leading citizens in town. If you're not careful, you could end up being the sheriff or mayor one day.''

''Oh, no. I'll see they have all the beer or whiskey they want, but I've got no patience for some of the newcomers and their squabbles.''

Gil glanced at the folded *Gridley Gazette* by the ledger. ''What did Mrs. Hampton have to say this week?''

''Nothin'. Abbott must've reined her in.''

After the scene she made earlier, Gil didn't agree. She was one spirited lady, and he didn't envy Abbott having to oversee her day after day. In fact, now that he thought about it, he ought to stand Abbott a few drinks.

''Good thing, too,'' Jack said, shaking his head. "If he hadn't, the women might've come out in droves to vote, and we could've had a rebellion on our hands, if we ever have an election.'' He jabbed his finger at the newspaper. ''You should look at his editorial. He's still moanin' about loggers strippin' the hills bare and dirtyin' up the river.''

''Good. It'll give me something to read while I'm gone.''

Gil finished his beer and stood up. "I'll be leaving tomor-row afternoon."

"Kiss Vonney for me."

"Ride out tonight and kiss her yourself." Gil went to the back room and brought out a fresh keg. It was the same each Saturday. The loggers hit town in the late afternoon. Some headed straight to the bathhouse, others for the Wedge.

Jack was right about Gridley. Seven years earlier, at the age of twenty-two, Gil had decided to go into the timber business. He started the loggers working and put up a small lumber mill. He didn't plan to establish a town, but it didn't take long to see that the crew needed a place nearby where they could carouse. He and Jack put up the saloon on the bank of the stream they named Mill River, then Gil built the livery.

Drifters found the saloon the first week it was open. Soon there was a small store, and then other businesses lined River Road. Four years later Gil sold his share of the Wedge to Jack with the agreement that he could continue working the bar a few days each week. He had been content living upstairs, over the saloon.

A wagon rattled to a stop out front, and he started draw-ing the beer. Jake and Willie burst through the doorway, headed straight for the bar. They were the youngest crew members and the rowdiest. Gil set two glasses of beer on the bar for them and began filling more for the others streaming into the saloon.

It was finally Monday. Sarah tossed the shawl across her shoulders and met Phoebe at the front door. "I'm ready."

"Me, too. I hope Seaton's has the new woolen goods they ordered. Clay and Cora are growing so fast. I want to start on their new coats for winter."

Sarah left the house with Phoebe at a brisk pace. "Re-member when we hounded our mamas for those matching cloaks?"

"Blue." Phoebe laughed. "Teal blue."

"Trimmed with black braid." Sarah momentarily stopped

in her tracks and grinned. "Did you keep yours? Cora might like it."

"I have no idea where it is now. Mama wouldn't have saved it. She passed all our hand-me-downs to the Tillibey family." Phoebe glanced at her friend. "Did your mama keep yours?"

"She may have. She probably did. She threatened to give it to my daughter and tell her what a little hoyden I was. I'll have to write and ask her." Sarah wouldn't mind passing her cloak down to Cora, who was almost like a daughter to her. At thirty-three, Sarah did not expect to remarry or have children of her own. They reached the general store.

Phoebe hurried over to where Mrs. Seaton was arranging a ready-made dress on display. "My, that's pretty." Phoebe reached out and felt the soft woolen skirt of grayish-tan with blue stripes.

"Hard to believe it'll be winter soon." Mrs. Seaton smiled at Phoebe. "The new winter woolen goods you ordered are here. Come with me." Mrs. Seaton led her to the back of the shop. "By the way, I read the new Miss Lucy article. . . ."

Sarah smiled to herself. Mrs. Seaton's opinion of Miss Lucy would be shared with her customers. Sarah fidgeted with an apple peeler and a coffee grinder and wandered around impatiently until Phoebe came out from the storeroom.

"Look at these new bolts. Think Cora will like the green?"

Sarah joined her at the yard goods table. "I do, but why not let her choose?"

Phoebe cast her a wry smile. "For someone who can write pages on why women should have the vote, it's surprising how you hesitate over decisions concerning the children."

"What do you mean? Oh, that's nonsense." Sarah ran her hand over the wool. "The green will look nice on her." While Mrs. Seaton cut the cloth, Sarah drew Phoebe away from the table. "What did she say about Miss Lucy?"

Phoebe glanced around and said softly, "Mrs. Seaton

thinks Miss Lucy is a delightful old dear and hopes to see more of her sage advice.'' She giggled, then quickly clamped her lips together.

"Old?'' Sarah frowned. She had pictured her "other self" as being charming, sophisticated, a woman to be admired and respected. "I'm hardly an 'old dear.' '' She was at least two decades away from reaching that description.

Twice a month Gil Perry checked on the logging camp, and while he was there he would spend the better part of a day riding through the woods. After he arrived early Sunday evening he walked through the bunkhouse, then went into the cookhouse.

Coffeepots, kettles, and pans hung from the rafters in the cooking area. It was warm and Dugan Moody, the camp cook, was standing at the stove. Gil walked between two tables to the kitchen area.

"Dugan, got any supper left over?'' He didn't know how old Dugan was; his gray hair and beard were as much a sign of a hard life as of age.

"Henry went huntin' with Choker and Dowdy. Brought back a real nice elk.'' Dugan glanced over his shoulder at Gil. "Tomorrow we'll have sourdough biscuits and stew. Got raspberry syrup fer the flapjacks in the mornin'.''

Gil chuckled. "If I stay more than a day or two I'll have to work off your meals.''

"Not a bad idear.''

"It's been five years since anyone could call me a woodsman. I'd just as soon keep it that way.'' Gil grabbed a cup and poured himself some coffee. "Have anything I can eat now?''

"Ya ain't gone hungry yet.'' Dugan grabbed a towel and opened the oven door. "Grab a fork and sit yerself down.''

"Are the supplies getting through all right?'' Gil took his coffee and flatware to the table.

Dugan set the supper plate in front of Gil and sat across the table from him. "You see what that Abbott feller said 'bout our strippin' the hills? He don't know nothin' 'bout trees.''

Gil shrugged and kept his thoughts on that subject to himself.

"An' tell me what he'd print his dern news on without paper."

Gil swallowed a tender bite of meat. "I brought the *Gazette* with me, but haven't read it yet. How did you get a copy so soon?"

"Dowdy came back last night."

"I didn't see him when I walked through the bunkhouse."

"He's likely at Vonney's. Surprised ya didn't see him there."

"Didn't stop by her house on the way up here." Gil finished eating and refilled his cup. "You need to go into town with the men. Can't spend all of your days in here."

"I don't," Dugan said and chuckled.

"Glad to hear it." Gil stood up with his cup in hand. "See you in the morning." He went to the office, where he also bunked down. After looking over the company books, he added a shot of whiskey to his coffee and sat back with the newspaper.

He read Charlie Abbott's editorial about loggers leaving hillsides barren, blonde hair being worth more than its weight in gold, and a Minneapolis man who had managed to put five hundred and four handwritten words on one postcard. Gil wondered if there was a limit to what some people would do to be noticed.

There were a couple of notices about stores going out of business. Too bad Sarah Hampton didn't have an article in the paper. Some of those peculiar ideas she wrote about gave him a chuckle.

She had become the butt of many jokes in the saloon because of her sharp-tongued articles in the *Gazette*, especially the ones about free love. He was folding the paper to put it aside, when he noticed a piece by a Miss Lucy.

Stifling a yawn, he leaned over the desk and read "How to Approach a Lady" with growing interest. It was almost as if this Miss Lucy had been eavesdropping on the incident with Sarah Hampton in front of the saloon. He set the paper aside and stretched out on the bunk. That was an entertaining article, but Gridley was a logging town, at least it had started out that way, not a big eastern city.

The next morning Mount Hood's snowy cap gleamed in the sunlight. After eating a stack of flapjacks drenched with Dugan's raspberry syrup, Gil rode into the hills beyond the logging camp. He guided his mount between the hemlock, pine, and red cedar trees. Although he was north of where his crew was working, their clamor carried through the trees—the whacking axes, the grating scrape of the saws, and above all the cry of "Timber!" just before the rending crack and crash of the tree shaking the earth when it landed.

The trees *talked* as the last fibers gave way and snapped, and Gil was glad he wasn't close enough to hear that. It sounded too much like dying. He preferred listening to the wind bend and whip the tops of the huge old trees, and the whispering of the branches.

Near sundown he rode into the logging camp. After tending to his horse, he went into the cookhouse. The tables were set but the lamps would be lighted just before the men arrived. He walked back to the kitchen and poured a cup of coffee.

Dugan came out of the storeroom carrying a tub. "Hi. Yer early."

"Thought you might need another hand." Gil grinned as he raised the cup to his mouth. Three large trays of raw biscuits were ready for the oven.

"Ya say that every time. Yer jist jawin'." Dugan set the tub on the worktable. "Did ya go by 'n' see how the men were doin'?"

"I watched from a distance." Gil took another gulp of coffee as he watched Dugan. "Why? Is there a problem?"

"Heard some rumblin' from the men." Dugan began spooning butter into bowls.

"I better talk to Henry again."

"Ask him 'bout the charred timber."

Once in a while Sarah dined at Elsie North's boarding-house. Elsie had outlived two husbands, and her four children had families of their own. She had five rooms to rent, and the house rules were enforced. She charged the "comers-an'-goers" a dollar and a half, and her regulars a dollar. Her gentlemen boarders felt at home, and her lady boarders felt safe.

On Wednesday, Sarah arrived early for dinner so they could visit before the boarders came in to eat. Elsie answered the door with her customary smile. "Hello. Is this a good day for me to drop by?"

"Come on inside. You're welcome anytime."

Sarah left her shawl on a peg near the door and went back to the kitchen with her. "Your sign's still out. I thought you had a full house."

"Mr. Settles said he'd only be here a short time. Mr. Rand and Mr. Bradly are salesmen. Each one spends two or three nights a month here." Elsie set a loaf of bread on the worktable. "But Mr. Pratt, the new schoolmaster, has taken a room. He should be here a while."

"I hope so." Sarah looked around. "Mm, that smells good. What can I do to help?"

"Slice bread?" Elsie handed her a knife. "I read that other woman's story—Miss Lucy, that's her name. She must be new in town."

"She's not from around here. I believe she lives in the East." Sarah sliced the bread, relieved that Elsie had mentioned the column.

"It makes no difference. I wish the men would take her advice." Elsie looked at Sarah. "You can tell Miss Lucy is a real lady. I bet her sons know how to behave."

Momentarily nonplussed, Sarah spread the bread slices on a plate. She wasn't sure what she had expected Elsie to say, but certainly not what she had. "Mm-hm." Sons?

"Of course. She sounded like my own dear mama." Elsie rang the dinner bell for the boarders. "I hope she writes more advice articles like that for Mr. Abbott."

"I could tell him what you said, but it might sound better coming from you."

"Yes, I'll do that. By the way, I missed your article this week. You aren't going to stop writing, are you, Sarah?"

"No—No, I'm working on the next one." Oh, figs, Sarah thought. If she could only change the spoken word as easily as the written. "Although, there aren't many more new ideas to tell about."

Elsie smiled at her. "You'll think of something. You always do."

Sarah nodded slowly, feeling the weight of her friend's confidence. She would continue writing under her own name, and she still felt women had as much right to the vote as men. Mrs. Woodhull's ideas were revolutionary, although some Sarah did not agree with, but women did have the right to know what others believed. That was why she had begun doing the series of articles.

"I'd like to hear more about that free love." Elsie laughed. "Long as it doesn't involve marriage. That isn't exactly free."

"It's been free for most men since time began." Sarah's grin slipped away when the image of Mr. Perry stepping toward her. She would be willing to bet love was free for him.

"If I weren't beyond an age to be interested, I'd sure think about it," Elsie said with a wink as she lifted the platter of meat to carry into the dining room.

Sarah chuckled. "According to Mrs. Woodhull and the National Radical Reformers, you're never too old." She had her doubts about that. She couldn't remember ever lying awake for want of a man's comfort, even John's—not after they moved to Camden, anyway.

When dinner was over, Sarah went to the *Gazette* office. Charles was seated at his desk reading an out-of-town newspaper. "See anything interesting?"

He lowered the newspaper and grinned at her. "Mrs. Rochester, of Boston, believes that the Women's Suffrage Association stands in the face of God and the laws of this country. Care to write to her?"

"I'm sure Miss Susan B. Anthony would be more eloquent. Besides, I have work to do." She sat at her desk.

He watched her a moment. "I recognize that look. What's happened?"

"I had dinner at Mrs. North's." She glanced over at him and grinned. "Elsie and the others believe Miss Lucy is a matron and must have raised at least two fine sons and probably a few daughters." She leaned back on the chair. "How about that?"

He laughed. "So you'll continue writing the column?"

"Oh, indeed, both of them. Elsie said she'd missed my article this week." She jotted down a couple of notes before they slipped her mind.

"She's likely the only one," he muttered.

Sarah smirked at him but continued with her own train of thought. "If others think Miss Lucy is real, I should keep writing under my own name, too. We don't want anybody to become suspicious."

"You may be right. But don't waste your time with that National Radical Reformers group. I don't care what she threatens, Victoria Woodhull will *never* be elected president of the United States."

"I agree, but some of her views on other subjects are intriguing. . . ." Staring at her notes, she remembered what Elsie had said. "It certainly would be interesting to talk with women who not only believe in, but who also practice free love," she mused aloud. "I'll ask women who believe in it to write me and share their feelings. Men, too. It might be very enlightening to see how men felt."

"You can't!" Slack-jawed, he stared at her. "You'll cause a riot."

"Charles, I'm not advocating war."

"You do know—*must* know—that some people actually believe every word printed in newspapers is the God's honest truth."

"Our readers should understand that I'm not reporting on events as much as sharing my views." She tapped the end of the pencil on the desk. "I need to check something at the lending library. I won't be long."

"That'll be a first." He sighed, as if relieved she was leaving. "Haven't you memorized every book on the shelves?"

"I just know where to look for the information I need.

Anyone that's been there more than twice does. The town needs to raise funds to purchase more books.''

He nodded, added to the list on his desk, and went back to reading the newspaper.

She grabbed her pencil and two sheets of paper, and walked to the Harrison Lending Library, named for the late Mr. Harrison. Actually it was a single, fair-sized room, lined with stained pine shelves, attached to the Timbers Hotel. Mr. Harrison's widow had donated his many volumes to encourage others to do the same. Charles gave a copy of each newspaper, and occasionally the library received other donations.

Sarah entered the hotel, which had been built to house loggers and mill workers. The present owner, Mr. Kenton, had added carpets, new paint, and watercolor landscapes of the Columbia River and Willamette Valley. As she crossed the lobby, she waved to Mr. Kenton and went to the library.

She had donated a booklet published by Victoria Woodhull and wanted to read it again. However, after searching through the shelves, Sarah realized someone must have borrowed the booklet. It would be nice to know who, she mused. She found one reference she needed, made notes, and left the library.

She stepped onto the boardwalk in front of the hotel, her mind on the opening sentence for her article. A gentleman passed and her arm brushed his.

"Excuse me." She glanced up and found herself staring at Mr. Perry. Stunned by his unhurried appraisal, her heart seemed to skip a beat. At least he hadn't covered her with muck this time, but he was as imposing. She instinctively stepped back from him.

He tapped his forehead, as if tipping a hat, and smiled. "Careful, Mrs. Hampton. I wouldn't want to be blamed for you falling off the boardwalk." Her gaze, a mixture of surprise and alarm, fascinated him.

His voice wasn't biting or mocking, as she might have supposed it would be when they met again—if she had given it any thought, which she hadn't—but that didn't change her opinion of him.

He looked up at Mount Hood. "It's a fine day, isn't it?"

"Yes." She glanced around. "Yes, it is nice." She stepped past him and nodded. She had no desire to stand there passing the time of day with him.

"I didn't see your article in last week's paper. Are you working on a new one?" He waited to hear her use *Miss Lucy's* suggested topics of conversation for just such a meeting. He had reread Miss Lucy's column. It had a familiar sound, almost as if Mrs. Hampton had written the piece, so much so that he had written to her. It would arrive in the next mail delivery and maybe then he'd find out if his suspicion was right.

So, he could read, or at least he claimed to know how. Evidently, he didn't take her seriously—no, not her, Miss Lucy. Drat, she must keep the articles straight in her mind. She turned and faced him. "I wouldn't have thought you would be interested in the women's suffrage movement." The papers she clutched in her hand rattled.

He grinned, not bothering to hide his amusement. "You'd be surprised what interests me, Mrs. Hampton."

She had already noticed the red cast in his wavy brown hair and felt the piercing gaze from his dark eyes. She certainly did not want to know what he thought about. "Let's keep it that way, Mr. Perry." Without waiting for a reply, she continued on her way.

He eyed the sway of her skirts as she hurried off. "I'll look for your article in this week's paper."

With no intention of replying to him, she went straight to the *Gazette* office and stepped inside. Glancing down at her chest, she half expected to see her wildly beating heart beneath her shirtwaist. She had the oddest feeling about their meeting. He behaved as if they were acquainted. Maybe he had mistaken sweeping dirt on her as an introduction. *Don't waste your time on him,* she thought, and turned her mind to her writing.

While she wrote the next Miss Lucy column, Sarah imagined her dear aunt speaking and worded it accordingly. She set the first draft aside and began working on the other article. She made two false starts before she felt she had found the right approach on the subject of free love and managed to work in a sassy comment about ladies who were so proper that their corsets would pop open if they actually were friendly with men.

In the last paragraph, she asked men and women who had personal knowledge of free love to share their experience with her. Charles had turned down two lights before she realized how late it was.

He shook his head. "You're enjoying yourself too much for my comfort."

"If I wasn't, I would do something else." She folded the pages, grabbed her shawl, and walked outside with him.

"You go on without me. Tell Phoebe I'll be home before long."

She had felt like his sister for so long that this comment prompted a a teasing, sisterly grin. "If you tell Phoebe and me what you overhear at the saloon."

"Not on your life, missy."

When he crossed the road, she laughed and glanced past him at the Wedge. Men milled about, but she didn't see Mr. Perry. Fine. She didn't know why she even bothered. Charles paused in the doorway, waved to her, and went inside.

She started walking down the street. She would love to eavesdrop on the conversations that took place in there and write a column enlightening women about men. Oh, if she could figure out how a man's mind worked, she might even write a book.

Gil walked through the lobby of the hotel and went into the lending library. If he had been a few minutes earlier, he probably would have found Mrs. Hampton in there. Just as well he hadn't. He didn't need the distraction, and she was that.

After following her columns in the newspaper, he felt he knew her as well as most people did, and couldn't resist teasing her a bit by breaking most of the rules in Miss Lucy's column. Her next one might be interesting, especially if it sounded as if she had witnessed his second meet-

ing with Mrs. Hampton. However, now he needed to
remember his reason for going to the library.

As Dugan had suggested, Gil had spoken with Henry
again, and learned that two small fires had been set or had
started at the edge of the camp. Gil knew that people who
liked to start fires tended to move around. Fires made news,
especially in small towns. Now he wanted to find out if any
other fires had been reported in the area.

He sat down in the upholstered chair with the pile of
newspapers at his side and reached for the most recent
Statesman. He could stop by the *Gazette* office and talk to
Charles Abbott, too. Not a bad idea, he thought, smiling.

3

$\mathcal{P}$hoebe finished reading and pushed the pages back across the kitchen worktable to Sarah. "You can make anything interesting, but do you really expect women to admit they practice free love?"

"I won't know if I don't ask." Sarah idly shuffled the papers. "I'd like to talk with women who believe in it. Maybe they would be more forthright about their experiences. Who knows, one or two men may write to a woman they don't know."

"Men have been practicing that for centuries, and so have women of easy virtue."

Sarah shrugged. "I'll weed out those responses."

Phoebe picked up her cup of coffee. "Gram told me about bundling. It doesn't sound that different."

"We missed out on that." Sarah laughed, trying to imagine her mother's mother and father as a young passionate couple lying in bed together with only a board the length of the bed separating them. No wonder couples married quickly. She glanced up. "Or it wasn't done with the families' permission."

"Don't say such a thing. What if the children heard you? They would likely think you're serious." Phoebe smirked as she raised the cup to her mouth. She had wondered if

Gram had bundled with Grandpa, but she hadn't been bold enough to ask her.

"It's strange." Sarah ran a finger around the rim of the cup. "I have the right to sleep with a man, if I truly want to, but I certainly wouldn't want Cora to think she can do the same with just any boy until she's wed—or, at the very least, well past twenty."

"Cora can wait until she marries," Phoebe said. "That's probably how our mothers felt when young men called on us."

"Remember Homer Leggett? He spent so much time pacing down the road to your farm, Papa said he made a new ditch for your papa to water his field."

"Mama didn't have to worry on his account."

"That's probably why she liked him better than the others." Sarah sipped her coffee. "I went to the library this afternoon. When I left the hotel, I bumped into the beer jerker from the Wedge." *Beer jerker* was the best way to regard him. It served to remind her, if she happened to be in need of a mental nudge, that he worked in a saloon.

"Why do you refer to Mr. Perry that way? He's nice enough."

"That is his occupation."

Phoebe shook her head. "What happened?"

Sarah frowned. "Nothing."

"What did he say?"

"He mentioned my articles." Sarah stared at Phoebe. "That's just it. The way he talked. We've never been introduced, have hardly even spoken, yet he acted as if we were acquaintances."

"He's friendly, but I doubt you've given him even the slightest encouragement. How do you expect to marry again? You haven't let any man get close to you."

"I don't expect to get married. Men want young brides, innocents they can train. Fifty-year-old men ogle young ladies fresh out of school." Sarah shrugged. "I'm certainly no innocent; I absolutely refuse to be 'trained' and I have no interest in domestic chores. You know that. You wrote those articles on housekeeping, I didn't."

"Yes, well, Charles couldn't tell I had, but that's beside the point. Even if you live alone, you must keep house. Wouldn't you rather share your home with a loving man?"

"No. Nearly twelve years ago I felt differently, but I've matured." Sarah swirled the last swallow of coffee in the cup and stood up. "I'd better go to bed."

"I didn't mean to bring up all those memories, Sarah. Are you all right?"

"Fine. I thought I'd forgotten how angry I was with him, about his drinking . . . so many things. . . ." Sarah patted Phoebe's shoulder. "He promised to cherish, love, and protect me, and I believed him."

"I'm sure he did his best." Phoebe stood up and hugged Sarah. "John wouldn't have wanted you to mourn him the rest of your life."

Sarah stared at her. "I'm not."

"Then why don't you stop by the lending library Monday night?" Phoebe decided it was about time to goad her into meeting men. They had challenged one another when they were much younger, so she hoped it would work now, too. "I understand Mr. Pratt, the new schoolmaster, is in the habit of reading there each Monday night."

"I'm certain I will meet him eventually." Sarah shook her head at Phoebe and walked to her bedroom.

"Yes," Phoebe said too softly to be heard. "Sooner than you know." She turned out the light and went to her room. After she slid into bed beside Charles, she whispered, "Don't you think it's time for an article about the new schoolmaster?"

"Mm-hm."

She pressed a light kiss on his shoulder. "Why don't you have Sarah interview him?"

"Yes, dear. . . ."

The next morning Sarah completed both articles. It was almost dinnertime when she handed the carefully penned pages to Charles, the one written under her own name on top.

"I took Phoebe's suggestion and poked fun at some of

society's restrictions, ones Miss Lucy would admire, so no one will suspect I'm writing both articles."

She gave him a wide-eyed glance and went back to her desk. The first story would upset him, but she hoped the second one would give him a chuckle. His eyes seemed to be focused halfway down the first page when he scowled. Next his cheeks had more color than usual, then he sputtered and gaped at her. She could almost hear him speak before he was able to form the words.

"Why—this is—" His hand shook. "Tell me you don't expect anyone to write to you, at least admit that much to put my mind at ease."

She granted him a slight smile. "I'm not sure. But wouldn't it be interesting if a few women did? I was too curious not to ask. Surely there's no harm in that."

"It'll give the boys at the Wedge a good laugh."

She shrugged. "Maybe some woman—as far away as the Arizona Territory—will read the *Gazette* and feel safe writing about her experience." When he rolled his eyes, she smirked. "Look at the Miss Lucy piece. It should make you feel better."

"I hope the dear old soul doesn't disappoint me." He sat on one corner of his desk and began reading.

"She wouldn't do that, not to you." Sarah dropped the first drafts of each article in the wastebasket and straightened up her desk.

He finished reading, laid the papers on his desk, and glanced at Sarah. "I'd sure like to meet Miss Lucy sometime. Think you could arrange it?"

"Hm, I don't know. She leaves almost before she finishes her articles."

He laughed. "That's true enough." He walked over to the front window and stared down the street. "I'd like you to do another article for this week's edition."

"Please, not an obituary. I'm not good at those."

"No, an interview. Mr. Pratt, the schoolmaster. He's new in town. People are likely curious about him." Charles meandered back to his desk. "You probably can see him after school lets out this afternoon. Shouldn't take too long."

"Just as bad. Wouldn't you rather do it? Man to man."

He started shuffling papers on his desk. "You'll do fine. Ask about his background, family, why he came west, how he came to Gridley."

"I see Phoebe's hand in this." Sarah glanced at the clock. "I should take her with me. She could chaperon us."

Sarah walked down River Road to the Methodist church, which served as the school during the week. The sun was warm and the light breeze felt good. School was out. She greeted several children in passing before she saw Cora talking with her friend Patsy and waved.

Cora was a happy little girl, so like Phoebe was at her age—large brown eyes, reddish-gold hair in a long braid down her back, and a smile that would drive the boys to distraction in a few years. Patsy had the sweetest face with caramel-brown eyes, a sprinkling of freckles, and curly blonde hair. Together, the girls could be a handful.

Cora ran over to her. "Are you looking for me, Aunt Sarah?"

"No, sweetie. I wanted to speak to Mr. Pratt. Has he left yet?"

Patsy leaned over and whispered near Cora's ear, and they giggled. Cora glanced at Sarah and quieted. "He cleans up and grades papers after school."

"Mrs. Hampton . . ." Patsy bit her lower lip before she continued. "Do you like Mr. Pratt?"

"We haven't met yet." Sarah smiled the girls. "Where are you two going?"

"To Patsy's house. Her mama promised to teach us how to make noodles."

"Watch carefully. Maybe you can fix some for us tomorrow night." Sarah took one step and turned back to the girls. "Oh, Cora, don't forget to ask your mama first."

"Yes, Aunt Sarah."

The girls skipped down the road, and Sarah continued on to the school. By the time she reached the steps, the yard was deserted. A rope swing, hung from a tree branch, twisted slowly in the breeze. She made her way up the plank steps quietly, as if she were late for church, and entered the classroom. She passed the cold woodstove as a tall gentleman walked toward the front of the room.

"Mr. Pratt?"

She paused halfway up the aisle, staring at the bundle of switches on the desk near the pulpit. Many were thin, but some were as thick as her thumb. A memory of another teacher, viciously switching a small boy's hand, suddenly flashed in her mind, and a shiver slid down her spine. She hadn't been more than seven at the time.

"Yes, I'm Mr. Pratt," he said, turning around. When he saw her, he straightened up. "I have met many of the students' parents, but not all. Which child is yours?"

"None." She stepped forward, pushing the memory to the back of her mind where it belonged, and focused on Mr. Pratt. He looked rather studious with his fine features, and a bristle-straight mustache almost overshadowed his small, square jaw. "I am Mrs. Hampton, and I write for the *Gridley Gazette.*"

"Sarah Hampton?" He put down the books he had been holding. "This is a pleasure, Mrs. Hampton. I have followed your articles with interest."

"Thank you. Men don't often approve of my articles."

"Oh, but they have been most interesting. History in the making. Mrs. Hampton, won't you sit down?"

She smiled and chose a seat at the end of the nearest bench. "Mr. Abbott, the editor of the *Gazette*, would like to publish an article on you, an introduction to the community for those who haven't had the opportunity to meet you."

"Oh . . ." He sat across the aisle and two rows up from her. "There isn't much to tell. Schoolmasters live rather quiet lives, at least I do."

"It won't be a biography, Mr. Pratt." She unfolded the paper and laid it on the desk in front of her. "How long have you been teaching?"

"Fifteen years last May." He looked away from her.

"That is a long time. Do you mind telling me where you grew up?"

"Maryland, originally, but I spent my youth in Chester County, Pennsylvania." He glanced around the room.

"My, you've traveled a very long way." Clever comment she thought sarcastically, and grimaced inwardly. Most everyone in the West had traveled across the country or had sailed around the Horn.

"Not all at once. I taught school in four different states and three territories." He shifted on the bench. "Do you need the names?"

"Oh, no, Mr. Pratt." She smiled, hoping to put him at ease. "That won't be necessary." She wrote *experienced* on the paper. He was such a mild-mannered gentleman, she hoped the switches were more for show than actual use.

He sighed and nodded.

"Do you mind my asking if you are married? I'm sure the ladies will be curious." She thought about asking what he thought about free love but dismissed that idea just as quickly.

"No, I am not married, Mrs. Hampton."

She knew of at least two women in town who would be interested. He wasn't offering anything but simple answers, and she didn't have enough information yet to fill the column. "When you were a boy, what was your favorite pastime?"

He smiled sheepishly. "Reading and fishing."

"You'll be able to do both here. What subject do you like teaching most?"

He glanced at a map hanging on one wall and smiled. "Geography."

"Have you always been adventurous?"

"One year I had the good fortune to be tutored by a gentleman who used geography to teach arithmetic, reading, and writing. He made learning fascinating."

"Ah, that's why Clay and Cora have been talking about the size of mountains."

"The Abbott children?"

"Yes. I am close to the family." She didn't want to become the interviewee and changed the subject. "I see you have Noah Webster's *Blue-black Speller* and *McGuf-*

fey's Eclectic Readers. Do you loan books to some of your pupils?"

"For use here in school if they have forgotten to bring their own. The children in Oregon are more fortunate than those in some other areas. This state stresses the importance of education." He shifted on the wooden bench. "Have you been here long?"

"Almost three months." So long, Sarah thought. She really needed to get her own house. "Is there anything you would like to add?"

He shook his head. "If the parents want to speak with me, I am usually here until half past four each afternoon."

Sarah added that to her notes, folded the paper, and stood up. "Thank you very much for talking with me. I've enjoyed meeting you, Mr. Pratt."

"It was my pleasure, Mrs. Hampton." He rose to his full height. "I hope I'll see you again soon."

She gave him a slight smile. "That is one advantage to living in a small town."

She walked to the door, the click of her heels resonating in the silence. It was an eerie sound, one that reminded her of how long it had been since she had gone to church. On the way home, she went over the interview in her mind. Belatedly, she thought of another question, but it would keep. He seemed to be a pleasant man and, she hoped, a good teacher.

That evening after supper, she and Cora helped Phoebe clean up the kitchen. While they talked about things that would not interest Charles, he enjoyed one of his frequent games of chess with Clay. As Sarah wiped off the worktable, she spoke to Cora. "You seem to like school better this year. Does Patsy?"

"Uh-huh. She sits next to me."

Phoebe gave Sarah a knowing grin. "The way you two like to talk, that may not be a very good idea."

Sarah picked up a tea towel and helped Cora dry the dishes. "Is Mr. Pratt strict?"

"Mm-hm. Bobby Jo put a frog in Mr. Pratt's lunch pail

and it wet all over his food." Cora giggled. "He got real mad and switched Bobby Jo good."

Sarah watched Cora. "I wouldn't have been very happy about that either." But I'm not sure, she thought, I would have used the same punishment.

Cora dried a fork and put it in the drawer. "Aunt Sarah, did you like Mr. Pratt?"

"He seemed nice, and he sounded as if he enjoys teaching. That's important."

"I think he likes Miss Lucy, the other lady that writes for Papa's newspaper. He told the older boys to read her story in the paper so they would learn how to behave."

Phoebe coughed but refused to meet Sarah's gaze. The children didn't know Sarah wrote those articles, and Phoebe knew that was best. As much as Cora tried to keep secrets, she rarely succeeded.

Sarah managed to conceal her surprise from Cora. "I wonder what the boys thought of that."

Cora shrugged. "I wish Miss Lucy would tell boys not to be such blockheads." Cora finished drying the flatware. "Mama, can I write to Miss Lucy and ask her?"

"I don't know. . . . Sarah, what do you think?"

"I don't see any reason why you shouldn't write to her. In fact, I'm sure Miss Lucy would like to hear from you." It would put that much more distance between her and the fictitious writer, Sarah thought, quickly warming to the idea.

"May I be excused, Mama? I want to write to her right now."

"Go on, sweetie. We'll finish here."

"Hang up your towel first." After Cora dashed from the kitchen, Phoebe looked at Sarah and shook her head. "Maybe you shouldn't have encouraged her."

Sarah glanced at the door and lowered her voice. "Don't you think it will confirm that Miss Lucy is real?"

"As long as she doesn't learn the truth."

"I'll speak to Charles after Clay goes to bed." Sarah put the plates in the cupboard. "Have you met Mr. Pratt?"

"Not yet. Do you think I need to speak with him?"

"Oh, no. I have the feeling you were behind my interviewing him, and I was wondering what you thought of him."

Phoebe smirked and picked up the pan of dishwater. "You don't sound as if you suffered through the experience." She dumped the pan of water outside. "I haven't heard any complaints. Have you started the article yet?"

"I will later, but I wanted to know what the children thought." Sarah hung up the tea towel she had used. "I think I'll see what Clay has to say, if you don't mind."

"No, go on. I just thought of something I need to do, too." If one letter would help Miss Lucy, why not two? Phoebe wondered. She liked writing letters, but she would have to sign a name other than her own. After all, a letter from the editor's wife might sound insincere.

Sarah went into the parlor and joined Charles and Clay. Clay was seated across from his father, in a very similar pose, studying the chessboard between them. His hair was darker than his father's, his smile favored his mother's, and he had the gangly physique of a youth burgeoning toward adulthood.

She sat on a slat-back side chair and watched them finish the game. She had tried playing chess a couple of times but didn't have Charles's enthusiasm. Their pieces seemed to be spread out in no particular pattern. One of Clay's knights was between his father's bishop and knight. Charles had six pieces remaining in the game, while Clay had twice as many. Charles mumbled, rubbed his chin, and made a move.

Two plays later Clay said, "Checkmate."

Charles looked at Sarah. "He's getting too good for me. Guess I'll have to forget he's my son and whop him good next time." He chuckled and helped reset the game pieces. "How about a game, Sarah? A nice friendly match."

"No, thank you. I think I'll work on Mr. Pratt's interview."

Clay looked at her. "You gonna talk to Mr. Pratt?"

"I did this afternoon. Now I have to write it up for your father." A pawn rolled off the board. She picked it up and handed it to Clay. "How do you like Mr. Pratt?"

"He's fair enough. Better than Mrs. Roberts. He doesn't scream, and he talks about different places he's been." Clay shuffled his feet. "He must be interested in logging. He's teaching us how to figure how many board feet of lumber are in a tree."

Charles snorted and moved the small table with the chessboard to the corner of the room.

Sarah read Charles's thoughts clearly and wanted to derail a forty-minute discourse on logging. "I hope he will also express an appreciation for the beauty of the land and trees."

"Pa, are you going to print more of Miss Lucy's articles?"

Charles avoided looking at Sarah. "Yes, I'm sure she has more advice to share with us. Why?"

"Mr. Pratt said we'd have to read her next one aloud in class. I wish she'd do needlework instead of write." He glanced at Sarah. "At least yours are funny."

"Why, thank you, sir." She couldn't resist smiling at him. "They weren't intended to be." He was a good boy, and he probably had been teased about her articles.

"Yeah, I know. But at least the fellows read them. One even said you were right." Clay stood up and stretched. "Good night. See you in the morning."

After he had gone, Sarah looked at Charles. "Thank you for not telling him. We don't want Cora to know either. She may write to Miss Lucy."

"I should have known you and Phoebe would corrupt my daughter." He grinned and shook his head. "How was the interview with Mr. Pratt?"

"It should make you happy. After I write a first draft, I can give you an idea how long it will be. I'm not sure right now." She had already formed a few sentences, but she needed to fill a couple of pages so it wouldn't seem as if he wasn't interesting or that there was not much to say about him.

"Can you have it ready for this week's edition?"

"Oh, yes. I'll get started now." On the way to her room,

she wished they would run a picture or drawing of Mr. Pratt, but that was a dream, a way to avoid having to fill both pages.

Phoebe took turns reading ten pages of *Little Women* with Cora before kissing her good night. After changing into her nightgown and robe, Phoebe sat down at her desk and withdrew one sheet of plain writing paper. She dipped the pen into the small, amber glass inkwell and wrote, "Dear Miss Lucy."

Phoebe referred to the first article and asked if it was wicked to speak to a gentleman in public, one whom she had secretly admired. They had no mutual friends to introduce them, and she desperately wanted his attention and his admiration. She signed the letter "Wary."

After rereading the letter, she folded the paper and slipped it into an envelope. She addressed it and put it in the drawer under a camisole. Her husband didn't need to know everything.

She was sitting up in bed reading when Charles climbed in beside her. "Mind if I keep the light on a while longer?" she asked.

"I do." As he snuggled up to her, he reached down and slid the hem of her nightgown upward.

"Oohh, Charles." The book fell closed. She put it on the night table and turned down the wick of the kerosene lamp. "I'm all yours."

4

When Sarah came into the *Gazette* office, Charles started shuffling through the papers on his desk. "Someone left a note here for Miss Lucy."

"Who was it?"

"It had been pushed under the door." He found the missive and handed it to her.

She unfolded the single page and read the signature. "It's from Cora. The other night she said she wanted to write to Miss Lucy. I'd forgotten."

"No wonder the writing looked familiar. What does she have to say to our Miss Lucy?"

Sarah grinned. "She wants her to tell the boys to 'stop being big blockheads.' "

"Good for her. Are you going to answer her?"

"Miss Lucy will, but Cora won't expect a reply today. Next week will be soon enough." Sarah put the note in the open box on the desk. "Oh, if she asks, tell her you sent it to Miss Lucy. She may have overheard Phoebe and me talking about Miss Lucy living back East."

"If she asks, I'll tell her."

She went to work finishing the interview with Mr. Pratt. Soon she handed it to Charles. "The Miss Lucy column's almost ready, too."

"Good." With a practiced eye he scanned the article. "Just what I wanted. I'll set this up on the first page."

"Mr. Pratt will be surprised."

Charles glanced over at her. "He did understand that you were writing about him for the newspaper, didn't he?"

"Yes, but he seemed to think no one would be interested in reading about him."

"Then this will be a lesson for him."

"Not a painful one, I hope. I believe he values his solitude, but that's just my opinion."

She began writing the final draft of the Miss Lucy column, the second part on street etiquette. Included were examples of three different situations. She was on the last page when Phoebe arrived.

Phoebe opened the door wide and breezed into the office. "It's such a nice day. You should leave the door open while the weather's so pleasant. We may be in for a harsh winter."

Charles cast her a bemused smiled. "What will the weather be like next week?"

"Sunny days, cool nights, and showers before long." She kissed her husband's cheek. "But the wooly-worm's coat isn't thick yet." She handed him the mail and walked over to Sarah. "I have a couple of letters for you." As Phoebe held the letters out to her, she winked, a silent message for Sarah not to make any comments.

Sarah glanced at the top envelope. She recognized Phoebe's penmanship, but it was addressed to Miss Lucy. "Wha—?"

Phoebe puckered her brows and shook her head to quiet Sarah. "I think you can answer those better than Charles."

Sarah shuffled the letters. Both were for Miss Lucy.

"Looks like you have gained admirers." At least one, Phoebe thought. The second one, which she hadn't written, piqued her curiosity.

Phoebe's letter was first, and it was signed Wary. Sarah grinned at her and read the single page.

Charles watched his wife and Sarah. "What's so funny?"

Sarah didn't dare look at Phoebe. "I'm reading a letter

from a sweet woman asking for Miss Lucy's advice."

"Sounds interesting. Care to share it with me?"

Sarah cleared her throat. She couldn't laugh. He would never understand, and she was not about to explain it to him. "There is a fine gentleman I have secretly admired for many years. None of my friends, who could introduce us properly, know him. Would it be terribly wicked of me to speak to him first? I am a spinster lady, Miss Lucy, and fear I will always be so if I do not say something to him. Signed, Wary."

Charles looked confused, and Sarah took pity on him. "We thought it would be from a man."

"Oh, that poor woman," Phoebe said, struggling to keep her composure. "You are going to answer her, aren't you?"

Sarah shrugged. "I don't want to be responsible for what this sweet woman may do." With a sideways glance at Phoebe, she added, "Besides, if she smiled at him a few times, wouldn't he acknowledge her if he were interested?"

With her back to her husband, Phoebe frowned at Sarah.

"Good idea, my dear. Include her letter and your answer in your column, Sarah. There may be other spinsters pining away for men because they haven't been formally introduced." He grinned at his wife. "That didn't stop us, did it?"

"Not for long. We couldn't keep our eyes off one another."

"That must've been messy," Sarah said, glancing at Phoebe, who just happened to look away at that moment. "I'll see."

"Open the other letter." Phoebe stepped around Sarah's desk and peered over her shoulder.

Sarah glanced sideways, a smile tugging at the corners of her mouth. "Would you like to read it?"

"No," Phoebe said, resting her hand on Sarah's shoulder. "Just open it."

Slowly, Sarah opened the envelope, withdrew and unfolded the plain sheet of paper. "Dear . . . *est* Miss Lucy—"

She looked from Phoebe to Charles. "Are you sure you want to hear this?"

Phoebe laughed but managed to say, "Don't you dare stop now."

"Enough of your teasing," Charles added. "Do continue, Sarah."

Sarah felt like a snoop going through someone else's mail. She wasn't, though. It was addressed to her. She began reading.

> *"Your article was most engaging, even if men were your unwitting targets. I believe a line from* Henry VIII *best speaks out for my gender; though the situation was not the same, I feel it applies. 'What sudden anger's this? how have I reap'd it?'*
>
> *"Yours respectfully, Mr. Brown"*

"Shakespeare," Charles said, laughing. After a long moment, he rubbed his hand over his mouth, as if trying to sober himself, and said, "Your readers are an interesting group, Sarah."

Sarah rolled her eyes. "I didn't handpick them. But I'll grant you this one is different. It's probably a prank."

"I'm not so sure." Charles shrugged. "Sounds like a challenge to me."

Phoebe clamped her lips together as she ambled toward the printing press. Could that gentleman have witnessed the scene with Sarah and Mr. Perry? She had given him a piece of her mind, and, knowing her, anyone within sight might have heard her. When Phoebe had overcome the threatening laughter, she calmly said, "I wonder who Mr. Brown is."

"I've no idea." Sarah leveled her gaze at Charles. "It is a common name. . . ."

"Wasn't me," Charles said, waving his arm. "I'm sure you can work it into your column."

Sarah shook her head. "Many more letters and the readers will be writing the column. Or you could ask a question of the week and then publish the readers' suggestions."

"If you quit working for me, I may do that."

Phoebe wandered back toward Sarah's desk. "Aren't you just a little curious about Mr. Brown?"

Sarah picked up the envelope, looked at the postmark, and released a hushed sigh. She was, but she wasn't about to add to Phoebe's curiosity.

"Was it posted here in town?"

"No. Fenton's Crossing." Sarah held the envelope out to Phoebe. "Do you know where it is?"

Phoebe shrugged and turned to her husband. "Charles?"

"It's north of here. Near the Sandy River." Charles eyed his wife and Sarah. "Enough speculation, Phoebe. Sarah needs to finish her column."

"Careful," Sarah said with a smirk. "You're starting to sound like a curmudgeon."

"We do have a paper to get out."

She watched him a moment. "Charles, are you sure you didn't write this letter?"

"Nettie's bustle," he responded, shaking his head. "I have enough writing to do. Why would you think I'd waste time on that ridiculous letter?"

Phoebe couldn't help herself this time and burst out laughing. "I wondered if it was written by someone here in town, but I didn't think of Charles."

She went over to Charles, put her arm through his, and leaned close. "You really didn't, did you?"

"No, Phoebe dear. You and Sarah have enough imagination for all of us."

While they spoke in hushed tones, Sarah reread each letter. It wouldn't be difficult to use the questions in the column. After considering Phoebe's spinster's question, she suggested the woman take a bold approach. Engage the man in conversation; invite him to a social; link arms with him and suggest a stroll through the park. She handed the page to Phoebe. "Think this will inspire Wary?"

Phoebe read the paragraph and burst out laughing. "You aren't really going to use this, are you?"

Charles looked at it. "No, she isn't. If that woman read

this she might never look at a man." He handed the paper back to Sarah.

"Charles, you have no sense of adventure." Sarah picked up Mr. Brown's letter.

Phoebe hugged her husband's arm. "I'll leave you two to your work. Sarah, have fun with Miss Lucy."

"Thanks. What if I disagree with her?"

"Listen to her," Charles said, winking at his wife.

Sarah frowned at Mr. Brown's letter. *Sudden anger? How have I reap'd it?* Being insulted or humiliated would be enough to cause a woman's customary sense of propriety to slip. However, Mr. Brown, *if* a Mr. Brown really wrote the letter, sounded like a gentleman. She picked up the pencil and began writing.

First she thanked Mr. Brown for writing with his concerns and suggested men choose their companions with care, and that if one should find himself the object of a woman's anger in public she should be quietly asked to continue the discussion in private. If she refuses, the gentleman should retreat with dignity—and trust that the woman will do the same.

And, Sarah thought, hope the woman doesn't run after him screaming for all to hear—but she didn't include that. She did, however, quote one proverb: He who keeps company with a wolf will learn to howl.

She ended the column with the spinster's letter, saying that if there was no one, not a mutual acquaintance, minister, or clerk, who could introduce the man to her, then she could introduce herself to the gentleman, exchange pleasantries, and go her own way. If the gentleman is interested in her, he will reveal his regard. She took out a clean sheet of paper and made the final copy.

When she finished, she handed the pages to Charles. "I like expressing my opinions, but I should not be telling strangers how to conduct their personal affairs."

Charles grinned at her. "You and Phoebe are always saying what so-and-so should've done."

"That may be true, but I don't go around saying *everything* I think." Well, she thought, not usually, and she had never approached a stranger and told them what to do.

Charles held up the Miss Lucy column. "This almost makes up for your other article."

"Goodness, I may have to speak to Miss Lucy about that."

Saturday morning, when Clay Abbott delivered the *Gazette*, Gil was waiting for him. "Mornin', Clay."

"Morning, Mr. Perry."

"You're out early."

"Yes, sir. Going up to the pond with some friends." Clay handed the newspaper to him and took off running down the road.

"Have fun!" Gil sat down on the bench in front of the saloon and unfolded the paper. The Miss Lucy article was on the first page. His letter should have arrived in this week's mail, but unless Miss Lucy lived in town, she wouldn't have had time to respond in this issue.

He glanced down the column, searching for a reference to his letter, signed Mr. Brown. If Sarah Hampton were writing as Miss Lucy, she could respond this soon. Near the end of the piece he found the answer. His suspicion was confirmed.

Outspoken, unbridled Sarah Hampton wrote the Miss Lucy articles. He lowered the paper, looked across the road at the *Gazette* office, and burst out laughing. "Oh, Sarah, this might be fun."

Jack stepped out of the saloon and stared at Gil. "How can I add yesterday's income with you makin' all that noise?" He surveyed the town from one end of the road to the other. "What's so funny?"

"Just reading what to do if I happen to anger a quick-tempered woman in public." Gil chuckled again.

"Oh, that Hampton woman again. Since Abbott took her on at the paper, I bet he started makin' a profit."

"He deserves it for putting up with all the gibes. Many at his expense. This time it's the Miss Lucy article."

"She writes like a mother. Think she's Abbott's?"

Gil glanced over at his friend, but Jack wasn't smiling.

He was serious. "Not likely. Who's to say?" Gil noticed Sarah's other article and started reading it.

Jack watched him a minute. "Guess I'll finish the books."

Gil read more about Victoria Woodhull's radical ideas for "female-women," as she called them. The woman wanted to revolutionize the all-male government. Did Sarah really believe the ravings of that female? She seemed to have more sense than that, but, he reminded himself, he really didn't know her.

The next morning, before going downstairs to the saloon, he sat down at the desk, took out a piece of paper, and dipped the pen in the inkwell.

Dearest Miss Lucy,

I am flattered you responded to my comments. I would hope the ladies will heed your advice, too.

"Her voice was ever soft, gentle, and low, an excellent thing in woman." I might add that it is also an endearing quality. I imagine your voice is music to your companions.

I would be interested to learn if you and your fellow writer, Sarah Hampton, share your opinions with one another. She does possess a passionate interest in subjects few ladies speak of, or does she dare to shock the readers' sensibilities? Or possibly to stave off would-be suitors?

I hope I do not presume too much by continuing our correspondence.

Yours respectfully, Mr. Brown

He reread the letter, chuckled, and blotted the ink. Matching wits with her was fun. As he addressed the envelope, he wondered how long it would take Sarah Hampton to realize it was all a jest and lambast him.

Sarah spread Phoebe's blackberry jam on a slice of toast and bit into it. Clay and Cora were in school, and the house was quiet. "Do you expect another letter from 'Wary' this week?"

Smirking, Phoebe shook her head. "She's barely had time to follow your suggestions from the first one."

"You haven't told Charles you wrote that letter, have you?"

"He liked thinking some poor spinster was pining away for a man who never noticed her. Chivalry isn't dead. It just needs a nudge once in a while. Besides," Phoebe said, before she took a sip of coffee, "if he knew I'd written that letter, he would've dismissed it as another silly scheme."

Sarah stared at Phoebe. "Did *you* write the Mr. Brown letter?"

"No. Quoting Shakespeare is one of the last things in life I would do, but I still want to know who Mr. Brown is." Phoebe recognized the mischievous expression on Sarah's face. When they were children, it usually meant trouble.

"Why, Phoebe Abbott, you're a married woman."

"Pshaw. You're as curious as I am. Don't pretend you're not." Strange, Phoebe thought, usually I am the one trying to dampen her interest.

"You've enough for both of us. We probably won't hear from him again anyway." By the time Sarah had finished eating her toast, she had forgotten about Mr. Brown and had turned her thoughts to an earlier concern. "Have you been to the lending library recently?"

"Not in the last month. Has someone donated new books?"

Sarah shook her head. "That's why we need to raise funds to purchase more. Do you think anyone would pay to attend a dance?"

"That's a wonderful idea. Everyone likes to dance."

"Or maybe we should require the men to buy tickets in order to dance with the women."

"That'd be fun. Where could we hold it?" Phoebe touched her finger to her tongue then dabbed at the crumbs on the plate. "The church benches were nailed down after poor Mr. Billings tipped one over backward last spring.''

"Why not outside? Remember the summer dances? There's nothing like a canopy of stars and maybe a full moon to embolden timid men and shy women.''

"You haven't lost your romantic notions after all. I'm so glad. But we cannot count on the weather, not this time of year.''

"If the night's cool, the men will have an excuse to put an arm around their sweethearts.'' Sarah set the lid on the bowl of preserves. "The rest of us can wear a warm cloak.''

"You'll need more than a warm cape if it rains.'' Phoebe refilled their cups. "The hotel lobby isn't large enough. The only place I know of that would be is the Wedge.''

Sarah stared at her. "You want us to hold a benefit in the *saloon?*''

"We wouldn't be likely to run short of men. I wonder if Mr. Young would give us the use of it for one evening.''

"If you don't care what kind of men,'' Sarah said skeptically, "you could be right.''

"You didn't used to judge them so harshly.''

"I'm not against people having a drink. What I cannot abide is men drinking to excess—balmy, spiffed, or tanglefooted—whatever you want to call it.'' Sarah sipped her coffee.

At times she knew she could be unyielding, especially concerning spirits, but after spending the last four years of her marriage with a man who was rarely sober, she had no patience with drunkenness. Nevertheless, she didn't want to ruin the benefit for everyone else. It had to be successful. "Would Mr. Young agree not to sell liquor during the dance? We couldn't very well hold a benefit there so he could profit from it.''

"I don't know.'' Phoebe raised her cup and glanced over the brim as she sipped. "I've only spoken to him in passing.''

"I'll talk to him. If reasoning doesn't work, I'll try charm, not one of my strongest traits,'' Sarah said, grinning. "If that fails, I'll badger and bully him.''

"We're going to need help with this, especially the night of the dance."

"We'll put a notice in this and next week's paper announcing the dance. We can also ask for volunteers to help us. Now we need to decide on a date. A Saturday?"

Phoebe checked a small calendar Charles printed for her. "The twenty-fifth would give us a little over two weeks to plan it."

Sarah took her cup and plate to the sink. "I'll talk to Mr. Young this morning."

She rifled through her wardrobe and withdrew the lapis lazuli-colored poplin dress. It had been stylish when it was made for her, some five or six years earlier, with its scalloped edges and the pleated hem on the underskirt. It would do nicely and best of all, it was comfortable.

She brushed out her hair and put on the dress. Yes, she thought, turning in front of the small mirror, I am presentable, but not conventional—she rarely wore a corset and preferred her hair unbound.

It was midmorning when she set off for the Wedge Saloon. The safest time of day for a woman to enter that establishment, if she must. She crossed the road, stepped onto the boardwalk fronting the saloon, and entered the men's refuge. The room was large, dark except for the lamp at the back and what little sunlight streamed through the doorway. She could make out chairs placed around tables, but most noticeable of all were the overwhelming odors— beer, stale smoke, and something she couldn't identify— that hung in the air.

As her eyes adjusted to the light, she saw that the top of the long bar was polished, which was more than she could say for the tables. Then she noticed the painting behind the bar. She had heard about such pictures, but she had never actually seen one.

The woodland scene was beautiful. However, it was the woman standing by a creek, her dark hair streaming behind her as if blown by a strong breeze, that claimed the viewer's attention. The only piece of clothing was a silky-looking wrapper draped over a log. The artist seemed to have caught the woman looking skyward in midstride. A slight smile softened her full wide mouth.

The voluptuous woman was apparently a nature lover.

Sarah gulped and forced her attention away from the strangely intriguing picture. Running her finger inside her collar, she started walking toward the doorway at the far end of the bar. As embarrassing as that image was, a small part of her envied the model's boldness.

"Don't hurry away, Mrs. Hampton," Gil said, leaning back in his chair.

That voice. Her heart leapt to her throat and her cheeks felt singed. She turned around and searched the darkness.

"Never thought you'd pay us a call, not in here." He had been as shocked to see her as he felt sure she was with that picture she'd stared at for a full two or three minutes.

"I—" *He's been watching me!* Her animosity overcame embarrassment. "What are *you* doing here?"

"Maybe I should ask you that question?"

She chose to ignore that attack. "I didn't see you."

"How could you?" He motioned to the painting. "That's the lovely Lorinda. Fascinating, isn't she?"

"I suppose her charms would appeal to the kind of men who frequent this establishment." Who was she kidding? What man wouldn't appreciate Lorinda's "charms." Even clothed, she would draw attention.

From Gil's point of view, Sarah Hampton was herself a fetching sight. "That's a pretty dress. I'da thought you would've worn a canvas apron to come in here." Her wind-tossed hair and that blue dress invited a man's appreciation. All those little black buttons, up the sides of the sleeves and down over her ample breasts, begged to be undone . . . slowly. Very slowly.

"It's soaking in the washtub." She looked away from him but not in time to miss his coarse appraisal and wicked grin. It was also reflected in a mirror near the end of the bar. His eyes sparkled and his lips parted. Why weren't his teeth tobacco-stained? Or at the least yellowed, like so many men's?

She brushed at one sleeve. "I came to see Mr. Young. Is he here?"

"Yes, ma'am." Gil stood up. He wanted to watch Jack's face when he saw her.

She heard the chair scrape on the plank floor and glanced over at him. "Simply tell me where he is, Mr. Perry. I'll find my way."

He nodded, not bothering to hide his amusement. "In his office, down that hall." Jack hardly ever closed his door, and Gil had never given it a thought. Now, however, it made it easy to eavesdrop.

"Thank you." She went back and paused at the open door. She had seen him around town, but they hadn't been introduced. "Hello, Mr. Young." His hair and mustache were dark blond, and he wore a brown vest over his white shirt. He looked no different from any other businessman.

Jack looked up, then came to his feet. "How can I help ya, ma'am?"

She walked to his desk and held out her hand. "I'm Sarah Hampton, Mr. Young." He was obviously stunned. She smiled at him and shook his hand.

He hurriedly shoved a chair over for her.

"Phoebe Abbott and I are organizing a benefit dance to raise funds to purchase books for the lending library—"

"Be happy to donate, Mrs. Hampton." Jack leaned over and opened the bottom desk drawer.

"Thank you, but I'm not soliciting a contribution, Mr. Young, not now. But I won't turn it down at the dance."

He closed the drawer. "What is it ya do need, Mrs. Hampton?"

"The use of your saloon. We want to have the dance the evening of the twenty-fifth, two weeks from this Saturday."

He stared at her and then looked past her to the doorway. "Ya want to have a charity dance *here*?"

She smiled. "It seems you have the only place large enough to hold a community dance."

He twisted one side of his mustache. "Saturday's our busiest night. 'Sides, ya really think the ladies of this town'll come to a dance in a saloon?"

"Oh, yes, indeed. You see, we'll advertise that the bar will be closed. We will provide punch and possibly a kind of potluck supper. Say five cents a dipper. And we will probably charge the same for each gentleman who invites a lady to dance."

"Pay t'dance?"

She nodded. "We need money for books, Mr. Young." She studied him for a long moment. She did not want to do it, but she realized she may have to make a concession in order to win his agreement. "Of course, the loggers would be welcome, too," she added. Remembering her comment to Phoebe about charm, she smiled.

"They're drinkers, ma'am, an' punch ain't exactly what they'll want."

"There haven't been any dances in town for a few months. I believe they might be willing to forgo liquor for one night to be in the company of ladies." More, she would not promise.

He leaned back in his chair, staring past her.

"You would be doing a service for the community. The lending library is in desperate need of more books, and it is open for anyone to use." Another minute passed, and she was contemplating grabbing his shirtfront, when he raised his hands.

"Okay, Mrs. Hampton. Ya can have your benefit here."

"That's wonderful." She stood and stepped around the chair. "Oh, one more thing. Will you agree not to sell any spirits during the dance?"

"I agree, Mrs. Hampton."

He didn't sound happy, but she was delighted. She held out her hand to him. "Thank you, Mr. Young."

He hesitated a moment and shook her hand. "I'll walk ya out."

"We'll publish the first announcement in this week's *Gazette*." They reached the boardwalk, and she paused, glancing back at the painting over the bar. "There is one problem."

"Yes?"

"You must remove that painting, the one behind the bar.

The ladies would definitely be offended.'' Laughter burst out in the darkness. She tightened her jaw and glared in Mr. Perry's direction.

"Lorinda?" Jack chuckled.

"She can hide in my room, Mrs. Hampton, upstairs," Gil called out. "She'll be safe with me."

"If you say so, Mr. Perry." A match made in a saloon, she thought. What more could a man ask?

$\mathcal{S}$arah and Phoebe made up a poster advertising the benefit dance, and Charles printed them while Sarah wrote an announcement for the newspaper. She and Phoebe then visited all the businesses in town and left each one a poster to display.

Phoebe returned to the *Gazette* office with Sarah. "We need to decide if we want Charles to print the tickets for the benefit or if we'll just use different-colored slips of paper. What do you think?"

"You're right. We will need to hand the men something they can drop into a bowl as they step onto the dance floor. Shouldn't we have two ladies collecting for the suppers? The men will pay for each dance, and we'll charge for each helping of food. What else?"

"Since they'll be paying to dance and eat, we should provide the punch."

Sarah grinned. "I agree. What about the music? Is there a band around here that usually plays at these affairs?"

"Last winter some of the mill hands got together." Phoebe looked over at her husband. "Charles, would you ask them to play at the dance?"

"We'll give them supper," Sarah added.

Charles peered around the newspaper he was reading. "I'll stop by the Wedge and ask tonight."

Phoebe rolled her eyes and shook her head. "Any excuse."

Sarah began noting their ideas on a sheet of paper. She was a good list-maker. The problem was keeping track of the lists. "I suppose we should form a committee to choose the volumes for the library. Charles, of course." Sarah glanced up. "Everyone trusts him. Mr. Pratt should have a say, also."

Phoebe nodded. "And I believe Mr. Riggs borrows books regularly. Why not include him?"

"The smithy? By all means. Anyone else?"

"Shouldn't the committee be made up of an odd number?" Phoebe glanced at her husband. "So there will be a majority if everyone isn't in agreement."

Charles put down the newspaper. "Will you two be on the committee?"

Sarah and Phoebe looked at each other. "I would like a say in the choices. Wouldn't you, Phoebe?"

"I thought we would be unwelcome." Phoebe shrugged. "But if you think there will be no objections. . . ."

Charles smiled at his wife. "Just wanted to give you both something else to consider."

"Goodness. Do you think we should have everyone in town vote on who should be on the committee? We could hold it at the dance."

"If this gets too complicated, we won't get anything done." Sarah sat back on the chair. "We could have a sheet of paper for anyone who wants to serve on the committee to sign." Looking from Phoebe to Charles, Sarah thought about the charities she had been involved with through the years. "But most people are satisfied or relieved when someone else steps forward to do the work."

"You're right. If anyone objects we can discuss it then."

Sarah crossed that notation off on her list. The idea of the benefit had been well received. Mr. Young offered the use of the saloon, though she was not sure he was truly interested in the cause. Then there was Mr. Perry. His taste in art ran to nude females, and she didn't want to contemplate his other interests.

There would be no need for a beer jerker at the dance, but would he attend? The unsettling, clear memory of his laughter and his cocky smile sent a shiver down her back. A moment later she comforted herself with the knowledge that he was just one man among many in town.

On the way back to town from the logging camp, Gil stopped by Vonney's place. A sturdy log house built to withstand the heavy rain and cold winters, it was set among the fir and pine trees near a stream that usually flowed year round. From the upstairs bedrooms the view of the Willamette Valley through the trees was a sight to behold. Of course, not too many men were interested in that when they were up there with one of Vonney's girls.

He hitched his horse to the rail out front and went into the house. The door had barely closed behind him, when Vonney saw him. Her titian-red ringlets were a bit springier than usual but her brown eyes were as bright as always. She didn't paint her face, as some women did, but she didn't need to cover any flaws and her figure was curvy enough to suit any man's tastes.

She and the other three women had been run out of Silver Creek, and liked the idea of being the only women within a day's travel from the logging camp. Later, when Gridley became a real town, Gil had offered to set her up in a business in town, but she wasn't interested.

"Hey, girls, look who's here!" Vonney ran over and threw her arms around him.

He swung her in a full circle and set her down. "You're lookin' real good."

"But how do I *feel*?" She wriggled against him and kissed the side of his jaw.

"Better than you have a right to, and you know it." He grinned, slipped his arm around her waist, and turned to the other girls: Frannie, Vi, and Jessamine, though most called her Jessie. "Have you ladies spent any time outside enjoying the good weather?"

Jessie wrinkled her nose. "Too much sun makes freckles, and red streaks in my hair."

She does have nice dark brown hair, he thought. "Then walk in the woods. I don't want you getting sick."

Vi thrust her shoulders back, her bosom out, and her hip to the side.

He chuckled. She was an incorrigible flirt, but they all were. That's how they chose to earn their money.

"Do I look peaked?"

They all laughed, and he did, too. "Take care of yourselves. I want you and the men to stay healthy."

"We take good care of those men, Gil." Frannie giggled. "An' I wouldn't mind givin' you a sample. A-n-y-time."

"He'll just have to take your word for that," Vonney said. "Now scoot, all of you. I haven't seen enough of this man lately."

She cast him one of her saucy smiles, and he had no doubt about what she had on her mind. It had become a kind of test of wills. She'd bait him to visit her room, and he'd turn her down, as gently as she would allow. "Got any fresh coffee?" He had sampled her pleasures in the past, until he realized she wanted more than he was willing to offer.

"Sure do. An' I made blackberry pie. It's still warm." She put her hand in his and led him into the kitchen.

"I still say you should open a baked goods shop." He released her hand and sat on a stool at the worktable.

She glanced over at him. "If I did, do you really think the women of Gridley would enter or buy anything made by me?"

"There are hundreds of little towns. How about west of the Willamette? Bridgeport, Dallas, and La Fayette are nice places." He leveled his gaze on her. "Surely you can't claim to be known in each of those small towns."

Ribald laughter was her only response. She liked to believe that her reputation had spread. He knew her well enough to be familiar with her overblown pride, a harmless trait unless it clouded her judgment. Deciding to save his argument for another day, he changed the subject. "Have you heard any talk about fires near the camp?''

She set a cup of coffee down in front of him. ''One of the men said something, but it didn't sound like there was much to it.'' She cut a slice of pie and handed it to him with a fork. ''Did I hear wrong?''

He tasted the hot coffee and shook his head. ''The men are careful. I was just wondering if any of the other logging camps had been having trouble.''

''If I learn anything, I'll let you know.'' She poured herself a cup of coffee and joined him at the table. ''Is Jack still seeing the Layton girl?''

''Yep. He said to say hello.'' He savored a bite of pie.

She worked a finger through one springy curl. ''Tell him for me that I said he should come out here and talk for himself.''

''I'll be happy to.'' He gulped the rest of his coffee and held up his cup. ''More?''

''Sometimes I think the only reason you see me is to fill your stomach.'' She refilled his cup and her own.

He gulped down a second bite he had been chewing. ''Aren't we friends?''

She held his gaze a long moment. ''We used to be more. Are you keeping company with someone?''

He cocked his head. ''Nope. Can't think of anyone.''

As she dipped one finger in the berry juice in the pie pan, she asked, ''When's the mill going to open up again?'' Then she licked her finger clean.

Ignoring her not so subtle gesture, he sipped the coffee. ''Hopefully, the end of the month. If it doesn't, we're going to lose some good men.''

''I just may take you up on that pie shop if they don't get back to work.''

He had finished the last bite of pie when he heard the girls hurrying down the stairs.

Jessie entered the kitchen and dropped the newspaper on the worktable near Gil. ''You know that editor fellow, Abbott, don't you?''

''Just about everyone in town does. Why?''

''How come he keeps goin' on 'n' on 'n' on about the

trees? They're all over. You could never cut 'em all down, even if you wanted to.''

"He has a right to his opinion. As long as he doesn't come after me with a gun, he's not hurting me.''

"No? You know he doesn't want the mill to open? That's low. Real low.'' Jessie planted her fists on her hips. "Think he'd try somethin' so it couldn't open?''

"Abbott's weapons are words. He's not a fighter.'' Gil felt confident the man wouldn't resort to violence. Hell, he liked Abbott, respected him.

Jessie tapped on the right side of the newspaper. "I like that Miss Lucy. She reminds me of my ma.''

"Jessie,'' Vi called from the front room, "Henry's here!''

Jessamine grinned. "See you later, Gil.''

He chuckled. "She's certainly enthusiastic about her work.''

Vonney shook her head. "About Henry.''

As she stood up, Sarah watched two parched cottonwood leaves float downstream. A gust of cool wind tousled her hair and billowed her skirt. Fall was in the air, and she felt its vitality. After three short months she knew this was where she wanted to live.

The riverbank at the eastern edge of town was one of her favorite places to daydream or ponder ideas for an article. Today she had done both. After shaking bits of dry grass and twigs from her skirt she walked up to the road.

With her mind on the next Miss Lucy column and her answer to Cora's letter, Sarah had not taken more than a half dozen steps when she heard an approaching horse behind her. Walking at the side of the road, she continued on her way.

The moment Gil saw her rich dark brown hair fluttering in the breeze, he slowed his horse. It had to be Sarah Hampton. He rode up to her and kept pace with her brisk step. "Mrs. Hampton.'' He tapped the brim of his old hat and smiled.

Of all the men, it would have to be him. She glanced

sideways without breaking stride. He flashed that ridiculous grin, as if that would make up for his covering her clothes with saloon sweepings and for the wisecracks he had made the other day.

"Nice day for a walk."

"That is why I'm out here," she said softly.

He leaned down near her. "What did you say?"

She gritted her teeth and stared straight ahead.

"Mrs. Hampton, you'll have to speak up. I can't quite make out what you're saying." She was one determined lady. However, when he noticed the deepening rose hue in her cheeks, he knew she was not as lost in thought as she pretended.

She paused at the corner of the smithy's shop and waited for him to pass so she could cross the road. Being a perverse sort of man, he halted his mount directly in front of her, which put his muscular thigh at her eye level. She did not want to be *that* familiar with him.

"We'll have to do this again."

She took a deep breath and started to walk around the horse.

He did admire her restraint but that wouldn't keep him from having some fun. "Next time, Mrs. Hampton, bring your fishing pole. We can have a picnic."

"When they have snowball fights in Hades, Mr. Perry."

"You never can tell what'll happen, Mrs. Hampton." He tapped the brim of his hat. As he rode the few feet further to the livery and watched Sarah walk down the road, her back as straight as an axe handle, he wondered how her laugh sounded. One day maybe he would hear it, but that sure wasn't going to happen today, he thought.

Sarah entered the newspaper office and sat down at her desk. Why was she suddenly always running into that man? In the fourteen or so weeks that she had been in Gridley she had only seen him two or three times—and even then at a distance—until recently. Phoebe said it was inevitable and that he was a "decent sort." Just because they were cherished friends did not mean they agreed on everything.

"Sarah," Charles said, looking up from the paper on his

desk, "I have an idea for a series of articles."

She looked up.

"Phoebe stopped by to tell me people liked your interview with Mr. Pratt."

She saw he wore that smug smile that was his way of saying I told you so. She said, "He hasn't been here long. You were right. People were curious about him."

"Mm-hm." He eyed her. "Each week we'll print an interview with a different businessman. New families are moving in all the time. The articles will introduce readers to the men who own the businesses and also serve as an advertisement for them."

"And everyone will buy the paper to read about their friends or themselves." She glanced sideways at him. "Who will you interview this week?"

"Gil Perry. He's worried about some fires near the logging camp. I told him we'd mention them in the article."

"You've already done the interview?"

"No, no," he said, shaking his head, "not me. You'll do that."

"*Me?*" She swiveled on the wooden chair and stared out through the window.

"I told him you would include the fires. Might help him find out who's starting them."

"I don't see how he can run a logging camp, let alone own one. He has the common sense of a seven-year-old. I can't do it."

"You might be surprised."

"I'll read about it in the paper."

Charles chuckled. "You'll do better than that. You'll write it." He picked up a newspaper laying on his desk, opened it, and sat back in his chair.

She glared at him, but of course he had safely retreated behind the paper. He usually sweet-talked her until they reached a compromise, but not this time. He rarely dug his heels in; however, when he did there was no coercing him out of it.

Was not wanting to do this article important enough for her to resign, or to threaten to resign, her position over?

No. As repugnant as the idea was, she was not going to allow her feelings for Mr. Perry to cause her to do something she would regret. Swallowing her pride wasn't easy, but she would get through the interview, write it up, and work on her next column.

"All right, Charles. I'll speak with Mr. Perry."

Charles lowered the newspaper and nodded. "I thought you would."

"Have you arranged a meeting?"

"Tomorrow morning. The saloon should be empty."

That was it. She shot up off the chair and planted her palms on the top of her desk. "*No!* I may have to interview the man, but I will *not* do it in the saloon. How could you even suggest it?"

"No one's likely to be there." He shrugged. "I didn't think it was right for you to visit his room over the saloon. Where else could you meet him?"

"The library. Since you arranged this, you can tell him. I won't step foot in that place."

"Not even for the dance?"

She just looked at him.

"Okay. The library sounds fair. I'll stop by the saloon on the way home." He grinned at her and added, "Don't forget to tell Phoebe it was your idea."

"As if you need one."

Later she would make a list of questions for Mr. Perry, but first she needed to finish the thoughts she had for her other article. When she was done, she noticed the other lists on her desk. Her life had certainly become busy.

Gil walked into the lending library early. When Charles had first suggested the interview, Gil had doubted that she would cooperate. He located the latest edition of the *Oregon Statesman* and settled into the upholstered chair to wait for Sarah Hampton.

Sarah hurried into the hotel. She had intended to be in the library when Mr. Perry arrived. Unfortunately, Mrs. Seaton had stopped her to talk about the dance. Sarah glanced at the clock in the lobby. It wasn't quite ten. At least she wasn't late. On the other hand, he might be.

She turned the corner and saw him seated by the table reading. She stopped in her tracks. All right, he had arrived first. Her confidence momentarily jolted, she reminded herself that he wanted the interview published in the *Gazette*, and he needed her to write it. "Good morning, Mr. Perry."

Gil stood up, staring at her. "Mornin', Mrs. Hampton." Compared to the pretty dress she had worn to the saloon last week, this morning's outfit was appropriate for mourning—a somewhat ill-fitting, no-nonsense gray blouse with a high collar and a drab sort of brownish skirt.

He smiled to himself. Charles had warned him that she didn't want to interview him. With her sense of humor she probably thought her outfit suited the occasion. "Take this chair. It's the most comfortable."

"No—Thank you," she said, the latter spoken softly. "I prefer the slat-back chair." Being too comfortable with him would put her at a definite disadvantage.

He moved one of the side chairs close to the table for her. "You like to walk. Why don't we stroll along the river?"

"This isn't a social visit. Mr. Abbott said you wanted to do this interview. If you've changed your mind, Mr. Perry, and would rather not, I understand." She wasn't there to chat, and he knew it. She stood beside the chair and waited for his reply.

"This'll do, Mrs. Hampton." Gil reclaimed his chair and leaned back. So much for amenities. There'd been a moment when he thought she might have loosened her stays.

Sarah sat across the table from him, her papers in front of her, and looked at him. "You are the beer jerker at the Wedge, and I was told you own a logging company. Is that right?"

He nodded.

"Do you also own the saloon?"

"Jack Young does, but you should know that."

"You could be his partner."

He chuckled and shook his head.

"I'm glad you're amused. Since I haven't lived here very

long, I'm not familiar with your background.''

"What'd you like to know?''

"Why do you work at the saloon? Isn't the logging business doing well?''

"Is that for the article or do you really care?''

"Both—'' The pencil slipped from her grasp and rolled across the table.

He picked it up, and she held out her hand. He hadn't noticed her fingers before. They weren't red or work toughened, nor were they pale from doing nothing more than holding a teacup. They were lightly colored by the sun, the nails rounded and smooth. As she took the pencil, her fingertips brushed his, a soft but cold sensation.

The warmth of his hand lingered in the pencil. She glanced at him, and he released it. For a moment he almost seemed gentle. An instant later that cocky look was back in his eye. Oddly enough, she was grateful and consulted her notes.

"How long have you lived in Gridley, Mr. Perry?'' He raised one brow as if he were surprised by the question, but she refused to let him intimidate her.

"A while.'' He smiled.

"How has the town changed from when you first arrived?''

"A lot more people.''

"And farms, houses, and livestock, I suppose.'' She put a check by the first question. "How long have you been in the logging business?''

"A few years.''

She put a question mark on her notes and tried to keep her frustration with him from showing. "Mr. Abbott said you have been concerned about recent fires near your logging camp. Have there been many?''

"Two I know about. Have you heard about any more?''

"No, but Charles keeps track of what's happening in other areas. I'm sure he would tell you. Was anyone hurt?''

He shook his head. "They were more of a nuisance than a danger.''

"I'd think a stranger in the area would be noticed. Could

one of the loggers have a grudge with you?''

He gave her a speculative glance. ''I see the men every week. They say whatever's on their minds.''

That must be interesting, she thought, and consulted her notes. ''I understand the mill will open soon. Are you involved with that?''

''What do you mean?''

''You have to do something with your logs. The mill sounds like it would be a good investment.''

''Yep, guess it would be.'' He watched as she clenched her jaw. ''You interested in owning a piece of the mill, Mrs. Hampton?''

''Me? No. If I—'' She stopped herself and waved her hand in dismissal.

He leaned forward, resting his forearm on his knee. ''If what?''

''Pardon me?''

''I'm curious what you were about to say. 'If I . . .' '' He held her gaze a long moment.

She shifted her position on the wooden chair. ''This article is about you, Mr. Perry. Not me. Now—''

''Can't you talk to me without writing down every word?''

''Of course, but this is an interview for the *Gazette*. It's about you, not me.'' *Thank God*, she thought. She wouldn't want him questioning her. ''Tell me about the logging business.''

''The name says it all.'' He shrugged. ''I'm a very simple man.''

That was what she had believed when she entered the library; now she wasn't as sure. ''Is there anything else you would like in the article that you haven't told me?''

''Can't think of a thing.''

''There's one question I forgot to ask. Are you married?''

''Definitely not,'' he said, wondering what else she'd want to know about him. ''Will that bit of information be in the article?''

''Why, yes, of course—''

He smirked, then shrugged. She shouldn't mind him turning the table on her. "Do you see Miss Lucy very often?"

"No. . . ." She glanced at her notes. "I understand she lives in the East. Why?"

"I liked what she said to Cora Abbott. It must've made little Cora happy, too."

She watched his eyes and lips. Was he serious or teasing her? "Yes, she was very excited." *He reads the Miss Lucy columns.* She felt dumbfounded, though she shouldn't be. The advice had been written for men, especially him.

"Well, if you're done," he said, rising, "I'll get back to work."

She gazed up at him. "Yes, I'm finished. This will be in the next edition."

He grinned at her. "Guess I'll have to read it to find out what I said." He gave her a slight nod. "Be seein' you, Mrs. Hampton."

6

*W*riting the interview with Gil Perry had not been as difficult as Sarah had believed it would be. Either the articles were having a positive effect on him, or he was not always as ill-mannered as she had first thought. The former was most likely true. By noontime Friday she handed the completed interview to Charles.

"This isn't bad. Not bad at all. No one would know from this what you really think of Gil." Charles dropped the two pages on his desk. "He should like it."

"Aren't the interviews supposed to be an advertisement? It wouldn't serve any purpose to insult the man in print." She had simply attempted to restrain her personal, possibly cynical, opinions.

Charles raised one bushy eyebrow. "Interesting *you* should say so."

"The Miss Lucy column's all but finished, too." She walked over to the window and looked down the road. "Shouldn't Phoebe be here with the mail?"

"She's probably visiting with Mrs. Seaton. You expecting something special?"

"No. . . ." But she was. Mr. Brown had written twice, and she couldn't help wondering if there would be a third letter.

She stepped outside onto the boardwalk and looked toward the general store. The stiff breeze carried her skirt out in front of her, and she fought to hold it down. A woman came out of the bank, but it wasn't Phoebe. As Sarah turned she saw Gil Perry standing in the doorway of the saloon. Didn't that man have anything better do?

Gil waved and called out, "Thinkin' about taking a walk before the rain starts?"

She glanced at Mount Hood. The snowy peak stood out clearly and there wasn't a cloud in sight. She looked at him and motioned to the mountain. Maybe he needed spectacles.

He shook his head and pointed to the southwest, beyond the rooftop of the newspaper office. She frowned at him and started to go back inside, hesitated, and walked to the corner of the building. He chuckled. She may be stubborn, but, like most women, she was also curious.

She stared over the trees. The sky was gray, and she could actually watch the clouds surging their way. Clutching her skirt with both hands, she spun around and shrugged at Gil Perry before she dashed inside. When the weather changed here, she thought, it didn't waste any time.

A few minutes later Phoebe hurried into the office. "Sarah, we have two volunteers to help us with the dance. Mrs. Seaton and Mrs. Myers."

"Wonderful. How about Elsie North?"

"I haven't seen her since we gave her the poster."

"I'll stop by the boardinghouse when I'm done and talk with her."

Phoebe went over to her husband and kissed his cheek. "Are you about ready to start the press?"

He patted her shoulder. "I still have to finish the editorial." He looked over at Sarah. "Any mail for us today?"

Phoebe handed him three letters and one newspaper. "Sarah, I do believe the Poet's written to you again." She stepped over to the desk, waving the envelope in the air.

" 'The Poet'?"

Phoebe grinned. "He has a preference for poetry."

Sarah grabbed the letter. "Honestly, Phoebe, we're not

sixteen.'' The penmanship was the same, so was the post-mark, with no sender's name.

"Well," Phoebe said, leaning over the desk, "open it."

Sarah lifted the flap on the envelope. The Poet, indeed. *Dearest Miss Lucy,* she read and smiled. It sounded so sweet.

"Read it aloud, Sarah," Phoebe prodded.

Charles shook his head. "She's been waiting for that letter. Allow her to read it in peace."

Phoebe smirked behind her hand. "Yes, dear." So, Sarah has been anxious to hear from Mr. Brown after all, she thought as she paced around the office. At last she is interested in a man.

"Don't worry, Phoebe. You may read it next."

Sarah continued reading.

> *You are most considerate in your reference to Mrs. Hampton. Your views are not so different from hers. The distinction lies in the elocution. You share your wisdom as a friend, and she like a valiant Amazon.*
>
> *Men and women have long struggled to understand one another. One gentleman, among so many, best described what man searches for in a mate. "A dancing shape, an image gay, to haunt, to startle, and waylay."*
>
> *I would be most interested to learn what women yearn for in their hearts.*
>
> *Yours respectfully, Mr. Brown*

Sarah fanned her face with the letter. *She Was a Phantom of Delight.* This time he'd quoted lines from a poem she had treasured in her romantic youth.

Phoebe couldn't wait a moment longer. "It must be something to make you blush like that." She held out her hand. "Come on, it's my turn."

"You might be disappointed." Sarah handed her the letter and watched her eyes.

When Phoebe finished reading she grinned at Sarah, the

way she used to when they were schoolgirls and shared a delicious secret. "My, my, my. This isn't something for the article. It's . . . uh, somewhat intimate." Phoebe folded up the letter and handed it back to Sarah.

Charles walked over to their desk. "Mind if I see that, Sarah?"

She gave it to him. "I can try to answer his question." She smiled at Phoebe. "What would you tell him?"

"Hmm. . . ." Phoebe had few secrets, but a woman had to hold some thoughts to herself. "I'm no William Wordsworth, but I'll just say a gentle man with a sense of humor, big, strong, adventurous." She grinned at Charles, though he didn't notice. "And a *wonderful* dancer."

"Yes," Sarah said, laughing. "There's nothing quite so romantic as being in a man's arms—" She glanced at Charles and shook her head.

"Well"—Charles handed her the letter—"I agree with Phoebe. This Brown fellow sounds smitten with you."

"How could he be? He doesn't know me, or Miss Lucy. I've never corresponded with him." Sarah frowned at the paper. She was curious about him, and his interest was flattering.

"I suggest you don't write to him, not unless we—you— find out more about him." Charles scratched the back of his head. "He's probably some lonely man who's more comfortable with books than people."

"He is well read." Phoebe glanced at one of their posters. "I wonder if he'll come to our dance."

"I'll mention balls, cotillions, and dances in the article. Suggest that it would be a good place to meet people." Sarah couldn't help hoping he would attend. If he asked about Miss Lucy, he would be the only one.

"Sarah, you might consider making friends with some of those loggers you insulted—just for protection."

"Charles! Don't frighten her. Have you ever known a poet who looked like a ruffian?"

He shook his head and walked over to the printing press.

Phoebe leaned close to Sarah. "How are you going to answer the Poet?"

Suddenly Sarah felt edgy. She stood up and pushed the chair under the desk. "I need to take a walk and think."

She tossed her shawl around her shoulders and left the newspaper office. She didn't know what possessed her, but she looked across the way at the saloon. *Botheration,* she thought, *what is wrong with me?*

She marched up the road. Who was she to say what another woman wanted in a man? Many women looked to a man for care and to protect them. Others worked alongside their man. She had no desire to marry again, but if she were to consider the possibility, she honestly didn't know what kind of man would interest her.

Of course, she did know the type she wouldn't look at twice, and glanced back at the saloon again.

The next two weeks passed with a flurry of preparations for the library benefit dance. Sarah interviewed Charles one week for the businessman series of articles, and Mr. Young the next. Most of her time, however, was spent with Phoebe, Jane Myers, Elsie North, and Ruby Jean Drake, Cora's friend's mother.

They made streamers to hang, arranged for the music, enlisted women to prepare food, made up dance cards for the ladies, and cut tickets for the men to purchase. In their spare time, the women chose their dresses and brushed and pressed their husbands' go-to-meetin' suits. Saturday morning, the day of the dance, Sarah and Phoebe arrived at the saloon at ten o'clock; each carried an overflowing box of supplies.

Gil was behind the bar when Sarah and Mrs. Abbott entered. "Welcome to the Wedge." He set two clean glasses on the bar. "What'll you ladies have?"

With a sideways glance at Sarah, Phoebe stepped forward and smiled. "Good morning, Mr. Perry. Maybe a glass of lemonade . . . later. . . ." As she held the box protectively against her body, she gaped at the picture of the woman behind the bar. She couldn't help herself. The woman had *no* clothes! Bare as a newborn babe. Sarah hadn't told her about *that.*

When Phoebe's voice trailed off, Sarah glanced at her, then followed her gaze. Then she glared at Gil and slammed the box down on the nearest table. "Mr. Perry. We had an agreement. That painting was to be taken down."

"I'll take her down before tonight." He cocked his head at Sarah. "Aren't you early for the dance?"

Phoebe stepped backward until she bumped into a table. Reluctantly, she set the box down on the table and looked around the room. So this was where Charles drank with his friends. It smelled awful, but at least there were no dancing girls, or maybe it was too early for them.

"We came to put up the decorations, Mr. Perry. Mrs. Myers and Mrs. Drake will be here shortly." Sarah glanced around. There was one man drinking at the far end of the bar and two more playing cards at a table. "It's nice to see we'll have extra help."

Gil smirked and set the glasses back behind the bar. "You better not count on them."

Sarah scowled at the men. Useless. Furthermore, Gil Perry and Mr. Young profited from men like these. "When will you close the saloon?"

"Jack didn't say."

The man at the end of the bar shoved his empty glass down the smooth bar to Gil. "You hirin' fancy girls t'keep us company?"

"Les, these are *ladies*."

"How come ya lettin' those wom'n in here? Ain't *nothin'* sacred?"

Gil drew another beer and took it to Les, who was too far gone to understand much. "We'll be closing up for the big dance here tonight."

Sarah began tapping her toe. "Mr. Perry—"

"Hey, Gil," one of the men at the table called out, interrupting her. "That dance fer ev'ryone?"

"Yep, sure is. In fact, these ladies are here to decorate." He eyed Sarah. "The notice in the *Gazette* said the dance'll start at seven."

"It would take us a week to give this place a good air-ing,'' Sarah said, her expression reflecting her feelings, ''and we have less than nine. hours.''

He looked from Sarah to Mrs. Abbott and shrugged. ''Figured I'd shut down the bar 'round six, maybe change shirts, and come to your shindy.''

''Shindy?!'' Sarah fairly shrieked. He was impossible! Change his shirt. Ugh—as if a clean shirt would make that much difference.

Phoebe immediately put her hand on Sarah's arm, then stepped up to the bar. ''Mr. Perry, do you have a stepladder we could use?''

''Yes, ma'am. There's one in the back room.'' He smiled at her. ''I'll get it for you.''

The moment he walked from behind the bar, Sarah whirled on Phoebe. ''How could you be so sweet to that . . . that *idiot*?''

Phoebe couldn't resist giggling. ''Can't you tell he's teasing you?''

''I'm glad you're enjoying yourself, but he wasn't teasing. He probably only changes his shirt every other Saturday night.'' On reflection, Sarah decided that he did possess a certain kind of cleverness. After all, he had Charles fooled, and that wasn't easily accomplished.

Gil returned carrying the ladder. ''Where do you want this, Mrs. Abbott?''

''By that door will be fine. Thank you.'' Phoebe turned to Sarah. ''We can set out the food on one end of the bar, and the punch at the other end. It's perfect.''

''Very convenient. The men won't have any trouble locating a drink.'' Sarah started unpacking the box she'd brought. ''We've got to do something about the stench. We'll need a couple of kettles, lemons, cinnamon—all the fragrant herbs you can think of.''

''Lime water would help, too.'' Phoebe looked at Gil. ''May we use your furniture polish? The tables really could use a good cleaning.''

''I'm sorry, ma'am.'' Gil cleared his throat to keep from laughing. ''We don't polish the tables.''

''Phoebe, do you honestly believe these men bother polishing anything?'' Sarah scraped the toe of her shoe over the planks. ''Too bad we can't cover the floor with ground cloves.''

Phoebe ran her finger over the surface of the table. ''It's clean, Sarah. It won't take much to bring up a shine.''

Shaking her head, Sarah took off her shawl. ''Think if we boil some wild mint it might freshen the place?'' She really should have taken a good look around when she was here the other day. However, she hadn't and now they would have to make do.

''I'll go home for the extra supplies and ask Cora to gather the mint.''

''Okay. I'll start''—Sarah glanced at the boxes—''somewhere.'' She grinned at Phoebe.

Phoebe peered over her shoulder at the painting. ''Walk outside with me.'' She led the way and paused at the end of the boardwalk. ''You didn't mention that picture. Why didn't you tell me?''

''He promised to put it in his room.''

Phoebe giggled. ''I'd never tell this to anyone else, but I'm glad he didn't. Can you imagine standing in the woods like that?'' She shivered. ''I've never even seen my whole body unclothed. Have you?''

Sarah nodded to Miss Layton across the road. ''No, I've never walked around nude or posed that way in front of the mirror, but it might be fun to see what it's like.''

''This time of year you'd be covered with gooseflesh.''

''I wouldn't parade around like that.'' Sarah giggled. ''Do you know what her name is?''

''Who?''

''The woman in the painting.''

''They *named* her?''

''Lorinda. The lovely Lorinda.''

''Oh, my.''

''It could be her real name.'' Sarah glanced across the road at the *Gazette* office. ''Why not ask Charles?''

Phoebe grinned at her. ''I just may do that.''

• • •

Sarah stood near the top of the stepladder with a hammer and nail in one hand, the streamer pinned above the door with the other. "Jane, should this be lower?"

"That's fine. I bet the men have never seen streamers in the saloon before."

Elsie joined them. "I'm glad you thought to bring flowers, Jane. All I had was blowballs, but the wind stripped their stems the other day."

Sarah pounded the nail through the streamer into the wall and leaned back to survey her handiwork. "It's so plain."

When Gil saw the stepladder start to wobble, he crossed the saloon at a run. "Sarah—watch out!"

Sarah dropped the hammer and clung to the ladder as it weaved from side to side. "Thunderation!" she exclaimed, clamping her eyes closed. "Please make it stop." Suddenly, it did. Someone's strong hands were on her waist and had steadied the stepladder. It had to be Jane Myers. She had the sturdiest build.

"Oh, thank you, Jane. I was sure I'd—"

"It's not Jane." Gil grinned up at her. "Open your eyes."

Gil Perry! Her eyes snapped open. No man had touched her so intimately in a very long time.

He chuckled. Her color had changed from pasty white to a nice shade of pink. "You can let go of the ladder, unless you want to stay up there." Her given name had slipped out, but he felt sure she hadn't heard him.

"When you remove your hands, I will be glad to step down."

"Yes, ma'am." He released his hold on her and stepped aside to steady the ladder for her. "I'd have figured you were quite a hoyden in your youth."

"Well, you"—Sarah noticed Phoebe's wide grin and relented—"weren't that wrong. But I didn't climb trees."

"Good thing."

Phoebe spoke up before Sarah's temper flared anew, "What do you think of the saloon now, Mr. Perry?"

Gil had to admit it was certainly more festive. "It's real pretty. The boys won't recognize it."

Elsie nodded. "That's what we were hoping for, weren't we, ladies?"

Ruby Jean Drake nodded. "It sure was."

Even Sarah was amazed. The polished tabletops gleamed, the windows sparkled, and a kettle filled with water and a generous portion of various spices simmered on the woodstove. And she had badgered Gil Perry until he had cleaned the spittoons.

"Well, ladies," Ruby Jean said, wiping her hands on a towel, "I say we go home and get ourselves ready for the dance."

"She's right. We'll need to be here early to set up the food and punch." Sarah dusted off her hands and picked up her shawl.

Jane started out but paused in the doorway to put her wrap over her head. "It's raining again."

"Our dresses will dry while we dance. Think of all the money we'll raise for the lending library."

Phoebe turned to Gil. "Thank you, Mr. Perry. We appreciate your help."

"You're welcome, Mrs. Abbott. See you tonight." He met Sarah's gaze. "You, too, Mrs. Hampton."

Sarah nodded and hurried outside. She had the strangest feeling that he'd been about to address her by her given name—but surely he would not dare to do that. Pulling her shawl over her head, she dashed home with Phoebe.

Gil pulled on his polished boots and looked out the side window of his room. The rain had stopped an hour earlier. The road was muddy but the roofs had stopped dripping. He couldn't remember seeing so many people in town at one time.

Townspeople had been arriving for the dance for the last half hour. Timothy Farmer, the barber and owner of the bathhouse, had enjoyed a brisk business the last few hours. Unless the men refused to dance, which was not likely to happen, Gil figured the benefit would be a success. There was a knock on his door.

Jack poked his head inside. "Ya ready yet?"

"Just about." Eyeing Jack, Gil picked up his vest. "You clean up pretty good. Change your hair tonic?"

"Bear grease isn't too popular with the ladies."

"I'll try to remember that." Gil shrugged into his vest. "Weren't you supposed to escort Miss Layton tonight?"

"On my way." Jack tugged on his stiff shirt collar. "How 'bout you?"

"I'll be down. Go get your girl before that collar chokes you."

"Take too long and the ladies' dance cards'll be filled up before ya get there."

"Don't worry 'bout me. Just make sure your name's on Miss Layton's card."

Gil sprinkled a dash of hair tonic on the brush and ran it through his hair. He put on his coat, left by way of the back outside stairs, and walked around to the front of the saloon. Laughter and the rumble of voices drifted outside.

He hung back until there was a lull and then entered. Sarah was stationed at the door greeting everyone. Her dress had a wide, low neckline, and when she moved, the lights caught a golden cast in the brown fabric. "Nice turn-out tonight, Mrs. Hampton." When the loggers see her, he thought, they just might forgive most of her insults.

She had begun to think Gil Perry might have changed his mind about attending the dance. She turned toward his voice. He had done more than change shirts. A great deal more, and she couldn't help staring at him. Indeed, his black suit had not one wrinkle. One could even think he looked dashing, she decided, and his spicy hair tonic had a wonderful scent.

"Good evening, Mr. Perry. Someone asked about you a little while ago."

"A young lady?" He grinned, eyeing her tempting neckline and appreciating her lilac scent.

"No . . . it was one of the men. A logger, I believe." She barely met his gaze. "I'm sorry. People have been arriving in a steady stream."

"There's quite a crowd." He motioned toward the bar. "Looks like you've set out quite a supper."

"The ladies have been cooking for days to provide enough food. Each helping is five cents. The punch is at the far end of the bar."

"All for a good cause, Mrs. Hampton. The loggers alone should eat enough to buy several books."

She watched him out of the corner of her eye. "I'd hoped they wouldn't be so angry about my articles that they'd refuse to attend."

"Angry?" He chuckled. "Don't concern yourself on that account. Who knows. One or two may even ask you to dance." Her dismay was immediately evident. "They don't usually hold a grudge."

"Good." When he flashed her a cocky grin, she wondered how many dances that leer would gain him. She consoled herself with the knowledge that he would not approach her. "I try not to, either." *Although I'm not always successful,* she amended to herself.

"How much is the punch?"

"That's free, Mr. Perry. Have all you want. It's quite good—Elsie North made it." Mr. Young and Miss Layton arrived and stood in line behind Gil Perry. She was a pretty young lady with pale blonde hair, doe eyes, and a sweet smile.

Gil chuckled. "You're quite a sales . . . lady."

She grabbed one of the pieces of red paper roughly the size of a pocket watch. "This is a dance ticket. They are five cents each and good for one dance with the partner of your choice."

"How many would you suggest I buy?"

"At least a dozen." She shrugged. "More if you are in a particularly amorous mood tonight."

He burst out laughing. Several heads turned in their direction, and she appeared a little uncomfortable. "Do I have to decide right now?"

"No. The tickets will be for sale *all* evening, Mr. Perry." He did enjoy being perverse, she thought.

She smiled at Mr. Young and Miss Layton as they spoke in whispers behind Gil Perry, who acted as if there wasn't a line forming behind him.

"Hey, Gil, what's takin' so long? Can't ya dance and talk with Mrs. Hampton later?" Jack Young winked at him. "We're hungry."

Sarah groaned inwardly, and picked up a dance card and pencil for Miss Layton. Sarah had chosen the post at the door in order to see each man who entered. On the off chance that Mr. Brown might be there, she wanted to insure an opportunity to meet him.

Gil eyed Sarah's wrist. "The lady isn't wearing a dance card. It's either already filled, or maybe she doesn't want to dance."

Sarah ignored him and smiled at Miss Layton. "This is your dance card." The cream-colored cards were illustrated on one side with a fan of books. Numbered lines were drawn on the other side, and a red silk ribbon hung from a corner.

"Thank you, Mrs. Hampton." Miss Layton slipped her left hand through the red loop of ribbon.

Sarah noticed the shy smile the girl gave Mr. Young, and then she noticed Gil Perry watching her, Sarah, with the strangest look in his eye. *Ignore him,* she told herself, grabbing a dance ticket. She held it up and smiled. "Mr. Young, this—"

"Excuse me, Mrs. Hampton"—Gil leaned in front of Jack—"is there anything else I need to know about tonight?"

If he *isn't* an idiot, she thought, he does a good imitation of one. "Circulate, Mr. Perry. Have supper. Visit with friends, or keep Lorinda from being lonely." She gave him her sweetest smile.

$\mathscr{P}$hoebe handed a glass of punch to Sarah and peered outside. "You don't have to spend all evening at the door. It looks like almost the whole town is here." The musicians started playing "Wait for the Wagon," and Phoebe tapped her toe. "Doesn't everyone look wonderful? The women were so glad to have an excuse to wear their best dresses."

"The men aren't hard on the eyes, either, in their stiff collars, black knotted neckties, and pressed suits. At first I didn't recognize the loggers." Especially Gil Perry, Sarah thought. He looked like a different man, but he behaved just as he always had.

"See, your articles are having a good effect on them."

Sarah remembered Gil Perry's mocking comments and shook her head. "I doubt that." He crossed her line of vision, and she was fascinated by his easy manner. He was speaking with Beth Kenton and her husband. When he said something, Beth fluttered her fan and flashed a coy smile. Sarah shook her head. "How does that man manage to charm women so easily?"

Phoebe turned around. "Who?"

"Mr. Perry. He smiles and the ladies simper." Sarah refused to watch an instant longer. "It's indecent. I'm surprised Mr. Kenton allows it."

"Why, Sarah, you sound a mite jealous." Phoebe regarded her speculatively.

"In a pig's eye."

"Be careful. . . ." Phoebe laughed, as she surveyed the crowd. "Not many of the married men are dancing. Maybe they don't want to pay to dance with their wives."

"That's possible, but they'll probably ask other men's wives—later." Sarah grinned at her. "Don't worry. Married men tend to drink or fill their stomachs before noticing women. Why not ask Charles to dance? Help get it started."

"What about you? Have you found the Poet yet?"

"I've no idea. I certainly haven't spoken to any man who sounds the way I imagine Mr. Brown would."

"There are men here I've never seen before. He could be one of them." Phoebe glanced sideways at Sarah. "That man talking to Elsie keeps looking at you. Why not smile at him? I bet he'd ask you to dance."

"I didn't notice anyone."

"You never do." Phoebe threw up her hands. "Several men have shown interest in you, but you cut them dead in their tracks with a glance and probably don't even know it."

"That's balderdash. I do no such thing."

"You do, too. I've seen that faraway look in your eyes, when your mind is on the next article or whatever."

Sarah shrugged. "I'm not about to play coy with every man I see." She motioned to Jane Myers. "Phoebe, dance with Charles before he feels obligated to ask someone else."

Phoebe studied her. Before Sarah married, she had loved dancing and always had a full dance card. "Well, try to have fun tonight and not think about books or the Poet all evening." The last few years of marriage and the death of her husband had changed Sarah, and not necessarily for the better.

Jane came over to Sarah as Phoebe left to find Charles. "Everyone's having a good time."

"I'm glad. Have you sold many tickets?"

"Most of what I had. The loggers and mill hands are buying five and ten at a time." Jane held up her reticule. "See how heavy it's getting?"

"I wish they'd use them." Sarah handed her more tickets. "I'll find a box for those coins before they weigh you down."

"Oh, I see two men who look like they want to dance. I'd better see if I can sell them some more tickets."

Sarah located a tin to keep the money from the sale of dance tickets and lightened Jane's reticule. Afterward, she fixed herself a sampling of the supper dishes, refilled her glass with punch, and took her plate to a quiet corner. The musicians seemed to be enjoying the festivities as much as everyone else.

Looking around the room, her gaze met Gil Perry's. He flashed his smile and nodded, and she continued studying the crowd. He probably had not even realized it was her. Being a beer jerker, he must be used to smiling at people for no reason, she decided.

She found the way people socialized fascinating. Women, who normally were almost retiring, smiled and conversed with ease. It must be the music. Even the men appeared comfortable, and not a drop of spirits had been served. Some of the children played near the door, a few of the older ones danced, and the little ones slept on folded blankets.

Charles and Phoebe danced by. She was as pretty, and almost as trim, as when they married. He still looked taken with her. Mr. Young and Miss Layton were also taking a turn, as was Mr. Pratt with a woman Sarah hadn't met.

She finished eating and refilled her glass with punch. It was really delicious. With another stack of dance tickets, she went over to Jane. "I'll spell you now. You must be thirsty."

"Thanks. Here's the reticule." Jane handed the black drawstring bag to her. "The women have been folding the tickets from their partners and putting them in here, too."

Sarah slid the drawstrings over her hand before she sipped the punch and set the glass on the nearby table. The

music stopped, and she found herself surrounded by men.
"Mr. Farmer, how many tickets do you want?"

"Ten for now, Mrs. Hampton." Mr. Farmer reached into
his pocket.

She gave him the tickets for the half-dollar piece. "Have
fun, Mr. Farmer." She dropped the coin in the reticule.
"Who's next, gentlemen?"

"Five for me, ma'am."

"I'll take fifteen. Don't want to miss a dance."

Sarah nodded. The last was said by one of the loggers.
She couldn't really keep track after that. Rough hands,
some sun-darkened, held out money, and as quickly as she
could manage, she took the coins and gave them tickets.
The music started, and she rushed to help the last two men.
They hurried off to find partners, and she wondered if one
of them could be Mr. Brown.

She reached for her punch and drank what remained. The
bag was heavy. Titles of books she would like to see in the
lending library spun around in her mind—*Tennyson's Poetical Works,* one dollar if clothbound; Thackeray's *Adven-
tures of Philip,* one dollar fifty cents; Louisa May Alcott's
Little Women; and Jules Verne's *Twenty Thousand Leagues
Under the Sea.* . . .

She was getting carried away. There wasn't enough in
the little bag to purchase all of those books, but probably
enough to buy three. Then, glancing at the food on the bar,
the many empty serving dishes, she doubled that number.
It would be a good beginning.

"Mrs. Hampton—?"

"Yes?" she responded spontaneously as she looked to
her right. "Mr. Pratt. Are you enjoying the dance?"

"Indeed I am. You and the other ladies have done a
splendid job organizing this affair."

"That's very kind of you." She smiled at the school-
teacher. He was so formal, not like most of the men in
town.

He held out a ticket to her. "May I have this dance, Mrs.
Hampton?"

"It would be my pleasure, Mr. Pratt." She folded the

ticket in half, tucked it into the little bag, and took his hand. "Have you any suggestions on which books the lending library should acquire?"

"There are so many noteworthy poets. John Donne; John Keats; Lord Alfred, Tennyson; William Butler Yeats . . ." He guided her in a slow turn. "And we should not forget one of the most revered, William Shakespeare."

She nodded. A chill slid down her back. Could his naming poets, particularly those poets, be a coincidence? Or could he be the Poet? He seemed to be well-read, and he was certainly more refined than many of the men in town.

"I apologize. Sometimes I think I should work in a library. A lifetime would not be long enough to read and study the outstanding works."

No, he couldn't be the Poet, could he? He didn't seem to be a ladies' man. "You should make a list."

"Oh, I would not presume to propose which volumes to purchase." He released her hand and ran his palm down the side of his coat. "My tastes, I fear, would not appeal to many people."

"I don't agree, Mr. Pratt. I enjoy discovering authors or books I've not read." The music ended. "I'm sure others do, too."

He blurted out, "May I have the pleasure of this polka, Mrs. Hampton?" and offered her his hand.

She tried not to let her surprise show. She hadn't considered . . . She nodded and placed her hand in his. He gave her another dance ticket and a moment later he began to lead her around the dance floor.

For a shy gentleman Mr. Pratt was an unexpectedly skillful dancer. He knew the proper steps, but he was so stiff and so very formal. Maybe she was expecting or hoping the Poet would turn out to be the carefree, dashing man of her girlhood dreams, the one who took her breath away and made her heart pound.

Gil watched Pratt whirl Sarah around the dance floor. When he'd taken her hand, she'd looked as startled as a robin caught in a cat's jaw. The polka ended, and she sold more dance tickets. Jess Drake struck a chord on his fiddle and called for a square dance. To Gil's surprise, Henry, his foreman, joined one square with Sarah.

The music was lively. While three squares of adults followed the calls, Gil noticed the Abbott and Drake girls, with arms linked, skipping around in a circle in one corner of the room. Several boys, too old to play with the younger children and not yet interested in girls, played mumblety-peg outside on the boardwalk. The sound of laughter drew his attention to one of the squares.

Henry turned Sarah around and sent her skirts flying out. Gil caught a glimpse of her ankles, but it was her broad smile that held his attention. When she smiled, hell, she was beautiful. He owed his foreman a drink.

The music ended. He filled two glasses with punch, walked over to her, and held one out. "Thirsty?" He nodded to his foreman, who left them alone.

"Oh, yes. . . ." Sarah stopped fanning her face and accepted the cool glass. "Thank you, Mr. Perry." She took a long drink and smiled.

"Congratulations, Mrs. Hampton. I'd say tonight is a success." He glanced at the musicians.

"Everyone does seem to be having a good time. I've seen more smiling people this evening than I usually see in a month." She took another drink of punch and drained the glass. "I'll have to ask for the recipe for the punch. It's delicious."

Gil set his glass on a nearby table. "I'd like to buy some of those dance tickets." He reached into his pocket and handed her a two-bit piece.

Noting the quarter-dollar coin, she handed him five tickets. "Will that be enough? I haven't noticed you dancing." My mouth will be the death of me yet, she thought, praying he hadn't been paying attention.

"If I need more, I'll be sure to buy them from you." He tucked four of the tickets into his coat pocket and eyed her wrist. "No dance card?"

She stared at her wrist, feeling rather stupid. "I got busy and forgot." The musicians, thankfully, began playing the next tune, "Beautiful Dreamer." She had no idea why she couldn't carry on an ordinary conversation with him. After all, he was being quite pleasant.

He reached out and pretended to check her imaginary dance card. "I see you have the next dance free." Holding up a dance ticket, he said, "Would you do me the honor?"

"Me?" she squeaked. Botheration, now her voice wasn't cooperating.

"It is for the lending library, isn't it?"

She nodded, but she couldn't say the usual polite response—*It would be my pleasure*—because she didn't have a fondness to be his partner. To feel his arms around her. "It's a waltz. Wouldn't you rather wait for a reel?"

"It'll do just fine." He held his hand a whisker's breadth from hers and waited.

"Yes, of course," she said, taking his hand. It was for charity and, besides, the dance wouldn't last all that long. Suddenly, he slid his arm around her, his strong hand flat and warm on her back, and they were dancing—until she misstepped and nearly tripped him. However, he was amazingly agile and swung her around without missing a beat.

At first she was skittish, he could see, but once she settled into the rhythm of the dance, she was light on her feet. "That's a nice dress. Makes your shoulders bluer—Gives your eyes a golden glow—" Hell, that came out ass-backwards. He never claimed to be clever, but he usually didn't act like a tongue-tied stripling.

She found it strangely comforting that he might be as confused as she was, and she grinned. "You clean up pretty nicely, too," she blurted out. "I barely recognized you at first." *Lord, take me now or allow me to swoon.* He laughed, and she was grateful. The deep rumble helped cover her embarrassment.

"Isn't it strange how a woman will agree to dance with a man she doesn't know?" He grinned at her. "An odd custom, but not a bad one."

Just as she glanced at him, he made a sharp turn. Instinctively, she held on to him and recalled the words to that passage of music: List while I woo thee. She caught a whiff of his hair tonic and took a deep breath. "As with most of society's rules, men have held women in submissive roles."

"Not all men."

She shrugged. "If a woman declines a gentleman's invitation to dance, she must sit that one out. If that rule applied equally for men, I wonder how long it would be before it was discarded."

He chuckled. "Point taken. But you must admit there are a good many conniving women."

She smiled at him. "I will concede there are many conniving people." He pulled her closer and executed an unfamiliar step. She felt as if she were floating, a very pleasant sensation. "Poor character traits are not limited to one gender."

He raised one brow. "Such as rudeness?"

"Why, yes." She met his gaze then narrowed hers. "Is this about my articles?" She tried to ignore the rich voice singing, "Beautiful dreamer, awake unto me. . . ."

Gil smiled at her. "It isn't hard to figure you aren't too fond of the men who come in here." He felt her back stiffen under his hand and stroked her with his thumb.

She stopped, lowered her arms to her sides, and took a step back from him. "Inebriates are loud, sloppy, smelly, and fixate on the first—or every—woman they see."

He looked around and faced her. "Careful, Mrs. Hampton." He motioned to one side.

Glancing in that direction, she realized she had drawn attention and the music had ended. "Do you go out of your way to be annoying or does it come naturally?"

"I thought we were having a conversation. Guess I was wrong." He took her by the arm to lead her off the dance floor.

She yanked her arm free and went over to the punch bowl. She almost gulped one glass and refilled it. When she turned around, Phoebe was bearing down on her.

"Sarah, whatever possessed you, speaking like that to Mr. Perry?" Phoebe poured a dipper of punch into her glass and took a sip.

"He brought up my articles—thought it was acceptable

to insult me in public." She took another gulp of her punch and looked across the room at him. "He nearly had me fooled—" *Those eyes, his voice . . . his dancing. . . .*

"Well, you haven't written about the loggers in the nicest terms." Phoebe sipped her punch. "This tastes odd."

"I think it's d'licious."

"Maybe it's me." The music started, and Phoebe watched Sarah a moment. She began humming and swaying to the music. "Are you feeling all right?"

"Why wouldn't I? Everyone's having a good time, and we're raising money to buy books." Sarah laughed. "You've taken a serious turn. What's come over you?"

When several of the loggers came over to the punch bowl, Phoebe touched Sarah's arm and stepped aside. "It is getting late. Perhaps we should think about leaving."

"I'm fine. Cora's asleep, and Clay's . . . well, he's around somewhere. Why don't you claim Charles for this dance?"

"I think I'll do that." As Phoebe wove her way over to Charles, she noticed everyone seemed very merry. She slipped her arm through her husband's and smiled at the men he was talking with. "Have you had any punch since supper?"

"Just finished one. Why?"

"Was it all right?"

Charles patted her hand. "Yes, my dear. It was fine."

She held up her glass. "Taste this. It seems off. But it can't go bad. Not within a few hours."

He took a drink, chuckled, and handed the glass back to her. "I'd say one of the boys added a little flavoring."

"Whiskey?" she gasp.

"Has someone complained?"

"Hardly," she responded. "I have to tell Sarah—"

"Don't make a scene, my dear. What she doesn't know will keep her content." He looked over at her. "She's happy now. Let her be."

"But she's drinking this concoction like it was water."

"Then she may not feel too good in the morning." He

pulled a ticket out of his pocket and pressed it into her hand. "Isn't this our dance?"

Phoebe set the glass down as she searched for Sarah. "I guess a few minutes won't make a difference."

"Promenade, two by two. . . ."

Gil watched Sarah dance by with Charles. She was laughing, playful, and she had evidently recovered from her irritation with him. Gil walked over to the bar where some of the younger loggers were doing their share to empty the punch bowl.

"Hi, boss. We saw you dancin'." Willie grinned and gulped his drink.

"How 'bout you boys? You behaving yourselves with the ladies?" Gil eyed him. The boy's spirits seemed a might high. But there hadn't been a dance for months, so that might be the reason.

"Yes, sir." Jake laughed and elbowed Willie. "Been real gentlemen, haven't we?"

Gil frowned at the boys. "Out front. Now, boys." He followed them outside. "Where's the bottle?"

Jake patted his pockets and grinned. "Haven't got one. Must be one behind that bar, right, Willie?"

"Should be. Ain't got one either. You wanna—?"

"You fools're spiffed. Where'd you get the bottle?"

Willie glanced at Jake. "We were gonna pay fer it. Here," Willie said, shoving two coins into Gil's hand.

"Where is it?"

Willie motioned to Jake.

Jake added two more coins to Willie's. "In the punch bowl," he said and burst out laughing. "Did ya see that uppity Mrs. Hampton guzzling it?"

"She didn't complain none."

Gil shook his head. "Sleep it off in the wagon." That explained Sarah's flushed cheeks and the change in her disposition.

Willie looked at Jake. "Hey, we're sober as a' under-taker, ain't we?"

Gil grabbed each one by the arm and marched them

down the road to the livery. "You can wait in the wagon
for a ride back to camp or you can start walking. The choice
is yours." Jake tried to wrench his arm free, but Gil held
firm.

"You can't tell us—"

"You've forgotten. I'm your boss, I pay your wages.
Since your pa isn't here to wipe your nose, it's up to me."
Gil stopped in front of the livery. "Which will it be, sleep
or walk?"

Willie and Jake staggered into the livery and scrambled
over the side of the wagon.

Gil walked back to the saloon. As he entered, the men
were singing, "Good Night, Ladies." Every woman was
dancing. One look at the punch bowl told him there would
be a few achy heads in the morning.

Sarah stepped away from her partner, twirled around on
her heel—and found herself face-to-face with Gil Perry.
"Hel-lo. Did you know thish is t'lasss dance?" He was
smiling at her again, such a nice smile, she thought, resting
her hands on his chest to steady herself.

"Thought it might be. Are you having fun?"

"Oh, yes," she said, waving one arm in a wide arc.
"You wanna finish t'dance wi' me?"

"It would be my pleasure." He fished a ticket out of his
pocket and handed it to her.

She made two attempts to drop it down the front of her
dress and succeeded on the third try. "Should be safe
there."

"Indeed, it should be." He took her in his arms, and she
began swaying against his body. If she were a little more
like this sober, she would be a definite distraction.

She leaned back, secure in his embrace, and wagged her
finger at him. "If yo'r tryin' to get a rise outta me, it won't
work." She nestled closer and followed his lead. He really
was the best dancer she had ever been with, and he smelled
wonderful.

When the music ended and she remained in the circle of
his arms, swaying, he smiled at her. "I think I'd better walk
you home, Sarah."

"Mm, that would be nice." She felt so sleepy and comfortable. "Can we dance home? You're a won-derful dansher."

He doubted she would remember this in the morning. "Did you bring a coat?"

"My cloak's o'er there," she said, waving her arm in the direction of the bar.

He looped her arm through his. "I'll help you find it." He ignored the curious stares, until Mrs. Abbott came up to them.

Phoebe could hardly believe her eyes—Sarah leaning against Mr. Perry's side with a dreamy smile on her face. "Sarah, are you all right?"

"Indeed—nev'r been better."

"Would you get her cloak, Mrs. Abbott? I'll walk her home. I don't think she'd be much help tonight."

"That's an understatement." She found Sarah's cloak and handed it to him. "She drank a lot of punch. Do you know who added the whiskey to the bowl?"

"The two men responsible are sleeping it off at the livery. They're young and thought it was a lark."

"Well, I hope they will feel as bad in the morning as I fear Sarah will."

He chuckled. "Don't worry. They will."

Charles came over to them. "Gil, looks like you have your hands full."

Sarah opened her eyes for a moment and looked at Gil. "He does?"

"I'll see her to the house." He glanced down at her head resting against his shoulder.

Phoebe put her hand on her husband's arm. "Don't you think we should take her home?"

"She's in good hands." Charles put his arm around his wife and urged her away. "See you later, Gil."

Gil wrapped the cloak around Sarah's shoulders. "Let's go." She nestled into his side. "Wish I had a photograph of this. You'll never believe it."

He led her outside. The breeze was cool and fresh, but she didn't notice. He put his arm around her shoulders, and they walked the short distance to the Abbott house. When they reached the stoop, he opened the front door for her.

"You're home, Sarah." He lowered his hands to her waist and turned her to face him. "Sleep well."

She rested her hands on his shoulders. "You're leaving?"

"I'd better or we'll really have a scandal on our hands." He steadied her and gazed into her lovely, bleary, blue eyes. She was quite a lady. Soft and cuddly, prickly as a berry patch, and so much fun to match wits with. He was just putting pressure on her waist to set her inside, when she wrapped her arms around his neck.

The sound of her soft gasps drew him closer. A shaft of moonlight pierced the clouds long enough for him to see her sultry gaze and her parted lips. He wanted to feel her lips on his. Ignoring the advice from his conscience, he bent down and slowly brushed his mouth over hers.

"Ooh," she murmured, her lips on his firm chin. "Kiss me. . . ."

That's just what he wanted to do. She ran the tip of her tongue along the rim of his chin, and a wave of dizzying desire stunned him. At twenty-nine, he was too old to experience such a rush of longing. Her fingers caressed the back of his neck. One kiss, he decided, and I'll leave.

As he wrapped his arms around her waist, he gently slanted his mouth over hers and licked the tender, moist flesh. He had never needed so much control to keep the rest of his anatomy bridled. She was satin and silk and a soft summer breeze.

She felt his hard body supporting her, pulsing against her—her own seemed to have turned molten. Her knee slid between his thighs. A surge of longing whirled below her belly, and she tightened her hold on him.

The raw intimacy she sparked jolted him. He broke the kiss and stepped back, his hands on her shoulders for balance. He filled his lungs with cool night air and the fog began clearing from his desire-numbed mind. Voices drifted down the street.

He lowered his arms. "Sweet dreams, Sarah." He adjusted his coat and walked away while he still possessed the strength and willpower.

She held on to the door frame with both hands and rested her cheek on the cool wood. "G'night, Gil." His lips felt warm and oh so very nice. . . .

8

*S*arah tied the sash on her wrapper and pressed her cool hands to her pounding temples. Her mouth was dry, tasted foul, and her head felt as if it were about to burst. She shuffled into the kitchen and headed straight for the pot of coffee on the stove.

Phoebe watched Sarah cross the room. "Good morning. Thirsty?"

"Don't shout," Sarah said in a hushed voice. "I'm not deaf." She reached for the cupboard door.

Coming up behind her, Phoebe picked up the cup she had set out for Sarah. "You look peaked. Didn't you sleep well?"

Sarah rubbed her forehead. "Must not have."

"Sit down. I'll pour the coffee."

Sarah eased a chair out from under the worktable and collapsed onto it. "Where is everyone?"

"Charles took the children out for a horseback ride." Phoebe filled the cup and set it in front of Sarah. "The dance was quite a success. We didn't count the money last night, but the bag was full."

"That's nice." Picking up the cup with both hands, Sarah raised it to her lips and sipped.

"I told the others we would count the money and deposit it in the bank tomorrow."

"All right," Sarah said, peering over the rim of the cup, "but can we do it later?" Lord, her head hurt. Coffee wasn't helping.

"It doesn't need to be done this minute."

"Good."

"We passed Mr. Perry as he left here last night, but you were in your room when we came inside." Phoebe sipped her coffee. "If I hadn't seen you leave with him, I would not have believed it."

Sarah stared at her, eyes opened wide. Slowly, she set the cup on the table. "You saw me do *what?*"

"Leave the dance with Mr. Perry."

"Phoebe, it's too early for jokes, and I feel awful."

"I'm not surprised."

Sarah frowned at her. "Why are you speaking in riddles?"

"Do you remember how much punch you drank?"

"I didn't count."

"I told you it tasted odd. There was whiskey in it. Lord knows how much those boys added."

"You mean I was *spiffed*?" She gulped down the rest of her coffee. "Why didn't you tell me?! Ohh," she moaned, grabbing her head with both hands.

"I didn't find out until the bowl was empty. By then you were past telling. . . . You were giddy."

"I'll kill Gil Perry!" She winced and lowered her voice. "I shouldn't've trusted him, but I never thought he'd spike the punch."

"He didn't. A couple of the young loggers did it—on a lark."

Sarah rested her head on her arms. "He's still responsible." She closed her eyes, wishing she could go back to bed and wake up yesterday morning. "I didn't embarrass myself, did I?"

"Let's say you surprised a few people. You were *very* happy." Phoebe refilled their cups. "Except when—" She really did feel sorry for her. Everyone who had read her article knew how she felt about inebriates.

Sarah stared at her. "When I what?"

Phoebe glanced at her, trying not to smile. "You were dancing with Mr. Perry and had a disagreement. At least it sounded that way."

"Please tell me I didn't make a spectacle of myself. I'll be the laughingstock of this town."

"No one seemed surprised by your disagreement. I'm not even sure there was any whiskey in the punch then."

"I remember dancing with Mr. Pratt, twice. . . ." Sarah sat up. "And later with Mr. Perry—a waltz, I think."

Phoebe waited. She had never had more to drink than a few sips of spirits. She felt sure Sarah hadn't either, especially since she was so against men drinking. "You two danced very well together."

As Sarah stared at the empty plate on the table her memory became clearer. "There wasn't much food left, and we sold almost all of the dance tickets." She finished her coffee and gave Phoebe a weak smile. "Men danced with their wives."

"Yes, they did. If they hadn't we might have had a riot on our hands." Phoebe poured the last of the coffee into Sarah's cup. "The last dance was particularly interesting."

"Weren't you with Charles?"

Phoebe nodded and chuckled. "One of the loggers led you onto the dance floor."

Sarah thought a moment but it was useless. "Well, which one was it?"

"I don't know his name, but you didn't finish with him."

Sarah groaned. "Just tell me what happened."

"About halfway through, you stepped back from him and twirled around. You stepped right into Mr. Perry's arms and finished the dance."

"I did?"

"You weren't too steady, so he volunteered to walk you home."

"Ugh, I thought that was a nightmare."

"Did anything else happen in your dream?"

"Nothing much. He said, 'Sleep well' or something, and I said, 'Good night.'" Sarah rubbed her forehead. "I'm not even sure who the man was, except that he smelled good." She didn't like the way Phoebe was grinning. "What is so amusing?"

"As we came up the street, we saw he had his arms around you."

"You must be wrong. I don't like the man. Why would I allow him such a liberty?" Sarah started to shake her head but immediately stopped. "You *have* to be mistaken. He's the last man I would—" She couldn't even complete that thought, let alone say it. She braced her hands on the table and stood up. "I think I'll have a cup of chamomile tea and lay down for a while. And hope no one remembers last night."

Sunday morning the town seemed to be recovering from the dance. The road through town was deserted and so was the saloon, except for Gil. The first thing he did was hang Lorinda back up behind the bar where she belonged. It didn't take him long to wipe the bar, sweep the floor, and rearrange the ladies' placement of chairs and tables.

When Jack returned late that afternoon, Gil was ready to leave. "You must've taken the long way home from church with Miss Layton."

Jack beamed at him. "We had a picnic by the bend in the river." He loosened his tie and removed it, then did the same with his collar.

"Wasn't it muddy?"

"We shared a log." Jack unbuttoned the top buttons on his shirt. "After last night, I thought ya'd be callin' on Mrs. Hampton by now."

"I don't have a death wish." Gil was curious as hell to know if she remembered kissing him. It wasn't something he'd forget.

"Goin' up to the camp today?"

"No reason to. I saw the men last night. Think I'll take a ride, though."

"Kiss Vonney for me."

"Not this time."

Gil went up to his room, put the letter in his pocket, and walked to the livery. A good ride should help clear his memory of Sarah—how she'd felt in his arms, her throaty sigh, the way her fingers had played on the back of his neck when she kissed him.

He paused outside the livery. Maybe he should *walk* to Fenton's Crossing to ease the lingering ache.

Monday morning as Phoebe finished cutting out the dress she was making for Cora for Christmas, she heard Sarah's bedroom door close and called out to her.

Sarah walked to the kitchen. "That will look good on Cora. I hope she likes it."

"Me, too." Phoebe folded the red wool skirt. "Are you going to the office?"

"Yes. I want to write my column about the dance."

"Would you stop by the bank and deposit this? Mr. Grebby said he'd open an account for the money we raised." She set a sturdy bag in front of her.

Sarah lifted the bag. "It feels like more than eighteen dollars."

"We would have raised more if we'd known those boys had added whiskey to the punch. We could've charged twenty cents a glass."

"Don't remind me." Sarah tossed the end of her soft woolen shawl over one shoulder and left with the heavy bag.

The weather had turned blustery again and there was more snow on Mount Hood. She would have to take the flannel petticoats out of her trunk tonight, she decided as she hurried into the bank. A sturdy counter ran the width of the room and the safe was in one corner.

Mr. Grebby, the owner of the bank, was working as the teller. Sarah stood in line behind the barber, Mr. Farmer. They both waited while Mr. Grebby helped another customer, Mr. Satterley. The bag seemed to grow heavier with each passing minute. She cradled it in her left arm for a while, then moved it to her right side.

Mr. Farmer smiled at Sarah. "Mrs. Hampton, you go ahead of me. I'm in no hurry."

"Thank you, but I don't mind waiting." The door opened, and Sarah casually glanced over her shoulder. Gil Perry. No. She was bound to see him around town, but she wasn't prepared to face him so soon. She looked at Mr. Grebby and silently pleaded that he would hurry.

Gil took his place in line behind Sarah. "Good morning, Sarah. You're looking very nice today." He motioned to the bag she was holding. "Is that the money raised from the dance?"

Sarah?! How dare he? "Yes, it is," she said in a stilted voice, then she caught a whiff of his hair tonic. Her dream. Phoebe swore she had seem them embracing. A shiver slid down Sarah's back. It couldn't be true, but it must be.

"You should be able to buy several books now. Will you pick them out?"

She stared at the counter as if hypnotized. "A committee will decide."

"Are you on the committee?"

"I—" Taken aback, she inhaled and exhaled slowly. She assumed she would be, but that hadn't been decided yet. Of course *he* had to be the one person in town to ask her. "I'm not sure, Mr. Perry."

"Well, you should be." He smiled at her. "You are in and out of the library all the time."

"How—?" she started, without thinking.

"To be honest, I've seen you go into the hotel. I just figured you were using the lending library."

She whirled around, glaring at him. "Have you been watching me?"

He chuckled. "You're kinda hard to miss." Mr. Satterley left, and Mr. Farmer stepped up to the counter. Mr. Grebby smiled at Gil, and Gil waved. "There aren't too many unmarried ladies in town, and hardly any running in and out of the hotel."

"How"—she began, then lowered her voice—"dare you imply that I—that I—Wipe that grin off your face, Mr. Perry."

"Yes, ma'am." He did try to keep a straight face, but he wasn't too successful.

"You buffoon, why don't you—" Suddenly the door flew open and banged against the wall. She started and tightened her hold on the bag. Two men darted inside. One was wearing a bowler and a stylish gentleman's overcoat, with a muffler pulled up over his mouth. The second man's face was nearly covered by a full, dark beard, and he wore course trousers, a well-worn woolen coat, and an old, stained felt hat.

"Gentlemen, and madam, please don't move or try any heroics. Sir," the man in the muffler said to Mr. Grebby, "fill up that bag, starting with the cash from the safe." The man nodded to his partner, who handed Mr. Grebby a large canvas bag.

The moment the bank robbers looked at Mr. Grebby, Gil closed the space between himself and Sarah. He put his left arm around her, with his hand firmly grasping her arm, and whispered, "Slowly pull the side of your shawl over the bag." Gridley had been so peaceful in the last few years, Gil had given up wearing a pistol except when he left town.

"Hey, yew, shut yer mouth." The bearded man waved his gun in an arc. "Don't nobody say nothin'."

Sarah's temper flared. "Who are—"

"Madam, do not speak," the mufflered robber said. "My friend may not know how to use words properly, but he can shoot that pistol, and I can assure you he can't miss you at this distance, and neither will I."

An icy quality in the man's voice convinced her to follow Gil's advice. She moistened her dry lips, her temper still simmering. Then Gil gave her arm a gentle but firm squeeze, and she nodded. His embrace felt comforting. Keeping quiet was not.

The mufflered bank robber looked at Mr. Farmer.

She stared at him and concentrated on memorizing his appearance. If he escaped, she would see that his description was in that week's newspaper.

"Hey, yew, we ain't got all day."

Gil was relieved that Sarah was being sensible and keeping quiet. The bank robbers were a strange pair. The bearded one was half-cocked, but the one with the fancy speech struck Gil as the more lethal of the two.

The wall clock chimed the half hour. The bearded bank robber turned and shot the clock.

Mr. Grebby dropped to the floor.

"Move, ol' man."

Mr. Farmer stumbled backward until the bearded bank robber fired in his direction.

"Stop it!" Sarah screamed, struggling against Gil's attempt to restrain her, and stared at the one in the muffler. "Can't you control him?"

Gil pulled her hard against his side and hissed, "You'll get yourself killed."

"Listen to him, madam." The bank robber wearing the muffler took a step closer to the counter. "You, clerk, if that bag is not filled and handed to my friend in the next thirty seconds, I will shoot the lady."

Mr. Grebby bolted to the safe.

The bearded bank robber sauntered over to Sarah and grinned at her. "Yew're kinda purty," he said, reaching out to her hair.

She wasn't about to let that filthy ruffian touch her. Gil wasn't wearing a gun, but she had the heavy bag of coins hidden under her shawl. She tightened her hand on the bag. The instant the bank robber's gun was near enough, she swung the bag upward and knocked the gun out of his hand.

She acted so quickly Gil couldn't prevent her rash action, but he managed to keep her from falling on top of the outlaw. The next moment he heard the faint click of a pistol being cocked. He wrapped his other arm across Sarah's chest and turned toward her.

A deafening shot rang out. She felt Gil jerk, then he fell into her. Caught off balance, she fell backward. She landed on the floor with him pinning her down; the back of his head rested against her cheek.

Dear God, he's been shot.

"Yew damn jackass! Yew kilt 'er!"

9

Another blaring shot reverberated. Sarah heard a thud, then retreating footsteps. Acrid gun smoke stung her nostrils. Craning her neck, she saw Mr. Farmer huddled in the corner with his back to the room, but she couldn't see Mr. Grebby or the bank robbers.

"Gil," she hissed in his ear, praying he was only stunned. "Wake up!"

Gil didn't move or make a sound, and he hadn't since he had fallen on top of her. He had her pinned to the floor. Unable to move without jostling him, and unsure of his injury, she couldn't very well just shove him aside.

"Gil, say something!"

"Sarah," Gil said, the pain in his side becoming worse by the second. "I'm not sure I can . . . move. . . ." Damn, his side felt as if he'd been split with an axe blade.

"Thank God, you're alive."

"Are you . . . okay?" He coughed and a godawful pain seared his side. When he caught his breath, he moved his free arm to brace himself, but the floor was slippery. "Sarah, can't . . ."

"Gil!" She could only reach his back with her free hand. He lay perfectly still, his breathing labored. "Mr. Grebby! We need help! Mr. Farmer! *Somebody help us!*"

Her arm was beginning to go numb and it felt odd, warm. Afraid to wait any longer, she struggled until she had all but her arm out from under him. She knelt at his back, free at last to see how badly he was injured. Then she saw the blood. It wasn't red but a brownish color, and it pooled out from under him.

She managed to ease her arm free and stared at it in horror. It was blood-soaked, and so were her clothes and shawl on that side. She studied Gil, and noticed blood welling through the back side of his shirt.

Mr. Grebby came from behind the counter and stopped, staring at Gil. "Good God A'mighty! Is he dead?"

"*No!* He's *not* dead!"

"What should I do?"

She crawled around to see Gil's face. It was pale, and he appeared to grow paler by the moment, almost gray-white. "Charles Abbott. Get him and Phoebe. *Hurry!*"

Charles had written for a newspaper during the war and spent those years with the army. She recalled him talking about helping surgeons with the wounded on occasion. There was no physician in town—he was her only hope. She was reluctant to do more than touch Gil, let alone to turn him over, but she knew that if the bleeding wasn't stopped, he would soon be dead.

"Are they gone?" Mr. Farmer asked from the corner.

"What? Oh, yes. How are you?"

"All right, I guess." Mr. Farmer stood up and looked around. "The bearded guy's on the floor. The one with the muffler must've got away."

"Is the other one dead?"

"Don't know."

She glanced at Mr. Farmer. "Get his gun, just in case he isn't."

She was frantic. She leaned down and touched her cheek to Gil's. He moaned and opened his eyes. Dear God, he was cool. He was getting worse with each breath. As panic threatened to unnerve her, she inhaled deeply, locked her jaw, and rolled him onto his side as gently as she could. He was covered with blood. Blood also gushed from a second wound in front. The bullet had gone straight through him.

Her stomach heaved. She felt light-headed. She had to stop the bleeding somehow. She ripped two strips of cloth from one of her petticoats and pushed his shirt out of the way. The wounds were not large but dear Lord, they were ugly. Bracing herself, she stuffed a wad of the cloth into each of the wounds.

Gil bellowed.

"Oh, Gil, I am so sorry. But I have to stop the bleeding."

Pain accompanied each breath he took and brought a wave of dizziness. "Hur-ts t' br . . . ea-the."

"Don't talk now." She moved her hands so only her fingers touched him. "Mr. Farmer, how far is the nearest physician?"

Mr. Farmer rubbed his jaw. "Damascus, I guess. About an hour away on horseback. Slower by wagon."

"He wouldn't survive." She stared at the blood running over her fingers. How much did a body have? How much could it lose before—? "I'll need bandages. Sheets will do—*clean* ones. Find something!"

"Yes, ma'am."

Holding her fingers over each wound, as if that alone would stem the flow of blood, she willed Gil to live. "Don't you die. Do you hear me? You *can't* die!"

She hung her head and closed her eyes. She had danced with him. They had laughed and been on friendly terms for a little while. She felt the tears running down her cheeks and realized she was crying.

"I . . .'ll try . . . not . . . to." Her touch was so gentle. Maybe he was dead and dreaming—but the pain in his chest countered that notion.

Charles ran into the bank and abruptly stopped at Sarah's side. "God in Heaven—" He swallowed hard. "Were you shot, too?"

She shook her head. "His blood . . . It's all his blood." She looked up at Charles. "There's so much. . . . And it's not all red. I don't know what it is. . . ."

"I've tried not to remember what I saw during the war."
He took a closer look. "But I believe the liver is there. The
bullet must have gone right through it. I recall a surgeon
saying something about bile turning blood brown, but I
could be wrong. It has been a long time."

"Your memory's usually accurate. Do you think he has
enough blood left?"

"Hard to say, but we have to stop the bleeding."

"How? I tried to stuff wadding into the holes but it's
dripping with blood, and when I pressed on the wounds it
was too painful for him."

"He could have a broken rib or two. Someone will have
to probe for bone fragments, bits of cloth, and metal
shards."

"You must have seen that done. You do it."

Charles held out one beefy hand. "You want to stick any
of these fingers in his chest?" He shook his head. "It won't
be easy, Sarah, but I think you should do it."

"How can I"—she bit her lip, trying to hold back more
tears—"cause him more pain?"

"The surgeons used chloroform." He sighed heavily.
"We don't have any but there's plenty of whiskey at the
saloon. And we need to move him over there anyway."

She stared at Gil's hand, so white against the brownish,
sticky blood. "The bullet was meant for me. . . . I'm the
one who angered them."

Charles gave her shoulder a brusk squeeze. "I'll get a
bottle of his best," he said and ran out.

Sarah felt an eternity had passed before Charles returned
carrying a bottle and one end of a door. Mr. Young held
the other end and a blanket. She bent her head, brushing
her cheek over Gil's hair, and whispered, "Charles brought
whiskey for you."

Gil tried to smile. That was one hell of a concession for
her. He must be close to death. Or out of his head. He
decided the latter was the most likely.

"Gil, Mr. Young is here, too."

"I brought a blanket," Jack said, staring at Gil. "Guess
he don't need it right now."

"Jack, bring your end around over there." Charles looked at Sarah. "You have to move so we can get him on the door. It'll do as a stretcher."

Phoebe flew into the bank and stumbled to her knees at Sarah's side. "Oh, mercy."

Sarah pushed Charles's hand away from her. "You said you wanted me to feel around in Gil's wound." She rested her hand on Gil's arm. "It should be done now before you move him."

"You're right. Better push your sleeve up a ways."

"Gil, can you take a few sips of whiskey?" She unbuttoned the cuff of her sleeve and rolled it up.

That must be a first, he thought. "Mm-hm."

Jack dropped down to his knees near Gil's head. "I'd better hold down his shoulders."

"I'll get his legs," Charles said. "Sit on them if I have to." He went down on one knee in front of Gil and uncorked the bottle. "Gil, drink as much of this whiskey as you can." He glanced at Sarah. "I don't think Sarah will mind."

"Goo-d." Gil felt someone's hand behind his neck and another hand raise his head. Suddenly, the bottle was at his mouth. He had never been so helpless or weak. He took one swallow and winced.

"This must hurt like hell, but it's nothing compared to how it'll feel when Sarah puts her fingers in your side. Jack, raise him a bit so he can drink." Charles tipped the bottle up for him.

After Gil had managed to swallow half the contents of the bottle, Sarah lowered his head and motioned for Charles to follow her outside. "Pour some of that over my hands."

He stared at her as if she had lost her mind. "This's good sippin' whiskey. Too good to waste."

"My hands are bloody and dirty. And maybe the whiskey will help numb his insides." She held her hands out over the dirt. "Pour."

Charles took a long drink before he did as she asked.

"Thank you." She shook her hands and went back inside.

Wordlessly, she knelt behind Gil and pulled his shirt up out of her way. The angry flesh had puckered closed. If only it were a hole she could see in to, but it wasn't. She met Phoebe's distraught gaze. "I can't imagine how painful this will be."

Phoebe put her hand on Sarah's shoulder. "It must be done. Would you rather I tried?"

"No." Sarah steeled herself for what she had to do—touch parts of his body she could not even envision—and pressed her first finger into the ragged flesh on his back.

Gil yelped and jumped—or tried to, but something held him down. Damn! That hurt like hell.

"Gil, hold still. If you move suddenly, my finger might jab something it shouldn't."

"Okaaay." All of a sudden Gil felt someone raise his head and pour whiskey into him. Three gulps were all he could manage; he nudged the bottle away with his tongue.

Charles met Sarah's gaze. "It'll help relax him."

She pushed her finger against something smooth and rope-like. Her finger slipped through a hole. *The bullet hole?* It tightened around her finger. Was that a muscle? She pushed her finger deeper and felt what must be a bone. It had to be a rib. Sliding her finger along the surface for a short distance, she came to a crack.

"I think he has a broken rib."

"I'm not surprised." Charles watched Sarah's face. "You *have* to feel around for any pieces of bone or metal or fabric from his shirt."

"I'm trying." As she turned her hand, her finger brushed something sharp. Gil bellowed and his muscle was instantly taut. God help me, she silently prayed.

Jack maintained his hold on Gil. "Mrs. Hampton, are ya okay?"

In case Gil could hear her, she didn't want her fear to alarm him. "Fine," she said softly, and with more confidence than she felt.

"Gil," she said, skimming the back of her free hand down his cheek. "Try to—" *Rest,* she was about to say, but that was an impossible suggestion. "Try not to flinch."

She heard him sigh. Amazingly, when she eased her middle finger into his body, the flesh stretched, as did the muscle, but more blood gushed out. She felt around and trapped the sliver between her fingers, and withdrew it.

"Phoebe, will you rip another piece off my petticoat? I want to put whatever I remove on it."

Phoebe moved over and reached under Sarah's shirt. "Does it matter which one?"

"I've already started shredding the top one."

Phoebe tore off three panels from the back and ripped a couple in half. She placed one at Sarah's right, tucked the other into her sleeve, and set the others on the counter. "What else do you need?"

Sarah met her gaze. "Experience and knowledge, but it's too late for that. I'll settle for courage."

Phoebe reached for Sarah's hand but drew back just before touching her. "You're doing what none of us could or would."

"Thank you." Sarah rubbed her blood-covered fingers on the swatch of cloth to dislodge the sliver. "Charles, would you check that? It was sharp." Again, she eased her fingers into Gil's back and blood oozed up over her hand.

Charles rubbed the small piece with the corner of the cloth. "Bone. Keep looking."

"How am I supposed to know when I've found any cloth or threads? Everything is moist and slippery."

Charles shrugged. "I left that to the surgeons."

"Oh, there's something—it's smooth and firm. Ugh," she said, and a shiver slid down her back. "Another hole."

"Might be the liver. Be careful."

She nodded, staring at Gil's side. "I feel blood and something thicker, like syrup, but I don't feel any more shards," she said, easing her fingers out. "Phoebe . . ." She held out her hand. Phoebe gave her half a panel of the petticoat, and Sarah lightly pressed it on the wound.

"Here." Phoebe handed another cloth to Sarah for her hands. "Are you finished?"

Sarah wiped her hands and walked around to face Gil. "I'll have to do the same on his chest, but first we need to move him. I can't kneel in that . . . blood." *His blood.* He enjoyed life so, and she prayed it wouldn't end here on the floor of the bank.

Phoebe grabbed the blanket. "Wouldn't it be easier to get the blanket under him and use that to move him onto the door?"

"Much." Sarah nodded. "Good thinking."

"I'd better get that mopped up before someone slips in it," Mr. Grebby said and rushed to the back room.

Sarah crouched by Gil's shoulder and brushed her forearm over his brow. "Gil, can you hear me?"

"Umh."

"Do you want more whiskey?"

He licked his lips. His head was swimming. " 'Nu . . . ff." Words drifted in his mind, but he couldn't get them out. He moved his hand and reached for her. "Sar . . . kiss . . . b'for . . . die. . . ."

She stared at his hand for a moment, startled, then took it in both of hers. "You're *not* dying. I—"

"Prom . . . ise."

She bent down and touched her cheek to his. "I promise, Gil." She almost kissed him, then realized he wouldn't understand it was only out of concern. "You'll be in your own bed soon." She felt his thumb brush the back of hers.

Jack and Phoebe spread the blanket behind Gil. "Okay, boys, do this real easy so he don't hurt."

"If you can raise him just a little, I'll pull the blanket under him." Sarah tucked her skirts between her knees and took a firm hold of the blanket. "Support his hips. There might be more scraps of bone in him."

Phoebe knelt on the other side of the pool of blood and held on to the blanket. She gave her husband an encouraging nod and in moments Mr. Perry was on the blanket. Sarah's color worried her. Her cheeks were nearly as pale as Mr. Perry's. "Do you want me to finish?"

"I will." Sarah looked at Phoebe. "This isn't anything like when we were midwives for Esmee and Linnet, is it?"

"I'd forgotten." Phoebe shook her head. "It's a wonder our dolls survived."

Sarah knelt in front of Gil.

Blood still ran from the wound in his chest. Without giving herself any more time to think about what she had to do, she began working her fingers into the wound. Gil yowled and grew rigid, but the men held him down.

In that instant she flinched and one finger scraped a jagged piece of bone. She pulled her fingers out and stared at a cut about a half inch long on her middle finger. "That bone could rip him up inside."

Charles patted her shoulder. "I'll help bind his ribs when you're finished."

She looked into Charles' gentle eyes and spoke softly. "What if I kill him?"

"Stop it!" he hissed. "He's dead if you do nothing."

"I'm trying. . . ."

Phoebe glared at her husband and tried to reassure Sarah. "You're doing just fine."

When Sarah plunged her fingers past the muscle, one slipped between two ribs and pushed into a smooth, slippery surface. Frowning as she concentrated, she worked her finger around to Gil's side. He yelled once, then, blessedly, he passed out.

"I don't know what this is behind his ribs, but there's something poking out of it."

"Good. I knew you could do it." Charles gave her a confident nod.

By the time she finished, she had removed small pieces of bone, metal from the bullet, and even a bit of fabric from his shirt.

Sarah went behind the counter and motioned Phoebe to follow. "Take my petticoat off for me and rip it into strips. We'll need it to bandage his wounds and bind his ribs."

While Phoebe made bandages, Sarah spoke to Gil even though he was unconscious. "We're almost done. I hope to God you don't remember this." She didn't want to remember it either, but knew that was not possible.

"The surgeons dressed a lot of wounds with lint," Charles said.

Sarah stared at Charles. "*Lint?* Put that on open wounds?"

"That's right. I don't recall why, though."

"Threads should be removed and lint put on? That doesn't make sense." Sarah looked at Phoebe. "Where are we supposed to find lint?"

"Fabric, yard goods? I'll see if Mrs. Seaton can help." Phoebe ripped the last strip and glanced at the counter. "Here's a pinch of lint." She handed it to Sarah and ran across the road.

Sarah looked at Charles. "How am I to remove this fluff later?" When she glanced at her hand, the lint had disappeared in the blood.

He shook his head. "I didn't spend that much time with the surgeons."

Mr. Grebby dropped the blood-soaked rags into a bucket and squinted at a spot on the floor. "Look here—is that the bullet that went through Mr. Perry?"

Sarah turned on her heel and tried to pick it up. "It's stuck in the floor."

"Leave it there so everyone'll know," someone called out.

"No." Jack took out a pocket knife and pried the bullet up. "He already has a reminder of what happened."

Sarah rubbed her hand on her skirt and held it out to him. "May I have it?" Jack dropped it in her hand, and she put it in her pocket to look at later.

Phoebe rushed back to the bank with a wad of lint. "This is all we could gather up." She put it with the other bit in Sarah's hand. "Is it enough?"

"It'll have to do." Sarah divided the fluff in half and with Phoebe's help soon bandaged Gil's wounds. His breathing was shallow. She ripped another piece from her petticoat and wiped his face. "We need to clean him up."

"That can wait till later," Jack said.

She wiped her arm across her forehead, then gently combed her fingers through Gil's thick hair. He looked so young, so near death, but she refused to consider that fate. He had saved her life. Surely he wouldn't have to pay with his own.

"He's ready to be taken to his room." She supervised as Charles and Mr. Young raised the blanket holding Gil and gently lowered him onto the door. "Don't jostle him. His ribs. . . ."

Jack nodded. "We'll b'careful, ma'am."

Mr. Grebby stared at Gil. "Somebody's got to go after the cutthroat."

Jack looked around. "Who'll go with me?"

Charles put his hand on Phoebe's shoulder. "I will." Seeing the fear in her eyes, he patted her arm. "I have to, my dear. We'll be fine."

Sarah wanted to see that the bank robber paid for his crime, but she did not want her friend to end up like Gil. "Charles, that robber isn't a stupid man. He's cold and calculating. Be very careful."

Sobbing, Phoebe rose and embraced her husband. She couldn't tell him not to go, but dear Lord, if anything happened to him . . .

Jack touched Sarah's arm. "Can ya describe that bastard for us?"

10

After Sarah had washed up and changed clothes, she hurried back to the saloon. She was halfway up the stairs when Mr. Grebby and Mr. Farmer started down. "How is Mr. Perry?"

"Holdin' his own so far," Mr. Farmer said.

"Mrs. Hampton, you shouldn't be here," Mr. Grebby said.

She moved up one step. "I don't want him to die because of me." She took another step. "Excuse me, gentlemen." She continued up the stairs, and they moved aside.

She walked down the hall to the only open doorway. Charles and Mr. Young were standing at the foot of the bed. "Is he still unconscious?" Both men started and turned, their expressions grim.

Charles nodded. "God willing, he won't wake up for forty-eight hours or more."

Jack glanced over his shoulder at Gil. "It's a wonder the move didn't kill him."

Sarah reached into her pocket and withdrew a bottle the size of her hand. "I bought a bottle of Dr. Mosebey's Syrup for Rheumatism, Inflamed Gums, and Back Pain. Mrs. Seaton said she knows people who swear by it."

Charles stared at the dark amber bottle and held out his hand. "May I see that?"

She handed him the bottle. "What's wrong?"

He read the label, removed the cork, and sniffed the contents. "Careful with this, Sarah. There's probably enough morphine in it to knock out a grizzly." He handed it back to her.

"I will," she said, examining the bottle.

Jack gave Gil one last hard look and started for the door. "I'm goin' after that bastard. Ya comin' with me, Charles?"

"Get the horses. I'll be right behind you." Charles studied Sarah. "You should get Mr. Farmer to stay with him. He pulls teeth and doses folks from time to time."

"You're sweet." She stood on tiptoe and kissed his soft cheek. "Don't you get shot. That outlaw's a devil."

"I learned how to duck real good in the war." He patted her shoulder and left.

She closed the door to Gil's room and pulled off her shawl. The drapes were dark green; the low-post bedstead appeared to be made from the same dark walnut as the chest of drawers and washstand, and there was a good woodstove. His room was comfortable. And the scent of his hair tonic sweetened the air. *Just what I should be thinking about right now.*

She draped her shawl over the back of the hide armchair, set the bottle on the little table near his bed, and stood at his side. From what she could see, Charles and Mr. Young had placed Gil on top of the bed in about the same position he had been on the bank floor, pulled a blanket up to the back of his neck, and wiped off his face.

She took the smashed bullet out of her pocket and stared at it. That small bit of metal had ripped up his insides. She looked at him as she rolled the bullet between her fingers and dropped it back in her skirt pocket. Her gaze followed the outline of his body under the cover down to his feet. Didn't they remove his boots? She reached out tentatively and touched one heel. His boot.

"I thought as much." She pulled the blanket back from

his boots, checked to make sure he had not wakened, and eased his leg over the side of the bed. She stared a moment, then hiked her skirt, straddled his leg, and hesitated.

This was not the first time she had taken off a man's boot. She had had to help her late husband, too many times, but this wasn't him. This was Gil, Gil Perry, and he wasn't an inebriate, he had been wounded. For her.

She grasped his boot with both hands. With her knees squeezing his calf, she loosened the boot and pulled it off. Before she could step away from him, he flexed his foot.

"Ooh," she squawked as she jumped over his foot. She clamped her hand over her mouth and listened to her pounding heart. Tiptoeing to the head of the bed, she leaned down and peered at his face.

He sighed and moved his hand.

She straightened up. "Any man with half a bottle of whiskey in him isn't going to wake up soon," she reminded herself.

After she had taken off his other boot, she added wood to the woodstove and wondered where he kept extra blankets. Bottom drawer of the chest? She opened it just enough to see folded trousers. Sarah didn't like snooping through his belongings, but she made herself peek in the next drawer and the next.

"You don't even know I'm here, so I suppose you won't miss me if I go after more covers for you."

There was no response, but she would have been shocked if he had spoken. She grabbed her shawl and quietly left his room. As she hurried down the stairs, she made a mental list of a few other items she wanted to bring back with her.

Phoebe closed the door to the newspaper office and prayed Charles would be home by morning to open it at usual. After the excitement earlier, the road through town was eerily barren. Word of the bank holdup had spread quickly and the men had gone after the bank robber with Charles and Mr. Young.

It was only midday. The children wouldn't be home from school before four. Anxious and worried, she went home and started cleaning house. She straightened up the parlor, dusted, filled the lamps' reservoirs, and washed all of the chimneys. When she heard the front door open, she ran to see if Charles had returned.

Sarah closed the door behind her as Phoebe raced around the corner. "What's wrong?" Sarah asked. Hadn't there been enough trouble for one day?

"It's you."

"Who were you expecting?" Sarah dropped her shawl over a peg near the door.

"Hoping is more like it. It's too soon to expect the men back, but Charles has never gone after an outlaw before."

Sarah put her arm around Phoebe's shoulders. "He survived the war, and he's a careful man. He'll come home safely."

"He'd better." Phoebe took a swipe at her skirt, and then looked at Sarah. "I thought you were going to sit with Mr. Perry."

"I came back for a few things."

"I'll help. What do you need?"

"A comforter and a blanket. I have extra in my room. Towels, some vinegar, a couple of cups, a pan to heat water . . . bandages."

"And more lint?" Phoebe couldn't help grinning.

"It doesn't sound very practical, does it? I wonder where the surgeons found all that lint." Sarah started for her bedroom. "And clean rags for pads for his wounds. I'll take paper and pencils, too. Might as well do some writing. I can't just sit and stare at him."

Phoebe set to work collecting things from the kitchen, adding a small coffeepot, coffee, tea, and honey, and packed them in a small crate. Realizing Sarah would get hungry, Phoebe sliced cold beef and bread and added a jar of her bean soup and some gingersnaps.

Sarah carried an armload of bedding to the parlor and went back to her room for her writing materials. When she looked at the mound of things she had to take to the saloon, she hoped that Gil would not wake up before she returned.

"I have to get back. I'll take what I can now and get the rest in a little while."

"No need to make another trip. I'll take the crate." Phoebe opened the front door and carried the crate outside.

Sarah followed her and pushed the door closed with her foot. "You realize everyone will be gossiping about us by suppertime."

"Good." Phoebe smiled. "I've always wondered about the rooms over the saloon." She glanced at Sarah. "Weren't you curious? Just a little?"

Sarah smirked. "Of course I was, but Gil's room is nice, not quite what I had expected."

" 'Gil'?"

Oops. Sarah carelessly lifted one shoulder. "Since I had my hand inside his body, 'Mr. Perry' seems a bit formal. Don't you think?"

"I won't argue. I would hazard a guess that many wives haven't been that intimate with their husbands."

"Lord, I hope not!" Sarah stopped in front of the saloon and peeked inside. "Still empty."

"Let's take the back stairs," Phoebe said, walking toward the side of the building.

Sarah hurried to keep up with her. "How do you know about the back stairs?"

"Haven't you walked along the riverbank and looked at the backs of the buildings?"

"No. Maybe I will if I need to stretch my legs."

They reached the stairs. Sarah led the way. The door opened to the hallway, and she continued to Gil's room. She shifted the bed covers in her arms and eased the door open.

"Is he still sleeping?" Phoebe whispered.

Sarah nodded, walked over to the hide chair, and set the covers on the seat. After Phoebe came in, Sarah closed the door and stepped over to the bed. Gil hadn't moved. When she lifted the blanket to check his wound, her fears were confirmed. There was fresh blood on the bed covers.

"Phoebe, we have to stop the bleeding. Do you know of anything that might help?"

"Alum stops bleeding in small cuts or nicks, and cobwebs are sometimes packed into a deep cut. I'm not sure about bullet wounds."

"Cauterizing might work, but I don't think I could do that to him."

"Want to try yarrow? It's sometimes called 'soldier's woundwort.' Many soldiers kept the leaves in their packs . . . *to treat wounds!* Why didn't I remember that before?"

"Do you have any?"

"Matter of fact, I do. I'll be right back."

While Phoebe was gone, Sarah looked at Gil's wounds again and noticed that the waist of his trousers seemed to be adding pressure to the wounds. He was still unconscious. She glanced around the room, as if fearing she weren't alone.

"I can do this," she said, bolstering her courage. She pressed one hand on the bed and worked the other under him to his belt buckle. She was working the belt loose when he groaned or growled. She yanked her hand out from under him and waited for him to say something.

He sighed, but he didn't wake up.

She watched him and decided it was safe to remove his belt. Slowly, she pulled the belt through each loop and set it on the chest of drawers. When she checked his wounds again, she was relieved to see that they were not seeping quite as much. She lowered the blanket.

"Hurry, Phoebe." Sarah paced across the room and back. Cobwebs. It couldn't hurt. She began searching. There was one lone strand on the ceiling but that wasn't enough. She walked down the hall and found more wisps of a web. However, added all together it would not make a ball bigger than a seed pearl.

Finally, she heard someone running down the hall. She opened the door as Phoebe slid to a stop. "Did you find the woundwort?"

"Yes," Phoebe said, thrusting a canvas bag into Sarah's hand and trying to catch her breath.

Sarah opened the bag. "What else do we need?"

"Cobwebs," Phoebe added, waving a linen towel. "The

old berry vines were covered with them.''

"Thank goodness. I only found enough to fill a pin-prick." Sarah put the bag on the floor by the bed and turned the blanket back. "I'll take off the bandages. I should've thought to bring a bucket, too."

Phoebe got the basin from the washstand and held it while Sarah unwrapped the bandages. "Has the bleeding slowed at all?"

"It doesn't look like it." Sarah removed the last strip of cloth and dropped it in the basin. "There's blood all over his side. I should wash it off with vinegar before we pack his wounds."

Phoebe set the jar of vinegar on the little table. "Do you think he'll be surprised to see us if he wakes up?"

Sarah closed her hand around the pitcher handle and turned to Phoebe. "He's likely to have such a headache that he might think he's imagining us. He consumed almost three-quarters of a bottle of whiskey."

"I'll go home and fix him some comfrey tea."

"That's a good idea, and add sugar. I have a feeling the patent medicine I got for him will taste bitter." Sarah poured vinegar over a clean cloth and applied it to the wound on his back. The vinegar was cold, but she didn't have time to warm it.

He flinched and let out a weak cry.

"Get mad, Gil. Fighting mad."

Working quickly, she made sure the blood had washed all of the lint from the wound before she packed half of the cobwebs into each wound. On top of that she added the dried, ground-up woundwort and wrapped him with fresh bandages.

He looked so pale, so weak and young. She ran her fingers through his hair, and he murmured softly. She placed her hand across his forehead. It was neither hot nor cold.

"Good. You're holding your own."

Gil's head hurt like hell, his mouth tasted as bad as a chamber pot smelled, and his side felt like a mule had kicked him down the road. "Musta been one hell of a fight," he muttered. The trouble was, he couldn't remember it.

His eyelids weighed a ton, but with the help of his thumb and finger he pried them open. He was in his own bed. Had he left the lamp burning? He hadn't been this liquored up in years, and he planned never to be again.

He planted the palm of his hand on the bed near his shoulder and pushed to lever himself up. His cheek left the bed, but he didn't have the strength to hold his head up. He relaxed his arm and sank back down. What time was it? He looked at the top of the chest of drawers, but the pitcher was in front of the small clock.

"Who in hell's been in here?" he asked, but it came out as a raspy whisper.

Sarah jerked upright on the hide chair. She must have fallen asleep, but what had startled her? The room was quiet. Setting aside the paper she had been making notes on, she went to the door and opened it. The hall was empty.

He hadn't imagined it. Someone was sneaking around in his room. "Who's there?" This time his voice was a bit stronger.

She whirled around. "Gil?" She crept over to the bed. His eyes were open! "How long have you been awake?" She stepped toward the head of the bed.

"Sarah?!"

"Yes, Gil?" She crouched at the side of his bed. "I'm right here."

"Wha—?" He felt light-headed and closed his eyes to get his bearings. "What're . . . you . . . doin' here?"

She knew after a deep sleep it was sometimes difficult to awaken completely alert, and since he had been soused on whiskey, she hadn't expected him to recall the bank robbery as clearly as she did. "I didn't want you to wake up alone." She didn't like the flushed look to his skin and laid her hand on his forehead. Fever. "You must be thirsty. I'll warm the tea."

"What's wrong—?" He rubbed his forehead on the bed. "So weak—"

She set the pan of comfrey tea on the woodstove. "Do you remember going to the bank?"

"Bank?" Strange images flashed in his mind, but he couldn't connect them. "Wha' day is it?"

She glanced at the clock. "Monday night." She swirled the tea in the pan and put it back on the fire. "You went to the bank this morning."

He felt as if her words were pieces of a puzzle he couldn't quite fit together. "Was there . . . fight? Feel like . . . th' devil."

"No, not a fight. The bank was held up." She half filled a cup with warm tea. Now that he was awake, they would have plenty of time to talk about what had happened. "Do you like honey in your tea?"

"Don't drink tea."

"You'll want this for your headache." She added a little honey to the cup, set it by the bed, and got the bottle of patent medicine and a spoon.

"How'd you know?"

"Anyone who gulps close to a bottle of whiskey is bound to feel its effects. Let me help you."

"In the bank?" It was a nightmare, he decided. It had to be. He never should've written to her. "Were you there?"

"Yes, I was."

"And you didn't knock the bottle out of my hand? Sarah, I'm sur-prised."

"Under the circumstances I thought it best. Now, you need to take this medicine and drink the tea. Try to roll onto your left side. I'll support your shoulders."

"Try?" He moved his right shoulder and a sharp pain shot through his body.

She pushed the blanket back. Fresh blood stained the bandage, but it had not soaked through the pad on the bed. She put one hand under his right leg. "It might be easier if you slide your knee up. I'll help you."

He tightened his jaw. "*I'll* move . . . leg."

"All right." When he couldn't manage it alone, she eased his leg up a little.

"Ugh!" He glared at her. "What th' hell's wrong?"

"You were shot by one of the bank robbers." She

poured the medicine in the spoon and held it near his mouth. "Now take this."

He had barely parted his lips, when she shoved the foul remedy into his mouth. "What was that?"

She showed him the dark amber bottle. "Dr. Mosebey's Syrup for Rheumatism, Inflamed Gums, and Back Pain."

"Back pain? Why in hell'd you give me *that*?"

"It's suppose to deaden pain."

"What's in it?"

"Charles said morphine."

"What? Good God, woman—" He closed his eyes for a moment. "That's potent medicine. For a woman who claims to dislike spirits, you're suddenly aw-fully free with them."

"One teaspoon every few hours shouldn't do more than dull the pain." She sat at the head of the bed and put her arm around him in order to support him.

"Just leave me . . . alone."

She held the cup to his lips. "This will sweeten your mouth. Maybe even your disposition."

He gritted his teeth and waited for the pain to let up. The tea didn't smell good, but she did. He took one sip, another, and another. It was sweet and it did taste better than the medicine, but now his stomach was roiling.

"Just leave me in peace." He straightened his bent leg as his stomach heaved, and as he covered his mouth, a wave of dizziness hit him.

"Try to finish the tea and then you can rest."

"No-o," he said weakly. "Hurts. Sick stomach."

She eased him down to the bed and stood up. "I'm not leaving until you are able to get around on your own."

He opened his mouth to speak, but couldn't.

"Sleep well. I'll be here if you need me."

She spread the comforter over him and caught herself as she bent down to kiss his cheek. Good Lord, she thought, backing away from him. What had she been thinking? He wasn't Clay or Cora. He was a man, cocky, irritating, and, on occasion, even . . . charming, in his own way.

•   •   •

When the early morning sun came through the bedroom window, Phoebe awakened with a start and sat up. She was still alone in bed. She drew up her knees and bent her head forward. This was the first night she hadn't slept with her husband since he'd come home after the war.

The same fears and frustration had returned twofold. Part of her wanted to pull the covers over her chin and sleep until he returned and woke her up, but she could not do that. Charles trusted her, depended on her to carry on, and so did their children.

"Mama?"

Phoebe rubbed her fingers over her eyes and tried to hide the worries she had from showing on her face. "Come in, sweetie."

Cora opened the door and stared at her papa's side of the bed, and then she ran over to her mama. "Where's Papa?"

"He's not back yet. Want to get in bed with me? It's too early to get ready for school."

"I kept waking up." Cora climbed over her mother and slid under the covers beside her. "I looked in Aunt Sarah's room, but she's not there. Did she go with Papa?"

Phoebe put her arm around her daughter's shoulders. "No. She's taking care of Mr. Perry. He was hurt yesterday."

"Is it true he got shot and bled all over the bank?"

"Oh, sweetie, is that what you have been thinking about?"

"All the boys were talking about it."

"Yes, he was shot."

"And Papa went after the man who shot Mr. Perry?"

"He didn't go alone. There are other men with him."

Cora snuggled at her mother's side and rested her arm on her tummy. "Mama, are you scared for Papa?"

"Mm-hm, but I know he's all right." Phoebe kissed the top of her daughter's head. "He's a smart man, and he knows how very much we need him and want him to come home to us." She comforted herself with the knowledge that Charles relied on his wits rather than brawn.

"Did Aunt Sarah have to stay all night with Mr. Perry?" Cora tipped her head back and looked at her mama.

"Yes. He's in a very deep sleep, and he has a fever."

"Does Aunt Sarah know what to do?"

"I believe she does. Why do you ask?"

"Remember when Clay was sick in the kitchen? She looked kinda yellow."

Phoebe smiled. "This is different. She's doing fine."

"Does she like him?"

"She is sorry he was wounded." Phoebe glanced at her daughter. "Why all the questions?"

"I just wondered if she likes him the way you like Papa."

"No, they're just friends." At least, Phoebe hoped they might be, if Sarah would only give him a chance.

Cora yawned. "He smiles a lot."

"Do you know Mr. Perry?"

"Uh-uh. But I see him sometimes." Cora yawned again and closed her eyes. "He was watching . . . Aunt Sarah at the dance. . . ."

Phoebe recalled seeing them at the front door, embracing. Sarah hadn't been fighting with him then. Phoebe closed her eyes and drew her knees up. *Charles, please return today. I need you.*

11

*G*il had awakened after midnight. Sarah gave him one more dose of the patent medicine and dripped a little more tea into his mouth. Recalling Charles's warning, she decided not to give Gil more of the medicine unless the pain became too much for him to bear.

Before the sun had crested Mount Hood, Sarah made a small pot of coffee and savored the first taste. After sleeping on the hide chair, she needed a long soak in a bathtub filled with hot water to work out the kinks. Tonight she would make up a pallet to sleep on in a corner of the room.

She checked his bandage. The wound was draining but there was less bleeding. However, he was shivering and his skin was hot and sweaty. The woundwort wasn't working, or if it was, not fast enough for her. Willow bark usually worked on fevers. She would try that next.

She didn't want to leave him alone, but neither of the two windows in his room opened to the street, and she had no way to flag down someone. She dampened a cloth and wiped his brow.

"I won't be gone very long," she said, knowing he couldn't hear her.

She wrote a quick note and set it where he would see it if he awakened, then she hurried downstairs. After rummaging through the storeroom, she left the saloon with a bucket and a large knife, and set out for the willow trees that grew just west of town.

Thirty minutes later she returned, out of breath but with a pail full of willow bark. Gil was restless and still shivering but not conscious. She scraped the inside of the bark into the pan, added water, and heated the decoction. When it was done simmering, he still had not wakened.

She dampened the cloth again and wiped his face. "Gil, wake up. Come on, open your eyes."

Why wouldn't she leave him alone. Her voice sounded as if she were calling from the edge of town. Raising his eyelids was more than he could manage. He moaned and that took great effort.

She watched him work his lips. She had the horrible feeling that if she didn't forcibly rouse him that he may never awaken. "Gil! Wake up *now*!"

He didn't respond.

"Do you want to die?" She waited and watched. "Don't you dare—"

"Sa . . ." He tried to move his hand, reach out to her.

"Oh, Gil, thank God." She bathed his face again. "I'll hold you up, just enough to drink."

She quickly poured some of the decoction into a cup and sat at the head of the bed. She lightly pressed the spoon to his lower lip and dribbled the tea into his mouth.

The hot liquid tasted foul, and he shivered.

"Try, Gil. One sip at a time."

He didn't want to frighten her but there was fear in her voice and that was enough to encourage him to try another taste.

When he had swallowed almost three spoonfuls of tea, she set the cup aside. "Rest now."

Desperate, and frightened he was slipping away, she decided to put the decoction on the wounds. He hadn't been able to take enough by mouth to be of much help. She removed the poultice and dribbled the warm liquid directly on his wounds.

He groaned and flexed a finger. He didn't struggle, and

that was even more unnerving. She knelt beside the bed and slid her hand beneath his. "Gil, I didn't mean to put you in danger. I am so very sorry, and . . . I did enjoy dancing with you." Her eyes filled with tears as she brushed her lips over the hot velvety flesh on the back of his hand.

"You don't deserve this. It should have been me." She gently withdrew her hand and stood up.

His desk was in front of the back window. She imagined him sitting there and gazing out at the river. She checked his fever and realized that she needed to step outside. Constantly staring at him would not help either of them.

She walked down the hall to the back stairs landing. The breeze caught her skirt and ruffled her hair. It felt wonderful.

As she stood on the landing she noticed a man fishing a distance upriver and recalled summers when she and Phoebe would spend the hot afternoons wading in the stream to cool off. She had wiped Gil's face but maybe she would need to do the same over his back and shoulders. She quickly filled the bucket and pitcher at the well and hurried back to the room.

She dropped three pieces of cloth into the basin of cold water, then pulled the covers back from Gil. Taking off his shirt was not as easy to accomplish. At first she was careful. However, considering he was unconscious, she ended up almost ripping the shirt from him. Thankfully, he was not wearing anything beneath. His chattering teeth gave her pause, but she plunged ahead and wrung out one piece of fabric.

The moment the cold cloth touched his fevered back, he jerked and made a weak crying sound but then as she wiped the cold, damp material over his back he quieted. The rag quickly became warm. She dropped it in the basin and continued with another one.

His back was lightly tanned and as smooth as satin. As soon as a cloth felt warm, she exchanged it for a cold one. At one point she soaked a towel and spread it over his back while she wiped his arms, face, and neck. She no idea how long she had been trying to cool him down when there was a tap on the door.

Phoebe eased the door open and poked her head inside. The moment she saw Sarah washing Mr. Perry's bare back, she hurried in and closed the door. "Sarah, did he—? Is he dead?"

"Too close. Would you help me cool him off?"

As Phoebe set the basket down, she stared at him in horror. "He's freezing. What are you doing to him?"

"The woundwort wasn't working, and he's only been able to take a few sips of tea." Sarah dropped the cloth she was holding into the basin and dragged her arm over her forehead.

"It takes time to bring down a fever."

"He was burning up." Sarah stared at Gil a long moment. "Remember how cool we felt soaking our feet in the stream?"

"Yes, but—"

"It might work better if we could sit him in a tub, but we can't." Sarah bundled up the covers at the end of the bed and dropped them on the chair.

"Lord, Charles will have more than a few words to say about our bathing Mr. Perry."

"Why tell him? We won't be *bathing* him in the true sense." Sarah studied his trousers but discarded the idea of removing them in front of Phoebe. "If he happens to remember this, he should be grateful." She picked up the knife she had used to collect bark.

Phoebe gaped at Sarah as she cut the back of one pant leg up to his backside. "*What* are you doing now?!"

"The more of him we can cool down, the better our chances will be to reduce his fever. Come on. Squeeze the cloth just until it stops dripping."

"What will he say when he sees what you've done?"

"I hope he bellows like hell."

"You may well get your wish." Phoebe picked up one rag. "I'll do his back and shoulders."

Sarah grinned at her. "Next summer you might try this with Charles."

"You have a wicked streak in you, Sarah Hampton."
Phoebe pursed her lips but couldn't remain stern. "His legs
were your idea. Better get busy."

"Remember his broken ribs. Don't press on him." Sarah
lightly wrung out a cloth and started at his ankle.

She rubbed the linen up his leg with both hands, over
his calf and the back of his knee, to his muscular thigh.
Turning her head, she pushed the cloth under the edge of
his trousers. All of a sudden her fingers slipped over the
edge of the cloth and pushed into his bottom.

Her heart seemed to lurch, and she yanked her hands
back. What she had not seen with her eyes, she had felt. In
an attempt to erase the memory, she dropped the cloth and
dried her hands on her skirt.

"My goodness, your face is crimson." Phoebe grinned
and wiped Gil's nearest arm.

"I've never been so familiar with a man." Sarah glanced
at Phoebe. "Have you?"

"No. There's never been a reason. . . ." Phoebe dropped
the cloth in the basin and rubbed her hands on her skirt.
"He's shivering so badly. Are you sure this will work?"

"Not really, but he was shivering before I started."
Sarah dipped the cloth in the water, wrung it out, and
worked on cooling his feet. "I wish I'd thought to bring
an oilcloth. The covers are getting damp, and we can't
move him."

"Together, we might change the bedding." Phoebe lifted
the edge of the cover. "It shouldn't be too difficult while
he's dazed."

Sarah dropped the cloth in the basin and arched her back.
"Would you mind staying with him? I want to get the
oilcloth before we move him."

"Go on. We'll be fine."

Sarah turned and nearly tripped over the basket. "What's
this?" She set it on the other side of the doorway.

"Since you didn't come home last night I thought you
would be hungry."

"You always look out for everyone else," Sarah said,

retracing her path across the room to Phoebe's side. "How about you? Did you sleep last night?"

"Off and on." Phoebe shrugged. "I had forgotten how lonely our bed could be."

Suddenly she looked as frightened as Sarah felt. She hugged her. "Charles won't take any foolish chances. He'll be home soon."

Phoebe nodded. "I keep telling myself that, but when I think of the men, all wearing guns—" A tremor slid down her spine. "Accidents happen. . . ."

Sarah held Phoebe's shoulders with a firm grasp and stepped back. "Don't you do that! Charles will ride in to town any day, and Gil's going to recover. We must believe in them."

Phoebe smiled. "I do—most of the time."

"Good." Sarah grinned at her. "Once we get Gil settled, I'll be starving." She stepped over to the door and paused, looking at him. He would live—he just had to. "We'll have to change his bandage, too."

Phoebe saw the pain in Sarah's gaze. "You aren't responsible for what happened to him."

"If I hadn't hit the bank robber . . ."

"Sarah, you didn't tell me *that*."

"The man was waving his gun in my face. I swung the bag of money at him and knocked the gun away." Sarah opened the door. "He made me so angry—Gil turned to me. I'm not sure what he was going to do. That's when the other bank robber shot him in the back."

She stared at Phoebe. "You see, I am responsible."

Sarah spent the remainder of Tuesday and the next two days applying cold cloths to Gil and changing the poultices. Even though he was groggy, she also managed to drip a little tea down his throat. Late Friday afternoon she refilled the bucket and prepared to rub him down again, when she discovered that his skin was cooler.

He had survived the fever.

She spread the comforter over him and smiled. "Now I am hungry."

She ate the rest of the bread, soup, and baked chicken Phoebe had brought her for lunch. Afterward Sarah filled a cup with willow bark tea and sat at the head of the bed.

"It's suppertime, sleepyhead." She combed her fingers through his hair, trying to rouse him gently. His color was improving.

Her voice seeped through the dense fog in his mind. He felt as if he had been asleep for days or maybe weeks.

She put her arm under his shoulders and lifted him. "Maybe now you can drink from the cup, even if you don't want to wake up."

She pressed the cup to his lower lip and dribbled a little tea into his mouth. He swallowed but before he had consumed very much, he seemed to be retching.

"Gil, can you hear me?"

She set down the cup, dipped her fingers in the bucket, and wiped his face. "Open your eyes, Gil. Look at me. Just once." He really was better. She wanted to shout for joy. He felt alive in her arms for the first time in four days.

"Mmm." The warmth and strength of her arm around him were so nice. He rubbed his cheek against her. "Sar . . . ?"

"Yes, Gil. I'm here. Oh, it's good to hear your voice." She watched him struggle. His eyelids fluttered, and then he opened his eyes. "Welcome back." She pressed her lips to his forehead, and it was much cooler.

"Wh . . . where've I been?"

"Resting. Sleeping." She couldn't stop grinning.

He tried to move and pain shot through his side. "Th' bank . . . Robb'ry."

"And you were shot," she reminded him.

He looked down and found himself staring at his arm. "Where's my shirt?"

"I had to take it off to bring down your fever."

That didn't make sense to him but it didn't matter right then. "Thirsty. . . ."

"I'll get a glass of water."

She eased away from him as gently as if he were a baby, and for a brief moment he wondered what was really wrong with him. When he thought about it, he realized he was as weak as an infant. While he waited for a drink, he tried to move. His arms didn't hurt, but moving his right one brought on a godawful sharp pain in his side.

Sarah set the cup of tea on the floor. "If I help, do you think you could turn a little so your chin's on the edge of the bed?"

"Why can't I sit up?"

She kneeled by the bed so he could see her face. "The bullet went in your back and came out through the side of your chest. It cracked at least two ribs, and you've lost a good portion of your blood. You shouldn't move unless it does not hurt." She helped him scootch closer to the edge and held the glass to his mouth.

He had only taken two small drinks, when she withdrew the glass. "Why can't I have the rest?"

"Too much at once seems to upset your stomach."

"If it feels queasy, I won't drink any more."

"All right. Just a little."

He took two greedy gulps and paused. "How much blood?"

"What?" she said, puzzled, then remembered the thread of their conversation. "A large pool on the bank floor," she said, extending her arms to give him an idea of the area. "A large pitcher full? And you've soaked numerous cloths, but the bleeding appears to have eased. That's one reason I don't want you moving about too much."

"Guess I'll be stuck here a while." He gave her a crooked grin. "*You* saved me?"

She shook her head. "Everyone helped. Charles is the one who knew what had to be done. I'm sure you would have died if not for him."

"I'll thank him next time I see him. Where's Jack?"

"He and the rest of the men in town went after the bank robber, the one that pretended to be a gentleman."

"Afraid I don't remember much, yet. How long was I . . . out?"

"You were shot Monday morning. It's now Friday evening. You haven't been conscious but a few minutes off

and on since then.'' She raised the cup to his lips and let
him drink.

He was so thirsty that he didn't taste the bitterness until
he had finished. ''What is that concoction?''

''Willow bark tea, for your fever.''

''Now that it seems to be cured, could I have coffee?
Never did like tea.''

She smiled. ''The first time I gave you some, you said
you didn't drink it.'' She dumped the tea in the chamber
pot, rinsed the cup, and poured coffee for him.

He inhaled the steam, smiled, and took a drink. Suddenly
there was a ruckus outside. ''What's that?''

She hurried to the side window. ''I can't see anything
from here, but I can hear voices.'' She turned to him. ''Will
you be all right while I go see?''

''I'll rest. Can't do anything else.''

''Please don't try to get up. Your ribs aren't healed yet,
and I'm sure your liver must feel quite raw, too.''

''Liver? How do you know about my liver?''

''Charles said he thought the liver was there,'' she said,
pointing to his side, ''under the ribs.''

''I'm not sure I want to know why you even care where
it is.''

''I wanted to know what I was feeling—'' A loud cheer
rose outside, and she darted to the door. ''We'll have time
to talk about this later.''

''We sure as hell will.'' So, he thought, she's become
familiar with my body. I didn't even have the pleasure of
enjoying her exploration.

She dashed down to the saloon and ran outside. The men
had come back! Dogs barked, children cheered, and the
women were running to their men. She spotted Charles just
as he took Phoebe into his arms and Clay and Cora held
on to them. Mr. Young broke away from the crowd, heading for the Wedge, and Sarah ran up to him.

''Mr. Young, didn't you catch him?''

''We did, Mrs. Hampton.''

''Well, where is he? In jail?''

''Dead.'' Jack walked past her into the saloon.

She dashed after him. "Tell me what happened! Please, Mr. Young. We've been waiting for days without any word."

Jack went behind the bar, grabbed a bottle of whiskey and a glass, and filled it with the amber-colored liquor. "We caught up with him outside Umitilla."

She smacked her hand on the bar to get his attention. "Then what happened?"

He gulped down half the glass of liquor. "The cocky bastard turned tail and ran. I got him in the back." He finished the drink. "Justice, wouldn't ya say?"

Shocked to hear it explained so simply, she nodded slowly. "I suppose it is." She had heard stories about Western justice, but the reality was quite different.

"You okay, Mrs. Hampton?"

"Fine." She swallowed and started toward the stairway, then paused. "Was anyone else hurt?"

"No, ma'am. Just that bastard."

"What . . . what did you do with him . . . his body?"

"I was for leavin' him for the buzzards. Some said that wasn't fair to the birds. He's buried with a marker at his feet: 'Here lies a thievin' murderer.' " He poured another drink and gulped it down. "How's Gil doin'?"

"He woke up a few minutes ago. He's anxious to see you."

"Still on his back, is he?"

"Mr. Young," she said, stepping over to the bar, "he has had a very high fever and has been unconscious since you and the other men left. He very nearly died."

Jack started for the stairs. "He's not—?"

"No," she said, catching up with him. "He is *very* weak. So weak he cannot move." She grabbed his arm. "Do you understand, Mr. Young? I won't allow you to aggravate him."

"You won't *what*?" Jack burst out laughing. "I'll be damned."

Sarah placed her hand on Gil's forehead and sighed. Looking at Mr. Young, she shook her head and motioned to the door. When they had stepped into the hall, she led him to the stairs and paused. "He's just sleeping, thank goodness. I'll let you know when he wakes."

Jack nodded. "I'm goin' to see Miss Layton. Be behind the bar later."

"Stop by when you return. He might be awake."

"I will. Thank ya, ma'am."

She went back into Gil's room and eased the door closed. Now she could finish her account of the bank robbery. Phoebe said she didn't want to publish the newspaper before she knew that Charles was safe. The paper would come out a couple of days late, but Sarah didn't believe anyone would complain.

There was a soft knock on the door, and Phoebe entered with Charles. "How is he doing?" she whispered.

Sarah walked over to the back window, and they followed her. "His fever broke. He drank some water and a sip of tea and some coffee. He's weak as a newborn, but he's sleeping quietly."

Charles looked over at Gil. "Phoebe told me about his fever. I'd say he's on the mend, thanks to you, Sarah. How are you doing?"

"Now that I know he's going to recover, I'll be all right."

"He's a fortunate man, that's for sure. Most men with wounds like his died."

Sarah shot him a venomous glare. "Charles," she hissed, "you didn't tell me that!"

"You had enough to worry about. Sometime you'll have to tell me how you did it."

"The lint was a bad idea." Sarah grinned at Phoebe. "She can tell you. She was a big help."

Charles looked from Phoebe to Sarah. "You two'll never change, will you?" He pulled his wife to his side. "Guess that's not so bad."

"I made beef soup for supper," Phoebe said, grinning from ear to ear. "I'll send Clay over with some for both of you."

Charles stared at each of them. "What are you saying?"

"She needs to eat, Charles, and she has her hands full taking care of Mr. Perry without having to cook on that little woodstove, too." Phoebe put the basket over her arm, ready to go home with him.

"Have you been staying in here with him, Sarah? All night?"

Sarah shrugged. "I suppose Phoebe could have taken turns with me, but I didn't think you'd like that idea."

"Mr. Young or Mr. Farmer can take over now."

"No," Sarah said, facing Charles, as adamant as she had ever been. "I've seen him through the worst of it, and I will see that he recovers."

"But, Sarah, it—"

Phoebe tugged on his arm and looked into his eyes. "It's up to her, Charles. The children are waiting for you." She willed him not to press the point, at least until she could explain the situation to him in private.

"Yes, my dear." He looked at Sarah. "I'll be back later with your supper."

"Thank you. Gil may be awake then. I know he wants to see you."

Phoebe started to leave, then remembered the letter. "I almost forgot." She pulled an envelope out of her skirt pocket and held it out to Sarah. "This came for Miss Lucy in today's post."

"From Mr. Brown?" As Sarah grasped the letter a thrill of anticipation made her heart race. So much had happened that she had forgotten about him.

"The penmanship looks the same." Phoebe smiled and left with Charles. She hoped that the letter would take Sarah's mind off Mr. Perry, if only for a few minutes.

When Gil woke up, the room was quiet. Had Sarah left? It took more effort than he would have imagined, but he turned his head toward the other side of the room. She was there, sitting in his chair reading. A smile curved her mouth, and she was idly winding strands of hair around one finger. What a nice sight to wake up to, he thought.

"Letter from home?"

"Hardly," she said, startled by his voice. She quickly folded the page and stuffed it into her skirt pocket. "Feeling better?"

"At least my head's clear. When can I get up?"

"I'm not sure. A few days. Maybe not for a week or more." She went over to the other side of the bed and raised the covers. "How does your side feel?"

"Hurts like . . . the devil. Have anything over there to remedy that?"

"The morphine syrup. I could give you a half dose. That might be enough to help and not put you to sleep."

He moved his left arm up and tried to roll over. A god-awful pain like a red-hot poker seared from his right side to his groin. He bellowed. Sweat dripped from his face. He gritted his teeth and waited for the agony to pass.

She grabbed the patent medicine bottle and teaspoon. She poured half a spoonful and put it in his mouth. "It should take effect soon." She wiped his face with a cool cloth and checked his bandage. "No more sudden moves. There's a spot of fresh blood. You may have started bleeding again."

"O . . . kay." The pain seemed worse when he gasped for breath, so he concentrated on breathing slowly.

"That's better. You'll have to think before you move."

"Uh-huh." He felt a wave of relief from the pain. "Since I'm not going anywhere, why don't you tell me about my liver?"

She picked up a blanket from her pallet at the other side of the room, folded it, and sat on it as a cushion on the floor beside his bed. "Blood must have poured out of you from the moment you were shot. I couldn't stop it. Since Charles had observed surgeons during the war, I valued his advice. He said there might be pieces of bone, shards from the bullet, and scraps of material from your shirt in the wound, and that they must be removed."

His eyes were wide open now. "Don't stop."

She had managed to force that memory to the back of her mind but now she drew on it for his sake. "I had to push my fingers—only two—inside you, following the path of the bullet. That's when I felt your liver, actually all of the way through it, and why I know you have broken ribs."

He rubbed his forehead on the covers. "Did you find anything? Besides my liver?"

She smiled. "I did, and I removed the fragments, mostly from in your liver."

"I've known doctors I wouldn't want poking around in me." What she had told him sank in slowly and, as he began to completely understand, he felt a bit uncomfortable.

"What's wrong? Do you feel sick?"

"No," he said softly. "You really pushed your fingers through the bullet hole? All the way through?"

"From each side. Charles gave you whiskey, your best, he said, but I know it hurt." She put her hand on his arm. "I tried to be gentle, Gil, but it had to be done."

"Thank you, Sarah." He closed his eyes briefly and gave her a slight nod. "That took courage," he said, watching her eyes.

"Not courage, desperation." She reached into her skirt pocket and withdrew the bullet. Holding it up for him to see, she said, "This was meant for me. Not you."

He glanced at the bullet, but watched as her beautiful blue eyes filled with tears. He had never felt so completely helpless, too weak to even reach out and dry her cheeks. "You can't know that."

"Oh, I do." She swiped at the tears with one knuckle. "You will, too, when your memory returns." Would he blame her for his injury? Or would he simply want nothing more to do with her? She hoped with all of her being that he would recover before that time.

"Would you help me into a shirt? I'm not too warm, now."

12

$\mathcal{P}$hoebe packed a bowl, spoon, napkin, and the clay jar filled with hot broth in the basket. "Are you sure you want to feed Mr. Perry? It won't be easy. I've watched Sarah."

Charles kissed her cheek. "I think I can manage. Sarah needs to get out of there for a while. I'll ask Timothy Farmer if he'll stay with Gil tonight."

Phoebe whirled around and planted the flat of her hands on his broad chest. "Listen to me, Mr. Abbott. Sarah *needs* to tend his wounds. She feels responsible."

"That's nonsense. She couldn't have prevented that murdering outlaw from doing anything."

"You won't change her mind so please, do not try."

"My dear, you know what people will say." He rubbed one hand over his hair. "Hell, they're probably already gossiping about her."

"If you try to bar her from his room, Charles, don't come home tonight."

"Now, Phoebe dear, before you invited Sarah to move in you said she wouldn't come between us."

"You're putting her there," she pointed out. "You were upset with her because you thought her dislike of Mr. Perry colored her articles. It's plain she's changed her mind.

Wouldn't you rather have them on friendly terms?''

"I'll wait until I find out how Gil feels about it. Now that he's awake, he may not be comfortable with a woman poking around on his body.''

She burst out laughing. "We *have* been married a long time, haven't we?'' She handed him the basket. "If you feed him soon, this will be warm enough. If not, you'll have to heat it a bit on the woodstove. And don't forget to tell Sarah I'm keeping her supper warm.''

"Yes, my dear.'' He wrapped his arm around her and held her close. "I've missed you very much.''

"Good,'' she murmured against his chest. "You can show me how much later.''

"I intend to.'' He kissed her and left for the saloon. When he reached Gil's door he grabbed the doorknob, then hesitated. After a moment's pause, he knocked.

Sarah opened the door and smiled. "Come in. You'll be good medicine for him.'' She reached for the basket Charles was carrying. "That smells good.''

He smiled at her. "I'm glad you think so. Phoebe's keeping your plate warm.'' He looked at Gil lying facedown on the bed.

"What did Phoebe send over?''

"Hot broth.'' Charles put his hand out, preventing her from closing the door. "Go eat at the house. Gil and I won't need supervising.''

"He can't feed himself,'' she said softly. "And more than a few teaspoons upsets his stomach.''

"We will be fine. Go on. Phoebe's waiting.''

"Hey, you two. Don't fight over me.'' Gil wanted to laugh, but it came out as a croak. "Leave us for a while, Sarah. You could use some fresh air.''

"I could?'' she said, walking around Gil's bed to face him.

"Put the color back in your cheeks. Besides, you must be tired of this room. I'll be here when you return.'' He was presuming she'd come back, but he couldn't be sure.

"All right.'' She snatched her shawl from the rack. Pale,

indeed. "Don't drink too fast. Retching would be hard on your wounds."

Gil croaked again. "Aren't those the sweetest words you ever heard, Charles?"

She whipped the shawl around her shoulders and walked out. Men. She went down the back stairs and wandered along the riverbank. It was as dark as pitch but the sound of rushing water and the breeze restored her spirits. It had been a long week. She was tired, and would dearly love to sleep in peace all through one night without being in constant fear of waking to find that Gil had died quietly during the night.

Maybe that was why she'd sniped at him. Or had he intentionally provoked her? She knew he enjoyed doing just that.

He had been wounded defending her but that did not change who he was, or give her a reason to believe that he would be any different when he recovered. She shivered and gathered the shawl tighter. Tears ran down her cheeks. Understanding the situation should have lifted the burden she felt.

It didn't.

Gil again tried to move his right arm, and again, failed. "Sorry, I can't get up. Pull the chair over. No reason for you to sit on the floor."

Charles set the basket down by the bed and pushed the blanket that Sarah sat on aside with his foot. "You're one lucky fellow. I was sure I'd have to pay my respects at the cemetery."

"Glad you were wrong." Gil worked his hand under his chcck, angling his field of vision upward.

Charles set the chair near the bed and sat down. "Hungry? Phoebe sent some broth. Think you could keep it down?"

Gil frowned at him.

"Sorry." Charles laughed. "I spent too much time with army surgeons."

"I understand I wouldn't be here if you hadn't. Thanks. That smells damn good."

Charles took the jar out of the basket. "Did Sarah cut a reed for you to drink with?"

"I've only been awake a short time. She used a spoon with the coffee and tea. Got any bread or meat in there?"

Charles opened the jar and poured part of the soup in the bowl. "After not eating for five days, the army surgeons would keep you on liquids for a while."

"Sarah told me you, Jack, and the others rode after the bank robber. What happened?"

Charles dipped the spoon in the broth and put it to Gil's lips. "Ben saw the crook crossing the Mill River and heading north. It took us a day and a half to pick up his trail near the Columbia."

"Did he try crossing it?"

"No. He seemed to know his way around. We rode spread out for a day before we spotted his cold camp."

Gil took another sip of broth. "Did anyone else get shot?"

"Only the bank robber. He took a few shots at us and turned tail. Jack got him."

"Wish I'd had the pleasure." Gil took another spoon of broth. So far it wasn't upsetting his gut.

"He won't be bothering anybody else." Charles dipped the spoon in the broth. "So, how do you like having Sarah nurse you?"

Gil smiled. "Almost makes this worthwhile. Guess I shouldn't've told her to get out. I usually tease her, and she dishes it right back. But she looked pretty miffed."

"You were right. She needed to get out for a while."

"I thought so. She's been stuck in this room with me all week."

Charles stirred the broth. "Oh, almost forgot. On the way back to town, we talked about electing a town council."

"Guess it's time. But I'd hate to see Gridley turn into a city. Look what happened to Portland." Gil took one more spoonful of broth. "If you don't mind, I think I'll rest."

"Not at all." Charles poured the broth back into the jar. "I'll leave this by the stove."

"Thanks. Never thought swallowing would wear me out."

"Bet you hadn't figured on a bullet ventilating your gut, either. You rest." Charles stood up. "I'll bring you a copy of the paper. It'll be a couple of days late."

"I'll be here. Thanks, Charles. Appreciate your help."

"Anytime."

"I'm sure you feel better now that you've washed up and changed clothes," Phoebe said, cutting a piece of honey gingerbread, "but wouldn't you like to sleep in your own bed tonight?" She set the bread in front of Sarah.

"Of course. That pallet's nearly as hard as the floor, but I can't sleep here until I *know* he is all right. That he won't start bleeding if he rolls over. I would love to see him sit up, or roll over—or have the strength to feed himself."

Phoebe stared, dumbfounded. She had not seen Sarah so dispirited in many years. "His fever is gone. He should be on the mend now."

Sarah held up the first two fingers on her right hand. "I jabbed these between his ribs and *into* his liver." For an instant she saw blood on her fingers, saw them as they had looked after probing for fragments inside Gil.

"Don't think about that. It's over, thank God."

Sarah grabbed the fork and cut into the sweet bread. "Mm, this is good."

Phoebe watched as Sarah devoured the bread, almost attacking it. "Did Charles say something to upset you in front of Mr. Perry?"

Sarah shook her head and gulped the last bite. "No. Why?"

"You're not yourself. The last time I saw you like this was when you caught John dancing once too often with Penelope Broderick."

Sarah thought a moment and smiled. "Golden ringlets and apple-green eyes. I wonder who she's bedeviling now."

Phoebe smirked. "With her accommodating manner,

probably any man within sight." She ate a crumb from the bread pan. "Want to tell me what's wrong?"

Sarah carried her supper dishes to the dry sink and began washing them in the pan of soapy water. "I suppose my vanity was pricked." Yes, she realized, her damnable pride.

"What are you talking about?"

"I was reminded that Gil is still Gil. His wounds haven't changed who he is." Sarah shrugged. "I'd forgotten that."

"Of course he is himself. What else would you expect?"

Sarah shook her head.

"Maybe he isn't the one who has changed."

"Me?" Sarah looked at Phoebe. "Do you think I have?"

"That's for you to say." Phoebe felt sure others would notice the difference and she wanted Sarah to realize it first. "If there hadn't been a bank holdup, would you give a fig how Mr. Perry was feeling?"

Sarah looked at her dearest friend and nodded. "You are absolutely right, as usual. Thank you. I'll see how Charles and Gil are getting along."

"Send mine home."

"I will." Sarah returned to Gil's room by the back stairs. She tapped on his door and peered inside. Mr. Young was visiting with Gil. "Hello."

"Ma'am." Jack stood up. "I'll leave now."

"No. Stay. It's all right. I was looking for Charles—Mr. Abbott."

"He left a while ago," Gil said.

"I'll be right back."

She went to the stairs leading to the saloon and descended, step by step, until the length of the bar came into view. She didn't see him and went back upstairs. She had passed Jack in the hall, when Charles came in the back door.

"I'm glad you're back," he said, meeting her in front of Gil's room. "Since Gil can't sit up to drink, I thought a reed might make it easier for him." He handed her the reeds. "I'd feel like a baby if Phoebe had to spoon coffee into my mouth."

"He'll appreciate this." She lowered the reeds and met

his gaze. "Phoebe's waiting for you." His cheeks turned a shade darker, but she didn't comment. It was quite endearing, she thought, as she opened the door to Gil's room.

Charles eyed her as if he were speculating about something. "That's a nice dress."

"Thank you." She glanced at the soft, brown wool dress, wondering why he had noticed that she had changed clothes. This one was old, loose, and comfortable. Perfect to sleep in, since she could not wear her nightgown to bed.

"Don't forget to dry them," he said, motioning to the reeds.

"I won't forget. I'm glad you're back, and that no one was hurt. You're going to write about your experience for the paper, aren't you?"

He nodded and grinned. "Tomorrow. I expect you to do the same."

"It's almost finished. G'night, Charles." She closed the door and spread out the reeds near the woodstove. Gil was in much the same position as when she had left, but he was sleeping.

His rest was peaceful, and his cheek was cool. "Sleep well."

Gil awoke with a start. A lamp was turned low. The room was warm. Sarah was asleep on her pallet. She snorted and sighed. The sound of rain made him uncomfortable. Damn. He had to piss, and he knew he'd never be able to stand.

Now what? Then it occurred to him to wonder how he had managed when he was unconscious. Had Sarah called Jack to help him? No, he hadn't been here. None of the men had been in town! Ugh—

She'd had to care for him like a baby, feed him with a spoon, and now this. Was there no end to his humiliation? He felt around under the bed for the chamber pot. She had to have put the damn thing close by, but he couldn't find it within his reach. And he didn't think he could hold his water much longer.

He slid one knee up and then the other, and leaned to his side. When he reached for the trouser waistband, he found the first three buttons unfastened. She must have helped with this predicament earlier. There was no way around it. He'd have to rouse her.

"Sarah—are you awake?"

She murmured in her sleep.

"Sarah," he said, a little louder than before. "Wake up! . . . Sarah!"

Her eyes were wide open and she was sitting up when she actually awakened. "Gil?" she whispered.

"Yes. I need help."

She tossed back the cover, and hurried over to his side. "Do you have a sick stomach?"

"I'm about to soak this bed. Get Jack—or help me."

"Oh!" she squeaked. "I'll get Mr. Young." She hurried to the door. "Which room is his?"

"Other side of the hall near front stairs."

She dashed to the door and tapped. There wasn't a sound from inside. Again she knocked. "Mr. Young. . . . Mr. Young, Gil requires your help." Was he in there? *Oh please,* she intoned, and banged her fist on the door. "Mr. Young!"

Nothing. "Forgive me, but I'm desperate," she said, opening the door. The room was black. This is a nightmare, she decided, stepping into the room. "Mr. Young! You must wake up." She stumbled over something, and very nearly fell onto the bed. "Mr. Young, you must help Gil." The covers didn't even rustle.

Gritting her teeth, she reached out to give him a good shake. She felt a blanket . . . nothing else. He wasn't there!

She ran back to Gil's room. "He's not there. I . . . will have to help you."

"Turn up the lamp—no, better not." This was a first for him. "What did you use last time?"

"Last time? You haven't had to relieve yourself."

He realized that he must've been close to death. "There's an old enamel pitcher. Look in the corner. I think that's where Charles put it." This was one hell of a situation— Sarah Hampton helping him piss.

She turned up the lamp, found the enamel pitcher, and

turned down the lamp wick so she could barely see the bed. "Where do you want me to put it?"

"You'll have to come over here."

Clutching the pitcher with both hands, she made her way around the bed. "Shall I hold this for you?"

"First, help me over to the edge of the bed."

She set the pitcher on the floor and stared at the dark outline of his body. "Can you lean on your elbows, just a little?"

He moved his arms forward. "I'm ready."

She pulled the blanket off him. "When I lift your hips, lean on your arms and try to keep your body straight." She placed one hand on each side of his hips and lifted, but she didn't have the strength.

He locked his jaw and waited. What he wouldn't give for a hole through his bed.

"I need to brace one knee on the bed." She raised her skirt enough and slid her knee on the bed between his. A strange sensation skittered down her back. She had never been in such a peculiar position with a man, but at least the room was dark and he couldn't see her discomfort. "All right. Let's try again."

He relaxed, a little. For one brief moment he feared her knee would pin his family jewels to the bed. If the situation were not so urgent, it would be laughable.

She put her weight on her knee, her hands on each side of his hips, and lifted. It worked. She lowered his hips at the edge of the bed. "I can't see your face to tell if you're in pain. You'll have to tell me when it hurts."

"I—I'm okay. Or will be." He straightened his left arm along his side and brought up his right knee. "Roll me back onto my side."

She moved her knee out from between his, and placed one hand on his hip and one on his shoulder. He didn't seem to have much padding over his bones. Against her wishes, the memory of him standing in front of her, with his cocky grin, was vivid. She applied pressure and, with his help, rolled him onto his side. "How's that?"

"Not bad."

"What now?"

"Get the pitcher." He reached into his trousers. "Hold it against the edge of the bed."

She held the pitcher near where she believed his hand would be and closed her eyes. "I'm not looking. You should make sure the pitcher's where you think it is."

"Guess I should." There was enough light on her face to see that her eyes were clamped shut. He felt the top of the pitcher pressed against the bed. "Better keep the bottom lower than the top."

She tipped the pitcher and pressed the side into the edge of the mattress, and then she silently pleaded that he would *hurry*.

He tilted his hips forward, gritted his teeth against the pain, and at last relieved himself. Damn, that felt good. He'd been close to drowning.

He seemed to go for a very long time. The poor man, she thought, gripping the pitcher with both hands. Then it felt as if he'd bumped the side. Was he done? She decided there was no delicate way to put it. "Finished?"

"Yes." He closed the front of his drawers and trousers, and sighed. "Thank you, Sarah. Tomorrow I'm going to work on sitting up."

She covered him with the blanket and set the pitcher by the door. "Can I get you something?"

"Some water? Broth? I am thirsty."

"I guess that's inevitable," she mumbled, walking over to the woodstove.

He started to laugh and ended up holding his side. "After I get a drink, I'll sleep. If you want to go home you can."

She closed the door on the woodstove a little harder than she'd intended and winced. "Maybe you would rather have Jack move in here with you, or I could give you a bell to call him."

He turned his head to face her, but he hadn't the strength to do more. "Damn, I hate this."

She finished pouring the glass of water and held it out to him. "The reeds aren't dry enough to use yet, but I'm sure you'll manage without them."

As he took the glass from her, his fingers brushed hers. She jerked her hand back, slopping water over his hand.

"Why haven't you offered to give me a bath?" he asked.

"How dare you—?" She stared him. He was giving her a little-boy look. She glanced at the ceiling and shook her head. "You buffoon. You can't help yourself, can you?"

He raised the glass in a salute. "You're irresistible." He tried to drink and almost poured it over his face.

She glared at him and walked over to her pallet, a part of her wishing there was a modicum of truth in his sarcasm. After all, no woman wishes to be thought as appealing as a toadstool.

He watched her and realized that maybe he had gone too far. "Sarah, exactly which comment made you so mad?"

"Which *one* comment?" She spun on her heel, scowling at him.

"Two? It isn't like you to hold back."

"You . . ." How could she tell him without making herself appear even more foolish? Or worse, pathetic. "You said I could leave. That is what I am trying to do."

"I thought you were tired." He watched her eyes and her mouth. He had pushed too far. "I don't *want* you to leave. Do you really think Jack could replace you?"

She met his gaze. "No I don't, but you're not my—Now that you are conscious, anyone you want can help you."

He smiled at her. "You're doing fine, Sarah. Stay?"

"Until you can sit up and eat and . . . take care of your personal needs."

"Good." He slid his hand to the bottom of the glass and tipped it to his lips. Water had never tasted so good. When he had finished drinking, he rested his head on the bed.

"Do you still want some broth?"

"If you don't mind."

She shook her head. "Twenty-four hours ago, I would have given anything to hear your wisecracking voice." She set the pan on the woodstove and poured broth into it.

"Really?"

As she retrieved the glass from him, she looked at him. "Gil, I am glad you're feeling better. I really am." She gave him a slight smile. "Do you want to write to anyone? Let them know what happened and that you will be all right?" While he appeared to consider that idea, she wondered who he was thinking about.

He did have a letter to write but not one she could post for him. "Not now. My family won't hear about this. I'll write them later."

"I'll be glad to write a letter for you if you change your mind."

He smiled. "I'll let you know."

She filled the glass halfway with broth. "I thought you would like to drink this rather than have me spoon-feed you."

"I did feel like a schoolboy in short pants."

She handed the glass to him. "You almost look like one when you're sleeping."

He clamped his jaw and grimaced. When the urge to chuckle had passed, he gazed at her. "Please, don't make me laugh. It hurts."

"I've never thought of myself as particularly funny."

"You're mistaken, Sarah. You definitely have your moments." He slowly tipped the glass to his mouth and gulped the broth.

"I'm flattered." She watched him, fascinated with his Adam's apple. It bobbed each time he swallowed. When he finished, she refilled the glass. He still looked young. "How old are you?"

"Twenty-nine. Why?"

"No reason. I thought you were older." She frowned. "You look older, when you're not sick in bed." She sounded like an imbecile.

He grinned. "I won't ask, but you're not so old that twenty-nine sounds young."

"It all depends on what happened during those four years." After the last week she felt a decade older than him.

"That's hardly any difference at all."

"Thanks."

He drank the second glass of broth more slowly. "I think I can sleep now. How about you?"

"It's been a long day." She rinsed the glass and set it on the table. "Will you be warm enough? I have an extra blanket."

"You take it. If it gets too cold, we can share." Her eyes grew wide and then narrowed. He grinned at her. "Sweet dreams, Sarah."

13

*S*arah woke up later than usual the following morning. It had taken her a while to fall asleep. The bed covers rustled, and she turned over toward Gil. Gazing across the room at him, with both of them lying in bed, created the strangest sensation in her belly. His eyes slowly opened and focused on her.

She smiled tentatively. "Have you been awake long?"

"A couple minutes." Long enough for him to observe her stretch like a contented cat. "You've been watching me. Thought I should have the same opportunity."

She left the warmth of the pallet, straightened the covers, and opened the curtains. After she built up the fire, she started the coffee.

As she tended to practical matters, he wondered if that was second nature for her or a way of breaking the intimacy. Whether it was intentional or not, the effect was the same. Having nothing else to do but look around, he noticed the subtle change in his room. It almost looked homey. "Is there any of that broth left?"

"A little." She poured the last of the broth in the pan and set it near the coffeepot. "Later I'll fix more," she said, glancing over at him. His mussed hair was rather endearing. "What else would you like to drink?"

"Can't I have something to eat?"

"You've only taken a little more than a cup at a time. Let's see if more upsets your stomach before you try eating."

"If you say so." He pulled the covers over his shoulder. "When you have the time, I'd like to change shirts. This one's kind of thin."

"The green flannel would look nice on you."

"If you say so." He smiled to himself as he pushed his left hand under the blanket and unbuttoned his shirt. "Sure wish I could roll over or sit in a tub."

"I wouldn't suggest that until after your wounds heal." She opened the drawer that held his shirts and ran her hand over the soft wool shirt on top. "Your back and limbs are fairly clean."

He looked at her. "How would you know that?"

"I wiped them with damp cloths."

"You bathed me while I was unconscious? And I missed the fun?"

"You did sleep through it, but I'm not sure you would have thought it was fun." And if I hadn't been so worried, she thought, I might have found it exciting.

"Are you blushing, Sarah? Just what did you do?"

"I certainly am not." She shook the shirt with a snap of her wrists. "I applied cold, wet cloths, which proves how ill you were. After the first one, you didn't protest at all." She began unbuttoning the shirt. "Phoebe helped."

"Must've been some sideshow," he said, eyeing her. "How many ladies did you invite to 'help'?"

She smiled. "I wish I'd thought of selling tickets. We could have split the money, and I imagine the ladies would have enjoyed comparing their husbands' physiques to yours."

"Guess I should be grateful for your lapse there." With more effort than he had supposed it would take, he pushed the sides of his shirt out from under him.

She pulled the blanket and comforter back, and grinned at the cuts she had made in his trousers. *He does have nice* legs, she thought. "Maybe you would be more comfortable in a nightshirt."

"I only sleep in one when it freezes."

"The nights are getting colder," she said, trying to pull the sides of one pant leg together, "and you can't move around to keep warm."

"What are you doing?" He moved his leg and it felt odd. "What's wrong with my trousers?"

"I cut the back of the legs."

"You ruined a good pair of pants?"

"I told you I had to cool as much of you as I could. Phoebe was helping me, and I didn't want to offend her sensibilities by removing your trousers."

"*Her* sensibilities?" he softly questioned. "Are you more accustomed to removing gentlemen's trousers than she is?"

She ignored his taunting. "At the time, your life seemed more important than a pair of pants. But I've been wrong before."

"You really were worried, weren't you?"

"I've never been responsible for a man's death. I didn't want to start with you."

"I'm glad."

"After your shirt, I'll help you change trousers."

"Now you offer, when I'm at your mercy."

She grinned, but merely said, "If you put your arms at your sides, I'll slip off your shirt." She resisted the urge to touch him but noticed the way he moved. "Does your right arm hurt?"

"My side does. When I use that arm it feels like I've been stabbed."

"I'll be careful." She slipped her fingers inside the neck of his shirt and pulled on the shirttail with her other hand. As she worked the shirt down past his bare shoulder blades, the back of her fingers skimmed his smooth, lightly tanned skin.

"Is something wrong?"

"No—not at all." Embarrassed to be caught ogling him,

she quickly drew the left sleeve free. The other came off easily.

When she dropped the shirt on the floor, he saw the bloodstain. "I thought I'd stopped bleeding."

"That's a small stain. When you move too much, you bleed a little." She eased the sleeve of the clean shirt up his right arm. "I washed the other shirt, the one with the bullet holes. It's on the desk."

"A souvenir? I'll wear it next summer. If it's cooler, I may shoot holes in a few other shirts."

"That might frighten off the next man who draws a gun on you." She pulled the second sleeve up his other arm and then smoothed the shirt over his back.

"Mm, that feels good. Do you give back rubs? I can't even scratch mine."

"I suppose I could, but wouldn't it hurt your ribs?"

"You said you rubbed wet rags over my back. I don't see how dragging your fingers over it would do any damage." He tried looking out of the corner of his eye but all he could see was her shirt. "If you're not going to rub my back, at least step aside so I can see you."

She had barely touched his back with one hand when he closed his eyes. *Good,* she thought. *Don't watch.* She trailed her fingertips up toward his neck.

"Better press a little harder, Sarah. That tickles."

"All right." Holding his shirttail with one hand, she rubbed with a little more pressure. When he murmured, a deep, almost purring sound, she continued with more confidence.

"That's nice. . . ."

She thought so, too, running her fingers across his shoulders. She massaged his neck. His hair was thick and soft. As she worked her hands down, the disquieting image of him doing the same to her almost seemed real. The idea of his large hands on her back sent a tremor down her spine.

He felt her hands tremble and he grinned. "That felt good. You must've had practice."

"Not recently." She raised her hands and flexed her fingers, her heart pounding with an anticipation she had all but forgotten. "Would it be easier to change trousers lying on your stomach or your back?"

He sure wished she weren't standing out of his line of sight. "Stomach, I guess."

"Yes, that might be best." She put her hands on the waist of his trousers and started to slide each around to the front.

"What are you trying to do?"

She froze, bent over him almost hugging his waist. "Unfasten your trousers."

"You should've asked." But he was glad she hadn't. "They're unbuttoned. Put your thumbs over the waist and they'll slide right down." Her hands trembled, and he realized that he wasn't numb below his waist after all.

She did as he suggested, with her eyes closed, but the image in her mind was worse than looking. She pushed the trousers to his hips and stopped. "I had better cover you with the blanket."

"Whatever you say," he stated dryly.

One memory I don't want haunting me is that of his backside, she told herself, spreading the blanket over him. She reached under the cover, eased the trousers over his hips and thighs, and slipped the pant legs off.

"Wish I had a pair of loose pants. Never laid around dressed in bed before."

"Where do you keep your trousers?"

"Third drawer. Pick the oldest pair."

She found a pair of soft, worn canvas pants. "These look comfortable." She held them out where he could see them.

"Good choice."

She uncovered his legs and left the blanket over his backside. Pulling the trousers up his legs without jolting his side took longer than removing them, but she slowly worked the pants up over his rump. "There. Feel better?"

"Much." He tried to crane his neck and look at her. "Do you know any reason why I have to stay on my stomach?"

"Not since you are feeling better."

"Good. I don't seem to be able to do much for myself

right now." He braced himself for the sharp pain he felt certain was about to grip him.

She studied him for a moment. "Hold your arms at your sides. I'll roll you like a log." She put pillows behind him and tipped him backward, then removed the pillows.

He sighed and smiled at her. "You have a gentle touch." He raised her hand. Her fingers trembled, and he rubbed his thumb over her knuckles.

She did not want to feel the warmth of his touch, and withdrew her hand from his. "I'd better get the broth. It must be boiling hot." At the stove, she poured the steaming liquid into a cup.

"Are any of those reeds dry enough to use?"

She checked them and chose one. "Have you used these before?"

"In my youth. We shot seeds through them."

She smiled. "At least you know it works. You'll have to let the broth cool or the reed will soften." She cut one section, then put it to her lips and blew to make sure it would work. "What else did you and your friends do?"

He grinned at her. "Put a live fish in the schoolmaster's coat pocket once, rode through town dressed like Indians, and," he said, chuckling, "snuck into—no, you don't want to hear about that." Some parts of a man's life weren't meant to be shared with a lady.

"You must have been a good storyteller, too." She handed the cup and reed to him. There was a knock at the door. "Come in."

Charles stepped inside. "Good morning. Glad to see you're both awake."

"Checking up on me?" Sarah poured coffee into her cup and blew on the hot liquid.

"Gil, you're looking much better."

"I'll have to take your word for that." Gil glanced at Sarah. "At least I'm awake."

Sarah noticed Charles was looking at her as if he were upset. She straightened up and studied him in return.

Charles stepped closer to Sarah. "I have a newspaper to

get out, and so do you. Oliver Grebby will stay with Gil for a while.''

"Surely you aren't worried about my reputation," she whispered.

"You've been here long enough." Charles turned to Gil. "Is that all right with you, Gil?"

Mr. Grebby entered and removed his hat. "Good morning, Mrs. Hampton, Mr. Perry."

"Good to see you, Oliver, but I don't need a nurse-maid."

Sarah smiled at Mr. Grebby. "He is not to move. It wouldn't take much for him to start bleeding again. I'll show you why." She motioned for him to follow her to the side of the bed.

Gil held the blanket secure at his side. "This isn't nec-essary."

"I don't agree." She lifted his hand, raised the blanket, and pulled his shirt up, exposing the bandage. "If you see his wound you will be less likely to let him talk you into leaving." She moved the bandage enough to expose the wound in front. Mr. Grebby blanched, and she knew she had accomplished her goal.

"Do not fear, Mrs. Hampton, I won't leave him alone." Mr. Grebby stepped back. "Will I have to . . . change that dressing? I'm not sure—"

"No, Mr. Grebby. Gil can have all of the broth, coffee, and water he wants. I'll send over more broth." With a glance at Charles, she added, "I won't be gone too long."

Charles walked to the open door. "They'll be fine, Sarah. Let's go."

She inched the bandage back in place and lowered Gil's shirt. After she had tucked in the covers, she met his gaze. "Behave yourself."

He put his hand over his side and chuckled. "I might as well, now."

She wrapped her shawl around her shoulders, picked up the paper with her article and the notes she had made, and left with Charles. On reflection she realized that the timing was right. Gil probably needed to use the pitcher again, and she'd just as soon leave that chore to Mr. Grebby.

After Sarah reread her article recounting the bank robbery, she put it on Charles's desk and peered over his shoulder. "Is that your editorial?"

"Just finishing it." He glanced up at her. "How about the Miss Lucy column? Think the old girl has something for us this week?"

"*Old girl?* She sounds too feeble to write!"

"Two pages would be enough. I don't want every story in the paper to be about the bank robbery."

"I'll see what 'she' can come up with." She didn't have the heart to lecture on decorum. The men had been gentlemen at the dance. Had it been only a week since that night?

"Didn't you get a letter from Mr. Brown? Maybe you can use that."

"I'll see," she said, and touched her hand to her pocket. "After I reread it." She glanced at his article again. "What is that about a town council?"

"The robbery made some of us wonder if it wasn't time to elect a town council. Maybe hire a sheriff or someone to act as one when needed."

"It's been so peaceful here, I hate to think we need a sheriff."

He looked up at her. "I guess some would call it progress."

"Toward what?" She shook her head. "Don't mind me."

"Why don't you take a stroll? That always helps clear the mind."

"I will." She took her shawl from the back of her chair. "Who do you want me to interview this week?"

"That's right! Let me see. . . . How about Timothy Farmer?"

"Okay. See you later." She had one errand to attend to before she took her walk.

She stopped at the general store, bought a plump chicken, and went home. The house was empty, and she set to work.

It didn't take long before she had the large kettle of water, chicken, and herbs simmering on the kitchen stove. Leaving a note for Phoebe, she put on her heavy cloak and stepped outside.

The east wind was brisk and so was Sarah's step as she followed the river to a small creek, where she veered into the woods. The tops of the tall hemlock and red cedar trees swayed. A doe cautiously approached the creek, and she paused to watch. She almost felt guilty enjoying the tranquil setting while Gil lay in bed unable even to roll over without help.

Holding the cloak tight around her, she walked between the trees, recalling the resonance of his voice and the tender way he had cradled her hand. She even remembered the warmth of his arms around her when he held her in his strong embrace as they danced together.

She quickened her step. He joked about everything. Couldn't he be serious? Her hand brushed against her skirt pocket. Not everyone thought life was a lark. She stopped long enough to reread Mr. Brown's letter. *A violet by a mossy stone, half hidden from the eye! Fair as a star, when only one is shining in the sky.*

Again, he had not written his name on the envelope. He evidently did not want to correspond privately. Curious. A little mystery may add spice to a situation—too much only frustrated her.

She started the trek back to town.

Just two pages, that's what Charles had asked her to write. As Miss Lucy. She had made a list of topics. She would address the next topic and close with a line or two for Mr. Brown. If he does happen to be interested, she thought, maybe the article will give him the courage to meet her.

She hurried back to the newspaper office for paper and pencil before going to the barbershop to interview Mr. Farmer. Twenty minutes later she left with all the information she had been able to coax out of him.

When she returned to the *Gazette* office, Phoebe was helping Charles lay out the front page of the newspaper.

"Phoebe, did you see the note I left you at the house?"

"Cora found it." Phoebe wiped her hands on a rag and walked over to Sarah. "She also tasted the broth and wants you to show her how you made it."

"That's sweet of her. Wish I'd written down the ingredients I used." Sarah searched through her notes and found the list of topics for the Miss Lucy articles.

"You haven't mentioned the letter. Was it from the Poet?"

"It was, as you well know." Sarah withdrew the envelope from her pocket and handed it to Phoebe. "If he writes again, want to ride over to Fenton's Crossing with me one day?"

"No, she would not," Charles said, looking at both of them.

Phoebe ignored her husband and read the letter. "He certainly does seem to be smitten with you. When do you want to go?"

"I should wait until Gil can leave his bed. Let's see if we hear from the Poet again."

"I don't think he'll stop now. We'll pack a picnic— make a day of it." Phoebe glanced sideways at Charles. He didn't take her bait. "We can wear our Sunday-best dresses and talk to every man in town until we find Mr. Brown."

"Sounds like fun," Sarah said, her mind on the article.

Phoebe glared at Charles, then at Sarah. "You two are the life of the party."

"My dear, the sooner I get this paper out—"

"I know." She walked over to him. "Want me to start on the advertisements?"

"Thank you, Phoebe." Charles smiled at her.

Sarah worked on the Miss Lucy article, the topic: the art of conversation. She concluded with a suggestion for the gentleman who had a particular fondness for a lady and felt uncertain that he might correspond with her. Once he establishes her affections, she advised, he should be more assured in his approach with her. She finished with a quote she'd once read: *"Love looks not with the eyes, but with the mind."*

She didn't completely agree with that quote, but she hoped it would encourage the Poet. She wrote the final copy and gave it to Phoebe. "Read the last paragraph."

Phoebe perused the end of the article and nodded. "Do you think the Poet will understand your meaning?"

Sarah shrugged. "It's tempting to say, through the column, that I would like to meet with him, but that sounds too brash, even for me."

"Stop the.press—we have a headline!"

"Charles Abbott, you're no help at all."

Charles shook his head. "Why don't you allow the poor man to conduct his affairs his way?"

Sarah chuckled. "What affair?"

"The first time Clay shows any interest in girls, I'm going to have a *long* talk with him." Charles walked over to Phoebe. "Is that the Miss Lucy article?"

She handed the pages to him. "I'd better see what Cora is doing. Should I come back and help you later?"

"No, I'm about ready to start. I'll see you at home, my dear." He wandered back to the printing press as he read the article.

"Are you ready to leave, Sarah?"

"Just a couple of minutes." Sarah pulled out the notes from her interview with Mr. Farmer and quickly wrote the short piece. She set it on Charles's desk, put the Poet's letter in her drawer with the others, and straightened the papers on their desk. "Now I am."

Phoebe glanced at her husband and walked outside with Sarah. "If I hadn't told him I was leaving he wouldn't have noticed."

"He enjoys his work, and he's good at it." Sarah linked arms with Phoebe. "Don't be too hard on him. He adores you."

Phoebe smiled. "That's why I put up with him."

"There's something I need to get at Seaton's. Want to go with me? It won't take but a couple of minutes."

Phoebe nodded, and they walked down the boardwalk to

the general store. "Don't forget the broth. It's still simmering."

"I wouldn't dare. Before I left, Gil was grumbling about not eating." They entered the store, and Sarah went to the side wall where the bolts of fabric were stacked on shelves.

Phoebe followed in her wake. "What are you looking for? Have you suddenly taken up sewing?"

"You might say that." Sarah ran her hand over the bolt of blue flannel and eyed the red. "If every woman should have a red petticoat, think Gil would like red drawers to sleep in?"

Phoebe stared at her. "Gil? You're going to make him flannel sleeping drawers?"

"They'd be soft and warm." Sarah looked at her. "No one would see them. What do you think? Red or blue?"

"I think you're out of your mind."

"Red." Sarah pulled the bolt off the shelf and carried it over to the counter.

Alice Seaton finished with a customer and stepped over to Sarah. "Isn't that a nice cherry red?"

"Yes, it is."

"Do you want enough for a petticoat?"

Since Sarah had never made a pair of men's trousers, she guessed on the length she would need. "Three and a half yards will do, and I'd like two needles and some thread. I'll pick out the buttons."

"Take your time, Sarah."

Sarah smiled at Alice, then she touched Phoebe's arm and they went over to the button case. "How many buttons will I need?"

"Don't you remember?" Phoebe lowered her voice. "It hasn't been *that* long, has it?"

"Three should be enough. He won't be walking down the street in them." Sarah chose the buttons. "May I use a pair of Charles's trousers for a pattern? It won't take long to cut them out."

"I'll do it for you."

"Thank you, but no. This is my project." If they didn't turn out right, Sarah decided, at least they would get a passel of red dust cloths out of it.

14

$\mathcal{S}$arah tapped on Gil's door, her arms ladened with fabric, her sewing box, and two jars of chicken broth. It being Saturday afternoon, the town was bustling. She felt sure by suppertime everyone within a half day's ride would have heard about the bank robbery and Gil having been wounded.

Mr. Grebby opened the door and smiled at her. "He's sleeping right now," he whispered.

She entered quietly and set her bundles down. "I'm sorry it took me so long."

"He's fine, just thirsty." Mr. Grebby said.

"Thank you for keeping him company. I'm sure Gil was glad to see you."

Mr. Grebby walked out into the hall and motioned for Sarah to join him. When she had, he pulled the door shut and whispered, "How long's he going to be on his back?"

"I'm not really sure. I thought Charles would know, but then he told me most men with wounds like Gil's didn't survive."

"Whew." He ran a hand over his chin. "If you need anything, Mrs. Hampton, just let me know."

"That's kind of you."

While Gil slept, she made a trip to the well for a fresh

supply of water and started stitching the flannel trousers. Since he would be wearing them only in his room, she didn't make pockets. As she stitched a side seam, she glanced at him and hoped he would sleep until she had finished.

It was foolish, but suddenly the idea of sewing sleeping drawers for him felt terribly intimate, even more than probing between his ribs. She finished the side seams and started on the inside seam, trying not to think of what it would cover.

Gil swallowed and rubbed the back of his hand over his mouth. Had he only dreamed he'd eaten chicken? It smelled so damn good he could taste it. He yawned and rubbed his face.

"Timothy—I must've fallen asleep."

At the sound of his voice, Sarah jumped and poked the needle through the middle of the crotch. "He left a little while ago." She dropped the drawers on the floor and went to the side of the bed, her heart still racing.

His eyes popped open, and he smiled. "You're back."

"I seem to be. Did you have a nice rest?" She stepped over to the woodstove and poured him a cup of broth.

"Mm-hm." He sniffed the air. "I still smell chicken. Don't think I've ever had a dream that real about food."

She knew he was grinning, and she couldn't resist a quick glimpse at him. "You must have smelled the broth."

"What are my chances of finding a few bites of the bird in there?"

"Slim to none." When she handed him the cup and reed, he slid his hand over hers. She didn't pull away. "How are your ribs?"

"Sore."

She raised the covers and his shirt. There were no fresh stains on the bandage, and she felt encouraged. She lightly pressed on his smooth, warm skin, and he flinched. "In a day or two maybe you can have some pudding, and maybe a few shreds of meat in the broth."

Her fingers were cool but her cheeks looked heated. He reached up and brushed her hair back. It was as soft as it looked, and he was reluctant to lower his hand.

He sipped the liquid through the reed and grinned at her. "Mm, as good as it smelled."

"I'm glad you like it. Don't expect the next pot to taste the same. I didn't use a recipe."

He chuckled. "You planning on cooking for me?"

"Someone has to. You can't."

He took another sip of broth. "Jack was here earlier. Did you see him?"

She shook her head. "He probably didn't have any reason to stay after you fell asleep."

"I don't blame him." He drained the last of the broth in the cup. "What time is it?"

"I'm not sure. Why?"

"The crewmen come to town Saturday afternoon. I need to know what's been happening in the camp." He stared at the window. "I've lost all sense of time lying here."

She set the clock on the front corner of the chest of drawers facing him. "Can you see the clock now?"

He looked over at the dresser and nodded. "Thanks. Did Charles get the paper out?"

"He's probably printing now. It was all but set up and ready when I left the office." She watched him drain the cup and smiled. "Would you like more?"

He held the cup out to her. "I hope you made a lot."

"There should be enough to last you until tomorrow." She refilled his cup and handed it back to him.

"What did you do with the chicken?"

"Do?" she repeated with a shrug. "I left it on a plate at Phoebe's. Why?"

"Wish I could get my hands on it for two minutes."

She laughed, then decided not to encourage him. "If you're finished I'll take that."

He held it with both hands and gave her a grin meant to intimidate her. "Not if you value your health."

"I'm glad you understand," she said, chuckling. "Broth is better than water or nothing."

They listened as a wagon came down the road and stopped outside the saloon.

He glanced over the brim of the cup at the clock. "That should be the men. You'll get to meet my foreman, Henry."

"I'll go home and have sup—I mean, leave you to visit with your friends."

He grinned at her. "Forget to bring your supper?"

She faced him squarely. "Yes, I did."

"I don't mind sharing. Have a cup of broth—on me."

"That is very generous of you, but I—"

"Would rather have something more filling." He smirked at her. "So would I."

A loud commotion erupted in the hall moments before someone pounded on the door. Sarah eyed Gil. "Your friends?"

He grinned. "Better let them in before they take down the door."

She snatched it open, but only partway, and stood in the doorway. One strapping man faced her and two others crowded in at his side. "Hello, gentlemen." The three men instantly froze, then stood tall and looked a little shame-faced.

The oldest and shortest of the three shouldered his way to the front. "Ma'am, we work fer Gil—at the camp. Could we see him?"

"Dugan, that you?"

"Yep. Who'd ya think'd bang on yer door?"

"Let 'em in, Sarah. I know the jokers."

"Please, come in, gentlemen." She pushed the door wide open and stepped aside. Dugan, a craggy-faced man of indeterminable age and not much taller than Sarah, nodded to her in passing, and she smiled at him. The others followed suit.

Gil tried to scoot up on the bed, but promptly gave up. "Sarah, I'd like you to meet some of the crew from the logging camp. Dugan's the best damn cook west of the Miss'ipp'. Henry is the foreman, and Beal is high climber. Men, this is Mrs. Hampton, my personal surgeon."

"Gentlemen, I'm happy to meet you."

"How do, Mrs. Hampton," the three men said in unison.

She looked at Beal. "Would you tell me what a high climber is? I haven't heard that term."

"A tree topper, ma'am."

"That sounds dangerous."

"Logging camps aren't for the faint of heart, Sarah." Gil spoke gently, then turned to his men. "Henry, how'd you pry Dugan loose from camp?"

Dugan scowled at Gil. "Nobody had t'drag me here."

"Vonney." Henry stepped over to the foot of Gil's bed. "Last night she heard you'd been shot. The drifter who told her didn't know if you were alive or dead."

"Damn." Gil glanced at Sarah. "How is she?"

Dugan walked to the side of Gil's bed. "The question is, how're *you* doin'?"

"I've been worse but thanks to Mrs. Hampton, I'll be harassing you before long."

Beal pulled a bottle out of his back pocket and held it out for Gil to see. "Bet you could use a swig or two."

Sarah eyed Gil and gave him a slight shake of her head. He was bad enough sober. She didn't want to see what he would be like tanglefooted.

Gil shrugged. "Thanks. I better not, but there's no reason you can't have one for me."

Sarah balled up the flannel drawers and stuffed them into her sewing basket. She picked up the empty jar, dropped the shawl over her arm, and excused herself. He needed to speak with his men and, she assumed, would appreciate a little privacy.

Gil observed his men watching her leave and didn't blame them. He enjoyed the view, too, and most times her feelings were unmistakably etched in her expression. When the door closed behind her, the men turned back to him.

Beal grinned, took a gulp of whiskey, and passed the bottle to Dugan. "How'd you manage to get such a pretty nurse?"

"Just lucky." Gil looked at Henry. "What's been going on at camp? Any more fires?"

"Nothing to worry about. We've had enough rain to keep things wet."

Dugan passed the bottle to Henry and moved closer to the bed. "We heard ya were shot in the side. I never see'd a fellow walk away from that."

"I didn't. They carried me." Gil put his hand on his wounds and rolled to his good side. "The ribs haven't quite healed."

Dugan shook his head. "Don't expect they'd be s'soon."

"What do you want me to tell Vonney?" Henry looked at the pallet at the far end of the room. "She's really worried about you, Gil, but she didn't think you'd want her coming up here." He took a swig and handed the bottle back to Beal.

Gil imagined Sarah's reaction to Vonney and chuckled. "I won't be riding a horse for a while, but tell her when I can, I'll stop by her place. Did you finish clearing that section?"

"Yep. We're working further south."

"It's been cold. Could snow any day now," Beal added.

Gil nodded. "Did you bring the books?"

"Figured ya wouldn't want t'see 'em till you was feelin' better. Put 'em in Jack's office," Dugan said. "I'll bring 'em up later if ya like."

"I'd appreciate that, Dugan. You better pick up supplies at Seaton's, too." Gil looked at Henry. "You'll have to take care of that for me."

"Don'tcha worry none. We'll git the supplies."

Gil nodded. "You fellows must be thirsty. You better get started before the others pass you up."

"We'll have a few for you, too, boss," Beal said, walking to the door.

"You do that." There was a knock at the door. Gil motioned for Beal to open it.

Charles entered, waving the latest edition of the *Gridley Gazette*, and handed it to Gil. "Now you can see what happened while you were unconscious." He looked at the others. "Didn't know you were up here. There're more papers in the saloon."

"Good," Henry said. "Better get one before they're gone. See you tomorrow, Gil."

"Thanks for stopping by." Gil glanced at the newspaper as his men left.

"Thought Sarah would be here."

"She stepped out for a while when the boys arrived."

"Well, I better get these papers delivered." Charles opened the door and looked over at Gil. "I'm glad you're better. Never did like lead stories about funerals."

"Me neither." Gil smiled. " 'Specially my own."

After a quick meal at home, Sarah returned to Gil's room. While he read the *Gazette*, she worked on the flannel drawers. As she drew the thread through the fabric, she glanced over and saw him smile. "I wouldn't have thought there'd be anything humorous in that issue."

"Charles's description of himself and the others tracking that outlaw just struck me as funny." He looked up from the paper and saw a wistful smile curving her mouth. If he weren't stuck in the damn bed, he would . . . But he was, and he couldn't. "What did you think of his article?"

"I haven't read it yet. After I finished mine, I left the office." She tied off the thread. "Did he interview Mr. Farmer and Mr. Grebby?"

"Yes, there are several quotes from them."

"Good. I'm sure none of us saw the robbery the same way." She fished through her sewing basket until she found a long length of cord.

For the first time, he noticed what looked like a red trouser leg, or a very long sleeve, dangling over her knee. "What are you making?"

She looked up at him as if she'd been caught with her finger in the pudding.

"Drawers . . ." She stood and held them up.

He eyed them skeptically. "Aren't they too large for you?"

"They're for you . . . to sleep in." She held out one leg for him to feel. "Flannel is soft. They should be warm, and I hope comfortable."

"You made them for me?" They resembled the baggiest lower half of a pair of long johns he'd ever seen. Without thinking, he rested one hand on his stomach. Did he look that big?

"I need to measure the length of a pair of your trousers before I hem these."

"But how will they stay up? The waist is—"

"Oh, I cut them large so they wouldn't bind. I have a cord," she said, picking it up, "which should make a strong drawstring, don't you think?"

"You're full of surprises, aren't you?" Hell, what was he supposed to say? He and Sarah could fit in there together—an interesting idea—or they could be half of a strange St. Nicholas suit. "You shouldn't have gone to so much trouble, Sarah. I'm sure Seaton's has nightshirts."

Maybe she shouldn't have made the drawers, but she had. "That would make it more difficult to check your wounds." She measured the flannel drawers against a pair of his old trousers and marked the hemline.

"That's true."

"You don't have to wear them." She returned his trousers to the drawer and slammed it closed. "Besides, who would see you?"

He smirked. "You never know."

"I suppose not," she said, ignoring his needling grin. "Since you're feeling so much better, would you like a bath?"

"That would be nice, but I don't think I can walk to Timothy's, and I sure as hell won't be carried."

"It can be done in bed. It won't be as nice as sitting in a tub of hot water, but at least you'll feel better." She sat in the chair and began pinning the hem of the drawers. "If you don't want a bath, I'll just change the bandage and poultice."

"I'm game if you are," he said, grinning. He drew his knees up and propped the newspaper against his legs. "Did Charles say how long it takes ribs to mend?"

"I don't believe he did." She cut a length of thread. "A few years ago a neighbor was thrown from his horse and broke a rib. It was about a week or so before he was comfortable."

"I can't lie here another week!" He glared around the room. "I've already counted the boards in three of the walls." *And to write Miss Lucy I'd need a book I don't dare ask you to hand me,* he thought. He quickly glanced at his desk and sighed in relief. He hadn't neglected to put away his volume of William Shakespeare nor the one of William Wordsworth.

"If you haven't the strength to get up, you'll have to remain in bed." She worked the needle through the cloth and looked over at him. "At least you're alive to complain."

Her bluntness momentarily surprised him. "You're right. Just feels damn strange being stuck here with nothing to do."

She understood his frustration, but she didn't like hearing him say he was "stuck here," even though he didn't add, with her. "Do you like to read? I can borrow any books you'd like from the lending library."

"I'll take you up on that offer. Not a book. I won't be here long enough to finish one, but I would like to see the latest issue of the *Oregon Statesman.*"

"The newspaper should've come in Friday's post. I'll check on it tomorrow."

"Thank you." Damn, it was galling to depend on her, or anyone else, for everything he wanted. "I don't want to bother you, but that broth sure smells good."

"Flattery isn't necessary." She jabbed the needle into the drawers and put them aside to pour the broth. "Is there a kitchen downstairs?"

"There's a stove and a cupboard."

"Does Mr. Young have a large kettle?"

"I wouldn't count on it. I'm not sure he knows there's a stove down there."

She handed the cup and reed to him. "I'll get one from home. Drink that slowly."

He took a sip of the fiery liquid and nearly spewed it over the bed. "If I don't, I'll scald my mouth."

She went to Phoebe's, collected what she needed for his bath, including a large kettle to heat water in, and returned to the saloon. Before going up the back stairs, she stopped at the well and filled the kettle. Making her way up the stairs, she prayed bathing Gil would be as easy as washing Clay or Cora when they were babies.

Gil watched Sarah struggle with the cauldron and felt helpless. "Do you really need that much water?"

"Probably not, but I didn't want to run short before I've finished." She set the kettle on the floor and dropped the facecloth, soap, and towels on the foot of his bed.

"*You're* going to bathe me?"

The tone of his voice was far more suggestive than the words, then she admonished herself for not recognizing another of his quips. "I've washed Clay and Cora. I believe I can handle you."

He grinned at her. "I've been doing it for years."

"That's quite an accomplishment." She cleared the top of the woodstove, put the kettle on to heat, and added wood to the fire.

"Gotten pretty good at it, too, but if you insist. . . ."

"I hope you'll share your experience with me." The only part of his body she had not seen in the past week was from below his waist to the top of his thighs. That thought caused an unwanted fluttery feeling, and she pressed her hand over her stomach. If he wanted that area washed, he would have to do it himself.

"When you change the bandage I'd like to see what the holes in my side look like."

She picked up the flannel drawers and sat down in the chair. "There isn't much to see now. Bruises and two small sores—where the bullet entered and where it came out. The skin and muscle have closed up."

"I've seen bullet wounds but never mine."

"I wish there was some way to see if your liver is healing over."

He glanced at the newspaper. "You can look if you want. I'll be happy to let you worry about that."

"I should have sent for a doctor after we got you settled here, but I've never known one with a cure for the fever that Phoebe didn't already know about. However, you may want to see one now.''

"Most doctors lance boils, set bones, and take a few stitches in a pinch. I'd rather keep my health in your hands.''

"Thank you, but you're the first and very likely the last person I will do that for.'' She gazed at him until he glanced up. "I do appreciate your faith in me, but I would much rather write about it.''

He watched her hands, those long fingers. He would rather imagine them working wonders on his body than poking around between his ribs. "You have a talent for both.'' She still wore her wedding band. What would it take for her to put it away, along with her memories? he wondered.

"What did you do before you started logging?''

He looked at her over the top of the newspaper. "Sold supplies in the mountains for a while, was a guide, hired on for any job that paid a fair wage. What about you?''

"Me?'' She stared blankly. No one had ever asked her what she had done, which was just as well.

He chuckled at the confounded expression on her face. "Which newspaper did you write for in the East?''

"None. When I was upset by an article or opinion, I wrote to editors of the Philadelphia papers. I sent Phoebe a copy of one, and she convinced Charles I could write for the *Gazette*.'' She shrugged. "He may feel hornswoggled, but he hasn't dismissed me yet.''

"A few of your ideas have shocked some people, but you also give the readers something to think about. Nothing wrong with that.''

She raised one brow. "I was under the impression you were not a fan of my writing.''

"I don't agree with all your ideas, but they're interesting.''

She considered his comment flattering, even though she knew he had laughed at her articles. Steam began to rise from the kettle, and she removed it from the stove. She poured hot water into the washbasin, and enough cold to make it comfortable.

"I'll need to take off your shirt and trousers." She remembered the oilcloth and spread it beside him. "If it isn't warm enough in here, I'll build up the fire."

"It's almost as warm as summer." Wondering how far this would go, he unbuttoned his shirt and trousers.

She helped him remove his shirt, then reached under the blanket for his trousers. This part had been easier when he was unconscious. She fumbled, trying to grip the waistband, and her fingers brushed over the front of his pants. The bulge beneath stirred, and she nearly jumped out of her skin. He definitely was no boy. Her hand shook so badly she almost pulled off his drawers along with the trousers.

Gil choked back the laughter that threatened and the sweet sensation her touch aroused. "Anything I can do to help?"

"No," she said without looking up, as she folded the trousers with great care. She grabbed the soap, determined to regain her composure.

After she wet the facecloth and rubbed soap on it, he took the cloth and scrubbed his face and neck. "Ahh. Feels good."

"I'm glad." She rinsed and squeezed the cloth. He closed his eyes as she wiped the soap off his forehead. His eyelashes were dark and long and turned up at the ends. She drew the cloth down his cheek and over his firm chin, but her attention was drawn to his mouth. She knew she had danced with him, and Phoebe said that he had walked her home, but had he tried to kiss her? *And,* had she allowed him to put his hands on her, press his body against hers, his lips over hers?

Damn, why had she drunk so much punch at the dance?

He felt her breath brush his damp cheek but her hand had stilled. "Something wrong?"

"No. . . . Stubble. You have a start on a full beard. If you want a shave, I'm sure Mr. Farmer would be glad to do it for you."

When he opened his eyes, she straightened up. As if he hadn't noticed, he felt his jaw. "You're right. Let's see about that in the morning." Her hair had fallen over her shoulders and hung down temptingly, almost inviting his touch. "I'll sit up so you can do my back."

"Let me wash your arms first." Adamant not to be distracted again, she soaped up the cloth and began scrubbing his arms and his hairy chest.

"Easy. I haven't been playing in the mud."

15

$\mathscr{G}$il knew his arms and neck had never been cleaner. While Sarah rinsed the facecloth, he moved his legs to the edge of the bed and slid them over the side. Pain shot through his side. "Agh!"

"What happened?" she said, spinning around to him.

"My legs . . . oh, my side . . ." As the waves of pain spread, he gritted his teeth.

She raised his legs back onto the mattress and bent his knees. His face was white and his forehead covered with beads of sweat. She squeezed the cloth and wiped his face. "What were you trying to do?"

"Sit up—" He held his side; the pain circled below his chest like a band of steel.

"I hope you don't try that again for a few days." She found the patent medicine and poured a little in the teaspoon.

"If that's the morphine, I don't—"

She pushed the spoon to his mouth, but he clamped his lips tight. "I won't be responsible for you opening your wounds."

He pushed her hand away. "I don't need that."

"Then lie still while I finish bathing you."

"I'm sick of lying here." He reached out and took her

hand. "Sarah, help me sit up. That isn't asking much."

She didn't blame him for wanting to sit up. It was such a simple request. "All right. I'll try."

She slid her arm under his knees. "Put your arm around my shoulders and hold on to me. I'm going to turn you. When I lower your legs, lean on me."

The pain was letting up, and he breathed easier. "That should be simple enough."

With her arm supporting his knees, she eased his legs to the side and lowered his feet to the floor. When she turned her head to look at him, his lips brushed her jaw. She froze.

"Whew." He raised his head and grinned. "This'd be better if my head wasn't spinning."

She held on to his upper arms and stood up. "Do you have a sick stomach?"

"No." He wrapped his arms around her legs and clung to her. "Wash my back if you're going to. I can't stay this way for long."

She grabbed the facecloth and quickly bathed his back, then dried him off. "It would be easier to put a clean shirt on you now. Can you brace yourself with your good arm?"

"I'm not moving." His eyes were closed to hold the spinning room at bay. Maybe if he pretended he was hugging her, the room would stop whirling around.

"I can't reach the chest of drawers." She searched for something to support him. Pillows were too soft, and his hold was so fierce that she couldn't move either leg. She ran her hand over his soft hair, but he didn't seem to notice. "Gil, if you let go of me with your left arm, I think I can pull the drawer open."

"All right." He let go of one leg and rested his cheek on her thigh. At one time he'd been sure she wouldn't't've spared a moment of her time for him, and now he was clutching her as if he were a little boy. And she was letting him. He had been so wrong about her.

She managed to stretch enough for her fingers to grab the edge of the drawer. She snatched at the first shirt. "Got it."

If he hadn't felt like a spinning top, he might have enjoyed her dressing him. It didn't take her long to get him into the shirt. "Thanks."

"Ready to lie down?"

"Definitely." He grinned. "Want to join me?"

She stared at the top of his head, amazed by his light-hearted teasing—yet somewhat intoxicated with the idea of her arms wrapped around him, her thighs caught between his, and his—

"I . . .'d better not." Then she decided to give him a dose of his own medicine. "I might fall asleep. What would Mr. Young think if he found us together in bed? Or Charles?"

Gil chuckled. "That would give the men something to dream about."

"Nightmares would be more like it." She bent down, placed his arm on her shoulder, slid her other arm beneath his knees, and eased him backward as she raised his knees.

He held on to her as he fell back on the mattress, and pulling her down with him.

She nudged his feet onto the bed with her leg. "You can let go now." The stubble on his cheek pressed into hers. Her lips were near his ear.

"Not yet." He slid his hand to the back of her neck and drew his lips along her jaw. "I've thought about doing this again since the dance." He took her mouth gently and buried his hands in her silky hair.

She didn't struggle. She wanted to kiss him. As she perched on the edge of the mattress beside him, she parted her lips. His large hand cradled her head as if she were fragile, while his other hand stroked her back and awakened her passions.

Having lived in a void of physical affection for the last few years, the sudden flood of excitement made her light-headed. The sweetness of his caress sent a delicious shiver down her spine and her body responded to him almost as if it was familiar with him.

The first time they'd kissed, he knew, her defenses had been weakened by the whiskey-laced punch, but not this time. She opened to him with a hunger that matched his.

Maybe he should've taken that dose of syrup so he couldn't feel his ribs, but holding her had almost the same effect.

He kissed the corners of her mouth and her chin. "I thought you'd forgotten or didn't want to remember." He skimmed a knuckle down her cheek, saying, "Glad I was wrong."

"Forgotten what?" She said, feeling a bit dazed. "What are you talking about?"

"Whoops." He should've kept his mouth on hers.

"You said 'again.' We have kissed before. . . ?" she asked. The memory was fuzzy, just beyond reach.

"After the dance. I walked you home"—he held her gaze, willing her to share his memory, the heart-pounding spark when their lips touched—"and we kissed good night at the door."

His low-pitched voice was like a caress. He had told her the truth. She felt it in her bones. "I wonder if Charles and Phoebe saw us?" Botheration, her body didn't have a problem recalling what she could not.

"I passed them on my way back here. They might have." He thought back. There hadn't been any sly smile or odd look to make him suspect they had seen him embracing Sarah. "I was busy."

She stood up and absentmindedly brushed her fingertips over her lips. "You rest while I finish your bath." Her body certainly remembered his first caress, but she knew her mind, too, would not forget this time. The taste of him still lingered on her mouth.

He watched her, smiling. She had that effect on him. She looked distracted, pleasantly distracted. He settled back, a bit surprised by her reaction. While she tossed the basin of cold water out the back window, he started buttoning his shirt but stopped after the first three. "Are you still going to change the bandage?"

She closed the window and walked over to the woodstove. "I'll do that next."

"Can I take a look?"

"I don't see any reason why you shouldn't." She

glanced down at her side but couldn't quite see where his wound would be. "Do you have a mirror?"

"Top drawer."

After she had the clean bandages and a fresh poultice ready, she gave him the hand mirror. She used the knife to cut the bandage, then peeled it away. "It's still draining." She gently bathed his side but as she dried him, the wound in his chest continued to drain.

He angled the mirror down and stared at small bruises on the side of his chest. "Looks like I've been kicked by a mule, not shot clear through. It's hard to believe you put your fingers through there."

"I'm glad you approve." She put one knee on the mattress and rested her weight on it so she could clean the other wound. "Wrapping the bandage around may seem awkward, but I want you to lie perfectly still."

"Yes, ma'am." She was all business again, he realized.

She fed one end of the cotton strip under his back and applied a fresh poultice to each wound, then continued wrapping the strips around him.

"Wouldn't it be easier if I sat up?"

"Maybe next time. I'm done." She tied off the bandage and pulled down his shirt. "Feel better?"

"Yes. It's warm."

"It's supposed to be." She folded the blanket back and pulled off his stockings.

Once the oilcloth had been spread under his legs, she lathered the facecloth. Such nice legs, she thought, and started washing his foot. The skin was pale, smooth, and soft. His ankle was slim, almost bony, but his calf was firm and covered with soft dark hair. The cloth slid over his knee, and she felt his thigh grow hard beneath her fingers. The breath caught in her throat. Body parts, she told herself. They are only parts of his body and, so far, not all that different from her own.

She tried to believe that, but her fingers trembled and her mouth was dry. If she couldn't fool herself, what must he think? *Don't think. Just wash,* she admonished herself.

He held the blanket firmly in place over his hips and

struggled to ignore the feel of her hands through the cloth working its way up his leg. When he was healed, he decided, he'd bathe her. As she rubbed the soapy cloth over the inside of his thigh, he pressed his fists into the mattress and pictured washing her slender neck, her bare shoulders, and her full breasts with his soapy hands. He'd span her waist, run his hands over her smooth belly, and sink his fingers into the curls he imagined—

"I'm finished." She took the oilcloth out from under him.

"Oh, Sarah. . . ."

His deep, velvety voice sent a tantalizing quiver through her belly. Her name had never sounded so beautiful. He had probably dosed off and was dreaming. "What trousers do you want to wear?"

"The red ones, of course."

She bundled up the soiled bandages and the towels and set them in the hall by the door. "Don't feel you have to. If it gets much colder, I may want to wear them under my petticoats."

"I'll share. You can wear them during the day, and I'll take them at night."

"A second pair makes more sense." She picked up the red flannel drawers and eased them up his legs until her fingers brushed his hips.

"Wouldn't be as much fun."

"Maybe you should pull them up the rest of the way."

Grinning, he reached under the blanket, grabbed the flannel, and tugged the drawers up to his waist. It reminded him of late-night forays in his misspent youth. "Where's the button?" He tossed the blanket aside and held up the ends of the cord.

"Just tie the drawstring. They won't fall off." The drawers were loose. Baggy, actually, but they wouldn't bind. She shook out the blanket and waited for him to finish tying the cord.

"No. This cord's sturdy." He watched her eyes as she spread the blanket over him. As the cover settled over his chest, he caught her hands. "Thanks for the bath."

She didn't know what to say. Unfortunately, she felt the heat of a blush stain her cheeks. She met his gaze and felt her defenses slipping away. *I enjoyed it, too,* hardly seemed appropriate. He already knew that.

"Why don't you sit beside me? We can read the paper together."

She smiled and nodded. When he pressed a kiss on the back of her hand, she felt it all the way down to her toes.

Sunday morning when Gil's friends began stopping by to see how he was feeling, Sarah left for a much needed walk. She wandered along the river, crossed the bridge to the mill, and strolled through the fields. Her thoughts darted about like a bee in a field of wildflowers.

In the last week she had learned a great deal about Gil and about herself. There was an unforgettable bond between them. She had not seriously considered there could be more, but neither could she deny the way she instinctively responded to him. When they had read the newspaper together, his arm draped around her shoulders, she had noticed him reading the Miss Lucy column, and felt a twinge of guilt about Mr. Brown.

Was it possible to love two men at once? Or had she become a fickle twit in her third decade?

The icy wind finally penetrated her wool shawl, and she went home. The house was empty, so she bathed, changed clothes, and started another pot of broth. As usual when she found herself at odds, she turned to books. This time she perused Phoebe's own receipt book of her favorite dishes. A few minutes later Sarah decided to make tapioca pudding for Gil.

She had gathered the ingredients, when Phoebe came in the kitchen, looking around with a bemused smile. Sarah quickly closed the cookbook. "You were out early."

"Not really." Phoebe turned to Cora. "Change your clothes, dear."

"Hi, Aunt Sarah. Are you making more chicken soup?"

"Yes, sweetie. Will you taste it later and tell me if it's good?"

"Mm-hm." Cora kissed Sarah and left the kitchen.

Sarah smiled at Phoebe. "I've missed all of you."

"I'm glad Mr. Perry's much better and that you're home." Phoebe hugged her. "Charles'll be happy you're back, too."

"I can't stay. While Gil's friends visit with him, I decided to prepare a few meals." Sarah put the cookbook away.

"So, you're spending another night with him."

"In the same room. Not his bed." Sarah stirred the soup and glanced at Phoebe. "He can't take care of himself. He can't even sit up yet."

"Why should he? You're waiting on him," Phoebe grumbled. "You didn't coddle John this way."

"There wasn't any need." Sarah looked over her shoulder at Phoebe. "This isn't like you. Don't you remember how much blood Gil lost? He's bound to be weak for a while."

"I've tried to forget seeing him on the floor. . . . I'm sorry." Phoebe shuddered. Lord, that had to be the worst sight she had ever witnessed. "It's just that you're acting like a doting wife—and you're not."

"If he hadn't shielded me, I would be dead. Isn't that reason enough?"

"Please remember who he is. You were barely civil to him before the dance."

Sarah shook her head. "Last night Gil tried to sit up when I was giving him a bath, but he hurt himself. He really doesn't like—"

"You didn't!" Phoebe said, staring at her.

"Phoebe, close your mouth." Sarah moved the pot to the side of the fire. "How else was he to get cleaned up? After having a fever for days, he needed a bath."

Phoebe put the teakettle on the fire. "Did you finish the drawers?"

"I did, and he wore them last night." Sarah added a little salt and pepper to the soup. "Charles's article was very good."

"So was yours." Phoebe set two cups on the worktable. "Tea?"

"Yes, thank you."

"He's talked with half of the men in town. Everyone seems to like the idea of a town council. Mr. Seaton wants to have a town meeting this week to decide how to handle the election."

"Good idea." Sarah sat down at the table. "Would you like to serve on the council?"

"*Me?* Men vote. They won't elect any women." Phoebe laughed. "You do come up with some interesting notions."

"Just because women can't vote for the president or governor, doesn't mean we shouldn't have a say in what happens in our own town."

"I agree, but how could we convince the men to let us vote? We might not agree with them."

"We'll have to attend the meeting," Sarah said, grinning, "and see that the other women do, too."

Gil set the empty bowl by his legs on the bed. "That soup sure was good. I'm full for the first time in a week. Thanks."

"I'm glad you liked it." She smiled. He really must have been hungry; the soup wasn't anything special.

"Surprising how two little bits of carrot, a bite of potato, one green bean, and a few slivers of chicken filled me up."

"It's more than you've eaten recently." She decided not to tell him about the pudding. No use getting his hopes up.

He eyed the hem of her skirt. "Did you wear the red drawers today?"

She grinned and shook her head. "I put them in the chest this morning. I'll check the bandage and help you change trousers."

"That's a deal." He unbuttoned his pants and pulled up his shirt. "I'm getting used to this. After I'm healed, will you check the scar once in a while? Just for old time's sake?"

She knelt at the side of the bed. "You are feeling better. As soon as you can sit up, you won't need me."

"Who says?" He'd gotten used to sharing his room with her. It wasn't as if they shared his bed, but her company sure was nice. "If I can't stand up, I'll still be stuck in bed. Alone."

She glanced up at him. "I'm leaving long before you're strong enough to entertain . . . in your room."

He held his ribs and chuckled.

"The bandage is stained. Did you try to sit up today?"

"Nope, but this mattress gets harder every day."

"When you don't have to spend all day in bed, it won't seem so bad." She mixed the poultice and set out fresh bandages.

With a groan, he rolled to his left. "How long before that heals up?"

"I don't know." She removed the bandage and the old poultice. "At least you didn't start bleeding." She washed his wounds, applied the fresh poultice, and rebandaged him.

"Good as new."

"As long as the wounds are open and draining there's still a danger of the fever starting up again." She pulled his shirt down. "I don't know about you, but I do not want to go through that again."

"I don't either, but it's nice to know you worried about me."

She shrugged. "I wasn't the only one. Everyone did, especially Jack. He turned white when he saw how much of your blood was spilled on the bank floor." She took the flannel drawers out and set them on the bed.

"When he sliced the end of his finger once, he threw up. Poor Jack. Guess I owe him. This's sure put a crimp in his social life."

She smirked and rolled back the blanket. "Why can't he close the saloon a few nights? The men don't need to drink every night."

"Good idea."

She pulled off his trousers and got him into the flannel drawers. "Did anyone tell you about the town meeting?"

"Yeah. They think a council's going to keep this town peaceful." He shook his head. The only way he knew that might help was to close the bank. Without a lure, there would be little there for an outlaw.

"You don't sound very enthusiastic."

"I should've been armed, but there hasn't been any trouble in years. I keep a pistol behind the bar. A lot of good it did."

"The robbery was horrible, but this is a *nice* town." She covered him with the blanket. "I'd hate to see everyone carrying or wearing a gun and ready to shoot the first person that frightens them."

"So would I." He caught her hand and held it. "You're going to the meeting, aren't you?"

"As long as you're all right I plan to be there."

"Good. You can be my eyes and ears." He gave her hand a gentle squeeze. "You won't let anyone get away with anything." He drew her down and slid his arms around her.

"Oh, be careful." Her heart was racing. "I don't want to hurt your side."

"You won't, Sarah," he assured her in a deep voice.

She wasn't sure if he was nudging her closer or if she wanted to think he was, but she leaned forward and brushed her lips over his. It was reckless, but she didn't care.

She drew his lower lip between hers and braced her hands on the mattress so as not to lean on him but, dear God, she wanted him to hold her close, to feel his body hard against hers. When he groaned and skimmed his hands down her arms, she deepened the kiss, desperate to ease the throbbing desire she felt for him.

He wanted nothing more than to please her, he had dreamed about it, but he couldn't love her the way he wanted—thoroughly, until they were spent. He stroked his palms over her breasts as he nibbled the side of her neck. This was maddening, almost cruel. He had to stop. He framed her lovely face and deepened the kiss until they were breathless.

She was dizzy and weak; only the tingling below her belly seemed to grow stronger. "You have the strangest effect on me.'' She had already seen his limbs, but she wanted to explore his body at leisure.

''So do you.'' Damn, he couldn't stop touching her and watching the delight on her face. He kissed each breast through her shirtwaist and covered her belly with his hand, rubbing gently. He slid his hand to her thigh.

Her breasts had never been so sensitive. Her insides were melting, throbbing for him to fill her, all of him. He was poetry and the sweetest music she had ever heard. Suddenly, some part of her mind intruded—reminding her of Mr. Brown. She summoned her willpower and pressed her hand over Gil's. ''Not . . . now.''

She was trembling with need, and he wanted to be the one to satisfy her. God, he thought, this was torture. Now he really understood that line from William Shakespeare's *All's Well That Ends Well:* ''A heaven on earth I have won by wooing thee.''

Sarah read the single page Charles had printed announcing the town meeting, set for Wednesday evening at the church. ''It looks fine, Charles, except you forgot to include the ladies in your invitation.''

''The women are welcome to come with their husbands.'' Charles scratched his head. ''I don't see any need to mention them.''

''Men usually don't, but I want you to add 'ladies' or delete 'gentlemen.' I'm going to the meeting, so is Phoebe, and we are encouraging the other women to join us.''

''Why all the fuss? We're only meeting to talk about electing a council. It will be more of a discussion.''

''I'm not married. Neither is Elsie North or Tess Layton, to name a few, and the wives may not agree with their husbands. It's our town, too.''

He groaned. ''Why does it sound like a revolt in the making?''

''A petticoat revolt?'' She smiled. ''That's an idea. I do believe we should have a voice in the running of our town. The Territory of Wyoming granted women the right to vote three years ago.''

"All right. No one said the ladies weren't welcome." He began resetting the type. "I want to pass this out to as many people as possible. Will you hand them out in town? I'll ride to the farms and over to the mill."

"Yes, as long as you change this. If I have extra copies I'll pass them out at school."

"You might leave some at the saloon, too."

"Don't worry. I'll make sure every business in town has one for its window and another for the counter. Word will spread soon enough."

A short time later she left the *Gazette* office with an armload of notices. Seaton's was her first stop. Mr. Seaton posted three of the announcements, one in the front window. Mr. Kenton took two, and she left two more in the library. She worked her way up and down the road passing out notices.

She stopped by the house for another jar of soup and a bowl of tapioca pudding and took them to the saloon. Mr. Young was seated at a table, and she walked over to him. "How are you today, Mr. Young?"

"Doin' fine, Mrs. Hampton. Whatcha got there?"

"The notice about the town meeting," she said, handing him one. "I would like to leave a few on the bar. We want everyone in town to attend."

"You do that. I'm closin' th' saloon. Wouldn't miss that meetin'."

"I'm glad you're going. I'll see you there." She went upstairs, tapped on Gil's door, and opened it a crack. "May I come in?"

"It's about time."

She stepped inside and closed the door. "I'm glad you're awake."

"I'm so tired of this. If I'd had any paper I would've written to Miss Lucy and asked her to come take care of me." He gave her a crooked grin, and noticed a momentary look of surprise on her face.

Was he teasing her again? It would be just like him, then she remembered that he didn't know that she was Miss Lucy. If he found out, she would definitely be laughed out of town. He would never let her hear the end of that. "You're supposing she has nothing else to do?"

"She seems to be a very kind lady."

Sarah set the notices at the foot of his bed and the basket on the floor. "By the time she arrived, I'd hope you wouldn't need anyone to stay with you."

"Don't be too rational, Sarah. Takes all the fun out of daydreaming."

"Not necessarily." She draped her cloak over the back of the chair. "Hungry?"

"As good as your soup is, it doesn't stick to my ribs very long."

"I brought you more and also a bowl of tapioca pudding."

"You're an angel."

She poured the soup into a cup and handed it to him along with a spoon. She set the bowl on the small bedside table. "I've handed these out all over town," she said, giving him one of the notices. "Charles is taking them out to the farms and over to the mill."

He quickly read the paper. "Should be a good crowd. Do you really expect many women will go?"

"They live here. I don't see why they—we—can't have a say in what happens."

He grinned. "I'm not surprised."

$\mathcal{P}$hoebe followed Sarah up the side aisle in the church, toward the front. "This's far enough. If we sit in the first row we'll have to keep turning around to see who's speaking."

"Mind if I sit on the end? I might as well take notes for my own reference."

Phoebe gave her a piercing gaze. "Did Charles ask you to write about this meeting?"

"No, but we may need an article in the paper to help us get a woman on the council, if that's what everyone decides."

"There's Elsie North." Phoebe waved and motioned for her to join them. "I wonder if she would like to serve on the council."

Sarah smiled to Elsie. "Ask her. Have you thought it over?"

"I would like to," Phoebe confided. "But I don't really think I'd have a chance. The men will vote for men."

"Hm. Don't count yourself out yet." Sarah glanced up as Elsie joined them. "Have a seat."

Elsie sat on the other side of Phoebe. "Alice and Beth are outside with their husbands, so we won't be the only women here tonight."

Sarah looked at the door. "Ben Layton just came in, but I don't see Tess."

Elsie leaned toward Phoebe and Sarah. "Jack Young's been courting her. She'll probably come with him."

"That's why Gil—"

"Oh, there she is," Phoebe said, "with Mr. Young. Don't they make a nice couple?"

"They do." Elsie tapped Sarah's knee. "What were you saying about Gil Perry?"

"It wasn't important." Not enough to recount, Sarah thought, but it did explain Gil's remark about Jack's social life.

"Finally," Elsie said. "The cold's driving everyone inside." She tapped Sarah on the arm. "Who's staying with Gil Perry?"

"He's alone. I'm hoping this meeting doesn't run too long. He was resting when I left."

"Look," Phoebe said, "the Ryans and the Udalls came."

"They have farms south of town, don't they?" Sarah searched the room and realized that she didn't recognize many of the people filling the room.

"That's right. I'm surprised so many have come on a weeknight on such short notice." Phoebe nodded to Mr. and Mrs. Pace.

"Where's Charles?" Elsie asked. "I don't see him."

"He and George are trying to get to the podium," Alice Seaton said, taking a seat behind Sarah.

Sarah spoke with Alice until the meeting was called to order, only a few minutes after seven. Charles introduced himself, and then George Seaton. George gave a summary of the thoughts that led to the meeting and asked for suggestions on how to go about selecting the town council.

One man called out, "Why not just hold our hands up?"

A man in the back of the room stepped forward. "I wanta know how this council coulda helped Gil Perry."

George spoke up. "The council would have the power to make laws, and hire a sheriff, if one is needed. It would give us leadership. Fortunately, when Gil was shot a few good men stepped forward. That may not happen next time.''

Sarah looked around the room waiting to hear what she thought was the first obvious question, but no one asked it. She stood up and glanced around. ''Has it been decided that the majority of people want a town council?''

George chuckled. ''No, Mrs. Hampton. That's why we're here tonight.''

''Then shouldn't you take a vote on that first?''

Charles glanced at George and shrugged. ''All in favor of holding an election for town council, raise your hands.''

Sarah searched the group and could not find one person who didn't have an arm in the air. She nodded at Charles. ''In that case, I nominate Mrs. Phoebe Abbott.''

Alice jumped to her feet. ''And I nominate Mrs. Elsie North.''

''I nominate Sarah Hampton,'' Mr. Grebby announced from the back of the room.

Everyone started talking at once. Charles stuck two fingers in his mouth and let out a screeching whistle. The crowd quieted. ''You'll have to take turns or we'll be here for the next week.''

''Whoever heard of a woman runnin' a town?'' a man called out.

''Well . . .'' Charles looked at George.

George stared at the women watching him.

''Mr. Seaton,'' Alice said. ''Why not put the women's names on the ballet and let the voters choose who they want?''

Phoebe stood up. ''I agree.''

Vernon Riggs stood up. ''I say Gil Perry. He'd be a good choice.''

Half the people in the room agreed. Sarah smiled. It was too bad Gil couldn't be here, she thought, adding his name to the list of nominees.

Phoebe stood up. ''I also nominate Alice Seaton.''

Alice shook her head vehemently. ''Thank you, but no. I've got enough to do now.''

By the time they had finished the nominations, Sarah had

seven men and four women on the list. There would be some difficult choices. She stood up again. "Have we decided how many people will make up the council?"

George glanced at Charles. "An odd number. Seven?"

"Five's better," Jack said, standing up. "Seven'd never agree on anythin'."

"You got a point, Jack," Timothy Farmer said.

Emmett Pratt stood up. "I suggest Mr. Abbott write a short biography or statement by each nominee and publish them in the *Gazette*."

Charles nodded. "That's a good idea. Did everyone hear that?" He looked around the packed church. "Each person nominated should write something about themselves and bring it to the office, or see me about writing it for you. I'd like that by Friday so they'll be in this week's paper."

"How about printing a ballot, too?" George asked. "Everyone could bring their ballots in and leave them in a special box at the post office."

Mr. Pace stood up. "Why not have everyone vote in town, the way real elections are held? Not everyone takes the paper. Sorry, Charles."

"No problem." Charles looked around the room. "Those in favor of voting in town, raise your hands." He and George counted, then spoke to one another. "Those in favor of a newspaper ballot, raise your hands."

"Guess we'll be holding the election in town," George announced. "Now we need a date."

By the time everyone agreed to vote on the twenty-second, the Saturday before Thanksgiving, when most people would come to town, Sarah had three pages of notes. The meeting ended and the townspeople slowly filed outside, chattering among themselves. Sarah was anxious to check on Gil and tell him all about the meeting.

Phoebe, Sarah, Alice, Ruby Jean Drake, and Elsie walked out together. At the bottom of the stairs, Elsie turned to the other ladies. "I think we should meet and talk about this election. How about lunch at my house?"

Alice glanced at the others. "What is there to talk about? People will make up their minds."

Elsie shook her head. "The one thing that no one mentioned was, will women get to vote. I say we should campaign to get every woman in town to vote."

Phoebe nodded. "You pick the day, and we'll be there."

"Good idea." Sarah faced Ruby Jean and Alice as she said, "You can count on me."

Ruby Jean waved to her husband. "When's this lunch?"

"Next Monday?" Elsie proposed.

"I'll speak to Mr. Drake. I'm sure he won't mind. See you then." Ruby Jean left to join her husband.

Sarah shook her head. "Convincing some women to think for themselves could be half of our problem."

Phoebe laughed. "You'll think of a way. I'd better get Charles or he'll be here all night. See you later."

Alice also said goodbye and joined her husband.

Mr. Pratt came up to Sarah and Elsie. "Good evening, ladies. It's nice to see you looking so well, Mrs. Hampton, especially after the bank robbery last week."

"Mr. Pratt." Caught unawares, Sarah hoped she didn't look too startled. "Congratulations on your nomination."

"And to you, both of you." He gazed at Sarah. "I have wanted to ask you about the library fund. I understand you have been busy. I would be very happy to help you with the decision about which books to order, if you would like assistance. Or were the funds taken during the robbery?"

"The money is quite safe, thank you. I'll have to let you know later about the meeting to choose the books."

"That will be fine." He tipped his hat and walked up the road.

Elsie glanced at Sarah. "I think he had more than library books on his mind."

"Oh, I hope you're wrong." Sarah and Elsie started walking back to town. "I think the first thing we need to do is write good biographies for each of the women candidates."

Elsie shivered and tightened her grasp on her shawl. "We may be hoarse by the time this's over."

• • •

Sarah stopped by Phoebe's for the rest of the pudding before returning to Gil's room. The room was almost as cold as the air outside. The woodstove was only warm to the touch.

"Gil." The bed covers were all jumbled up on top of him. She quickly added wood to the stove.

"I'd about given up on you," he said, pushing the covers back from his face. "Almost feels like an icehouse in here."

"I'm sure I fed the fire before I left." She started a fresh pot of coffee. "How did you manage to get all of that on top of you?"

"Wasn't easy." He tried to move and winced.

"Guess I won't have to worry about changing the sheets, will I?" One by one she pulled off the blankets and sheets.

"Why would you? I haven't been lying on them. I've been under them." He grabbed the last blanket. "You want me to freeze?"

She laid her hand over his forehead. "You'll survive another few minutes." She yanked the cover away from him and spread one of the sheets over the length of him, including his face.

He lay still as she layered the blankets and comforter on him in a more orderly fashion than he had done. "Good thing I'm wearing these flannel drawers," he said through the bedding. "Too bad there isn't a matching shirt."

"I am sorry about the heat. Next time I leave, I'll make sure there is plenty of wood in the stove."

The coffee was ready. She handed him a bowl of tapioca pudding and poured each of them a cup of coffee. "I wish you could've been there this evening. The benches were full and people stood in the aisles and along the back of the room."

"At least you must've been warm." He didn't care if he scalded his mouth on the steaming coffee, as long as it warmed him. He ate a spoonful of pudding and sighed. "I didn't think there were enough people around here to fill the church." And, he thought, I sure as hell wouldn't want to be trapped in a room with them.

"I didn't recognize a lot of them, but I'm still new to town." She sipped the hot coffee.

"Are you going to tell me what happened?" He scooped up another bite. "Or do I have to listen to a detailed account of the evening?"

"You're in fine spirits, aren't you?" She picked up her notes and quietly stared at the top page. If he wanted to behave like an overindulged youngster, she would treat him as such.

He glared at her. "Want to change places? You lie here for a few days and see how much you like it."

She arched one brow at him. "You can read about the meeting in the newspaper. It will give you something to look forward to."

"Oh, Sarah, I'm looking forward to many things." He grinned at her. "Hearing about that meeting's down near the bottom of the list."

She glanced out of the corner of her eye at him and felt her cheeks grow warm.

"Aren't you curious about what tops the list?"

Lord, her heart was pounding hard. She met his gaze, praying her expectations weren't evident in her expression. "Should I be?" He chuckled, a deep, rich, suggestive laugh.

"Soon as I'm able, I'll show you."

He tried to change his position—big mistake. He ended up pulling something in his side. He gritted his teeth.

She gulped, wondering if she was again misunderstanding his meaning. "Then both of us have something to look forward to," she said, meeting his piercing gaze.

"Yes, we do." He set the bowl on the table by the bed. "Have you ever been stuck in bed, unable to do *anything?* Not even add wood to a fire." He waved his arm at the window. "I can't see anything from here. I'd welcome a crow on the windowsill."

"Why not ask Jack to move your bed by the side window? You could see the river or the street."

"When he comes back, I will." He looked at her. "Do you ever lose an argument?"

"No one's right all the time." She grinned. "Not even you."

He held his side as he chuckled. "Since I have to guess, I'd say a few people have their sights on being on the council."

She nodded. "Eleven people were nominated and then it was decided that five will be on the council." She added another piece of wood to the fire.

He picked up the bowl of pudding and raised the spoon to his mouth. "Who are the lucky eleven?"

"Charles, George Seaton, Jack, Mr. Drake, Mr. Pratt, Mr. Riggs, Phoebe, Mrs. North, Mrs. Drake . . . you, and me."

He choked on the pudding. "Good God—not me. Tell Charles to scratch my name off that list."

"I don't know if that's possible. Everyone approved of your nomination, but I'll tell him. I'm not sure I want my name on the ballot either."

"Jack must've had a good laugh." He gulped down another bite. "There's some paper in my desk. Would you get one sheet for me, and a pencil?"

"Which drawer?"

Not the right one, he silently commanded her. Would she recognize the paper Mr. Brown's letters were written on? "Top left. A scrap will do." He watched her, hoping there wasn't anything in that drawer to interest her.

She found a pencil and a piece of blank paper on top of a small wooden box. "Will these do?"

He nodded. "Would you mind writing it?"

"What do you want to say?"

"Must see you now. Underline *must.* Would you put this in Jack's door?"

"He stops by each night before he retires. Why wouldn't he tonight?"

"I don't want him to forget."

"Oh—of course." Since he's feeling better, she decided, he's embarrassed to ask her for help with the pitcher. "*In* the door?"

"Unlatch the door and stick the paper between the door and jamb—the frame."

"All right." She went down the hall and tapped on Jack's door. When there was no answer, she opened his door a crack. There wasn't a light in the hall. How was he supposed to see the note in the dark?

Gil finished eating and wondered what was taking her so long. "What the devil are you doing?" he called out.

The light spilling into the hall from Gil's room wasn't much help inside Jack's room, but she managed to locate a lamp. After she put the note in the door, she lighted the lamp and left it on the floor in the hall.

"Did you call me?" She closed Gil's door and stood in front of the stove warming her hands.

He gazed at her a long moment, remembering how good she felt in his arms. Then he caught the glint of her wedding ring in the light. "It wasn't important."

Thursday morning Phoebe packed breakfast into a basket and went to see for herself how Mr. Perry was doing. She had wanted Sarah to be pleasant to him but it seemed to her that the situation had gone way beyond common kindness. Phoebe had raised her hand to knock on the door, when it opened.

"I'll see if Jack's awake," Sarah was saying as she stepped into the hall, nearly bumping into Phoebe. "Phoebe! I didn't expect to see you here."

"Last night a few ladies asked if you were well—they said you looked peaked—and I realized you probably hadn't had a decent meal since dinner last Saturday." Phoebe held up the basket. "I brought breakfast for you, and for Mr. Perry."

"How nice. I *am* hungry. Set it by the stove. I'll be just a minute." Sarah knocked on Jack's door and went back to Gil's room. A moment later, Jack arrived. She smiled at him, then glanced at Phoebe. "Take a walk with me. We'll be right back."

Phoebe followed Sarah down to the saloon. "What are we doing here?"

"Jack's been helping Gil with . . . ah . . ."

"Oh, I hadn't thought about that. The poor man."

"It will be easier for him when he can sit on the side of the bed." Sarah stopped at the end of the bar. "Was Charles satisfied with the meeting last night?"

"He thought it went very well, but he did mutter something about a 'petticoat revolt.' " Phoebe grinned at Sarah. "Want to tell me what he was talking about?"

"I don't know why I said that aloud. We were talking about women voting in the election, and he said it sounded like a revolt."

Phoebe's smiled slipped. "Every man will be against us by the end of the day."

"It's no secret. Four women were nominated to sit on the council. It shouldn't be difficult to realize at least some women will be voting for the women."

"Look at Charles's reaction. And I believe he's more broad-minded than most."

"Last night no one complained about our being nominated. I expected an argument then."

"The men are probably confident that men will vote for men, which will block the women."

"And I can think of several men who'll likely tell their wives they can't vote—that's if their wives even mention an interest in the election." Sarah heard a door open and close. "We can go back now."

Phoebe paused at the bottom of the stairs and looked back at the painting behind the bar. She hadn't asked Charles about it yet. Maybe tonight. She put her hand over her stomach and smiled. She would brush out her hair, pinch her cheeks, and wear her lacy chemise to bed, and then she would ask him.

She hurried up the stairs and walked into Gil's room behind Sarah. "Sarah, you sit down. I'll serve."

Gil grinned and shrugged one shoulder. "Will you join me, Miss Sarah?"

"Why, thank you. I wonder what the special of the day is." Sarah took her seat and watched Phoebe. "You don't have to wait on us."

"I'm just dishing up the eggs." Phoebe set the bowl of custard on one plate and served them. "Do you drink coffee or tea, Mr. Perry?"

He handed her his cup. "Coffee, please, Mrs. Abbott. This meal looks delicious."

"Yes, this is wonderful." Sarah compared their plates. Phoebe had given her sausage and toast with scrambled eggs, and Gil eggs and custard.

Phoebe refilled their cups. "Oh, Sarah, Charles wanted me to ask you to stop by the office this morning. I think we should do our best to see that the women's statements are in his office in time for this week's paper. It'll be easier to speak to the ladies about"—she paused, glancing at Mr. Perry—"their voting if they have read about us."

"You're right. Have you written yours yet?"

"I will when I get home, but I'd better stop by Elsie's first."

"Then I will see Ruby Jean before I go to the office." Sarah scooped up another bite. She was starving.

"You're a good cook, Mrs. Abbott," Gil said He could have easily eaten a portion of sausage and toast, but he wasn't complaining. At least now he was eating, not drinking, his food.

"I put a little cinnamon in the custard, so it would taste more like a breakfast dish."

Gil dipped the spoon into the custard and grinned. "I wouldn't mind some more of this."

Sarah shook her head. "Don't get greedy or you'll be back on broth."

He sipped his coffee. "Yes, ma'am." He grinned at Phoebe. "Bossy, isn't she?"

Phoebe couldn't resist his charm and smiled. In that instant, Phoebe saw why Sarah enjoyed being with him. He was a tease and a rogue with an endearing smile. "Well, I had better get busy. You won't forget to go by the *Gazette*, will you?"

"I'd planned to see Charles anyway." Sarah recognized Phoebe's disapproving tone, which shouldn't have been a surprise. Phoebe and Charles tended to agree with one another. "Thanks again for breakfast."

After Phoebe left, Sarah ate the last bite of eggs and sausage. "Mm, that was delicious."

"It was good." He smiled at her. "Each meal gets better. Can't wait to see what we're having for lunch."

"I'll bring you some soup. I have a lot of work to do."

"That's fine. What about supper?" He raised the coffee cup to his mouth and gazed at her over the brim. "You won't work through supper, will you?"

Oh, that smile, she thought. Is he using it on me because he needs an amusement? "Don't worry, Gil. You won't go hungry." She really had to remember to stop by the library and borrow a few newspapers for him. Anything to get his mind off food.

$\mathcal{S}$arah smiled at Ruby Jean Drake. "Phoebe and I thought it would be a good idea if we could get our statements in the next issue of the *Gazette*. Have you thought about what you would like to say in yours?"

Ruby Jean twisted her handkerchief. "I was going to speak to Mr. Drake about it this evening. This may be a mistake. What do I know about being on a town council?"

"You'll learn. We don't know if any of the candidates have experience. That doesn't seem to be a concern."

Ruby Jean chewed on the side of her lips. "I'm not sure what to say."

"I'll be glad to help, if you would like."

"Oh dear, I don't know...." Ruby Jean twisted the handkerchief tighter. "What are we supposed to say?"

With Sarah's gentle encouragement, Ruby Jean eventually articulated some thoughts and put them down on paper. Sarah felt a wave of relief when Ruby Jean finished.

"That wasn't too bad after all. Thank you, Sarah." Ruby Jean blotted the page and folded it in half. "Have you written yours yet?"

"That's one of the things I have to do this afternoon."

Ruby Jean handed the paper to Sarah. "I appreciate your help. Mr. Drake'll be surprised."

"And proud of you, I am sure." Sarah walked to the door. "Good luck in the election. You are planning to vote, aren't you?"

"*Vote?* We can't vote."

"I intend to. If we can run for an office, we should be able to vote." Sarah patted Ruby Jean's hand. "You think about it. There will be quite a few of us voting. I hope you'll join us."

"I'll see. Are we still meeting for lunch at Elsie's Monday?"

"Yes. See you there." As Sarah walked to the newspaper office, she thought about her own statement.

The more she considered serving on the council, the more doubts she had. By the time she entered the office, she knew just how to word the short paragraph. If there was ever a time to irritate people, she thought, it was now.

"Charles, Phoebe gave me your message," Sarah said as she settled herself at her desk.

"I need your help with the council nominee statements. Emmett's the only one who wants to write his own. George, Jess, and Vernon asked me to handle theirs. Did you speak to Jack about his?"

"No, but I brought Mrs. Drake's. Phoebe is probably working on hers right now, and mine will be ready soon."

She laid several sheets of paper on top of the desk and started writing her profile in pencil. By the last line she had stated her interest in men helping with domestic chores, free love, spiritualism, and right of women to run for the congress, senate, and the office of president of the United States. She grinned. The women wouldn't even vote for her.

She penned the final copy and handed it to Charles, along with Ruby Jean's. "I thought I would interview Mr. Kenton this week for the business column. If it'll help you, I'll talk with Mr. Riggs and Mr. Young about their statements."

He looked up and smiled. "I was hoping you would." He tapped her profile. "What's this nonsense about?"

"Voters deserve to know the candidates and their interests. Isn't that what you had in mind?"

He shook his head. "If every politician were this honest, there would be few complaints."

"Oh, I nearly forgot. Gil said he wants his name removed from the list." She grinned to herself. "He isn't interested in local politics."

"I'm not surprised. He'll probably get the most votes." Charles brushed his hand through his hair. "I'll speak to him."

Sarah stuck the draft of her profile in her pocket. "I'll start on the interview now. Oh, may I see yours to get a better idea of what you want?"

He shuffled through several pages and handed one to her. "People read my opinions every week. There wasn't much more I could add."

As usual, he'd struck the right balance between his background and his views. "It's good," she said, handing it back to him. "I won't be back until I've spoken to everyone on my list."

He grinned. "Feel good to be back at work?"

"I never left."

She collected paper and pencils, and walked down the road to the Timbers Hotel. When she entered, Mr. Kenton was behind the desk speaking to a man wearing a yellow-and-brown checked suit. A drummer, she decided, noticing one large and one smaller case near his side, and wondered what he was selling.

After the man went up the stairs carrying his cases, Sarah walked up to the desk. "Hello, Mr. Kenton."

"Mrs. Hampton, how nice to see you again. How can I help you?"

"I'm here on behalf of the *Gazette*. We've been running interviews of local businessmen, and I would like to interview you for this week's paper. That is, if you would like to participate. It also serves as an advertisement." She was not disappointed with his reaction. He stood a little taller, smiled, and puffed out his narrow chest.

"Well, yes. Thank you, Mrs. Hampton. I would like that." He put a box in his office and locked the door. "Why don't we go into the library? It should be quiet."

She nodded and walked ahead of him into the Harrison Lending Library. As Mr. Kenton crossed the lobby, a lady stopped him. While he was detained, Sarah found the last two editions of the *Oregon Statesman* for Gil and put them under her paper.

"Now," Mr. Kenton said, taking a seat across the small table from Sarah. "What would you like to know?"

"You have made many changes since purchasing the hotel. It's so bright and the watercolor paintings are lovely."

"Mrs. Kenton will be glad to know you like them. I've told her she's a good painter," he said with a shrug, "but I'm her husband."

"Mrs. Kenton painted all of the watercolors in here and in the lobby?"

"Yes, she did," he said, his voice hearty and proud. "Soon there will be one in every room."

"I'm sure the people who stay here appreciate the changes you've made." She glanced at her notes. "What brought you and Mrs. Kenton to Gridley?"

"We heard stories about Oregon and wanted to see it for ourselves." He grinned and leaned back on the chair. "One night in Albany, I was in a saloon and struck up a conversation with this drummer. He'd just come from Gridley and was a talkative sort."

"It was lucky for us you went into that saloon that night." She scribbled notes and hoped she would be able to read them later. "How do you like living here?"

"It's beautiful and people are friendly."

"Do you have any special plans for the hotel?"

"Three rooms still need paint, and the roof's going to need work." He shrugged. "I'd just like to keep it clean."

She thanked him and left the hotel. It was midday, and Gil was probably worried about his stomach. She went by the house, packed a lunch, and returned to Gil's room.

She tapped on the door and opened it a crack. "Are you awake?"

"I'm alone. How am I supposed to get tired?" He used his feet to push himself up higher on the bed. She bustled inside, her cheeks rosy and her hair windblown. Oh, to catch her in his arms, he mused, and kiss her until they both were breathless, naked, and had made love until they'd fallen asleep in each other's arms.

She dropped the armload of papers on the foot of his bed. "You're looking good. I brought you something." She moved her papers aside and handed him the newspapers.

"Thanks." He glanced at the papers and looked back at her. After she left, he would have more time than he needed to read. "What did Charles want?"

"He's going to publish the candidates' statements in this week's paper, and I had the business interview." She served him soup with hot coffee.

"Potato soup." He tasted it and grinned. "Did you have time to make this?"

"Goodness, no," she said, watching the steam rise from the bowl. "Phoebe did." She set a bowl with a baked apple on the little table. "That, too." He ate the soup with such enthusiasm her own stomach protested. "Do you need anything else?"

"You aren't leaving yet. Sit down and have a cup of coffee." This was the Sarah he was used to seeing around town, distant, her mind seemingly a step ahead of her.

"I have to interview several of the candidates." She gazed into his eyes. She could stay a few minutes. She poured a cup of coffee and sat down. "I told Charles you weren't interested in running for the council."

"Good. That's settled."

She shrugged. "He wants to talk to you about it."

He traded the empty soup bowl for the baked apple. "What are the interviews for?"

"Charles is publishing short statements by each candidate for this week's paper. Hopefully, it will balance the ballot so it won't be just a popularity vote."

"Written yours?" He dug the spoon into the tender apple.

She nodded and sipped her coffee.

He noticed a mischievous glint in her eyes. "May I read it before the paper comes out?"

She met his gaze. "Why not? I would like your opinion." She pulled the paper out of her pocket and handed it to him.

He quickly read the paragraph and looked at her with one brow raised. "You really want to be president?"

She stared at him. "Did you *believe* that?"

"It's right there," he said, tapping the paper. "If you want admirers, the free love should get their attention."

She stared at him, appalled. "That's what you think I was trying to do?"

He lifted one shoulder. "Isn't this supposed to attract voters to you?"

"No! It's supposed to convince them how unsuitable I would be. . . ." She cocked her head, assessing him. "Can't you be serious?"

"Aren't I?"

"Lord, I hope not." She slumped back in the chair. "Sometimes you're impossible."

"You know better than that," he said softly.

"That's not what I meant. . . ." His leer and voice were positively indecent, she thought, fighting the tremor that slithered down her spine.

"Don't worry, Sarah." He chuckled. "Wouldn't it be easier to drop out of the election?"

"I nominated Phoebe, and after I encouraged the others to vote, how could I?"

"That would be ticklish." He reread her statement as he ate the last bite of apple. "You might take out the part about domestic chores. Don't you support Victoria Woodhull's principles?"

"Some of her ideas, certainly, but not all."

"When you wrote about her, you were criticized most."

She smiled. "I like that. Thank you." She really had misjudged him. "I'd better get busy." She refilled his cup, put the dirty dishes in the basket, and added wood to the stove. "Will you be okay?"

He reached for the newspapers she'd brought him. "I'll keep busy. See you this evening."

• • •

Phoebe sat by the fire in the parlor working on a plum-colored sweater for Clay. No one paid any attention to the click of the knitting sheaths. Cora struggled to embroider delicate stitches on her sampler, and Charles and Clay were playing chess.

Glancing at her husband, Phoebe smiled to herself. There had been times during the day when she'd wondered if night would ever come. "Charles, do you have all of the nominees' statements?"

Charles shook his head. "I'll see George and Jess in the morning." He moved his rook. "Not sure about Gil. I meant to speak to him this afternoon. Guess I'd better see him tomorrow, too."

"I thought Sarah would write his statement if he didn't want to."

"She said he wasn't interested in serving on the council." Charles kept a straight face when his son captured one of his knights.

"He's suffered a lot." Phoebe smoothed the back of the sweater. "It will be a while before he's able to attend any meetings."

"We'll see. He's quiet but smart, just who we need on the council." Charles stared at the chess pieces.

Phoebe wished with all her heart that Mr. Perry would recover quickly. If he didn't see so much of Sarah, if he stopped spending most of his waking hours with her, maybe he would realize that his interest in her grew out of the situation. For some reason Sarah's normally sound mind had forsaken her when she needed it most. Feeling guilty and responsible for his injury she let her guard down and temporarily forgot her sense of propriety. Phoebe finished off the neck and put her knitting in the basket.

"Cora, it's time for bed." She smiled. Her daughter was half asleep.

After Cora kissed her papa good night, Phoebe helped her dress for bed and tucked her under the covers with a kiss. Next, she sent Clay to his room, and sat on the hearth by Charles's chair. "It's been a busy day."

He nodded, without looking up from his book. "Tomorrow won't be any better. Not sure when I'll get home.''

"I'll bring your supper to the office." She saw him yawn, which of course caused her to do the same. "I think I'll go to bed. Are you ready?"

"Soon, my dear." He smiled and patted her arm. "I won't be long."

Rising, she bent over and kissed his cheek. "I'll be waiting," she whispered in his ear.

The image of the lovely Lorinda hadn't been far from her thoughts all day. She turned down bed covers, took off her dress and underclothes, and dabbed a little rose-scented toilet water on her neck. Wearing only her lacy shimmy, she brushed out her long hair, turned down the light until it barely broke the darkness, and slipped between the cold sheets.

Charles pushed the bedroom door wide open and stared at the bed. "Phoebe?"

She leaned on her elbow, a pose she hoped would intrigue him. "Come to bed, dear." She pulled back the covers on his side and patted the mattress.

He walked over to the dim light and turned up the wick. He gaped at her, then grinned. "What's all this?"

Part of her began to feel foolish, but she was determined to see her plan through. "Take off your clothes, Charles." His gaze seemed to pierce the silky-soft fabric of her shimmy. She pulled the satin ribbon holding the sides together in front and gave him a peek at her breast. Seeing him yank his clothes off gave her more satisfaction than she could have imagined.

Charles stripped down to his drawers and turned down the lamp wick.

"You won't need your drawers, Charles." Her heart was pounding in her throat.

Charles unbuttoned his drawers and paused. "Have you been tasting the brandy? In all our years together, you've never—"

"It's time, don't you think?" She smiled at him seductively. "Have a brandy, if you wish to."

"I won't need it." He dropped his drawers on the floor

and climbed in beside her. "Oh, my dearest," he murmured, pressing his mouth to the base of her throat.

If I wait any longer, she thought, I won't care. "Do you think Lorinda is beautiful?"

"What?" He mouthed her nipple through the thin fabric, his hand kneading the other breast.

"Lorinda. 'The lovely Lorinda.' Do you think she's beautiful?"

He rested his forehead against her breast, gasping for air. "Why are you asking me? *Now?*"

"I've seen her hanging in the saloon. I just wondered why you never mentioned her to me."

He lifted his head and stared at her. "*You* are the most beautiful woman I have ever seen, but I sure as hell don't want your picture in any saloon."

"Thank you." She slipped her arms around his neck. "I needed to hear you say that." She skimmed her hand over his hip. "Is Lorinda really her name?"

He groaned. "How the devil should I know?"

She grinned.

"Enough about damn Lorinda."

She parted her lips as he pressed his head down to hers. She was quite satisfied with his response.

"Oh, God, Phoebe, I feel eighteen again. . . ." He hastily pulled off her shimmy and began showering her naked body with kisses.

She had always liked making love to him but this time it was different, even better than in the early days of their marriage. He was eager, forceful, and she relished his nibbling, taunting caresses until she thought she might go mad. "Please . . . I need to feel your weight on me, inside. . . ."

He wrapped his arms around her and rolled to his back, with her on top. "Tonight, I want to feel you on top of me."

"Oh, do you think—" Suddenly he filled her. In one glorious instant all of her sensitivity was centered where their bodies joined. She gasped, then mewed as ripples of pleasure washed over her. Then his hands were on her waist, guiding her.

"Yes, oh yes. . . ." She braced her hands near his shoulders and followed the rhythm of her body.

"Not now," he mumbled. "God, no. . . ."

She spent the last of her energy in one frantic, fulfilling burst and collapsed on him. When she caught her breath, she pressed kisses on his shoulder. "No wonder you like being on top."

"You won't hear any complaints from me if you want to take turns." He brushed her hair back. "I love you more than life, Phoebe dear."

Sarah hurried back to the house to make breakfast. This morning Gil wasn't the only one who was hungry. The first thing she heard when she entered was whistling. Charles whistling? She trod lightly as she approached the kitchen and peered inside. He was at the stove. Cooking? What on earth?

She stepped back and went down the hall to his bedroom and tapped on the door. It drifted open. "Phoebe?"

"What're you doing here?" Phoebe said, tying the sash on her wrapper.

"I still live here. Thought I'd make breakfast, but Charles beat me to it." Sarah grinned, almost smirking. "Did you sleep well?" Phoebe's hair was still in disarray and now she was blushing.

"Yes, indeed." Phoebe caught a glimpse of herself in the small mirror and grabbed her hairbrush.

"Good for you." As she watched Phoebe, Sarah wondered if she had ever glowed the way Phoebe did now. Gil would have that effect on a woman, Sarah thought.

Phoebe finished brushing her hair and stepped into the hall. "I think I'll help Charles."

Sarah grinned and followed her into the kitchen. "Where are Clay and Cora?"

"On their way to school." Charles handed Phoebe a cup of tea and Sarah, coffee. "Hotcakes sound okay?"

"Mm, yes," Sarah said, wondering what to fix for Gil.

"I'll scramble eggs with bacon." Phoebe set a skillet on the stovetop and kissed Charles's cheek as she passed him.

"Sarah, did you tell Gil I'd be by to see him?"

"Yes, but he said it wouldn't do any good. His mind's set." Sarah filled a bowl with applesauce for Gil. "What are people saying about the election?"

Charles looked over his shoulder at Sarah. "Some are saying that women running for the council's a joke. Don't expect many votes."

"As long as whoever counts the ballots is fair, we won't complain." Phoebe turned the sizzling bacon.

"Charles, I don't remember choosing the committee in charge of counting the votes." Sarah looked from him to Phoebe. "Do you?"

"No, I don't."

Phoebe blended the eggs in a bowl. "There are plenty of people who aren't candidates. How many do we need?"

"Well, I could recommend three men—put it on the front page and see what the reaction is." He chuckled. "Of course, that's probably playing fast and loose with the legalities of the election process."

"What about Mr. Grebby?" Phoebe asked. "We trust him with our money."

Charles smiled at her. "Good choice. Ben Layton's another good man."

"I'd suggest Aunt Lucy, but she doesn't live in town." Sarah chuckled. "Alice Seaton is good with figures. There should be at least one woman on that committee."

Phoebe nodded. "I agree."

Charles beamed at Phoebe as if he didn't want to deny her anything. "Okay with me."

Gil hardly noticed the plate of food Sarah was setting in front of him; he clasped her hand. "You look like you're not planning on staying."

His thumb stroked the inside of her wrist, and she found it difficult to think. "There's . . . still a lot of work to do. . . . The mail comes in. . . . Charles prints on Fridays. . . ."

"You get a lot of mail?" he asked softly.

"No, not a lot. Sometimes a reader writes." *And when he stops writing,* she added to herself, *I have no idea why.*

"You'll be working all day, then." He traced the length of her fingers, one by one.

"Y-es. . . ." She felt mesmerized by his tantalizing touch.

"Come here," he said, gently tugging her down to his level, and captured her mouth for his tender invasion.

It was all she could do not to curl up with him in bed. His lips and tongue were even more persuasive than his voice.

He kissed the end of her nose and smiled. "So you won't forget me."

"I doubt you've ever suffered with that particular problem," she said, and stood up. "Has anyone ever told you you're a silver-tongued devil?"

"Not lately," he said, laughing.

"I'll see you later." She put on her cloak and opened the door.

"Sarah, don't be afraid of your feelings. You can't keep running away."

She gave him a puzzled look and left.

Long after Gil had finished eating, there was a rap on his door and Charles came in. "Sarah said you'd be by. Have a seat."

"What's this about you not wanting your name on the ballot?" Charles turned the chair around and sat down.

"Can you honestly see me on that council? I'd rather keep a pistol handy." Gil shifted his position. "How's the election coming along?"

"Hard to tell. Too bad we didn't vote Wednesday night when everyone was at the meeting. Maybe the articles in the paper will bring them back to town on election day."

"Everyone likes a show. They'll come to see what's going on."

Charles nodded. "Hope it doesn't turn into a circus."

"Where're you holding it?"

"Depends on the weather. If it's not raining outside. Otherwise, we may end up in the livery." Charles leaned forward, resting his arms on his knees. "Withdrawing from the race will be a problem. I've already printed the ballots."

Gil shook his head. "Bring them to me. I'll cross out my name."

"I know you don't want this made common knowledge, but this is *your* town. You've put too much into it to turn your back now. This is still just between us. I'm not going to publish a story about how you own the town. Hell, if I was going to do that, I'd have done it when I first found out."

Gil stared at Charles. "Thanks."

"Let the people decide who they want. You're only one of eleven. You may not win." Charles grinned and stood up.

"I won't write any statement for your paper."

"Don't have to. Sarah or I can do it for you."

"No. No statement."

Charles shrugged. "Whatever you say." He glanced at the empty cup on the small table. "Want more coffee before I go?"

"Yeah, I would appreciate that."

18

$\mathcal{P}$hoebe went by Seaton's and picked up the mail. She rifled through it on her way down the boardwalk to the *Gazette* office. There were letters but none from the Poet—again. She went inside and felt relieved when she didn't see Sarah.

As Charles walked over to his desk, he bumped into Phoebe. "Oh, sorry. I didn't hear you come in."

She stood on tiptoe and kissed his cheek. "If I hadn't stood in your way, you still wouldn't know I was here." She started to lay his mail on his desk but paused. "You'll never find it," she said, staring at the mass of papers covering his desktop.

"What?"

"Nothing," she said with a smirk. She searched through the supplies and finally found a small wooden box. She dropped the mail in it, set it on his desk, and propped up in it a tall piece of stiff paper with the word *mail* written on it. That may help him to find it, she decided.

She walked over to the worktable, where stacks of papers covered the surface. "How are you doing?"

"I'm ready to trade places with that juggler we saw last spring." He ran his hand through his hair and sighed.

"Yes, dear, of course you are." Holding her hands behind her back, to resist the urge to straighten the mess, she sauntered the length of the table. "This will be a big issue."

"Mm-hm."

Sarah dashed into the office. "I'll have the last interview ready in ten minutes. Sorry it's taken so long." She dropped her papers on the desk and saw Phoebe. "Did the mail come already?"

"Two letters came for you, there under your papers." Phoebe went over to their desk. "The Poet didn't write. I'm sorry."

"He didn't? Well, I guess I misunderstood his intentions." Sarah dropped down on the chair. If he wasn't interested, why had he used that particular quote in his last letter? Maybe it was one of his favorite lines, nothing more.

Phoebe put her hand on Sarah's arm. "Are you all right?"

"Was I that wrong about him?" If I was, Sarah thought, can I trust my judgment with another man? With Gil?

"You saved his letters, didn't you?"

"Yes."

"Want to reread them? When the dust settles around here."

Sarah nodded. "Thanks. We'll do that."

She slid the letters out from under her notes. Both had been postmarked in Oregon. She opened the one posted in Salem from a Mr. Jenkins and read. "Charles, I think you'll like this man's comments about free love."

"Is he for or against it?"

"He wants to call on me and also to give him names of other women who also practice free love."

Charles eyed her. "I warned you."

"Men," Phoebe said. "What about the other one?"

"This's from Sally Timmons in Albany," Sarah said, taking out the letter. " 'You are surely the Devil's spawn. Your vile interests are a sin against God. Repent and pray for His mercy.' "

With a quick glance at her husband, Phoebe put her hand

on Sarah's shoulder. "I guess you were bound to hear from crackpots. Don't let these bother you."

"Miz Timmons should stick to reading her Bible." Sarah shrugged. "It was worth a try, but I have work to do."

Phoebe knew the moment Sarah lost herself in her work, and couldn't blame her. The Poet was no gentleman after all. "See you later."

"Okay." Sarah reached for a sheet of paper and began writing up Mr. Drake's statement. When she finished she handed it to Charles. "I'll do the Miss Lucy column now."

"Wait. I'm not sure there'll be room for it this week."

"That's fine." She watched him mentally laying out the paper. "Want me to start the back page?" It was a relief not to have to write the column right then. She didn't know if she could summon any enthusiasm for it.

Saturday morning Sarah felt the light on her eyes and pulled the covers over her face. By the time she brought Gil's and her supper back last night, it was almost eight o'clock and they had talked until midnight. She drifted back to sleep. The next time she roused, she heard what sounded like Gil relieving himself.

Her eyes popped open. She hadn't heard Jack come in the room. She waited and listened. It sounded as if Gil was done. The room was silent. She peered out from under the covers. Jack wasn't there, but Gil was sitting up. His back was to her, and he was propping himself up on the side of the bed!

She threw the covers back and jumped off the pallet. "How long have you been sitting up?"

"A couple of minutes." As he glanced over his shoulder, he hastily buttoned his drawers. "Good morning. Sorry I woke you."

"You didn't." She walked over to the bed. "You haven't answered my question. When did you start sitting up on the side of the bed?"

"Been trying the last two days, but this's the first time I didn't get dizzy."

"That's . . . wonderful." No more reasons. No more ex-

cuses. She would move her things back home this morning.
"How's your side?"

"Sore. Still hurts to raise my arm or put much pressure
on it." He put his hand on the mattress and pressed. Pain
spread outward like ripples on a pond, and he grimaced.

"Don't!" She dashed around the bed to his side. "Don't
you undo all we've accomplished. Give yourself time."

He nodded as the pain began to recede. "If you say so."

"Have you tried to stand?"

He braced himself with his good arm. "Not yet."

"I'd better check your bandage."

He pulled up the side of his shirt and waited to feel her
fingers on his tender side.

She inched the strips of cloth down. "It looks good."
She pulled the bandage back in place and smoothed her
hand over his side.

"You're a good doctor."

"You're getting dizzy again. You'd better lie down."

"I think you're right." He eased himself down to the
pillow. "Do you mind? My legs. When I try to raise the
right one it pulls on my side."

She moved his legs for him. "I'll brew some coffee for
you." Once she put the coffeepot on the woodstove, she
went down the hall to Jack's room and knocked. "Jack,
it's just me, Sarah."

Jack pulled the door open. "What's wrong?"

"Nothing. Has Gil asked you to move his bed?"

He scratched his head. "Don't think so."

"Sometime today, could you get one of the men to help
you move his bed by the side window? He can sit up now
and it would be nice if he could see the road and the river."

"Sure thing."

"Thank you." She returned to Gil's room and began
folding the covers on her pallet.

"What're you doing?"

"Straightening up."

"After almost two weeks, you decide to make up your
bed?" He glared at her. "You been talking to Miss Lucy?"

"If I had, you probably would've been sharing your

room with Jack the last week.'' She stacked the folded covers near the door.

''What're you saying?''

''You can sit up and see to your personal needs. You don't require much care anymore, but don't worry. You won't go hungry.'' She forced a smile, hoping he wouldn't notice her lack of enthusiasm. ''I'll bring your meals each day until you can walk.''

''I'm not that steady. What if I fall?'' Damn! He knew it wouldn't last forever, but another week would have been nice.

''I'll find a bell for you to ring.'' When the coffee was ready, she poured him a cup.

''You'll hear it?'' He raised one brow. ''*Wherever* you are?''

''Not unless you open your window, and I happen to be walking down the road.''

''Some doctor you are,'' he grumbled halfheartedly.

She grinned, in spite of herself. ''I think you'll survive.''

''If I don't, you can rest easy knowing you did your best.''

''That's generous of you. I'll try to remember.'' She surveyed the room and picked up the pile of bedding. ''You have everything you need. I'll see you later.''

''Not *everything*,'' he said, and moved as if to go after her. ''Damn it!''

''What?!'' She dropped the bedding and hurried to his side. ''You didn't—''

He wound his arm around her waist and pulled her down to the bed. ''If I could . . .'' He grinned and slid one hand to the back of her neck. ''Can you be bribed? No one knows but you and me. I won't tell.''

His touch had the power to fog her mind and cause her to question her own decisions, the way he was at that moment. ''You aren't going to make this easy, are you?''

''I'm trying my damnedest not to.'' Slowly, he drew her closer until his mouth captured hers. God, she was sweet. And exciting. She trembled each time they kissed and with each caress her passion increased his vigor.

Shivers of desire flowed through her belly and her breasts longed to be crushed against his hard chest. His intimate caress on her mouth aroused a hunger for him that threatened her better judgment. She pulled back and gazed into his eyes, her heart pounding as her breath came in short gasps. "You know I can't stay here any longer."

He could have lost himself in her passion-dazed eyes. He eased her head to his shoulder and ran his fingers through her hair. "I don't have to like it."

"Neither do I."

When Phoebe saw Sarah coming through the door loaded down with bedding, she couldn't believe her eyes. "You're moving back?"

Sarah peeked around the covers. "You didn't think I would?" She walked back to her room.

Phoebe hurried after her. "He can take care of himself?"

"He can sit on the side of the bed." Sarah dumped the covers on top of her bed.

"What's wrong? Aren't you glad he's doing better?"

Sarah grabbed her hairbrush and began swiping at her hair. "Why wouldn't I be?"

"Maybe because you remind me of Mama when Will left home."

"She was afraid of losing your brother in the war," Sarah said, putting down the brush. "I'm fine. Is Charles working today?"

"He's taking Clay and Cora with him when he delivers the paper to the farms. Do you have any plans?"

"I haven't thought about it. Gil's waiting for breakfast, and I need to stop by Seaton's." Sarah glanced around her room. "Guess I'd better do some laundry, too."

Phoebe grinned. "Welcome home."

"Thanks. It'll feel good to sleep in a bed tonight." But it's going to be awfully quiet, Sarah thought, and lonely.

"I'll go with you. If the rain holds off, we can stretch our legs a bit."

•   •   •

Sarah took Gil three meals every day and stayed to talk with him more often than not. She knew she couldn't continue spending all day and evening with him, and decided to keep so busy she wouldn't have time to think about him so much. Between mealtimes, she cleaned and reorganized her bedroom and polished and waxed everything in the house.

The activities kept her body occupied, but not her mind. She'd look over her shoulder, expecting to see him, but he wasn't there. She'd hear him tease her about cleaning house, and once she thought he had touched her sleeve.

She was not staying in his room, but she hadn't left him.

Monday she decided to iron, and put the irons on the stovetop to heat. When she had finished she would rent a buggy and go for a long ride. Maybe the fresh air would help to sort out her feelings for Gil, and about Mr. Brown.

Phoebe went into the kitchen for another cup of tea. "Why are you ironing now?"

"Because it needs to be done."

"Have you forgotten about the lunch at Elsie's? We said we'd be there early to help her."

Sarah turned to her. "It's Monday? Already?"

"Mm. Follows Sunday every week." Phoebe blew on her tea. "I thought we'd leave in a little while, but I can go ahead, if you'd like."

"No. It won't take long to press the petticoats and a pair of drawers."

"Have you arranged for Mr. Young or someone else to take lunch to Mr. Perry?"

"Oh—no."

"I'll put something together for him."

Sarah set up the ironing board Charles had fashioned for Phoebe. It didn't take her long to finish; she stepped into the still-warm undergarments and slipped the bronze poplin dress over her head. She brushed her hair and found Phoebe sitting at the kitchen worktable. "I'm sorry I forgot."

"You've been running yourself ragged since you moved back home. Guess it isn't surprising you forgot what day it is." Phoebe stood up and set her cup in the dry sink.

Sarah peeked under the cloth covering Gil's tray. "Looks good. He's already spoiled with your cooking." She smiled and picked up the tray.

Phoebe followed her through the house. "Where did he eat before?"

"I didn't ask. He must've cooked on the woodstove." When they reached the road, Sarah paused. "I'll take this to Gil and meet you at Elsie's."

Phoebe nodded and walked down the road.

Sarah hurried around to the back of the saloon and up the stairs. She knocked on Gil's door and eased the door open. "Are you awake?" she asked softly.

"No," he growled, "go away." He watched the door and waited for her to burst inside.

"Oh," she said, and paused outside, frowning. "You're not alone." Who could be visiting him that he didn't want her to see?

"What the devil do you think I'm doing? Entertaining soiled doves in here?"

She cocked her head, listening. "I've always wanted to meet one," she said, shoving open the door.

He moved to sit on the side of the bed and said, "Sorry to disappoint you."

"Maybe next time she'll stay longer."

"I'll see what I can do."

She set the tray on his lap and almost gave in to the temptation to sit beside him. "I'm still not used to how different your room looks with your bed under the window." He could just reach the coffeepot on the woodstove, and she made sure everything else was within his reach.

"You haven't spent much time here lately." He clasped her hand. "Been busy writing?"

"Taking care of things I've neglected."

He pointed to the *Gazette*. "Has Charles heard from Miss Lucy? She didn't have an article in this paper. Hope she's not ill."

"I would imagine her letter was held up somewhere along the way." As his thumb lightly massaged the inside of her wrist, she felt the flutter of expectation wending through her breasts and belly.

He noticed her glance at the door. "You look ready to run off."

She stared at their joined hands, and then gazed at him. "I'm meeting Phoebe and Ruby Jean at Elsie's for lunch."

He grinned at her as he continued to graze the tender skin on her wrist. "Map out your strategy?"

"That's the idea." She gave his hand a little squeeze and slipped hers free. "I'll put on a pot of coffee and come back after lunch for the dishes."

"I'll be here."

She prepared the coffeepot and set it on the stove, then she hesitated. One step forward would bring her close enough to caress him, hold him, kiss him, but it was that that kept her rooted to the plank floor out of his reach. It was almost as natural to kiss him as smile at him. That frightened her. "See you in a little while."

When Phoebe saw Sarah hurry through Elsie's front door, she sighed. Must be a record, she decided. Sarah always lingered with Mr. Perry while he ate. Maybe she was coming to her senses. "You're just in time."

"You look surprised," Sarah said, and smiled at Ruby Jean.

"I'm glad you could come," Ruby Jean said. "I thought maybe you had changed your mind, what with having to take care of Mr. Perry and your work at the newspaper."

"No, of course not." Sarah passed her and went to the kitchen. "Sorry I'm late. Elsie, what can I do to help?"

"Hello." Elsie picked up the breadbasket. "Set this on the table and have a seat. I'll be right there."

Sarah took a seat at the table with the other ladies. Over lunch they talked about the new yard goods at Seaton's, family receipts for Thanksgiving dishes, and Sarah was asked about Gil's condition. They cleared the table, and Elsie served spice cake.

"That smells delicious," Ruby Jean said, staring at the cake.

"It's still a bit warm. That's why the frosting isn't as nice as I'd like." Elsie sliced the cake and passed out the pieces.

Phoebe glanced around the table. "Does anyone have an idea how we can get the ladies out to vote?"

Ruby Jean looked at the others. "Don't most of the farmers' wives come to town with their husbands to shop?"

"Usually," Phoebe agreed.

Sarah raised her fork and paused. "The election will be held in the middle of the month. Many won't come to town that week."

"Then we'll have to convince them to come in to vote."

Elsie nodded at Phoebe. "Sarah, will you write an article for the women? I think it may make the difference. The men won't encourage them."

"I'll start on it tonight."

Phoebe scooped the last bite of cake onto her fork. "We could make sure there are at least two women available to hold babies, so the ladies can vote."

"Yes," Elsie said, "good thinking."

"What about refreshments?" Ruby Jean asked. "Wouldn't it be nice to have coffee and cake or cookies?"

Sarah glanced at Phoebe. "It's an idea . . . but it isn't really a social. We don't want the men thinking we're turning the election into a tea party."

"I didn't think about that."

By the time the lunch ended, all of the women were excited about the upcoming election. As Sarah and Phoebe walked home, Sarah remembered she was supposed to see Gil. "I have a stop to make. I'll see you at the house."

"Tell Mr. Perry hello for me." Phoebe turned the corner and hoped Sarah wouldn't forget to return home.

Gil shook his head at Jack. "What do you think I can do about it? Sarah isn't going to change the way she writes. Not for me—I wouldn't ask her to—and especially not because a handful of men laugh at her opinions."

"Damn it all, I've seen the way ya look at her. Don't ya care what's bein' said about her?"

"Hell, *I've* called her 'that Hampton woman.' " Though that had been before he really knew her, Gil thought. "That's nothing new or all that insulting."

"Don't it depend on how it's said?"

"She'd probably laugh if she heard them. Don't worry about it, Jack." If he told Jack that she'd intentionally written her statement to have that effect on people, Gil knew word would spread faster than fire. Jack meant well, but he had trouble keeping confidences.

"Jist thought ya'd want to know."

"How's Miss Layton?"

Jack grinned. "Fine. Jist fine."

"I'm surprised Ben hasn't taken you aside. You're not the only single man in town."

"Been expectin' it myself." Jack laughed. "T'tell the truth, I nearly asked her the night of the dance."

"Good for you." Gil held out his hand and shook Jack's. "When're you going to start on the house?"

"What house?"

"The one you and the future Mrs. Young will share."

"S'ppose I'd better, huh?"

Gil chuckled. "If you expect her to say yes."

Jack grinned. "Help me, 'n' I'll help you."

"I don't need a house," Gil said, making it clear he didn't want to discuss it. "Still have my shack. If this town keeps growing, I'll move back up there."

Jack shrugged. "Well, better get back behind the bar. Need anythin'?"

"I'm fine."

"If ya do, jist pull that string."

"I will." Gil looked at the twine strung from the windowsill to the top of the stairs leading to the saloon, where it was connected to one of the bells Sarah had brought him. He could see out through the window, and he could call for help. What he couldn't do was move around his room, get to his books, or post a letter without help.

He grabbed his right trouser leg with his strong hand, raised his leg to the bed, and stretched out. From the moment Sarah had seen him sitting up, she'd begun pulling back from him. Maybe she was right. He sure as hell wasn't ready to build a house and picket fence, but he didn't want to go back to waving to her as she walked down the road, either.

Tuesday morning Sarah went to the *Gazette* office anxious to continue the campaign for the women.

Charles smiled at her. "I wondered when you would get tired of cleaning."

She grinned and sat at her desk. "I think Phoebe was ready to kick me out."

"She's not used to you taking over her chores." He shuffled a few papers on his desk. "I'll need both articles from you this week. We'll have to keep the election on everyone's minds."

"I've been thinking about doing just that."

He eyed her. "That sounds ominous."

"Don't worry. I'm not out to shock the women or men of Gridley, simply to get everyone to vote."

He shook his head. "I just wish your writing would read the way you describe it."

"I always try to put down my thoughts accurately. Alas, I sometimes fall short of my expectations." She grinned at him. "Yours, too, evidently."

When she opened the drawer to take out fresh paper, she saw the letters from the Poet. Maybe he had only needed a diversion for a short time. She stuffed the envelopes in her skirt pocket and grabbed her pencil. The devil with him, for now.

She filled two pages with the first draft of her article and quoted Abigail Dunaways, the editor of the *New Northwest*. Mrs. Dunaways's editorial and fictional stories emphasized the inequities between the sexes in the laws. If only, Sarah reflected, I had thought about inviting her to speak here, but now there wasn't time to arrange it.

Next Sarah checked her list of topics for the Miss Lucy column. Dinner parties and evening visits. However, there would be no cloaked message for the Poet. She finished writing the column and straightened the papers on the desk.

Charles looked up. "Will you be back this afternoon?"
"Not unless you need me."

As she stepped onto the boardwalk, she heard a bell and glanced at the side window over the saloon. It rang again, and she felt as if his finger had slid down her spine. Had Gil been waiting to see her? She smiled and waved to him. On the way back to the house, she looked at her correspondence from Mr. Brown. She had to settle her confused feelings.

When she arrived home, she smelled stew cooking and went to the kitchen. "Phoebe, would you like to take a ride with me to Fenton's Crossing on Saturday?"

19

$\mathscr{S}$arah surveyed the gentle slope of the meadow and the rich forest that seemed to cover so much of Oregon. "Are you sure you don't want me to drive? You still look a bit peaked." Phoebe hadn't been feeling very well before they'd set out that morning.

"You can have the reins on the way back. Fenton's Crossing's just ahead, or should be, according to the directions." Phoebe glanced at the newspaper on the seat between them. "Are you really going to use that story you made up for Mr. Brown, that is, if we manage to locate him?"

"He should be flattered we drove all the way over here to deliver his copy of the *Gazette*."

"He hasn't written in the last two weeks, or is it three? Whatever, I hate to see you chasing after the man."

Sarah grinned at her. "Aren't you the least bit curious? I am, and so I can put him out of my mind, I need to see him." *And I need to prove to myself that I am not fickle.*

The Poet's letters had been flattering and intriguing. She had begun to feel her heart softening and believed she was falling in love with him—and then she'd found herself enthralled with Gil. They argued, laughed, and even danced well together, and when he kissed her she felt beautiful, cherished, and desirable.

"His name isn't on the mailing list. If I were him, I'd be suspicious of anyone hand-delivering a newspaper I don't have a subscription to."

"We'll cajole him. Remember how we distracted Henry Finch so Odette could slip outside with Mr. Carey?"

"We were seventeen and foolish. If we hadn't helped her, she might not have had to marry so suddenly." As they came to a bend in the road, Phoebe pulled in on the reins and slowed the pair of horses. "There's the ferry, up ahead."

"The town's larger than Gridley."

"It's probably older, too." Phoebe stopped at the landing and the ferryman waved her forward.

When they reached the opposite bank, Sarah handed the ferryman the twenty-five-cent crossing charge. A few minutes later they were in the center of town. "Why don't you pull over here? The post office is in that dry goods store."

Phoebe guided the horses to the side of the road. "What are you going to do?"

"I considered claiming to be The Poet's second cousin," Sarah said, watching a bearded man coming toward them on the boardwalk. "But that could get complicated." The man went into the dry goods store.

"And embarrassing. His name's Mr. Brown." Phoebe snickered. "What if he's in there and overhears you?"

"I'll be careful," Sarah agreed, "and stick to the truth, as much as possible." She climbed down from the wagon. "Aren't you coming in with me?"

"There's a general store on the other side of the bank. I'll see what I can find out there." Phoebe set the brake and wrapped the reins around it.

Sarah looked up and down the road. "There's a restaurant next to the hotel. Why don't we meet there in half an hour?"

"Have you forgotten we packed a lunch?"

"I'll treat you to a cup of tea. We can stop and eat on the way back."

Phoebe smiled. "I'll meet you there. Good luck."

"You, too." Sarah went into the dry goods store and glanced around. The man she had seen outside was looking at axes and shovels.

She waited until the postal clerk was not busy and stepped up to the counter. "Excuse me," she said, hoping her smile appeared natural to the woman and not as contrived as it felt. "I've been corresponding with Mr. Brown and wanted to surprise him. Have you seen him today?" She glanced at where the bearded man had been standing, but he wasn't there.

"Mr. Brown . . . ?" The clerk stared off into space. "You must mean Teddy Brown. I haven't seen him lately, I'm sorry."

"Oh, dear. I've come such a long way, and I don't know when I'll be able to return." Sarah placed both her hands flat on the counter. "Does he live nearby? I would be so grateful for any help you could give me."

"Last I heard, he was living in the woods across the river, but I couldn't swear to it." The woman shrugged.

"Thank you so much." Sarah beamed at her and fairly danced outside. She looked at a couple of window displays and waited in front of the restaurant for Phoebe, too anxious to sit still.

Phoebe was staring at the tobacco, when the clerk came over to her.

"Can I get something for you, ma'am?"

"Tobacco. For his pipe." She smiled at the clerk and tried to gain his sympathy. "My husband wanted to try the brand his friend uses, but I don't remember the name." She cast a pleading look at him. "It's Mr. Brown's brand. I believe the only one he uses. Does he shop here?"

"Brown? Common enough name, but I don't know him."

"Oh, dear, then maybe I should wait. Thank you."

She left the dry goods store and walked down the boardwalk. After she used the same approach in two more stores, she went to the restaurant. Sarah was pacing up and down out front, grinning so hard it looked painful. "Did you find him?"

Sarah clasped Phoebe's hands. "Yes, well, almost. He may live in the woods we passed before the ferry crossing."

"That's wonderful! Do you want to ride out to his house?"

"Let's have tea first. I think it would have been easier to simply run into him. Guess I'm a little anxious." Sarah opened the door to the restaurant, and they entered.

A few minutes later, Sarah ran a finger around the rim of the cup, held it, and even raised it near her mouth, but she never tasted her drink. "I forgot to ask what you learned."

"I didn't talk to anyone who claimed to know him. Who told you where he lives?"

"The post office clerk."

"She should know." Phoebe finished her tea. "We might as well leave, since you don't want your tea."

Sarah handled the reins as they rode out of town and crossed the river on the ferry. She watched closely along her side of the road. "Do you see a trail leading into the woods?"

"Not yet, but shouldn't you slow down?"

Sarah eased back on the reins. "Has Mr. Pratt asked you about meeting to choose the books to purchase for the library?"

"No—I had forgotten about it, what with the bank robbery and all."

"I did, too, and I even interviewed Mr. Kenton in the library. Maybe we can meet at the school one day next week."

"I'll tell Charles. Do you want to speak to Mr. Pratt?"

"I will see him Monday after school."

Phoebe spotted a scorched tree stump. "Look at that. Are those ruts leading off the road?"

"We might as well try it." Sarah pulled on the rein and

turned the team to follow the rough trail into the forest.

The farther they traveled into the woods, the more uneasy Phoebe became. "I don't think this is right. I don't see the ruts now."

"Maybe he rides horseback." Sarah smiled. She liked that image.

"Or maybe we'll drive around in here until we admit we're lost," Phoebe said, eyeing her.

Sarah shivered. "We'd never hear the end of that."

"*If* someone found us."

When they turned around, Sarah noticed a trampled patch of undergrowth and stopped. "There's a path, but we'll have to walk."

"Oh, Sarah. There's no one out here."

"Wait here. I'll just look beyond that big hemlock tree."

Sarah climbed down to the damp ground, shook out her skirt, grabbed the copy of the *Gazette*, and took off down the path. She hadn't gone far when dried berry vines snagged her skirt. Determined to find the Poet, she bunched her skirt with one hand and continued.

When she passed the hemlock, she saw an old, ramshackle cabin with a spindly column of smoke rising from the chimney. "Lord, please surprise me," she whispered, marching to the door. She knocked and stepped back.

After what seemed like an hour, she turned to leave. Just then she heard a creaking sound. Her heart pounded and her palms were suddenly damp as she looked back. The door was open partway.

"Mr. Brown?" she said, slowly approaching the shack. "Oh, merciful heaven," she muttered, staring up at a giant of a man who appeared old enough to her grandfather.

"Yeah. What ya lookin' fer, missy?"

She was momentarily speechless. The story she had improvised seemed foolish now. "Are you familiar with Gridley?"

"What's that?"

"I'm sorry I bothered you. Evidently, I made a mistake with the directions." She noticed him staring at the newspaper in her hand. "Would you like this?" she asked, holding the paper out to him.

"Yessum, sure would." He snatched the paper from her, darted his hand back inside, and closed the door.

As she hurried back to the wagon, she muttered, "That was not the kind of surprise I had in mind." Her heart still beat like a drum roll.

Phoebe heard Sarah running through the underbrush and climbed down from the wagon. "What's wrong?!"

When Sarah marched into the clearing, Phoebe ran up and hugged her. "Phoebe, what happened?"

Phoebe stepped back, studying Sarah carefully. "With me? I heard you running, as if—I thought he'd attacked you."

"No. Wrong Mr. Brown. This one must be well over sixty and about seven feet tall. He was more interested in the newspaper than in me, thank goodness." Sarah smiled at her. "Let's go home."

Phoebe watched the undergrowth, thick enough to conceal a man and his horse, as they retraced the track back to the road. "Maybe your Mr. Brown is that man's son."

"He was frightened, almost as if he wasn't used to seeing people. If the Poet is his son and neglects his father that way, I don't want to know him." Sarah turned onto the road. Could she have been so wrong about the Poet? He's an educated men, she thought, but that did not necessarily reflect on his character.

Now she was more confused than when she'd ridden in to Fenton's Crossing.

Gil watched Sarah dish fried chicken, mashed potatoes, and green beans onto a plate. Looked like she had enough to feed several people. Her dark green skirt swayed gently, giving him a glimpse of ankle. "Are you going to a party this evening?"

She glanced over her shoulder at him. "I thought I'd keep you company tonight, unless you have other plans."

"I like yours just fine."

She grinned. "I hope you're hungry." She cleaned off

the little table and moved it to the side of his bed. "I felt like cooking."

"Smells wonderful. Almost as good as you look," he said, eyeing her playfully. "Too bad I'm not up to dancing yet."

Basking in the warmth of his compliment, she set her plate across from his. "Have your men been up to visit you yet?" His color was better and his eyes were bright. Lord, he was handsome, even when he wasn't flashing his roguish grin.

He swallowed a bite of fluffy potatoes. "A steady stream."

"You were worried about them. Is everything all right?" She sat down on the chair, across from him.

"There was another fire. The men put it out before it reached the bunkhouse." He picked up the fried chicken leg and bit into it. There wasn't a damn thing he could do to track down whoever was plaguing his logging camp, not until he could at least stand the jostling of a wagon to get up there.

"That's good. Wouldn't your men notice a stranger prowling near the camp?"

"They've taken turns walking the perimeter, but whoever it is is clever or lucky." He stabbed green beans onto his fork. "Or crazy enough to be wily."

"That's a frightening thought. Who would want to burn down your camp? Half of the state is covered with trees, so it couldn't be for the logs."

"Makes no sense. My camp seems to be the only one being harassed."

"Is there any way I can help?"

He shook his head. "If I think of something, I'll let you know. Enough of this. How was your afternoon?"

"The weather was so nice, Phoebe and I took a ride, and came close to getting lost in a forest." She didn't see any reason to tell him what a fool she had made of herself.

"Didn't you stay on the road?"

"I thought I was on a trail." She grinned at him. "At least I followed our wagon tracks out."

He nodded. "Next time you want to wander through the woods, let me know. I'll be happy to take you."

"I would like that. Thank you." She smiled. I must look like a grinning idiot, she thought. I shouldn't have wasted my time searching for the Poet. He didn't want to be found anyway.

"Good. As soon as I can ride again I'll show you around the logging camp, if it hasn't been burned down." He winked at her and was rewarded with the laughter shining in her eyes. "Have you been up on Mount Hood?"

"Do any roads lead up there?" Still smiling, she gave up her pretense of eating and sipped her coffee.

"Not a road, but there's a trail. Do you ride?"

"I haven't been on a horse lately, but I think I can stay in a saddle."

"Sidesaddle?" He tried to picture her in a riding outfit, seated with her leg hooked around the horn, her full skirt covering her legs, and her hair fluttering in the wind. Somehow, she didn't fit that image. In her youth he figured she was more likely a hoyden.

"Astride." She felt his gaze on her and wondered if he felt the tension growing between them.

He nodded slowly. One of the most erotic images he knew was that of a woman mounted astride. "I think you'll like the view." He shifted on the mattress. "There's nothing quite like it."

When he grinned, a slow, unrestrained grin that curved his mouth, there was a glint in his eyes that was decidedly improper, and arousing. Her stomach felt as if she had suddenly slid across an ice-covered pond. "I made brown Betty for dessert," she said clearing their plates, their meal only partially eaten.

"How about sharing one helping with me?"

She smiled at him and nodded.

"Don't feed that to the pigs just yet. I may get hungry later."

She set his plate back on the table and put hers in the basket. The room was so quiet that she heard when he drew in a sharp breath. Her pulse quickened, and she hoped he

wouldn't notice her shaky hand as she dished out one serving of dessert and set it in front of him.

"Smells good. The whole meal was, and you're all
dressed up. Too bad we can't make this a special occasion."

"Celebrating your recovery?"

"Or standing? Come here, Sarah." He scooted toward
the end of the bed.

"Are you sure?"

"My ribs don't hurt. My side's just tender."

She stepped over to him. "What do you want me to do?"

"Stand next to me," he said, holding out his arm, "in
case I'm not too steady." That's something he'd never said
to a woman before.

She stood next to him. When he rose and wrapped his
arm around her, she put hers around his waist.

The room started spinning. He grabbed her shoulder with
his hand and closed his eyes. "Can't—"

She lowered him to the bed. "What's wrong?"

If not for her, he would have fallen. "Reeling. Guess
I'm not as ready as I thought." He held on to her and bent
his head as the room continued whirling around him.

"You're doing so well. You'll be on your feet soon."
Beads of sweat covered his forehead and he was breathing
hard, but his arm wasn't weak. He held her close, though
not exactly how she would like it.

The room finally righted itself, and he sat up. "I'll wait
a couple days before I try that again." He loosened his grip
on her, but not his hold. "Never had to use an excuse to
hold a woman in my arms."

"That doesn't surprise me," she said, losing herself in
his incredible gaze.

"Mm, lilacs." He skimmed one finger under her chin.
"They never smelled so sweet." He captured her mouth
with the hunger of a starving man. She quivered against
him and ignited a surge of longing akin to a lightning bolt,
but he was unable to satisfy her the way he had in his
dreams. Surely he must be paying for his youthful mischief.

She moaned and clung to him, hearing nothing but the

pounding of her heart. He took her breath away and awakened every desire she had ever felt or imagined. She held him close and pressed her breasts against his chest. His muscles tightened beneath her hands, and she drew his tongue into her mouth. She wanted to push him down onto the mattress, but a small part of her mind stopped her.

Leaving her swollen lips, he seared a path down the column of her neck as he unbuttoned the top of her dress. His lips grazed the smooth creamy flesh and his hand circled her full breast. He was reaching for the hem of her skirt, when Jack's voice intruded.

"Hey, Gil," Jack called out, "ya wanna come downstairs? Figured I'd carry ya if I have to."

"Not now. Just had supper." Gil grinned at Sarah. "Kinda wore me out."

"He almost walked in!" she whispered, fumbling with the buttons.

"Ya sure yer okay?" The latch clicked, and Jack started to open the door.

"Get the hell out, Jack!"

"Okay. See ya later, then."

Jack's footsteps receded, and Sarah sagged against Gil.

He smiled. "I'll put a lock on that door." He lifted her chin and gently caressed her lips.

His kiss was slow and reassuring. Smiling, she said, "You'd better rest, and I don't want Jack walking in on us."

"I thought you believed in free love." He kissed the side of her neck, his hand lightly tracing the length of her arm.

"I do, but . . . I don't want it discussed by everyone in town."

"Me either. I was teasing."

She kissed his chin. "I don't want to wear you out."

"That won't be a problem much longer." She was glowing, and so lovely. He brushed her hair back from her eyes and nibbled on her earlobe.

She rested her hand on his thigh to steady herself. "Ohh, that's not fair, Gil."

He covered her fingers and inched her hand upward. "Who's trying to be?"

"Please, my legs are already soft as butter, and I have to walk home." She raised his hand and rubbed her cheek over his knuckles. "I'll see you in the morning." She stood up on wobbly legs and put on her cloak.

"Sweet dreams, Sarah."

She grabbed the basket. "You, too." She darted out before he could change her mind. Lord, she wanted to stay with him. Free love. She had shared her views through her articles, but her belief had never been tested.

Until now.

She went down the back stairs and stopped at the well. Maybe if she didn't care for him so much it would be easy to make love with him. Her problem was that she had fallen in love with him, yet a small part of her clung to the memory of the Poet's letters and the feelings he had inspired.

She pressed her fingertips to her lips and trembled with the memory of Gil's caresses.

Phoebe and Sarah hurried out of the rain into the school. Three children were hanging around Mr. Pratt. Phoebe stepped over to the woodstove. "Charles should be here by now."

"Don't worry." Sarah turned her back to the heat. "He won't be too late. I left a note where he couldn't miss it."

"Good." Phoebe nodded. "He said he would ask Mr. Riggs to come, too."

"All right now, off with you," Mr. Pratt said to the children. "Don't forget to do your arithmetic. There will be a test tomorrow."

"Hello, Mrs. Abbott," he said, walking over to the woodstove. "Mrs. Hampton. I haven't seen you since the town meeting. I hope you are well."

"Fine, thank you. The children looked happy."

"Yes," Phoebe agreed. "They must like school to stay after class is out."

He shrugged and added two pieces of wood to the fire. "Some are slow to go home to chores. Please, sit down."

He walked to the desk and returned with paper and pencils. "I thought each of us could list books we would like to have in the library."

Sarah withdrew her list from her cloak pocket. "I brought mine."

Phoebe laid her list on one desktop and sat down. "I make lists for everything." She heard the door and looked back. Finally, Charles and Mr. Riggs.

"Hello, Emmett." Charles took the seat behind Phoebe.

Vernon Riggs pulled off his hat. "Sorry I'm late, folks."

"Hello, Charles, Mr. Riggs. I guess we can start now." Mr. Pratt handed paper and a pencil to each man.

Sarah had the feeling Mr. Pratt had forgotten that school was out for the day. "We raised eighteen dollars and forty cents to spend on books and, of course, the postal charges."

"That is a good beginning, Mrs. Hampton," Mr. Pratt said, smiling at her.

Charles cleared his throat. "One book every library should have is a dictionary." He looked at each of them. "I say the latest edition of Noah Webster's is a must."

"I agree," Mr. Pratt said, nodding.

Phoebe stared at her list. "I think *The Swiss Family Robinson* and *Andersen's Fairy Tales* would be interesting for the younger children."

Sarah began to write down each of the titles or authors being mentioned. "Why don't we each read our lists so I can make up one to work with?"

Mr. Pratt took his list from his desk drawer and sat down in front of Sarah. "Mrs. Hampton, why don't you start?"

"All right. Tennyson's *Poetical Works,* Louisa May Alcott's *Little Women, Twenty Thousand Leagues Under the Sea,* and . . . I guess that's enough from me." Sarah looked at Phoebe.

Phoebe smiled at Sarah. "I like *The House of Seven Gables,* Nathaniel Hawthorne."

Charles rubbed his chin. "*Silas Marner,* George Eliot. Vernon, what do you have to say?"

Mr. Riggs cleared his throat. "I like Mr. Jules Verne's books. "Mebbe the children would, too."

"Well, several of my choices have been mentioned, but I'll add *Meteorology* by Charles Wilkes, *The Pathfinder,* by James Fenimore Cooper, a good atlas, and a volume of William Shakespeare." Mr. Pratt laid his list down on the desk. "There are so many poets, too."

Phoebe waited for Sarah to finish writing. "Sarah, would you read the list?"

Sarah read the titles. "I count thirteen. We'll need to take a vote. I'll keep a list of the books we can't buy now so we can order them later." Had Mr. Pratt emphasized Shakespeare or had it only sounded like it to her? And he kept smiling at her. She had been sure he couldn't be the Poet. Oh, hell. What difference did it make? The Poet had stopped writing, but Gil was real, and she couldn't deny her love for him.

"Sarah, you know what a couple of the books would cost, but what about the others?" Phoebe asked.

"They ranged from eighty-five cents to almost two dollars. I believe we should be able to purchase at least eight or nine."

"Well," Charles said with a shrug, "let's vote. Sarah, write down the number of votes each gets. We'll order the books with the most votes."

"That sounds reasonable." Mr. Pratt cast another smile at Sarah. "If you don't want to count the votes, Mrs. Hampton, I'll be happy to do it."

"It's no trouble, I assure you." Sarah stared at the list, wondering if he heard the annoyance in her voice. Mr. Pratt's attention was becoming embarrassing.

She began naming the titles, starting with the dictionary. She voted for James Fenimore Cooper's title and the atlas that Mr. Pratt had suggested. The other two he posed she didn't vote on.

Mr. Riggs stood up. "If we're done, I better get back."

"We appreciate your help, Mr. Riggs," Sarah said as he started for the door.

"Thanks for coming, Vernon." Charles got to his feet and held his hand out to Phoebe. "That's settled. Phoebe, would you place the order with Seaton?"

"Tomorrow morning." She took his arm. "Ready, Sarah?"

"Yes." Sarah folded her notes and left the pencil on the desk. "I think we did very well. Thank you for your help, Mr. Pratt."

"It was my pleasure, Mrs. Hampton. I would—"

Sarah, who didn't care for his fawning or the gleam in his eye, interrupted him. "We'll let you know when the books arrive, Mr. Pratt. Good evening." She pulled on her cloak as she left with Phoebe and Charles.

Mr. Pratt could not be the Poet, Sarah thought. He just couldn't be.

20

$\mathcal{S}$aturday morning Sarah awakened early. It was election day. After rekindling the fire in the kitchen stove, she started a pot of coffee and put water on for tea. She looked outside. The ground was damp and the sky gray. They would be voting in the livery. She washed up, put on a half dozen petticoats and her wine-red wool dress trimmed with black braid, and brushed out her hair.

Phoebe smelled coffee and went to the kitchen. Bacon was sizzling in the skillet, and Sarah was pouring water into the teapot. "Morning. Thanks for starting the tea."

"Hi. Is Charles awake?"

"Mm-hm. Getting dressed. He, Mr. Seaton, and Mr. Kenton are meeting at the livery to clean and set up tables." Phoebe put another skillet on the stove and got the bowl of eggs. "Can Mr. Perry stand up on his own yet?"

"He did last night. He's been trying each day, but that was the first time he didn't become dizzy. He even took a few steps with me." Sarah smiled to herself. They had walked to his desk and back to his bed, then he had crushed her against him, from chest to knee. His arousal was unmistakable, even through the layers of her clothes.

Phoebe glanced at Sarah. "The look on your face is positively indecent."

Sarah's gaze snapped up and caught Phoebe's knowing expression, and saw she didn't appear pleased. "What's wrong?"

Phoebe shook her head. "I'm glad you won't have to wait on him anymore."

"I don't *wait* on him, and in another day to two he'll be on his own." Sarah sipped her coffee. Only two more days.

Phoebe turned around and a wave of light-headedness made her sway. She pressed her palms on the worktable to steady herself. She couldn't be sick, not today with so much to do. A moment later it had passed. She poured the tea and sipped it. When she looked up, she saw that Charles was watching her from the doorway. "Breakfast will be ready soon."

He went over and kissed her cheek. "Are you feeling all right?"

She smiled at him. "Just trying to wake up."

He poured a cup of coffee. "You rest. Sarah and I'll fix breakfast."

"Charles, I am fine." She stood on tiptoe and whispered in his ear, "I'll prove it tonight."

"Oh, it's going to be long day, my dear." He winked and tasted his coffee.

Sarah sliced bread and spooned berry jam into a small dish. "The skillet's hot," she said, reaching for the bowl of eggs Phoebe had whipped.

"I'll do it." Phoebe picked up the bowl and poured the eggs into the hot pan, then added the crumbled bacon.

Cora joined them, and Clay was right behind her.

"Good morning, you two." Sarah set two glasses on the worktable.

"Aunt Sarah," Cora said, walking over to her, "can I help you feed Mr. Perry?"

Before Sarah could answer, Clay laughed. "You ninny. He feeds himself. She just takes food to him."

Sarah hugged Cora. "Clay's right, sweetie. I'll leave the tray for Mr. Perry. Your mama and I have a lot to do this morning."

"Cora," Phoebe said, "you can come with us when we

vote. You better get dressed." She grinned at Charles. She didn't want their daughter believing women must stand in the shadows when it came to politics.

"Yes, Mama." Cora skipped out of the room.

Sarah looked up. "Charles, why can't Clay help you set up for the election?"

"Can I, Pa? We've been talking about it in school."

"Good idea, but let's eat first."

Cora ran back into the kitchen. "I'm ready."

"Sit down, sweetie. You have to eat." Sarah set a plate on the table for her and finished packing the basket for Gil.

"Here, Sarah." Phoebe held out a plate for her.

"Thanks, but you eat it. I won't be long, then we can meet Elsie."

Gil woke before daybreak. As he stirred the fire and fixed coffee, he almost felt like himself. He washed up, dressed, and put on his socks and boots before buttoning his trousers. His side bothered him most when he tried to bend over. He stretched out on top of the bed to wait for Sarah.

Sarah tapped on the door. She unlatched it and remembered Jack doing the same thing the night before. "Gil?"

He went to the door and watched her face when he opened it for her. "Morning."

She stared at him, then smiled. "You look wonderful." Standing face-to-face with him felt strange after his confinement in bed. He seemed taller, his shoulders broader. She swallowed as a familiar weakness seeped through her. She walked in and set the basket on the end of his bed. "You started the fire."

"It was cold in here last night." As he closed the door he realized that they were no longer limited to passionate caresses, his injury no longer a barrier.

She grinned at him. "I'll bring you a comforter this evening."

"That'd be my second choice." He felt like a tongue-tied youth.

She stared at his bed, the memory of lying beside him as they read the newspaper so fresh in her mind that she could not respond, and began unpacking the basket. "I can't stay. Elsie, Phoebe, and I are going to the livery to see if we can help after we vote."

"And I thought you dressed up for me," he said, stepping up behind her.

She glanced over her shoulder. "I would have but . . ."

He claimed her mouth tenderly as he turned her within the circle of his arms. She nestled in his embrace as if she had anticipated it. He was amazed by the depth of his desire for her. "Oh, Sarah . . ."

"Gil, I . . . must leave." She pressed her lips to his chin. "I'll see you later."

"Wait," he said, holding her with one arm by the waist. "I'll need your help to—"

"Of course. When I bring your lunch?"

"Fine." He stood in the doorway and watched her dash down the hall. "Guess you're too busy to walk down to the livery with me." He wanted her to walk with him to the livery. It might have been the last time she would help him. After he voted, she may not be back. Damn, maybe he shouldn't vote.

"Cora, come back here!" Phoebe called, as she walked down the boardwalk with Sarah, Elsie, and Ruby Jean. "I'm glad it stopped raining, if only for a little while."

Ruby Jean stared at the people. "Gracious, do you believe the number of wagons? Mr. Abbott must be very pleased his newspaper reaches so many people."

Sarah nodded. "We should be, too. I don't remember ever seeing this number of women in town in the middle of the month."

Elsie glanced at the saloon. "The Wedge is certainly busy, considering the loggers aren't in town yet."

"They usually don't arrive till late afternoon." Sarah looked back at the room over the saloon. "I wish they'd come early today."

"Isn't that Mrs. Price waving at us?" Phoebe asked. "I don't know the others with her." Some women carried babies, others led small children.

"Looks like they've just come from the livery." Sarah frowned. They appeared to be unhappy about something. "Grab your skirts, ladies," she said, stepping into the muddy, rutted road. Her foot sank down and the mud squished up over her ankle. She stepped back onto the boardwalk.

Phoebe looked at Cora. "You climb on my back and I'll carry you across. One pair of muddy shoes is all I'll want to have to clean later."

Ruby Jean gaped at Sarah. "*What* are you doing?"

Elsie laughed. "Taking off her shoes. I will, too."

"Feet are easier to wash off than shoes." Sarah shrugged at Ruby Jean and removed the muddy shoe. "I don't see any reason to keep my stockings on either. The newspaper office is empty. Let's go in there and take off our shoes and stockings."

"Oh, Sarah." Phoebe shook her head. Sarah looked so like she did when she was ten and doing the very same thing. "Get inside before you start a riot."

Sarah marched into the *Gazette* office with Elsie and out a few minutes later. Both were barefooted. "Phoebe, what about your shoes?"

"I'd rather wash them."

Sarah gathered her skirts, tossed them over one arm, and waded across the road with Elsie. "We can rinse the mud off in the horse trough."

Elsie chuckled. "I didn't realize crossing a muddy road barefooted would be so entertaining."

"Then they'll probably get a good laugh when we rinse our feet." Sarah stepped onto the boardwalk and held her hand out to Elsie.

Phoebe bunched her skirts with one hand. "Hold on tight, Cora, and don't wiggle or we'll both land in the mud." She picked her way across with Ruby Jean.

Mrs. Price rushed up to Phoebe. "We were coming after you and Mrs. Hampton. They won't let us vote!"

"*Who* won't?" Sarah lifted her foot from the horse trough and dropped her skirt.

Oh, no, Phoebe thought. "Was it Mr. Abbott?"

"It wasn't him. Don't know who he was. We'll go back to the livery with you, won't we, ladies?" Mrs. Price glanced at the others, who nodded in agreement.

"Come on, Phoebe." Sarah set off for the livery, her jaw set and her temper barely in control. Not once had she heard a comment about preventing the women from voting. "Was Mr. Abbott there?" she called over her shoulder.

"I didn't see him," Mrs. Price said.

"Thank goodness," Phoebe mumbled.

Sarah paused at the corner of the livery long enough for the others to catch up, then they all marched through the wide doorway. The odors of horses and manure hung in the damp air. She stopped at the table, where Mr. Drake sat with another man she didn't recognize. She didn't bother with formalities. "We came to vote."

Mr. Drake shook his head. "Sorry, Mrs. Hampton, can't let you do that. You know you ladies haven't the right."

Ruby Jean Drake shrank to the back of the group.

"My name's on that ballot, and that gives me the right." Sarah reached for a ballot, but Mr. Drake smacked his hand over the two stacks of ballots.

"If any of you ladies get enough votes, you can serve on the council." Mr. Drake eyed each of the women before his disdain settled on his wife. "Now, why don't you go home where you belong."

Sarah leaned forward and brought her fist down on the table. "Who elected you judge and jury?"

Mr. Drake jumped back. "Just one damn—"

Sarah snatched a stack of ballots.

At the same moment, Phoebe grabbed the other stack.

"Here now," the other man said. "There's no need for a ruckus. Mr. Drake is following the letter of the law."

"Who, sir," Phoebe said, "are you?"

"Mr. Rice, madam, a friend of Mr. Drake."

Mr. Drake seized the wooden ballot box, as if he thought it was not safe on the table.

Sarah held the ballots behind her back and waved her other hand. "Do you live here?"

The man shook his head. "Just visiting."

"*You* don't belong here! Leave or be silent." Sarah glared at him, hoping he could read her thoughts. Phoebe had always told her her face said what her mouth didn't.

"This is a local election," Elsie said, easing between the crush of bodies to reach the table. "We have as much right to vote for ourselves as anyone else. Where's Mr. Abbott? I bet he won't stand for this."

"We don't need anyone to fight our battles—"

"What the hell's going on here?" Gil slowly walked in through the back, with Ben Layton and Jack at his sides. He saw that Sarah looked ready to maim someone, and the other ladies appeared just as ready to pounce. God, she was a woman to be proud of.

Sarah spun around. "Gil! What are you doing here?"

"Came to vote." He walked up to the end of the table. "Well, Drake, this your idea of campaigning?"

"Gil, you reason with them. I told them they couldn't vote. Wouldn't be legal."

"Why? Four of these ladies' names are on the ballot. You weasel. Sure picked a good time to tell them their voice doesn't count."

Some chuckled.

"Don't blame ya none," a man's voice called out.

Gil winked at Sarah. "That's why I wanted no part of this election."

Sarah dropped one of the slips of paper. "Oh, look. A ballot. This must be yours." She handed it to Gil.

"How about you and the rest of us?" Phoebe asked Sarah.

Sarah looked at Phoebe as she turned to face the other women. "Do you want to vote now or discuss this first?"

"We should talk it over," one woman in back called out.

"I agree." Sarah grinned at Phoebe. "Since we have the ballots, I say the men can't vote until we can."

Gil chuckled. "Congratulations, Drake."

"Abbott can print more ballots," Mr. Drake countered.

Sarah spun around, tempted to grab for his throat, but he was out of her reach. "You'll have a long wait—"

"I can promise you Charles will never!" Phoebe shouted.

Charles hurried around the group of women, carrying two chairs. "Gil? Phoebe? What's this all about?" He set the chairs down and motioned for Clay to do the same.

"Oh, Charles, thank goodness you're back. Mr. Drake refuses to allow us to vote. In fact he seems to think you'll print more ballots to prevent us."

"And Mr. Rice has no business here." Sarah felt a tap on her shoulder and looked behind her. "Miss Layton, I'm glad you're here."

"Mrs. Hampton, there're more men coming down the road."

Charles stared at the table and at Jess Drake. "But where're—" Then he noticed the ballots in his wife's hand.

Mr. Drake took a step toward Charles. "Women don't have the right to vote in this state or city!"

Charles frowned and addressed Gil. "Do you know if Gridley was chartered by the state?"

A slow grin spread over Gil's face. "Don't believe it was. Jack, you remember anything about a charter?"

"Nope."

Gil shrugged. "Guess you can't use that excuse, Drake." Whoops of joy resounded through the livery, and he nodded at Sarah. He picked up a pen, marked his ballot, and walked around the table to deposit it in the ballot box.

"Who's Perry to know about charters?" Drake asked.

"Who knows a town better than the bartenders?" Charles grinned. "Ladies, I see no reason why you can't vote."

Sarah faced the women. The babies were fussy and the children were restless. "Ladies," she said, holding up the ballots, "if we form lines, it would be more orderly."

Phoebe smiled at Charles. She wanted to talk with him, in private, not in front of half of the town. At least he had known how to handle Drake. She set the ballots on the table, keeping one for herself.

Sarah did the same and filled out hers. Mr. Seaton was at the table with Charles and Mr. Kenton. "Mr. Seaton, would you be kind enough to set the ballot box on the table?"

"Yes." Mr. Seaton nodded. "Of course, Mrs. Hampton."

Mr. Kenton placed the box in front of her. "Ladies, after you drop your ballot in the box, please sign the roster." He grinned, almost nervously. "We wouldn't want anyone voting more than once, would we?"

Sarah smiled at Phoebe and held out her ballot.

Phoebe dropped hers into the box as Sarah did. *We did it* was evident in their gazes. Phoebe stepped over to her husband's side, and the women began casting their votes, one by one. The tension seemed to melt away, and soon the murmur of voices filled the livery.

Sarah walked over to Phoebe. "We need to see who's willing to take turns standing by in here, just in case other women come and need help with children, or their courage."

Phoebe put her hand on Charles's arm. "We also think it would be fair to have three women help count the ballots."

"No one will object." Charles glanced around. "Drake and his friend left in a huff. I don't expect any more trouble."

Phoebe sighed. "Thank goodness."

"Well, Sarah, Gil looks good. I'd write to one of those army surgeons, but he probably wouldn't believe me." Charles grinned at her.

"I'm grateful I didn't add to the damage the bullet did." Sarah said, then excused herself to look for Gil.

She had about given up, when she found him standing in the back doorway, pale and obviously fatigued. He went outside, and she followed him. Smiling, she stepped into his waiting arms. "Mm, this is nice."

"I missed you, too." He kissed her silky hair and the pulse at her temple, her soft cheek, and explored the warmth of her mouth.

She responded impulsively, heedless of their lack of privacy. His fingers teased the back of her neck and sent waves of pure pleasure through her belly. She pressed her hips against him, and froze. He was as ready as she was." I didn't mean to . . ."

He smiled at her. "I didn't either, at least not here."

"Why did you walk down here? One of us would've brought you a ballot."

"Thought I'd surprise you."

"You succeeded." She kissed his chin.

"Sarah? Where are you?" Phoebe called.

"Be right there." Sarah rested her forehead on his chest.

"What you did in there took courage, Sarah," he said, lightly massaging her back. "I'm damn proud of you."

She smiled. "Me, too. But I honestly didn't expect it to get out of hand." She ran her fingers over his forehead. "You look tired. Will you rest now?"

"On my way." He gave her a gentle kiss. "See you this evening?"

"I did say I'd bring you a comforter, didn't I?"

21

At six o'clock the election was declared closed. Sarah clasped Phoebe's hands. "We did it."

"What surprised me most was when Mrs. Tilly—and then Mrs. Gary!—sneaked back after waiting for their husbands to vote."

While Alice Seaton, Beth Kenton, and Tess Layton counted ballots with Ben Layton, Oliver Grebby, and Timothy Farmer, Sarah, Elsie, and Phoebe went to their homes to prepare supper. They all returned an hour later. Phoebe stood by Charles. "Have they announced the winners?"

"Not yet. They're about finished with a recount."

Sarah stood nearby with Elsie. Ruby Jean returned and joined them. "Mr. Drake isn't with you?" Sarah asked.

Ruby Jean shook her head. "He went to the Wedge. I'm sure he'll get the results there."

Mr. Grebby stood up, and there was silence. "All right, everyone. We have counted the ballots twice and the number of signatures. You'll be happy to know that everything balances."

Phoebe whispered to Charles, "Please tell him just to get this over with."

"I agree," Charles said, and motioned for Mr. Grebby to hurry.

"I'll read the five names with the most votes," Mr. Grebby said. "Gil Perry, George Seaton, Phoebe Abbott, Emmett Pratt, and Elsie North are our new town council members." He started the applause and everyone joined him.

Sarah congratulated Elsie, then hugged Phoebe. "Good for you! You and Elsie will be wonderful on the council. Glad I voted for winners."

Phoebe felt a bit stunned by the announcement. "I didn't really think any woman would be elected."

"I'm happy for you. It'll be exciting, and I'll write about it," Sarah said, grinning.

"I'm happy it's over." Phoebe wasn't sure if she shared Sarah's excitement or not. "Maybe now I can start preparing for Thanksgiving next week."

"You won't have to do it alone. I'm going to help, Phoebe. We'll have a wonderful dinner."

Phoebe shrugged. "I hope so, but I've been so tired lately."

"Rest. Supper's ready, and I'll cook tomorrow."

Phoebe smiled. "Maybe I will." Cora and her friend Patsy lunged for her, hugging her with all their strength. Phoebe braced herself and slowly pried them loose. "My goodness, girls."

"Oh, Mama," Cora said, beaming. "I'm *so* proud of you!"

Sarah joined Charles. "I'm sorry, Charles. I voted for you. I was confident you would be on the council."

He chuckled. "One in the family's enough. How about you? Regret your candidate's statement?"

"Absolutely not." She grinned, very glad that it was over. She wondered if the news about his election would change Gil's mind. "I'll see you later."

Phoebe caught her hand and stepped away from the well-wishers. "Where are you going?"

"To congratulate Gil—"

"Don't, Sarah. Let Mr. Young or one of the others tell him. Mr. Perry's all but well. He doesn't need your care now."

"Oh, for pity's sake. I'm not going to bathe him. I'll see you at the house." Sarah hurried to the saloon, up to Gil's room, and burst in without knocking. "You won! You're on the council!"

He stared as he advanced on her. "Tell me you're joking."

"I'm sorry. Mr. Seaton, Phoebe, Mr. Pratt, and Mrs. North are also on the council." She closed the door. "I suppose you could refuse to serve. The person with the next highest vote would take your place." The gleam in his eyes was a clear message that he was no longer thinking about the election.

He eyed her playfully and grinned. "I'm glad you brought my first choice." He framed her waist with his hands.

"First choice? But I thought . . ." She didn't understand, but then his hands were warm, and working their magic on her.

"To keep me from freezing tonight."

She started to laugh, but it died in her throat. "You aren't serious." She leaned up and brushed her lips over his. "I wanted to be the first to congratulate you. Now I'll get supper and a comforter."

He drew circles with his thumbs under her breasts. "I'm not interested in food, Sarah." He felt her heart race as he bent to kiss her.

"But you haven't completely healed yet . . ."

On Sunday Gil made his way down the stairs to the saloon. "Jack, why don't you get out of here for a while. I can pour whiskey and draw beer."

"Gil! Good to see ya down here."

"If you'd just drag a chair behind the bar for me, you can get the hell out for a while. Call on Miss Layton or go for a ride." Gil chuckled. Damn, it felt good to be there instead of alone in his room.

"Ya sure?"

"I don't mind my own company, but I've had enough."

Jack set a chair behind the bar and got a cup of coffee for Gil. "Thanks. Oh, I'll have to go after supplies, prob'ly

Tuesday." He gave Gil a half salute as he started for the door.

Gil grinned. "I'm going with you." *About time I reclaim my life.*

Sarah refilled her cup with coffee and Phoebe's with tea. "I don't see why you're still upset about my inviting Gil for Thanksgiving. If the idea was so unpleasant, why didn't you say so when I asked if I could invite him?"

Phoebe shrugged. "I hoped it wouldn't bother me as much as it did."

"Dinner was lovely. Charles and the children seemed to enjoy his company."

"Thanksgiving was a week ago, Sarah, and you're still spending evenings with him."

"I suppose everyone would be happy if he had spent the day by himself. Oh this is pointless," Sarah muttered. "Only a few weeks ago you wanted me to be nice to him."

"Well, it never occurred to me that you'd lose your common sense over the man." Phoebe rolled her eyes. "People are whispering. You spend so much time with him, *and in his room.*"

Sarah stared at the woman whom she had trusted with her most intimate secrets since they were six years old and felt her stomach tighten. "What do *you* think?"

"I try not to, but I'm worried about your reputation." Phoebe gave up the pretense of drinking her tea. Her stomach was already upset. "Honestly, Sarah, what do you expect people will think?"

"Some people always think the worst. Maybe because that's what they would like to do themselves." Sarah sprang to her feet and the chair fell backward. "It seems I've overstayed my welcome." She righted the chair and looked at Phoebe. "It's time I look for another place to live."

Phoebe swallowed hard, hating herself for what she was thinking and about to say, but it had been keeping her awake at night. "Maybe it is," she said softly.

"Fine. I hadn't planned to take advantage of your hospitality for so long.'' Sarah dashed to her room as tears began to fill her eyes. Phoebe's suspicions hurt, even more so because there was no reason for her to feel guilty. A few stolen kisses. Phoebe had done as much herself with Charles.

As much as Sarah wanted to make love to Gil, she hadn't. Hell, if she wanted to cause a scandal, she could move in with him, or at least suggest it to him. She splashed cold water on her face, brushed her hair, and hurried out of the house.

She walked by the boardinghouse, but the ROOM AVAILABLE sign wasn't out. The money from the sale of her home in Camden had been set aside for another house. Last summer she had thought about where she would like to build a plain house. Now it was time she decided exactly where she wanted her home.

After wandering up and down side streets from the church to beyond the blacksmith's, she continued up the road a ways. There were no houses for sale, and she hadn't found that piece of land that cried out to her. A brisk ten-minute walk east of town brought her to a rise overlooking the river. It was perfect. She could see the town and the mill. This is it, she thought, listening to the river. Now to find out who owned the land.

When she returned to town, she went into the *Gazette* office. ''Charles, who owns the land east of town, where the road turns south?''

He looked up at her, but he did not look surprised by the question. ''I'm not sure. Who wants to know?''

''I do.''

He nodded. ''Talk to Gil.''

''All right.'' Since Gil had lived there longer than most people, she wondered why she hadn't thought of asking him. ''Thanks.''

She went to the saloon and stood outside until she caught Gil's attention. ''Meet me out back,'' she mouthed, pointing, and walked around to the well.

Gil came out the back door and found her pacing.

"Something wrong?" He stepped into her path and took her hand.

She shook her head. "I just need to find out who owns the land east of town. I thought you'd know."

"Why? Working on a new article?"

"No, I want to see if the land is for sale. It's time I have a home of my own." She leaned against the edge of the well.

He smiled. "Glad you want to stay here. Is this a sudden decision?"

"Not really. I can't live with the Abbotts indefinitely."

He nodded. "That's a good piece of land."

"Do you know if the owner would consider selling it?" She stared at the river, then at him, wondering why she had the feeling he was being hesitant.

"It's possible. I'm partial to that spot myself."

"Oh," she said, not bothering to conceal her disappointment. "That's why you seem reluctant to tell me the owner's name."

"I own it." He sat beside her on the rim of the well. "I didn't know you were looking to purchase property."

"*You?*" She let out a long sigh. He had not mentioned owning land along with his other interests, and it hadn't occurred to her to ask. "Is it an investment or are you going to build on it?"

"Not sure." He traced the length of her thumb with his own. "Want to tell me why the rush? Sounds as if you'd like to buy it today."

She watched his thumb, almost mesmerized. "Living with a friend, even a dearest friend, can be difficult when you don't agree on certain things. I'm used to having my own home." She met his gaze. "It's time I do."

"I noticed the rift between you two on Thanksgiving. I had the feeling she wasn't happy I was there. Does it have anything to do with me?"

"No sense fabricating. She believes I spend too much time with you, but that's my business, not hers." Sarah gave his hand a squeeze. "If I weren't living with her, she wouldn't know when I left the house or care. That's the way it should be.''

''I should've guessed. I figured she didn't want a bartender in her home.''

''If Charles had invited you, there probably wouldn't have been a problem.'' She leaned against his side. ''I was hoping you hadn't noticed. I'm sorry.''

He chuckled. ''Would've been pretty hard not to. Don't worry about it.'' He kissed the top of her head. ''If you want that land, I'm sure we can strike a deal. Have you anyone in mind to build this house?'' Knowing she loved the land as much as he did made his decision to sell it easy.

She sat up. ''I can buy it from you? Oh, Gil, thank you so much!'' She wrapped her arms around him, hugging him tight. ''You'll be welcome anytime, I hope you know that.''

''Sounds good, but it won't be part of the deal.'' He glanced around, wondering if anyone was watching. ''What about the builder? Know anyone?''

''I haven't thought that far ahead.'' She couldn't stop smiling. She was a landowner, or soon would be. ''Who built the buildings in town?''

''Jack and I put up this place. Beaton did a couple more, but he's long gone.''

''There must be someone.''

''My crew might like the work when the logging stops in the next few weeks, depending on the weather.''

''Do they—have they any experience?''

He chuckled again. ''Yes, Sarah, they'd do a good job for you.''

''Wonderful! It's hard to believe.''

''What kind of house do you want?''

''Traveling across country on the train, I passed the time drawing some very simple plans. Nothing elaborate. Just a modest house is all I need.''

He stood up and pulled her with him. ''Mind showing me later?''

''Not at all.''

''Feel better?''

"Definitely, but I'm not going to rely on you to handle this for me. It's my responsibility."

"All yours." He raised her hand to his mouth and kissed the back.

While the children completed their schoolwork, Phoebe paced around the house. She picked up Cora's doll and left it on the table in the entryway when she grabbed her apron and started rubbing a spot on the small mirror. "Always something," she grumbled, shaking out her cloak. .She found a copy of the newspaper and took it into the parlor, where she saw an empty glass on the table between Clay and Cora. Phoebe grabbed the glass and continued into the kitchen.

Clay looked at Cora, then at his father. "Pa, why's Ma acting so funny? She won't even talk to Aunt Sarah."

"Stay here." Charles followed his wife and closed the kitchen door behind him. "Sit down, Phoebe." He pulled a chair out from under the worktable for her and one for himself.

"What are you doing, Charles? Christmas is next week. I've got to get the house ready."

"Have you looked in the mirror recently? The children are worried, and so am I." He leaned back in the chair. "You're wearing yourself out, my dear. You've been darting around this house and avoiding Sarah for two weeks now. And she's no better. When's it going to stop?"

"It's Mr. Perry." Phoebe sat down and looked at him wearily. "He's fine now. He doesn't need her waiting on him, but she continues seeing him."

"They're keeping company. Can't you see that? Gil's a good man, and he doesn't appear to mind her outspoken manner at all." He chuckled. "In fact, I'd say they're a good match."

She gaped at him. "He's happy working at the saloon, which can't earn him enough to raise a family on, and I frankly do not believe he's thinking about marriage. If she isn't careful, she'll ruin her reputation."

"Shouldn't you let her worry about that?"

"But she's my friend—"

"Phoebe, didn't you read her interview with Gil?"

She brushed at a crumb on the table. "Of course I did—but Sarah *had* to make him sound prosperous. Isn't that the point of those articles?"

"Yes, but she didn't elaborate. This is strictly between you and me," he said, evenly. "Do you agree?"

She nodded. All of a sudden she felt worn out.

"Gil's the one who founded this town, built it for the loggers. He even provided Vonney and her girls with a place to live rather than seeing them live in a shack." He leveled his gaze on her. "Most every man around has owed him at some time or other."

"Vonney and her girls? Who the devil are they?" She thought she could guess, but she couldn't believe what she was hearing. Or that he was talking about it so easily. Too easily for her liking.

"Such language—" He lurched forward, bringing his arms down on the table. "I thought you knew about her. She and the other women live in a nice cabin Gil built for them."

"He owns a . . . parlor house?" She gulped down some of her cold tea. "You say it's 'nice'? Oh, Lord—you went out there? You—You . . . *slept* with one of them?" She jumped off the chair and lunged for him with her hand out. *I'll kill him*, she thought.

He raised his hand in time to block her wide-arced swing. "Easy, Phoebe." He gently hauled her down on his lap and held her in the circle of his arms. "You've got it all wrong. I have no need to see any other women. You're more than enough woman for me and all I want."

He tried to kiss her, but she turned away. She wasn't about to let him off that easily. Nevertheless, she wouldn't forget his sweet words.

He sighed. "Anyway, one day Gil asked if I'd like to ride along with him, and I went."

"He's worse than I thought. And you didn't warn Sarah? Or me? What were you thinking?"

"Nettie's bustle," he muttered. "She's a grown woman.

She's been married. Let her make her own decisions."

"When she doesn't know all the facts? That's cruel, Charles, and not at all like you." She rubbed her forehead. "What have I done?"

"Talk to her. You two are closer than sisters." He kissed her cheek. "She'll listen."

Phoebe waited up for Sarah, but by nine o'clock she had to give up. She dozed off and on through the night, and woke with a start the next morning. She fought the morning queasiness as she pulled on her wrapper and hurried down the hall. She tapped on Sarah's door, praying it wasn't too late to mend the rift in their friendship. "I must speak to you, Sarah."

Startled to hear Phoebe saying her name, Sarah dropped her hairbrush and opened the door. "Come in."

Phoebe unclutched her hands. "Charles just told me. Last night. He didn't—" She glanced up, her lower lip caught between her teeth.

"Sit down," Sarah said, motioning to the chair. "What did he tell you?"

Phoebe perched on the edge of the chair, facing Sarah. "Did you know Mr. Perry owns a parlor house?"

"Make sense, Phoebe. You know he has the logging business. What makes you think—"

"Charles went there with him. Charles *saw* it. He was *there*."

Sarah shook her head slowly, backing away. "Not Gil. He wouldn't—"

"The way Charles talked, it sounded like Mr. Perry and that Vonney woman are close friends." Phoebe stepped over to her. "You're too good for him, Sarah. I've tried to tell you."

"It can't be true. Charles must be mistaken."

"He's never lied to me. You know that almost as well as I do."

Sarah shrugged. "I'll ask him about it."

"Charles? Of course. He'll tell you. Speak to him, Sarah."

"Not Charles. Gil."

"He won't admit it. Not if he hasn't before now." Phoebe recognized the set of Sarah's jaw and the steely look in her eye. "Be careful. You don't know him as well as you think." She reached out to touch Sarah's arm, then lowered hers. "It's in his eyes. He's too engaging."

"You're doing it again, Phoebe, stop it. I've changed my mind about him, but so have you. That's the problem." Sarah walked two paces and paused. "I believed you wanted me to be happy. I don't know what's wrong with you lately." She whirled around, facing her. "All you've done is criticize and scold. If you and Charles are at odds, it's no reason to gripe about Gil."

"We're fine, thank you very much." Tears suddenly filled Phoebe's eyes, and she swiped at them angrily with the back of her hand. "You and I have always looked out for each other, but you've made it clear you no longer care about my opinions."

Sarah inhaled and exhaled slowly. "Phoebe, I'm happier than I've been in years. Is that so wrong?" She didn't expect an answer and wasn't sure if she even wanted one, so she left the room.

"Of course it isn't. . . ." Phoebe bolted after her. A wave of dizziness threatened her balance, and she grabbed the doorjamb. She hadn't felt like this since . . . She laid her hand on her stomach and smiled.

As Sarah stared across the road at the saloon, Phoebe's comments tumbled through her mind. Did he own the parlor house? More important, had he been seeing this Vonney before the bank robbery? Sarah preferred facing problems head-on, but for once, she decided, she would give herself time to think over exactly what she wanted to say to Gil.

She went to the *Gazette* office and worked on the Miss Lucy article. The subject this week was courtship. "Perfect," she mumbled, "I've had so much experience with it."

Charles looked at her over the rim of his cup. "You say something?"

"Do you really want to continue the Miss Lucy articles?

Can't the poor old dear pass away in her sleep?''

He choked on his coffee. ''Kill off every reader's favorite mother or grandmother? What are you thinking?''

''Let Phoebe write it. She wrote the housekeeping columns, not me.''

He shook his head. ''I wondered about that when your writing style abruptly changed.''

''She's good at it. Give her a chance.''

''She hasn't been well. For now, you'll have to take care of this week's article.''

Gil carried his coffee into the saloon. Each day he felt stronger. Except for lifting crates, he was almost back to his former self. It was too early to open for business, but he'd spent a restless night. Seeing Sarah and trying to keep from touching her was detrimental to his sanity. He went outside and sat on the bench.

His cup was nearly empty, when he saw her walking up the road. He left his cup on the bench and stepped to the end of the boardwalk. ''Morning, Sarah.''

She hurried across the road. ''Just the man I wanted to see.'' This morning she had decided she couldn't wait any longer to speak to him, but she hadn't expected him to be watching for her.

''Have time for some coffee?''

''I'd like that.''

''Have a seat. I'll be right back.''

''I would rather go inside, if no one's in there.'' Her palms were moist and her heart felt as if it had leapt into her throat, but she had to ask him about that house.

''Sure.'' He followed her rigid stride inside. He wouldn't say she was angry. Possibly peeved, he decided, pouring her coffee. ''What's on your mind?'' He set the cup in front of her and sat down.

She wrapped both hands around the warm cup and raised it to her lips, then paused and blurted out, ''Do you own the bawdy house?''

He gulped and nodded. So that was what had her tied in knots. ''Yes. What made you ask?'' He kept his business to himself and hoped others would do the same. Not everyone knew that about him, but he thought she had understood.

Her heart seemed to plummet to her toes. "Does it matter?"

"Guess not," he said with a shrug. "It's just a log house."

"And the women?"

"What about them?"

She met his gaze, his intense, wonderful gaze. "I suppose you and Vonney are good friends."

"You could say that. Does it bother you?"

She straightened her back. "It all depends on how *close* you two are."

"Close? If she needs anything, she knows she can count on me." He had a hard-and-fast rule: He never repeated a friend's confidence. Trust was important to him, and he wouldn't violate it. Not even for Sarah. If she couldn't trust him, he'd better find it out now rather than later.

"I see." Her hand began trembling so badly she had to put down the cup. "Thank you for being honest."

"You're welcome. Now will you tell me what this is about?"

"I didn't know you had been seeing her—" *Oh, my damnable tongue*, she thought. "I shouldn't have said that. You're a single man. It's only natural for you to—"

He started chuckling. "You jealous?"

"Why should I be?" She tried to sound offhanded, but she was no good at deception. "Yes—I am."

"You've *no* reason to be." He stood and pulled her up into his arms. "You're friends with at least one man. Charles. I'm not jealous of him, and he's your friend." Holding her close, he covered her flushed lips with his.

She raised her arms to his shoulders, then lowered them. He hadn't denied owning the bawdy house or knowing that woman. His tongue teased hers, and she was almost ready to forgive him anything—after just one more question. She tore her mouth from his. "You haven't seen her . . . as a customer? Not that you'd have to pay—"

"God, Sarah!" He burst out laughing, lifted her up, and whirled her around. "You're priceless." He kissed her hungrily and grinned. "She might not charge me—if I were interested, which I am not." He kissed her again. "Satisfied?"

She flung her arms around his neck and raised her mouth to his. Thank goodness Phoebe had been wrong. So very wrong.

"Hey, Gil . . ." Jack said, walking into the saloon.

Sarah jumped back from him, but Gil reached out and clasped her hand. "What can I do for you, Jack?" He winked at her and squeezed her hand.

"You gonna check on the camp this week?" Jack looked up and froze in his tracks. "Sorry, Mrs. Hampton. Didn't know ya were here."

"Good morning, Jack." She looked at Gil. "I'd better leave." *And do so with as much dignity as I can manage,* she thought. When she made a fool of herself, she knew no limits.

He walked her out front. "Don't mind Jack. He won't say anything. Are you okay?"

She looked into his eyes, and then she smiled. "Much better than when I arrived." As she crossed the road she realized she was. She loved Gil, and there was no reason to be embarrassed about that.

Phoebe stopped by Seaton's and picked up the mail. There were the usual newspapers, and a package and two letters . . . for Sarah. The penmanship on one of them Phoebe would recognize anywhere. Oh, thank you, Lord, she thought. She rushed out of the store and went directly to the newspaper office.

22

*S*arah stuffed Mr. Brown's last letter in her pocket and handed Charles the Miss Lucy article. "I have to leave for a while, but I'll be back."

He leaned back and looked at her. "When are you and Phoebe going to patch things up?"

"Eventually," she answered, then left. It wasn't that simple, but he didn't understand that. She marched down the road to the school. If only Emmett Pratt hadn't talked so about his interest in Shakespeare and poetry, at that meeting where they'd chosen the new library books, she would not have given him another thought. After this morning's talk with Gil, she needed to discover if Emmett Pratt was the Poet. Once and for all.

Other than two boys climbing through the bushes in the yard, the school looked deserted. She went up the stairs and into the classroom. Fortunately Mr. Pratt had not left. It would be too embarrassing to discuss this with him at the boardinghouse.

She walked up the aisle, determined to resolve her suspicions about him. "Mr. Pratt—"

"Mrs. Hampton," he said, rising to his full height. "What a wonderful surprise. Please, have a seat. How may I help you?"

She smiled and withdrew the letter from her pocket. "A gentleman has been writing to m—Miss Lucy, and she asked me if I could find him for her. I'm hoping you might know." She started to hand the letter to him, but hesitated.

"Interesting. Doesn't he sign his name?"

"Well, yes, but I have a feeling he may be shy and using a pseudonym."

He held out his hand. "May I?"

She gave him the single page. She observed him carefully, but he didn't react as if he knew anything about it. She perched on the edge of a seat, anxious to learn the Poet's identity, yet worried that this man might be the writer. A moment later, his face turned red. Surely, the author wouldn't react that violently to his own sentiments.

"I had no idea—The gentleman's amorous feelings are quite evident, aren't they? I would say he is not only well-read but a highly educated man. The penmanship is beautiful, certainly not learned in a country school."

"That's what I thought. I haven't been able to match his writing with any gentleman's speaking voice."

"In my experience people tend to write with more care than they use in everyday conversation." He folded the paper and handed it back to her. "I'm sorry I can't be more help."

"You have been, thank you."

"May I walk you home? I will be ready to leave in a few minutes."

"I'm sorry. I have another appointment," she fabricated. She needed to be alone to think.

"Visit me any time, Mrs. Hampton."

She nodded and made her escape. She believed him, and relief spread over her like a summer breeze. Strolling along the riverbank, she wondered what difference it would make if she never discovered the Poet's identity. If she did, would it change her love for Gil? She stopped and looked at the saloon.

She wanted to talk with him again. After their earlier discussion she believed that she could tell him just about anything. She climbed the back stairs, went to his room, and knocked on his door, though she felt certain he was behind the bar. A moment later, she stepped inside and closed the door.

Using a scrap of paper from his drawer, she wrote a quick note asking to see him. When she was dipping the pen in the inkwell before signing her name, the door opened and startled the daylights out of her.

Gil grinned at her. "Sarah? You're full of surprises today." He closed the door and walked over to his desk.

"I shouldn't have just walked in, but I wanted to leave you a note." He looked uncertain for a few moments, then he smiled, and she sighed. This was the last time she would enter his room uninvited.

He put his hand on her waist as he leaned over and read her note. "Why not now?"

She smiled up at him. "You don't have to work?"

"Jack's behind the bar." He kissed her temple. She was uneasy about something. This time he wanted to make sure he answered all of her questions. He took her in his arms for a slow and thorough exploration. She came alive in his embrace, and felt so good.

She swayed her hips over his, feeding her desire for him. That sweet ache that began the moment he touched her now spread, rippling through her belly and her breasts. She clung to him for strength and support on rubbery legs. "I really need to talk with you about . . . a letter."

He swallowed a groan. "Now?"

She nodded.

"Must be important." Holding her hand, he led her to the bed and sat down on the side with her. "What's this about?"

She pulled the letter out of her pocket. "A certain gentleman has been writing letters." She met his gaze. "They're rather . . ." No, she thought, let him decide what to think of them.

He recognized the paper instantly, but had she figured out Mr. Brown's identity? "I'm not surprised you have admirers, but you didn't mention him this morning when you asked me about Vonney."

"Oh, he's not . . ." She felt about two inches tall, and crushed the letter in her hand. "I don't know him."

"How can I help you?"

"I tried to find the man but no one seems to know him. I—" She smoothed out the letter and opened it. Miss Lucy. *It was sent to Miss Lucy, remember that,* she silently intoned. "I'd like your opinion of it. Do you think he's serious? Or amusing himself?" She laid it on his knee.

"Oh, it's Miss Lucy's letter. Why didn't you say so?"

"She asked me to help find him." Oh, Lord, she sounded so muddled. "She's not sure if she should trust his intentions."

He slid his arm around her as he looked at the page and realized it wasn't his newest letter. "Sounds serious to me. Why doesn't she believe him?"

"Maybe she's afraid. She might be suspicious of such passionate declarations. It seems he wrote to her every week, then stopped. I think she may care for him more than she admitted."

"Ah, a woman scorned." He glanced out of the corner of his eye at her. He'd have thought she would've grown suspicious before now. Considering their passionate embraces, why hadn't she forgotten about 'Mr. Brown'? *But I'm Mr. Brown,* he suddenly reminded himself. It was galling to be in competition with himself. "Her articles have had an edge to them recently."

"It's . . . possible. . . ." She sat a moment listening to the fire in the woodstove, wondering if she had allowed her feelings to affect the articles. "I've never been introduced to her. I can't say."

That's good, he thought. She thinks on her feet, or in this case, on her nicely rounded bottom. "Did she tell you about what she's written to him?"

Questions and more questions. All she wanted . . . What was it that she had expected from him? "I believe she responds through her column, but doesn't he seem overly secretive?"

"Could've seemed romantic to him." Gil had wooed her with poetry and wanted to end what had begun as a prank and become a courtship in the same way. Besides, he knew she wasn't being completely truthful—about the elusive 'Miss Lucy'—either.

"At first I thought so." She rested her hand on his leg. "But no one in Fenton's Crossing seems to know him. Since it's not that far from here, I would think he'd ride over here. Try to see her." She shook her head. "It's strange."

Oh, Sarah, he thought, you have been busy. "Maybe he didn't want to risk having his pride wounded in person."

She skimmed her hand over his trousers, remembering his muscled thighs. "What should I tell her, when I write?"

"Mm, I don't like giving advice, but playing it safe can be lonely. Sometimes you have to take a chance." He trailed his finger along her jaw and traced the line of her lips. "Don't worry about Miss Lucy now. She'll do what she feels best."

Yes, let Miss Lucy worry about the Poet, Sarah thought, nibbling on his finger. I'd rather have Gil, a man who is warm, funny, clever, and so tender—not pretty words and empty promises from a man who hadn't the courage to meet her. All of a sudden the cloud of doubt vanished. She was free. Free to love and be loved.

She put her hands on his shoulders. "You're right. I think Miss Lucy should follow her heart." Her breasts tingled for his touch, and a liquid heat seemed to pool below her belly. *Sometimes you have to take a chance. . . .* Did he mean her or Miss Lucy?

He buried his hand in her glorious, silky hair and let it slip through his fingers. She moaned softly and trembled as she rubbed her palms over his shoulders. He drew his parted lips over her cheek, the bridge of her nose, her pulsing temple, taunting himself as much as her. Her hands slid down his chest and his muscles tensed, making it difficult for him to breathe. Responding in kind, he drew circles around her breast with his fingers until her nipple strained against his hand.

She held on to his waist and leaned back, reveling in the heat he generated. His knee pushed between hers. The rustling of fabric vied with the rush of blood pounding in her ears. Wherever his mouth or his hands touched, sparks of desire coursed through her. Never had she been so sensitive or hungry for a man's touch.

As if she were as fragile as fine china, he lightly outlined her curves and clefts with his fingertips, engraving her image in his soul. He felt the buttons on his shirt give way, then her mouth pressing kisses to his bared chest. She nibbled and licked, and he groaned from deep within.

She rubbed her breasts over his chest and moaned. Clamping her thighs over his knee wasn't enough. She wanted, needed more. She wrapped her arms around his neck and fell backward, pulling him with her. His weight felt wonderful.

He captured her parted lips with a hunger she alone aroused. She twisted beneath him, almost drawing him into her. He slid to her side and raised the hem of her skirt in response to her unrestrained invitation. He ran his hand over the soft fabric of her unmentionables, stroking her inner thighs. She murmured so beautifully. He slipped his hand between her thighs, and his fingertips grazed the edge of the damp split-legged undergarments.

She leaned against his hand and reached for the buttons on his trousers. He throbbed against her palm, growing harder, larger, and she felt as if she were melting against him. A tremor began in her belly and grew stronger and stronger. "Yes, oh yes, Gil—" she cried as the shudder gripped her in the most incredible burst of pure fulfillment.

He watched her. She was so incredibly beautiful in her bliss, and he fought to control his instinctive response to join her. Never had he struggled so hard against his need for release. He held her trembling body until she lay limp in his arms, then he felt her working the buttons free on his pants.

He raised her hand and pressed his lips over her fingertips. "I hope my advice will help Miss Lucy."

"It will," she gasped. "I'm certain it will." She gazed into his beautiful dark eyes, her body still throbbing with the need to take him inside her. Again, she reached for his buttons, but he gently restrained her. "What's wrong?"

"I hadn't planned this. I told Jack I wouldn't be gone all afternoon. You deserve more." He kissed her. "So much more." He held her in a loose embrace. He didn't have the strength to stand just yet.

She lay in his arms as her energy slowly returned. "I have to go back to the office, too." She kissed his firm jaw. "Though I'd rather not move."

He dragged his lips across her forehead. "Sunday I'm going up to the camp. 'Bout time I went to check on things."

She leaned on her elbow, coming almost nose to nose with him. "Christmas is next week. I was thinking about asking Elsie North if she'd have room at her table for guests. Have you made any plans?"

"Nope. We could fix something here, or spend the afternoon at camp. Dugan usually makes a feast, if only for himself."

She ran her hand down his chest. "Ask him if he would mind some company." She sat up slowly, her body still throbbing in the aftermath of their intimacy.

Sarah put the Poet's letter on top of the others, shoved them to the back of the drawer, and straightened up her desk. Miss Lucy is back, Sarah thought, and we'll keep our feelings separate. The office door flew open, and Phoebe dashed inside.

"Look!" Phoebe said, thrusting one of the letters at Sarah.

She stared at the handwriting. "The Poet?"

Phoebe stood it as long as she could. "Don't just stare at it. Open it!"

Sarah dropped the envelope on the desk. "I'm not sure I want to. When Miss Lucy comes in, she can read it. It's addressed to her." She glanced up. "What's that?"

Phoebe put the other letter and the package on the desk. "This box looks like it's from your mother."

"My dear," Charles said, coming up beside her. "You must be feeling better."

"Oh, fine. Never better." She kissed his cheek.

"Anything there for me?"

She beamed at him. "The usual."

He took the newspapers back to his desk.

Oh, Charles, she thought, *if I'd told you my news you wouldn't have heard me.* After supper, she would make sure she had his attention. She looked at Sarah. "What's wrong with you? Don't you want to know why he stopped writing? You have to be curious."

"He must've had his reasons. I'm not so sure I want to know what excuse he dreamed up." Sarah grabbed the other envelope and tore it open. After reading the first line, she looked at the postmark and grinned at Phoebe. "This's from a woman in Hollister, California. She wrote about my article on free love." She waved the letter. "Charles, another one."

Phoebe groaned inwardly. "Is she for or against it?"

"She says she came across country on a wagon train. After a woman has walked hundreds of miles beside a wagon, chopped firewood, and shot any four-legged creature in sight to keep from starving, she has the right to feel good in any man's arms she chooses." Sarah eyed Charles. "Did you hear that, Charles?"

"Let's hope she stays in Hollister, wherever that is."

Sarah folded the letter. "I'll have to write her."

She pulled the twine off of the package and opened the box. "The cloak," she said, lifting it up for Phoebe to see. "She did have it." She smelled the faint scent of lavender, her mother's favorite fragrance. It was as if a floodgate had opened to so many childhood memories.

Phoebe lifted the hem. "Your teal-blue cloak. . . ." Her eyes began to tear up. Wonderful, she thought. Lately I'm either carping or crying.

"It looks just the way I remembered, even the braid trim." Sarah opened the cloak and found her embroidered initials, S.S., on the lining. She and Phoebe had had few disagreements over the years and none as serious as their current one. Phoebe had never been so stubborn, but Sarah knew in her heart that Phoebe was wrong about Gil.

She folded the cloak and put it back in the box, then held it out to Phoebe. ''Do you want to see if Cora would like it?''

Phoebe nodded and tears streaked down her cheeks.

Sarah stood up and pushed the chair over to her. ''Phoebe, sit down.''

''My dear,'' Charles said, hurrying to her side, ''that's enough. I'm taking you over to Oregon City to see a doctor.''

Phoebe gulped and shook her head. ''It's the cloak.'' She tried to smile and stop crying. ''This is so sweet of you, Sarah. I'll save it for when you have a little girl.''

''Don't hold your breath for that to happen.'' Sarah saw the Poet's letter lying there. They had seemed romantic, as Gil suggested, but Gil was the man for her. It made no difference what the Poet had written.

Watching Sarah, Phoebe understood her doubts and fear and was determined to help her. ''If you're not going to read it, I will.'' She loosened the flap and slipped out the letter. ''My dearest Miss Lucy . . .''

Sarah set her jaw and paced over to the window. Step outside for a moment, Gil. Please. Of course he didn't, but Phoebe continued reading the blamed letter.

''I can only hope you will forgive my lapse in correspondence. I must beg your patience and understanding. I assure you it was unavoidable, though I would not blame you for thinking me a cad and complete scoundrel.

'' 'If I were loved, as I desire to be,
What is there in the great sphere of the earth,
. . . Clear Love would pierce and cleave, if
thou wert mine.'

''Yours with great fondness, Mr. Brown''

''Whew,'' Phoebe said, fanning herself with the letter. ''Doesn't sound like he's forgotten you.''

"Flowery words, nothing more. He didn't even bother to give an excuse for not writing."

Phoebe put the letter on the desk. "I hope you reconsider. He does sound contrite."

Sarah looked at her and tried to control her irritation. "You're doing it again. Just stop. I simply don't care what he says."

"You may change your mind, Sarah. Don't do anything you may regret later." Phoebe stepped over to Charles, kissed him, and left the office.

Sarah glanced at Charles. He was buried in the newspaper he was reading. She stuck the Poet's letter in the drawer and closed it. She had already finished the Miss Lucy article, and in it she had made no reference to any of his letters and had not written a word to encourage his interest. That should be the end of it.

Phoebe hugged Charles's arm to her side as they strolled across the field. "Isn't this nice?"

"It's freezing out. What are we doing here instead of in front of the fire?" He shivered and raised the collar on his coat.

She smiled and rubbed her cheek on his sleeve. "I've been remembering how disappointed you were when you couldn't get home from the war in time for Cora's birth."

"That was a terrible time, my dear." He patted her hand. "I tried to get home." He shook his head. "That was almost ten years ago. Why dredge up all that now?"

"Would you like another chance?"

"To do what?"

"Bring a child of ours into this world." Gracious, her heart was pounding loud enough to wake the crows.

"How—" He froze in his tracks, staring at her. When he found his voice again, it was quivery. "Are you . . . ? Are we . . . ? No, not after all these years."

"Yes, we are. I believe sometime in August, if my calculations are correct."

He swooped her up in front of him. "Phoebe, you're

beautiful!'' He crushed her to him. ''That's why you've been so cranky lately!''

She laughed. ''It took me a while to figure it out, too.''

''Our baby may be warm, but its Mama and Papa aren't. Let's go inside. What did Sarah have to say?''.

''She doesn't know yet, but I'll tell her soon.''

''I take it you haven't told the children either.''

''I thought we should do it together, but Cora's so happy with Sarah's cloak I don't think she'd even hear us tonight.'' She rested her head on his shoulder.

''They don't need to know for a while, and I've other plans for tonight.''

''I was hoping you would.'' She felt like dancing. He was happy about her pregnancy. It must have happened the night she asked him about Lorinda. The lovely Lorinda. Sarah would get a chuckle when she learned about that.

Sarah sat on her bed looking at the new house plans Gil had helped her draw. He didn't quote Shakespeare or Tennyson, or write her romantic letters, but she felt so alive with him. Even when they disagreed, or especially when they did, she thought.

Simply remembering his caress awakened her body; clamping her thighs together, she could almost feel Gil's fingers stroking her moist, tender flesh. Her only regret was that he had not shared in her satisfaction.

The lamplight caught her wedding ring, and she stared at it. It's time, she thought, twisting the gold band and pulling it off. It belonged to the past, in the little wooden treasure box her mother had given her a lifetime ago.

Where had she put it when she packed her things? She looked through the drawers in the chest, the valise, and even beneath her underclothes. She did find the bullet that had wounded Gil, tied in a handkerchief, but no box. She studied the room. Her trunk was the only other place it could be.

She dropped down in front of it, raised the lid, and began emptying it, spreading the contents on the floor. Under a nightgown and two sheets she found the little box. When she lifted the lid, she saw the little silver necklace her father had given her on her twelfth birthday. She set the box on her bed and straightened clothes she had not bothered unpacking since she arrived in Gridley.

As she dug through the contents, she discovered Linnet. Phoebe's doll. Sarah cradled the doll in the crook of her arm, fluffed her little mob cap and straightened the skirt dotted with tiny flowers. "Oh, Linnet, how could I have forgotten you, and my promise to Phoebe?" She placed the doll lovingly on her pillows.

"It's late. In the morning we'll talk to Phoebe."

Saturday morning Phoebe awoke to find herself alone in bed. Charles had let her sleep. For the first time in nearly three weeks she had slept soundly. She stretched and left the warmth of their bed. While she dressed, she realized her waist seemed to have grown overnight. Clothes. She would have to make a couple of dresses with drawstring waists.

She had finished her toilet before she found the note from Charles. He had taken Cora with him to work, and Clay had gone fishing with friends. *Charles is so sweet*, Phoebe thought, going to the kitchen. He had heated water, and she made tea. She needed to speak to Sarah, and there was no better time. While the tea steeped, she went to see if Sarah was still there.

Phoebe raised her hand to knock, when the door opened.

Sarah smiled. "Come on in."

Phoebe nodded.

"You look better this morning. In fact, you're almost beaming."

"I had a good night's rest." Phoebe sat on the chair. "Cora can't wait to see you. She loves the cloak. She even wanted to sleep in it."

"I'm glad she liked it." Sarah sat on the end of her bed. "Phoebe, I'm sorry I lost my temper. You meant well, and I shouldn't have reacted the way I did. Will you forgive me?"

Phoebe felt the tears before they blurred her vision.

"That's why I wanted to see you." She wiped at her eyes. "I shouldn't've kept harping at you about Mr. Perry. Can you forgive me?" She held out her arms as she stepped toward her. "He makes you happy. That's all that's important."

Sarah hugged her. "Oh, Phoebe." She had to wipe her eyes, too. "You were right about the parlor house. Gil told me about Vonney, too."

Phoebe nodded. "I'm glad he did. How do you feel about it?"

"They're friends. I'm not sure I'll like her, but I believe him."

Phoebe kept swiping as the tears continued. She would say nothing about that. Only Sarah's opinion counted.

"I found someone I think you might like to see."

"Who? Someone from back home?"

"Mm-hm." Sarah moved a pillow aside and picked up the doll.

"Oh, my goodness. Linnet. Where did you find her?" Phoebe ran her hand over Linnet's skirt. It was sprinkled with tiny lilac flowers, which Phoebe had embroidered.

"In my trunk. I always kept her with me, even if I didn't always remember her."

"I've got Esmee packed away in mine." Phoebe grinned, holding Linnet tenderly in her arm. "Want to have a tea party?"

"That would be fun, but let's have it in the parlor instead of under a tree. It's too cold out."

Phoebe sobered. "Sarah, I have to ask: If you're truly happy with Mr. Perry, will you not encourage the Poet anymore?"

"I didn't this week, and if he writes again, we'll burn the letter." Sarah cocked her head as she studied Phoebe. "Are you sure you're feeling all right? You're looking a bit peaked again."

"It's nothing to worry about, quite natural, in fact."

Sarah frowned at her. "That's gibberish. What aren't you telling me? You're grinning like a drooling fool."

Phoebe rested her hand on the swell of her belly.

"You're going to be an aunt. Again. Next summer—"

"Oh, Phoebe!" Sarah threw her arms around Phoebe, and new tears filled her eyes and spilled down her cheeks. "I am so happy for you. It's wonderful! You're such a good mother."

"I thought that part of my life was over." Phoebe giggled. "Charles was surprised, too. Oh, you will be my midwife, won't you?"

"If that's what you want, I will. But I'm out of practice. Cora's almost ten." *And I was ten years younger then,* Sarah thought.

"We'll do fine together," Phoebe said, smiling, their disagreement now a memory. "We always have."

Gil drove the wagon across the mill bridge and headed east up into the foothills of Mount Hood. He was still within sight of Gridley when he noticed a burst of gray smoke rising above the trees. Too close to be the camp. Vonney's house. It had to be. Damn! The loggers were still in town, and he couldn't fight a fire that size alone.

He turned the horses around and raced back to town. The logs in Vonney's house were stout, wouldn't burn quickly, but he didn't know how long the fire had been burning. It took him less than an hour to send out the alarm and ride back toward the fire.

Gil drove the wagon with the loggers and tools to fight the fire. Jack and several men from town rode ahead on horseback. The closer Gil came, the worse the smoke looked and the more fearful he became. An oil-lamp fire couldn't have caught hold to raise smoke that thick.

He came to a halt in the yard. Flames were shooting up at the far corner of the house, and the sheds were blazing. Vonney, Frannie, Vi, and Jessamine, in various states of undress, were passing buckets of water to throw on the fire. Both outbuildings were ablaze, along with one end of the house.

At least the women were safe. No one would be able to say the same for the bastard who started this inferno.

23

*G*il jumped down from the wagon. A stitch in his side brought him up short. Two months since the shooting, and he still hadn't regained his former strength. The men grabbed axes, buckets, canvas, hoes, pails, and shovels and took off. Gil went over to the women. Vi's blonde hair was gray with ashes. Frannie's face was tear-streaked, and Jessamine was barking orders like a foreman. Everyone continued working together until the fire had been put out.

The east end of the log house had been charred but not burned all the way through. Out of the corner of his eye he noticed a streak of light run by. He turned and saw Vonney dart around the girls and into the house. He hurried after her.

"Vonney!" He charged down the hall toward the burned area of the building, struck by the smell of the charred walls. "What the hell're you doing?"

"Just checking to make sure it isn't smoldering." She spun around and bolted into his arms. "Gil, your wonderful house. . . . We were so scared," she said through sobs.

"Shh, now. It'll take a while to air out the smoke, but I think you've saved the house. I'll get a better look when the fire's out." He walked her outside. "How did it start?"

"Olley Russell came by early this morning. He wanted

to see Frannie, but she refused him. Said she wanted no part of his games or marriage proposals." Vonney shrugged.

Vi grabbed Gil's arm. "I saw that dumb jackass scoot behind one of the sheds. Thought the fool was just spyin' on Frannie. He could see her window from there."

"You're sure it was this Olley Russell?"

"Damn right."

Gil put his hand on Vi's soot-blackened arm. "Are you all right?"

Leering at him, she ran her hand over her breasts and down past her hips. "What do you think?"

He chuckled and winked. "You're saucy as ever, Vi. Did you see him light a fire?"

"Nah. Doubt he'd know how to strike a match."

He nodded. "Are you okay now, Vonney?"

She snuggled up to his side. "I sure could use a little comforting from you. You're looking pretty fit for a man I heard was dead." She nuzzled his neck. "I'm real glad you're not. I missed your handsome face."

He looked around. "When was the last time you had this many men up here at one time?" He swatted her backside. "I'll see you later."

He walked through the nearby trees and surveyed the ground around the back side of the two burning sheds. The ground was damp and most of the dense covering made it difficult to find tracks, except in the muddy patches. Behind a huge pine there were marks on the ground that could have been made recently, but it was hard to be sure.

One shed had burned to the ground, and the men knocked down the other. Dirt was shoveled over the smoldering timbers, while Jake and Vernon Riggs continued dousing water on the end of the house. Gil went back to the front of the house and found Frannie rinsing her face at the well.

He filled a dipper and held it out to her. "You better drink some, too."

"Oh, Gil." She gulped the water and hung the dipper on the hook. "You goin' to catch that weasel?"

"I'll try." He couldn't help but wonder if the same man had anything to do with the rash of fires at the logging camp. "Are you certain Olley Russell started the fire?"

"He was di'mented! Always threatenin' to do somethin' terrible."

"Do you know where he lives?"

"I was only with him once," she said, shuddering. "He told me to dress up in nothin' but a' apron and mob cap, and pretend to be bakin' bread," she hissed. "Then that no-account says I'm 'so purty' he's gonna marry me!"

Gil rubbed his chin. He didn't want to know what men wanted the women to do for them. "Frannie, think. How was he dressed?"

She bent over and brushed her fingers through her hair, shaking some of the ash from the long brown strands. "Homespun trousers, store-bought shirt."

Gil nodded. Now she was making progress. "What kind of boots?"

"Worn hobnail." She shrugged.

"How did he smell?" He figured if she had been in a room with him, she must remember something.

"Ugh! Like he'd been rollin' 'round with hogs."

He smiled. "Thanks, Frannie. You take care of yourself."

She grinned. "Ah try, Gil."

After the men had put out the fire, Vonney served coffee to everyone. When they heard the women complaining about Olley Russell, tempers flared. The loggers were sure he was the man they had been tracking for the fires at camp.

"Let's go!" Willie yelled. "Won't come back till we have him!"

"Come on, fellas, what're we waitin' for?" Jake grabbed Frannie, kissed her hard, and ran to the wagon.

Gil grabbed Willie's arm in a vice grip. "Stop this. It's insanity."

Willie shook his head and dropped a heavy hand on Gil's shoulder. "Sorry, boss. We got to protect these women. I know you mean well, but you just ain't up to doing it yourself." He wrenched free and ran off.

"Damn fools. The damn fools," Gil said, but no one listened.

Phoebe clamped her hands on the side of the rig. "Sarah, this is insane. What do you think you're going to do at the parlor house that the men haven't?" Lord help her, she thought, Sarah was at it again.

"I've no idea, besides take them some food." Sarah couldn't stand watching the smoke without doing something. "I've never been in a bawdy house. This's the best opportunity I may have to meet Vonney, and I can make sure Gil's okay."

"You and your curiosity. *Be careful.* Lord knows what could happen to you."

Sarah laughed. "I'll write an article and you can read all about it."

"That just may drive Charles over the brink. Do you have a hat pin?"

"Whatever for?"

"Protection. Here," Phoebe said, pulling one out of her hat. She handed the six-inch-long pin to Sarah. "Don't forget to use it if you need to."

"This is lethal. I might as well take a sword." Sarah stared at her. "I'm not wearing a hat." She handed the rapier hat pin back to Phoebe.

"Sarah, you must take it."

Sarah shook her head and picked up the reins. "I'll be back by suppertime."

"I'll come after you if you aren't!" Phoebe called, as Sarah took off down the road.

Sarah crossed the mill bridge and followed the road leading up into the hills. After her begging and pleading, Ben Layton had given in and told her how to reach the bawdy house. Phoebe had been right. Everyone—all the men, anyway—evidently was very familiar with it.

Not long after she entered the forest, Sarah turned toward the creek and saw a large, log house. The acrid odor of charred timbers hung in the air and grew stonger the closer she came. She carried one of the crates to the door and knocked. The door flew open and a woman's large bosom seemed to fill the space.

"Why s'formal, sug—" Vi stood up straighter, eyeing Sarah from head to foot. "What do you want?"

"I would like to see Vonney." The woman shoved the door closed, and Sarah feared her surprise showed on her face, but she couldn't help it. The woman apparently was wearing only her shimmy and corset. And black stockings. No lady went out without her stockings. *Wait till Phoebe hears about this*, Sarah thought.

The door opened again. This time a woman with a riot of brilliant red curls faced her. Sarah smiled. "Vonney?" So this was Gil's *friend,* she thought, not quite sure what she had expected.

"Yes. What can I do for you?"

"I'm Sarah Hampton, from Gridley. I brought two crates of food. No one in town knew how bad the fire was. I thought you might need it." At least this woman's attire was a flattering violet muslin dress, the neckline more suited for evening wear but nonetheless rather attractive.

Vonney looked her up and down. "From the *Gazette*? That Sarah Hampton?"

"I believe most people are glad there's only one," Sarah said, grinning.

Vonney reached for the crate. "Let me take that, Mrs. Hampton. Come on in," she said with a broad smile. "This's a real pleasure."

Momentarily stunned, Sarah stood mute, then finally recovered from the warm welcome. The woman's smile was difficult to resist—it was easy to see why Gil hadn't. "I'll get the other crate."

"Don't you bother." Vonney poked her head around the door. "Vi, get the other crate out of Mrs. Hampton's buggy."

Vi ran to the door. "Mrs. Hampton? Sorry I wasn't so nice to you. We don't have many real lady callers here."

As Vi dashed out to the wagon, Sarah stepped inside. "Was there any damage to your house, Vonney?"

"You better come in the kitchen." Vonney led the way

through the house. "Some outside, but Gil—Mr. Perry built this place real solid."

Sarah recognized the tone in Vonney's voice when she said Gil's name. She felt more than mere friendship toward him. "That is good news. We saw the smoke from town. I was afraid half the hillside was ablaze."

"If Frannie hadn't gone out for water to wash her hair when she did, it might have been." Vonney set the crate on the floor. "I'll pay you for the food, Mrs. Hampton. Saved me a trip for supplies."

"No need, Vonney, and please call me Sarah."

Vi sauntered in with the second crate and set it by the other one. "Look, tapioca pudding. Thanks, Mrs. Hampton."

"Sarah." She heard hushed voices behind her, and glanced at the door. Two more women stood there. One, dressed in a pretty white shimmy and a half dozen or more petticoats, grinned.

"Hi. I'm Frannie. I can't believe you came up here to see us. We read every one of your stories. Never miss 'em."

"I'm glad you've enjoyed my articles." Their praise seemed genuine, and Sarah felt a bit bowled over by it.

Jessamine walked up to Sarah and held out her hand. "I'm happy to meet you, Sarah. I'm Jessamine. You wrote a real nice story about Gil."

Sarah smiled and shook hands. Jessamine wore a frothy yellow dressing gown that complemented her pretty, dark eyes. "He's an interesting man. I understand all of you know him."

"He's like our brother," Frannie said. "Well, almost," she added, looking at Vonney.

Vonney scowled at Frannie, and softened her gaze for Sarah. "Would you like coffee, tea, or blackberry brandy, Sarah?"

"Brandy sounds good." Sarah smiled. Since this was a day of firsts, why not try the brandy, she reasoned. "Do you mind me asking how long all of you have lived here?" She had no talent for guessing ages. However, Vonney appeared to be the oldest and Frannie the youngest.

Vonney poured two little glasses of brandy. "Almost eight years." She handed one drink to Sarah. The front door opened, and Vonney looked at the girls.

"See you later, Sarah," Frannie said, with an almost childish grin.

All three women scurried into the parlor, and Sarah overheard their purring voices, so different from moments before. She raised her glass. "To no more fires."

"I second that." Vonney drank to the toast. "How long have you been in Gridley?"

Sarah tasted the brandy and grinned at her host. It was delicious. "I arrived last summer." She ignored the obvious sounds of the women drifting to other parts of the house with the men who had arrived. "I interviewed Mr. Perry. Since you know him fairly well, would you tell me what you thought of the article?"

"It was real nice, but I could tell you didn't know him too well. He doesn't say much about himself, but he's always giving someone a hand." Vonney sipped the brandy. "You can't help but like him."

Sarah nodded. "So I've noticed." She had another taste of her drink.

"We heard about what you did in the bank to save him. I have to admit I've been curious about you. That took real courage."

"I was scared to death. If I'd kept my mouth shut the bank robber wouldn't have shot him." Sarah took another little taste of brandy. "It was the least I could do for him." Vonney gave her a knowing smile, and Sarah realized that the woman had guessed how she felt about Gil, too.

"Well, I couldn't've done it, but I'm sure glad he had you to take care of him."

"Have you seen him today? I heard that he and others came up here to help fight the fire."

"Yeah. He was here. The loggers took out after the scum that started the fire. Gil had me bind his side so he could ride horseback up to his logging camp. He wanted to see old Dugan."

Sarah gulped, instead of sipping, the brandy. It burned going down, and she coughed. "I didn't know he had recovered enough to ride."

Vonney smiled. "He didn't either. That's why he had me wrap his chest." She reached across the table and patted Sarah's hand. "Don't worry, Sarah. He'll be okay. That boy knows how to take care of himself."

The front door opened with a bang and a deep voice called out, "Vonney, where are ya, darlin'?"

She grinned and shrugged. "Sorry."

"I'm glad I met you, Vonney," Sarah said, standing up. She finished the tasty brandy.

Vonney downed the last of her drink, also. As she started past Sarah, she put her hand on Sarah's arm. "Come back any time, Sarah Hampton. It's a little quieter here during the week."

"Thanks. I will." Sarah waited until she heard Vonney lead the man away from the door, then she quietly left.

As she hurried to the rig, she felt the effects of the brandy and giggled. It wasn't something she would want to drink every day, but it would be nice on occasion. She climbed into the rig, raised the reins, and paused, wondering where Gil was and if he would stop by the house later. She turned the horse around and started back to town.

Gil stared at the burned corner of the bunkhouse. "Dugan, why the hell didn't Henry send word to me? Or tell me yesterday? The bastard could've killed one of you this time."

Dugan shrugged. "What could you do that we couldna done?"

"That's beside the point. I should have been told." Gil now understood why the men had reacted so violently when they heard the women complaining about Olley Russell being the one who'd probably started the fire at Vonney's.

Dugan eyed him. "Don't figure yer ready t'brawl yet. The men been itchin' fer a fight. Let off some steam." He chuckled. "Weren't sa long ago when you were leadin' the pack."

"You make me sound like an old man. I'll be twenty-nine for another month yet."

"Yer a babe."

Gil shook his head. "You got anything decent to eat?"

"Guess I can share my dinner," Dugan said, walking to the cookhouse. "Wasn't 'spectin' no one till supper."

"After I eat, I won't bother you. Might as well check the books while I'm here." Gil entered the cookhouse, glad that hadn't changed during his absence.

Dugan went into the kitchen and returned shortly with a steaming plate he set in front of Gil.

"Creamed chicken and biscuits. Sure smells good." Gil poked his fork into a juicy piece of chicken. "Want to tell me what else's been going on here?"

"Ya ain't missed nothin'. How's that Mrs. Hampton?"

Gil smiled as he broke open a biscuit. "Mrs. Hampton's fine." *Better than fine*, he thought, *much better*.

Dugan chuckled. "Heard yer on that new town council. How'd ya git roped inta that?"

"Damned if I know." Gil bit into the biscuit and reached for his coffee.

Willie ran into the cookhouse. "Boss, you gotta hurry. The men don't want to wait—"

"For what?" Gil jumped to his feet and grabbed another biscuit as he advanced on him.

"Henry sent me t'fetch you. They strung up that Russell fella, but Henry and Dowdy's tryin' to make 'em wait to hang him till you get there." Willie threw up his hands and ran outside.

Gil took off after him. He grabbed his coat as he passed the pegs.

"Yer rifle's in yer office!" Dugan bellowed, charging after them. "I'll get it fer ya!"

Gil mounted the horse and met Dugan in the yard. "Thanks. All right, Willie, go!"

They rode north through the trees along the upper foothills. At last they reached the small clearing where the men were gathered. Gil rode into the center and raised his rifle.

"You damn well better tell me what's going on right now! Henry?"

Henry wiped his coat sleeve across his brow. "These hotheaded jacks are decorating a cottonwood with Russell!"

"Cut him down, Dowdy."

The men grumbled and started crowding around.

Gil raised his Winchester and cocked it. "I'll shoot if you're dumb enough to try me." He rested his other hand on the saddlebag. "You know I never come up here without my Colt. Who wants to be first?"

Jake stepped forward. "Dang it all, that bastard's been lightin' fires at camp for months, and coulda kilt the women!"

"He's going to spend the night in the Oregon City jail." Gil guided his mount over to Olley Russell, who was himself mounted, with a rope around his neck, and literally shaking in his boots. "Russell, I'm the only one here who doesn't want to hang you. Tell us why you're bent on burning us out or I'll let them have you."

Olley Russell raised his head, eyes glazed. "Frannie's mine," he croaked. "Those dumb-ass pups kept sniffin' 'round her. Had t' stop 'em."

"You're the dumb-ass. The lady wanted no part of you." Gil nodded to Dowdy, who then pulled the noose off of Russell, none too gently.

"Dowdy, better check his hands. Make sure the rope'll hold him."

"Aye, boss." Dowdy tightened the rope around Russell's wrists. "They'll fall off 'fore he gits that loose."

Gil saw Vernon Riggs in the group. "Vernon, want to ride partway with us?"

"Right you are, Gil."

A few minutes later, Gil started down the hill with Russell in tow and Riggs behind. Gil hadn't really thought he'd have to shoot anyone, but he would have done it. It was going to be a long night, and he wasn't likely to get back to Gridley before morning.

It was dusk by the time they left Mount Hood behind.

After they crossed the mill bridge near town, Gil stopped. "Thanks for your help, Vernon."

Vernon nodded. "I'll even have a whiskey or two for you. Sure you want to go on alone with him?"

Gil looked back at his prisoner. "That sorry excuse for a person couldn't fight his way out of a barrel of water right now."

He pressed his heel to his mount's flank and continued on to Oregon City. *Sweet dreams, Sarah,* he thought, wishing he could tell her himself.

"Let's browse through the fabric at Seaton's. I think you could use a new dress or two," Sarah said, assessing Phoebe's midsection.

"I was just going to start fixing supper. Why don't we go in the morning?"

"So I can start sewing tonight. After last night, Gil will likely sleep until the morning." She shrugged into her cloak and handed Phoebe hers. "I need something to keep me busy tonight."

"Guess I should take advantage of your free time." Phoebe grinned as she donned her cloak. "I lent my old dresses to Mary Hoffman, thinking I wouldn't need them again."

Sarah laughed. "You should've known better than that." They left the house and walked up the street.

"Sarah, I'd like to go with you next time you visit the parlor house." Phoebe grinned. "It's not that I don't believe you. I just want to see it for myself."

"All right. I wonder what Charles will say."

Phoebe laughed. "When the time's right, I'll tell him."

Sarah paused on the walkway across from the saloon, gazing at Gil's side window. "He must be dead tired."

"At least he took that man to jail before they hung him. I haven't heard of a hanging anywhere around here." Phoebe tapped Sarah's arm. "Come on. I can't be too long."

Reluctantly, Sarah walked on. She didn't care what anybody thought. In the morning, she would take breakfast to

Gil and hear all about what had happened. They went in Seaton's and over to the bolts of yard goods. "Any special colors you'd like?"

Phoebe reached out to one bolt. "The salmon's pretty."

"That red mahogany would look good on you, too."

"Sarah," Alice Seaton called, hurrying over to her, "the library books arrived!"

"Today?"

"No. Friday, but we were busy and didn't unpack the crates until yesterday. I'll put them on the counter for you."

"Thanks, Alice. I'll take them to the library soon as I'm done here." Sarah smiled at Phoebe. "What a nice Christmas gift for the town."

"And we didn't even plan it that way." Phoebe pulled the two bolts out from the stack.

Alice came back. "I see you've decided."

"A dress length of each, and make it a generous amount," Phoebe said, glancing down.

Alice looked at Sarah and back to Phoebe as growing comprehension and a smile spread across her face. "Oh, congratulations, Phoebe. That's wonderful news."

"Alice, I would just as soon not announce it yet. We still have to tell the children."

"I may strangle on my tongue, but I won't say a word till you say it's okay."

Phoebe smiled. "I would appreciate that." She couldn't resist feeling the flannel. There was plenty of time before she needed to buy that, at least until after the holidays.

Alice unrolled the salmon fabric first. "Sarah, have you seen Mr. Perry since he came back from Oregon City?"

"He's probably sleeping. I understand he returned just after dawn."

"Are you going to interview him for another article? Everyone wants to read all about the fire at *that* house." Alice leaned closer to Sarah. "Should have let it burn to the ground. We don't need that kind of trash 'round here."

Phoebe cleared her throat, but Alice had no idea why Sarah suddenly became decidedly cool and walked away. "The library books are paid for, aren't they?"

"Oh, yes. When you and Sarah ordered them. Remember?"

"That's right." Phoebe looked over in time to see Sarah, her arms loaded with the new books, starting for the door. Phoebe hurried over and opened the door for her. "She doesn't know them, Sarah."

Sarah gave Phoebe a little smile. "How about taking that ride with me Wednesday morning?"

"That's Christmas Eve. Will next week be okay?"

Sarah sighed. "Yes. I'm taking these to the library before I say something I won't regret."

"I'll see you at home."

"This won't take long." Sarah walked down the boardwalk to the hotel and directly into the Harrison Lending Library. Maybe she should wait until they could arrange a ceremony for adding the books to the shelves. When she set the books on one of the tables, she noticed Gil seated in the comfortable chair. His back was to her.

"Gil? You're awake!"

He recoiled and glanced up. "Sarah—I didn't hear you enter." He laid the pen down across the paper he'd been writing on as she wrapped her arms around him.

"It's so good to see you. I thought you'd be sleeping." She bent down and gave him a chaste kiss, then she saw the letter. *My dearest Miss Lucy,*" it began. The penmanship. She would recognize it anywhere! She planted her hands on his shoulders and shoved him back. *"You!"*

"I can explain. In fact, that's what I was doing when you came in." God, she was angry. He wished he'd had time to complete the letter.

"How stupid I've been. You must've had a good laugh when I brought one of your own letters to you for advice." She paced the width of the room. "I was so foolish. It never occurred to me—that you could—"

"That I wasn't just a dumb beer jerker?" He gave her a mocking grin. That gave her pause, but only for a moment. "I'll admit it started out as a joke, but it quickly became more, Sarah, so much more."

"Oh, a parlor game?" She raked her fingers through her

hair as she resumed pacing. "Lord, I was thickheaded."

"We didn't really get to know each other until after I was shot." He knew he risked further wrath and embarrassment to do it, but it was better than dragging her outside. As he stepped into her path, he wrapped his arms around her and kissed her tenderly, hoping she would remember how well suited they were.

She stood unyielding, her arms pinned at her sides, her hands balled into fists. As he caressed and taunted her mouth, she raised her fists ready to pummel him, but she couldn't. Lord, she loved him. But how could she, after his trickery? But, oh, he was melting her resistance with his tender assault on her senses. No—

"No, no, no," she said, pushing him away. "I concede. You completely befuddle me when we're this close, but why didn't you tell me Friday when we were being so honest with one another?"

He turned and picked up the letter. "I came in here to look up a poem, 'Lucy Grey.' " He grinned at her. "But I didn't have time."

Taking a second look at the letter, she realized that he had just started it. " 'What's in a name?' " She met his gaze. "It is appropriate, isn't it?"

He nodded. "Very, my dearest Miss Lucy." That made her blush. "Seems we both had a secret, didn't we?"

"How did you know? I tried so hard. . . ." He was flashing his devilish grin again, and she wanted to shake him.

"Your writing. The style. I suspected with the first Miss Lucy article. That's why I began writing to her—you, hoping to trick you into admitting you wrote under both names. I got caught in my own trap."

"Serves you right, Gil Perry," she said, wagging her finger at him.

Her hand was naked. She had taken off her wedding band. His heart pounded as he posed the question, "What're we going to do about this? I have it on good authority you're a staunch supporter of free love." As he gazed into her beautiful blue eyes, they grew as big as saucers.

"Yes. . . ." She moistened her lips. "I did say that, and-I-meant-it," she said last the part as if it were one word.

"Men have been practicing it for centuries. Nothing new for them." He kissed her pale, sleek neck, then skimmed his lips upward and nibbled on one earlobe, whispering, "But I'd rather have you for my wife."

She trembled so violently he had to steady her. "Yes, Gil. I want that, too." She wound her arms around his waist and held him tight.

His caress quickly grew heated, and he pressed his lips to her pulsing temple. "We're attracting an audience." He nodded toward the doorway, where people were gathering.

"I wonder what Miss Lucy would suggest?"

He laughed. "A graceful exit, I'd imagine, with heads held high."

She nodded, grinning at him. "I didn't mention it, but Phoebe and I referred to Mr. Brown as 'the Poet.' " She started giggling. "I can't wait to see her face when I tell her you're him. She'll pop her buttons."

"The Poet, indeed." He offered her his arm.

Smiling, she slipped her arm in his.

"Why don't we see her now? I'd rather be alone with you later." He escorted her past the curious onlookers gathered in the lobby. When they stepped onto the boardwalk, he hugged her arm. "We can try out that new lock I put on the door."

Phoebe stared at Mr. Perry in disbelief. "I—How do—Are you sure, Sarah? I'm sorry, Mr. Perry, it's just that—" She wasn't making any sense at all, but she felt so flummoxed she couldn't even collect her thoughts.

Sarah grinned at Gil. "Didn't I tell you?" She laughed. "I don't recall the last time you were this befuddled. It never occurred to me even to suspect Gil, and I hadn't seen his handwriting until a few minutes ago." She handed Phoebe the letter he had started in the lending library.

The moment Phoebe saw the lovely penmanship, she recognized it. "Your deception was very good. You certainly hoodwinked Sarah and me."

"It started out as a good-natured ribbing, Mrs. Abbott."
He winked at Sarah. "I was certain she wrote the Miss
Lucy articles, and I wanted her to admit it."

Phoebe had not seen Sarah that happy in many years.
She had to admit it, Charles had tried to tell her that she
was judging Mr. Perry too harshly. "Did Charles know?"

Gil shook his head. "No one did. That's why I posted
the letters in Fenton's Crossing."

"That's right," Sarah said, belatedly remembering the
day she and Phoebe had spent searching for Mr. Brown.
"Why there?"

"It wasn't too far out of the way back to town from the
camp." He grinned at Sarah. "I thought she might try to
find Mr. Brown sometime. But I hadn't figured on being
shot and unable to post the letters." He covered her hand,
which was resting on the sofa near his leg.

Sarah skimmed her thumb over his finger. "So Jack
didn't know either?"

"I told no one. Besides, who would've believe it?"

"You both have to stay for supper." Phoebe handed the
letter back to Sarah and stood up. "Make yourselves comfortable."

"I'll help."

"No need. Everything's ready. I just want to speak to
Cora." Phoebe hurried through the kitchen to the backyard.
She found Cora and sent her to bring her father home for
supper with Mr. Perry. Phoebe lingered in the yard, still
astounded with Mr. Perry's ability to fool them so completely. Sarah had fallen in love with him twice, Phoebe
realized. No wonder Sarah had not stopped beaming.
Surely, she had more to tell her. Later.

Gil enjoyed the supper with the Abbott family. Phoebe
hadn't been cold or distant this time. As close as she was
to Sarah, he was sure they would spend more evenings with
them. However, he wanted to spend the remainder of this
one with Sarah. Alone.

"Mrs. Abbott, thank you for a wonderful meal, but it's
getting late." He stood and drew Sarah up beside him.

"Yes, we really do have to leave." Sarah kissed Cora good night and hugged Phoebe. "We're going for a walk. I'll see you later."

Charles shook Gil's hand. "It isn't often someone gets the best of Sarah. You have my admiration."

"I have to admit it was fun."

"Good thing she didn't know, when she poking around inside you."

"Hadn't thought about that," Gil said, laughing. "I'll have to be more careful."

Gil and Sarah said their goodbyes and walked toward the river, arm in arm as if it were a summer's night, not a blustery winter's eve. "Did you tell her we're getting married?"

She rested her head on his arm. "No. Sharing that you and the Poet are one in the same was enough for one night, but do you mind if I tell her tomorrow?"

"From the way she kept eyeing you, she probably already suspects." He stopped and turned to her. "I don't want a long engagement, Sarah."

"I have a nice dress packed in my trunk." She slid her hands under his coat and held him close. "I was saving it for a special occasion. Nothing can compare to this."

"I'll take you in your shimmy, as long as we can see a preacher in the next day or two." He covered her mouth gently with his own.

She quivered at his tenderness. "I'll talk to Phoebe in the morning. We could leave by midday. Where do you want to get married?"

"How about Fenton's Crossing? I think there's a justice of the peace there. And it isn't far."

She laughed. "Sounds perfect."

"Let's see if that lock on my door's going to work." Holding her hand, they dashed to his room. He rekindled the fire in the woodstove.

She lighted the lamp on his desk. It was as uncluttered as the first time she had seen it. There wasn't one note in sight, nothing handwritten, no sample of his penmanship for her to recognize. The bolt clicked on the lock. She smiled and turned as he reached out to her. "Were you going to work tonight?"

"No." He slipped the cloak off her shoulders and dropped it on the desk. "I'd planned on giving you the letter tonight," he said softly. His hands drifted down her arms, and he gazed into her glimmering eyes. "You are so lovely," he said, threading his fingers between hers.

"I don't know about that, but I'm glad you think so." Holding his hands, she wrapped her arms behind her. "You have no idea how I've tried to ignore your devilish grin. When I heard about the parlor house I couldn't imagine you needing to go there for companionship. You must be used to women flirting with you."

He chuckled. "The way you did?"

"You were far too confident." She crossed their wrists, pinning her body against his. "My curiosity got the best of me yesterday. I drove up to Vonney's."

He raised one brow. "And?"

"I like her. Frannie said you were like their brother, though I don't think Vonney's admiration is exactly brotherly."

He chuckled and hugged her with his upper arms. "Is it safe for me to go back?"

"Not tonight." She pressed her hips to his and felt him respond to her unspoken plea. Blood coursed through her veins, feeding her need for him.

With feather-light strokes he brushed his lips over hers until she groaned, then his mouth covered hers hungrily, a probing exploration as he swayed his hips in counterpoint to hers. She yielded and taunted and seduced him, and he struggled to control his body's searing need she ignited.

Her lips tingled. He lifted her as his lips made a smoldering path down to her breasts. She twisted and turned, increasing the heat between them. Tiny tremors shot through her, a harbinger of the pleasure building within.

He released her hands and led her toward his bed as he unbuttoned the waistband on her skirt. Next he loosened the ties on her many petticoats, and felt her hands brand him hers alone as she worked the buttons on his trousers.

"If we're not careful, we'll end up shredding our clothes."
He pulled off his coat and tossed it across the room.

"I keep remembering bathing your body."

"That is one debt I look forward to repaying," he said
fervently.

The rich timbre of his voice weakened her already un-
steady knees as she stepped out of her skirts and peeled off
her shirtwaist and her drawers. She stood before him, quivering with need in her shimmy, and stared at his magnetic
body. She reached out and lightly touched his scar, then
she pulled her shimmy over her head and dropped it on the
floor.

He tensed against the fierce swelling and consuming need
for her. With the soft glow of lamplight behind her, she
seemed a shimmery image. There was neither conceit nor
embarrassment in her stance as she allowed him to appreciate the extent of her curving, shapely body. Beauty beyond his imagining . . . A tremor shook his frame.
"Sarah. . . ."

"I've yet to see one very important part of your body."
She freed the button holding up his drawers and with intense pleasure regarded his readiness for her. "I much prefer you in this condition to the one I became so familiar
with."

He yanked back the rough blanket and held his arm out
to her. "Come here."

She went to him, a slight smile curving her lips. The
instant he took her in his embrace, the heat of his body
eased and heightened the frenzy of desire churning in her.
She sank down on the bed with him and finally felt the
weight of his taut body cover her. She ran her fingers over
his smooth back and skimmed the arch of her foot up the
side of his leg.

He nibbled and tasted and explored each inviting curve
and hollow, and stroked her satin-soft inner thighs. Her
nipples peaked against his tongue, and he brought her to a
fevered pitch with his mouth. Her scent was rich, and she
tasted like honeyed wine.

She was a quivering, molten mass of sensations, each

exquisite and driving her to the brink of her strength. Suddenly, a momentary release swept over her and left her panting. "Gil, . . . please, now."

"Yes, Sarah," he said, thrusting into her. He groaned as she tightened around him and arched her back. He pulled back and drove deeper, and again, and again. She writhed and cried out with her fulfillment as he gave in to the throbbing power of his release.

She was winded, gasping, and so was he, and deliciously weak. Lifting her hand to comb her fingers through his thick hair nearly spent what little strength she had left. When he shifted slightly, another wave of silvery pleasure soared through her.

He lay beside her, his head resting on one arm, his other holding her snug against the length of him. "Guess it's time I build a house."

"Mm, that sounds nice." She opened her eyes. "On the land I'm buying from you!"

He grinned against her shoulder. "Are you sure?"

"Oh, yes. With you, it really will be absolutely perfect. Do you want to live here or at Elsie's until it's ready to move into?"

"I can't ask you to live here. You know what people would say." He gave her a slight grin.

She nudged her leg between his and wound her arms around him. "The men will wink and slap you on the back, and the women will whisper behind their gloved hands, wondering what it's *really* like up here." She pressed her lips to the curly hair covering his chest. "I've been happy here with you."

He skimmed his hand over her belly and the side of her hip. "I love you, Sarah Hampton . . . Perry."

"And I, you," she said, tipping him on his back. "It's my turn to be on top."

He laughed, holding her firmly on top of him. "Oh, Sarah, you were worth waiting for." He framed her beautiful face and kissed her with unrestrained lust.

This would be no marriage of convenience.

Epilogue

It was Lucy Perry's eighth birthday. She grinned at Clarinda Abbott. "Now I'm as old as you!"

"I'm still two months older, but that isn't much. And we'll always be in the same grade at school."

"I heard Mama and Aunt Phoebe talking about taking us for a visit back to where they grew up. Jackson County in Illinois. We'll get to ride and sleep on the train."

Lucy brushed grass off Linnet's blue cloak and held the doll on her lap. "Mama said she and Aunt Phoebe had cloaks just like this. Isn't it pretty?"

"Maybe they'll make us coats alike." Clarinda sat Esmee on her lap and spread out the doll's skirt. "For Christmas."

"We'll ask them before my birthday party."

"Okay," Clarinda said. "Mama told me about when she and Aunt Sarah promised always to be friends, but I can't picture Mama as a girl."

Lucy giggled. "All ladies had to be girls sometime."

Clarinda glanced around, then whispered, "Did you find those letters we heard our mamas talk about?"

Lucy nodded. "Mama has a pretty red ribbon tied around them. I brought one so you could see it." She pulled the rolled envelope out of her pocket and handed it to Clarinda. "It's just a bunch of silly lovey stuff."

Clarinda flattened the letter on the grass. " 'My dearest Miss Lucy,' " She sighed. "That's so romantic." She fell backward and stared up at a lone cloud in the clear blue sky. "My dearest Clarinda—"

Lucy giggled again. "You want me to tell Thomas Wells to write you a letter like that?"

Clarinda sat up. "Don't you dare! I'd perish!"

"I won't." Lucy rolled up the letter and poked it back into her pocket. "I wonder what kind of cake Aunt Phoebe made for my birthday party?"

"Berry, probably. That's your favorite," Clarinda said, picking up Esmee. "Did you ask Aunt Sarah about my name? I asked Mama again, but she just smiles funny and says, 'It's a nice name.' "

"My mama said, 'It's a *lovely* name,' then she and Papa grinned at each other and she asked him if *she* was still in the saloon."

Clarinda stared at her. "You mean some lady's been in the saloon? Mr. Young wouldn't allow a woman in there."

"That's what she said."

Clarinda grinned. "Let's sneak in there. I want to see her."

"Oh, I don't know. What if we're caught? Papa'd tan my backside good."

"Come on," Clarinda said, rolling to her knees. "It'll be fun. As long as we're together we'll be safe."

"Somebody'll see us."

"We'll just take a quick peek. Besides," Clarinda said, "Aunt Sarah wouldn't get mad. She's a freethinker."

"What's that?"

"She doesn't have to do what other people say."

Lucy rolled her eyes. "I know *that*. Papa always says he never knows what she'll do."

"Don't you want to see the woman?"

Lucy shrugged. "I guess so."

"Clarinda! Lucy!" Cora called, walking up the path. "Where are you two?"

"Here, Cora!" Lucy shouted, standing so she could be seen.

Cora hurried up to the girls. "Happy birthday, Lucy." She kissed Lucy's cheek and held out a box to her. "This is for you."

Lucy stared at the pretty box. "Aren't you coming to my party?"

"Yes, but I wanted you to have this now. It's not a real present." Cora smiled at both girls. "Open it."

Lucy untied the yellow satin ribbon and lifted the lid.

"What is it?" Clarinda asked, frustrated with Lucy's slowness.

Lucy set down the box and picked up the cloak, then she looked at Cora. "Did you make this for me?"

"No, your grandmother made it for your mama when she was about your age." Cora put her arm around her little sister. "Our mama had one just like it, but it was lost. Aunt Sarah gave that to me when I was nine. I thought you'd like it, Lucy."

"Oh, I do. I do, Cora." Lucy gave Cora a quick hug and put on the cloak. "How does it look?"

"It's nice," Clarinda said softly.

"We'll share it." Lucy put the cloak around Clarinda's shoulders. "It's pretty on you, too."

"Come on, you two, or you'll be late for the party."

"Tell Mama we'll be right there." Lucy smiled at Clarinda.

Cora gave them a stern look. "You better be."

Clarinda frowned at her. "Just because you're grown up doesn't mean you have to sound like Mama."

Cora shook her head and a smile softened her expression. "That's not so bad."

As soon as Cora was out of sight, Lucy picked up Linnet. "Why don't we trade dolls, just like our mamas did. I'll always be your best friend. No matter what."

"I'll be yours, too, Lucy." Clarinda kissed Esmee and exchanged dolls with Lucy. Then Clarinda put the cloak on Lucy. "You wear it. It's your birthday."

Lucy put Esmee in the box and they started walking back to the house. "Think we'll ever be as old as our mamas?"

TIME PASSAGES

*Presenting all-new romances—featuring
ghostly heroes and heroines and the
passions they inspire.*

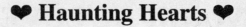 Haunting Hearts

❑ *A SPIRITED SEDUCTION*
   by Casey Claybourne   0-515-12066-9/$5.99

❑ *STARDUST OF YESTERDAY*
   by Lynn Kurland   0-515-11839-7/$6.50

❑ *A GHOST OF A CHANCE*
   by Casey Claybourne   0-515-11857-5/$5.99

❑ *ETERNAL VOWS*
   by Alice Alfonsi   0-515-12002-2/$5.99

❑ *ETERNAL LOVE*
   by Alice Alfonsi   0-515-12207-6/$5.99

❑ *ARRANGED IN HEAVEN*
   by Sara Jarrod   0-515-12275-0/$5.99

FRIENDS ROMANCE

Can a man come between friends?

❑ A TASTE OF HONEY
by DeWanna Pace   0-515-12387-0

❑ WHERE THE HEART IS
by Sheridon Smythe   0-515-12412-5

❑ LONG WAY HOME
by Wendy Corsi Staub   0-515-12440-0

All books $5.99